THE PAVILION

THE PAVILION

HILDA LAWRENCE

PENGUIN BOOKS

Penguin Books Ltd, Harmondsworth,
Middlesex, England
Penguin Books, 40 West 23rd Street,
New York, New York 10010, U.S.A.
Penguin Books Australia Ltd, Ringwood,
Victoria, Australia
Penguin Books Canada Limited, 2801 John Street,
Markham, Ontario, Canada L3R 1B4
Penguin Books (N.Z.) Ltd, 182–190 Wairau Road,
Auckland 10, New Zealand

First published in the United States of America by
Simon and Schuster 1946
Published in Penguin Books 1984
Reprinted 1984

LIBRARY OF CONGRESS CATALOGING IN PUBLICATION DATA
Lawrence, Hilda.
The pavilion.
Reprint. Originally published: New York: Simon and
Schuster, 1946 (An Inner sanctum mystery).
I. Title.
PS3523.A9295P3   1984   813'.52   83-17298
ISBN 0 14 00.6964 X

Printed in the United States of America by
Offset Paperback Mfrs., Inc., Dallas, Pennsylvania
Set in Janson

FOR MARGOT JOHNSON

THE PAVILION

Chapter One

THEY came to the house on different days, at different hours and by different routes, and the first two came by train.

At noon the sun was high and hot. The southbound train moved sluggishly between brown fields. The windows of the day coach were open and the smell of burning leaves and late ploughing filled the car.

In the middle of the coach a man and woman sat close together on the worn plush seat. They ignored their sprawling neighbors and looked at each other silently from time to time. It was as if they shared a secret too fragile for words. They turned their thoughts over and over with their eyes, accepting, rejecting, wondering. Sometimes the woman sighed and once she opened her handbag in answer to an unspoken question. The man checked its contents until he found a packet of cinnamon drops. He crunched these with a satisfied smile on his face.

They looked exactly alike, too fat, too white, too elaborately dressed. They rode in the day coach because there was less than a dollar in the handbag.

The others came on the following day, by ferry, by plane, by trolley. The first of these drove his station wagon on to the ferry while the early morning fog still covered the bay. He stood by the railing on the lower deck and listened to the lapping water that he could not see. Spray struck him in the face and he knew it had the taste of tears.

Somewhere out in the cold, gray dawn a bell buoy mourned gently for no one. He listened to the bell, his eyes straight ahead, one hand on the wet railing. Then he turned and went over to his car.

The fog was defeated there. A single oil lamp hanging from a beam poured yellow light on the lean figure and the muddy car. There was a pile of pigskin luggage on the driver's seat and the tonneau carried a spectacular freight. There were oysters in a dripping barrel covered with seaweed, eggs in a wicker hamper, limp, white geese, bronze turkeys, chickens, hams. The man looked at them all, absently, before he crossed to the opposite side of the boat. But the voice of the bell followed him like a thin, sweet requiem.

The plane that left New York at nine a.m. had one empty seat until two minutes before it took off. When the last passenger arrived he walked stiffly to his allotted place. He walked as if he were the only man aboard and the plane was his. He was not an old man, perhaps sixty, and there was a continental elegance in his dress and bearing. He limped, and his thin, curling lips were pressed together with an effort that was plain.

For the next hour and a half he sat with his hands on the knob of a silver headed cane, his chin sunk into the folds of a black scarf.

It was four o'clock in the afternoon when the girl climbed down from the interurban trolley at the four corners and stood undecided on the curb. A broad street lined with yellowing maples stretched before her. It looked like the right street but she wasn't sure. The last time had been so long ago and it had been summer then.

She set her suitcase on the pavement and tried to get her bearings. The church on the opposite corner, that was right. The undertaking parlor next to the church, that was right too. The small shops across from the church were new and so were the tearoom and the movie theater. She turned

doubtfully. The drug store was still there. She remembered
the colored lamps in the window and how they had looked
at night.

An elderly man in a white jacket stood in the doorway
and she crossed to speak to him. He began to smile before
she reached him but the smile faded when she started her
eager questioning.

"The Herald place?" he repeated. He pointed up the
maple lined street. "Cross over to the church, then straight
ahead on the other side. You can't miss it."

That was all. You can't miss it. She supposed he was
thinking of the iron deer on the lawn. Some people thought
the iron deer were funny. She thanked him and went on her
way.

The yellow leaves drifted down in lazy spirals, turning
themselves in the air, sometimes clinging to her coat before
they sank to the ground. She scuffed happily through the
ankle-deep leaves, forgetting she was tired. Behind her were
a day and night on an overcrowded bus and a jolting trolley
ride out from the city, but straight ahead were welcome and
affection. After a long time she would have both of these
again. She hurried a little when she thought of that, then
slowed down childishly to prolong the pleasure of arriving
at last.

A few yards farther on the iron fence began and she
knew she was almost there. She boasted quietly to herself.
A whole, long block of iron fence with a beautiful gate
in the middle, the biggest garden and the biggest house, the
thickest carpets and the heaviest lace curtains, the finest
place in town. She had heard her mother say so many times
and far in the back of her mind she could remember some
of it, too. Things like the iron deer, the blue bay that
rippled to the edge of the back lawn, the holly trees and
the crepe myrtles, the swamp magnolia that hid its droop-
ing blossoms, the colored lamps in the drug store window
that stained the red brick walk at night. In the summertime.

How old had she been that time? Six? Yes, six and a
little over. And smart, too, Hurst had said. They'd told her

to call him Cousin Hurst and she'd refused. He'd liked that.
That was when he'd said she was smart. She must be smart
this time too, in appreciation.

Some child had left a stick propped against the railing, a
fine, peeled stick. No, she told herself triumphantly, it
wasn't a child! He had done that! It was a part of his welcome. He hadn't forgotten the game they used to play. And
he hadn't known when she was coming, so he must have
walked across the lawn every morning and put it there for
her to find. That was like him, that was exactly what he'd
do.

There was no one in sight; the trees on the lawn grew
close to the fence and the house was still invisible. She
picked up the stick and ran it lightly along the railing. The
low, hollow ring brought a sudden radiance to her face. To
have it sound the same, as she remembered it, was like an unexpected gift. It was lovely, it was right. She put back her
head and laughed up at the clean blue sky.

He'd called it a magic stick, a wand. He'd said it could
do anything. He'd rattled it along the railings when they
walked together. He'd said it sounded like—what did he
say it sounded like? Like ghosts in a cellar. Disobedient
ghosts tied up in chains, living on bread and water. Somebody had scolded him for telling her that and he'd taken
her down to the big, dark cellar and shown her the hams
and bacon hanging from hooks in the ceiling. No ghosts.
He'd given them their freedom, he said.

She tucked the stick under the strap of her suitcase and
walked quickly on. The gate was just ahead. As she drew
abreast, a cloud moved over the sun and darkened the path.
It covered the path like a veil. It happened so suddenly, so
deliberately and accurately, that she dropped the hand she
had extended to the latch. The air was momentarily still;
even the leaves hung lifeless on the trees. She reached for
the latch again but before her hand could touch it the gate
swung open, slowly and without sound. There was no wind.

She passed through, not wondering or thinking because
at last she saw the house through the trees. First the tall

chimneys, then ivy and Virginia creeper on the walls, then balconies and pillars, and last of all the great carved door that had come from Italy. She had reached the foot of the steps before she saw the door.

A wreath hung in the center. Undimmed, unfaded, fresh and sweet, the white roses bloomed against the oaken birds and scentless garlands. Behind her the gate closed silently.

Chapter Two

MRS. MUNDY sat at the foot of the long kitchen table and surveyed the room with satisfaction. Everything was running smoothly, upstairs and down. No noise, no confusion, no—as Mundy himself had said—no people trying to get in that didn't belong. Everything proper and the reins in her own hands, except for the matter of all that food. They wouldn't be able to eat it in a month. She'd told Mr. Fray so, not mincing words, either. But that was the Heralds all over. Always bringing geese and things for somebody else to pick, looking down their long noses as if they owned the world. Upstarts.

Mrs. Mundy looked down her own nose at the table. It was set for the servants' tea, a heavy tea because dinner would be late. Behind her two tall windows let in the fading light. Plenty of light, she told herself. Plenty until the maids came down. The room was full of shadows but she liked it that way. She was fifty-six, not wearing well, and shadows were her friends.

It was a vast room, with dark walls and low ceiling. It was also a repository for everything in the house that was considered too good to throw away. Steel engravings hung on the walls, and rocking chairs, a sagging sofa, and a whatnot crowded with fancy shells and souvenir cups and saucers filled the corners. An old-fashioned coal range stood along one wall, flanked by a white enamel gas stove and an electric refrigerator. The coal range glowed and the copper kettles hissed.

Over the dumbwaiter shelves a long wooden box was set

6

into the wall. Its rectangular dial, like the face of a clock, listed the rooms in the house. The center indicator, like a little, pointing hand, was motionless. Mrs. Mundy hoped it would stay that way. It was an old contraption, known as The Box, and sometimes it got out of order. Sometimes the little hand would spin around and point to a room that was empty. Not only empty, but locked up, so nobody on earth could have pushed the service bell. When the little hand did that the maids always screamed and refused to answer the summons. If somebody could ring a bell in an empty room, they said, then that somebody could float right back where it came from.

Mrs. Mundy told herself The Box would have to go. It made trouble. You couldn't keep good Negro servants with that thing in the kitchen. They were afraid of it. Because of that, The Box had been directly responsible for Mrs. Mundy's hurried trip to town nearly two months before, a trip that had resulted in the Crain sisters, white.

When Mrs. Mundy saw the Crain sisters in the employment agency she knew at once that they were what she wanted. They told her they were fifty years old, in one way or another, and said they were very strong. They were in their late sixties and they were strong because they were desperate. Mrs. Mundy had noted how the younger one, Katy, had gripped her sister's skirt in an agony of hope, and she knew she could get them both for the price of one.

"It's a large house," she'd told Jenny, the older one, "but we keep a lot of it closed up. Two adults in the family and other help living in, myself and husband. Outside help comes in by the day and won't bother you. Room of your own with bath, good table and no heavy lifting. Mr. Herald don't like women to do heavy lifting. Mr. Herald"—she'd hesitated slightly—"Mr. Herald is foreign born. He pays for the doctor if you're sick."

Jenny's eyes had filled then. "We'll come, thank you," she'd said.

The Box gave off an angry, whirring sound and Mrs. Mundy jumped. A small red light glowed like an eye above the dial. She got up and crossed to read the summons. Dining room, directly above. That would be Mundy himself. She put her head into the dumbwaiter shaft and called up softly. "That you?"

Mundy's voice came from above in a whisper. "Ready."

The wire cable began to move and the waiter slid down, revealing empty shelves. Mrs. Mundy hooked it securely, collected two covered trays from a side table and put them on the top shelf. She unhooked the waiter and Mundy drew it up out of sight. She returned to her chair.

"They'll be coming soon now," she murmured. "When they see Mundy stepping around with cake and wine they'll look at the clock." She looked at the clock herself, an ornate bronze that had fallen from grace in easy stages from the second floor hall to the shelf over the coal range. After four.

A cloud moved over the sun and darkened the windows. Mrs. Mundy turned an angry face. At first she thought someone was looking in, someone who had no business on the grounds. People did that sometimes, fishermen from the bay, and the rough element from Water Street; they were curious, always had been. Curious about the house because you couldn't see it from the street. And now they'd be worse than ever.

But there was no one at the windows. The cloud moved on and the light returned. Mrs. Mundy shrugged her angular shoulders. October weather, she told herself. Winter'll be on us before we know it.

She got up again and turned on the hanging lamp that swung from the ceiling. The warm, red-shaded light fell on the white fringed cloth, the platters of cut bread and butter, cold meat and cheese, jam and cake. She poured four cups of scalding tea from the Rebecca pot that stood on the back of the range, for herself, for Jenny and Katy, for Miss Etta Luders. Miss Etta would be full of port and sherry and everything else she'd been able to snatch in passing, but she'd come down with the maids and fill up all over again.

Slow moving footsteps sounded on the stairs and the three women came into the room. Miss Etta Luders was first, as was proper for a pensioner of the family. She was eighty-two, frail and hennaed, with black velvet bows, obviously temporary, decorating bosom and flaming hair. She also wore a black feather boa.

She dropped into the nearest chair and covered her raddled old face with none too clean hands. "I can't swallow a mouthful," she said.

"But you will," Mrs. Mundy replied. She filled a plate and pushed it across the table.

The two Crains sat close together on one side. Their eyes were red-rimmed and their hands trembled as they folded bread and butter and jam and stuffed it in their mouths like eager children. After nearly two months in the house, with four huge meals a day, they were still hungry, still fearful of their good fortune. Last night had increased their fears. Last night and today had been nightmares. If they lost this job, if the good clean beds and the food stopped— Jenny avoided her sister's eyes; she was afraid Katy would see what she was thinking. Katy was thinking the same thing. She too looked away. No use worrying Jenny.

They ate steadily and silently. Only the clatter of knife and fork broke the stillness. Mrs. Mundy, toying with the tea she didn't want, watched her three companions with smug condescension. She had nothing to fear. She belonged to the other faction, the one that was left.

Someone knocked lightly at the garden door. The sound was trebled by the silence in the room. All four women jumped slightly. Mrs. Mundy cast a disapproving look around the table, got up and went to the door. She opened it wide. A girl she had never seen before stood on the flag-stone. Her young face was white and leaves clung to her plain brown coat. She carried a suitcase.

"Well?" said Mrs. Mundy.

"I've come," the girl answered. "I'm Regan Carr."

Mrs. Mundy stared. "You've what?"

"I've come. My cousin expects me. My Cousin Hurst.

But the front door—" She broke off, and her eyes completed the sentence as she looked from one old face to the other.

She was too young for everything in the room, for the ancient rocking chairs, the stained engravings, the useless clutter on the whatnot, the hot, close air. The lamplight that lay gently on her own round cheek dug deep and cruel furrows in the faces turned to stare.

Miss Etta's chair whined on the waxed linoleum as she pushed herself away from the table and darted forward.

"Regan," she exulted. "Regan! Poor baby, poor baby." She took the girl in her arms. "I'm Miss Etta. Old Miss Etta. Haven't you heard of me?"

Mrs. Mundy stood back. "What does this mean?" she demanded. She tapped the old woman's shoulder. "Go back to your place. Sit down, Miss—Miss Carr. Now maybe you'd better tell me what you're doing here."

Regan found a chair; it was heavy and she pulled it up to the table herself. No one tried to help her. It was too low, and sitting in it she looked like a child for whom no preparation had been made. It was Jenny Crain who brought a pillow from the sofa and tremulously offered it.

"I'm Jenny," she said. "This is Katy."

Mrs. Mundy watched. "Well?" she said. She stood by the coal range, arms folded, watching and waiting with outward detachment.

Miss Etta's voice traveled shrilly down the table and across the room.

"You heard her!" she shouted. "You heard her say she was Regan Carr! You know as well as I do what that means!" The sound of her own voice, crashing against the ceiling and coming back, frightened her into a pause. She ground a soiled white handkerchief into her eyes, blurring the mascara.

"You know who she is," she went on in a lower tone. "I never saw her before in my life but I'd know her anywhere. It's a Herald face. It's his own face. You can take her up to the front parlor this minute if you don't believe me, and stand her there beside the casket. It could be her own head on that satin pillow, her own face with the eyes closed."

Regan spoke to Miss Etta. "Is the wreath for him?"

Miss Etta nodded.

Regan waited. Then—"I didn't know what it meant. I didn't like to ring the bell . . . I hoped it was somebody else."

"No," Miss Etta said. "Suddenly. Last night."

Mrs. Mundy moved back into the light. "You say he expected you? Why was that? I always look after the mail and I don't remember any letters from you. And he'd stopped writing to people long ago. I'm only asking because I'm surprised."

"Regan," Miss Etta began, "Regan—"

Regan drew back from the table. "Will you take me upstairs?" she said to Mrs. Mundy. "I'd like to talk to Cousin May." She stood up and collected her gloves, her purse, her suitcase.

Jenny and Katy exchanged relieved and sober nods. That was the right thing to do, their eyes said to each other. The young lady was a relative and she'd had a shock. It was only proper that she should be taken up to Mrs. Herald. She never should have come to the kitchen in the first place. It wasn't fitting. Jenny took the suitcase in a bony hand; she even smiled a little at the peeled stick.

"I'll unpack for you," she said.

"Leave that here," Mrs. Mundy said. "No, keep your gloves and purse, Miss Carr. We won't be long." She led the way to the alcove where the stairs started upward. The other women listened to the retreating footsteps until they died away.

Miss Etta squared her thin shoulders and gave the Crains a long look. "I'd like to follow them," she said. "I could, too. I have the run of the house. I'm the same as the family. The Herald family," she emphasized.

The Crains waited respectfully for her to say more, but

Miss Etta's rouged mouth shut like a trap. They returned
her look with eager approval of whatever she was thinking,
and wordlessly acknowledged her superiority. Then they
reached hungrily for the remains of the cake.

While they ate, they thought. They had seen Miss Etta
Luders only once before, shortly after their arrival. She'd
come to the house to collect her monthly check from Mr.
Hurst Herald. She was a connection of some sort, born in
the same European village as Mr. Hurst's father, and her
own father had worked for the Heralds in the old country.
The Heralds never forgot the people who had worked for
them . . . Jenny and Katy didn't look at each other but
their thoughts traveled side by side. If Mr. Hurst hadn't
died maybe there would have been checks for them too.
When they were too old to work and couldn't lie about
their ages any more. Maybe once a month they could have
walked up the front path in their best clothes, turned their
steps at the side of the house where the conservatory was,
and moved on securely to the kitchen door. Maybe Mrs.
Mundy would have given them a big tea like this one, and a
neat bundle to take home, the same kind of bundle she gave
Miss Etta. A little frying chicken, a good piece of country
ham, beaten biscuit and some eggs. All good, all fresh,
straight from the farm across the bay. Thinking of the farm
made them think of Mr. Fray Herald. Mr. Hurst's youngest
brother. Today they'd seen Mr. Fray for the first time.

He lived across the bay on the old farm. It used to be the
Beauregard place, a big show place, and Miss May, poor
soul, had been born there. Mrs. Mundy had told them all
about it. She'd said the Beauregards were aristocracy and
never could learn to work for themselves the way the
Heralds did. So after the War Between the States they'd
begun to lose everything, sell off bits of land and fine horses,
until in Miss May's time there wasn't much left. That was
when Mr. Hurst Herald, out with some friends on a hunting
trip, saw Miss May, saw the farm, and took both.

Mrs. Mundy had told Jenny and Katy the whole story.

She knew it all. She and Mundy had been with the Beauregards all their lives. They'd always be here, too. They were the lucky ones.

Then—Jenny pushed the platter of cheese closer to her sister's hand—then Mr. Hurst had brought Miss May over to this house, which was his father's, and they'd lived here happily ever after. Mr. Hurst had loved this house and always said he wanted to die in it. Well, he had.

Jenny raised mournful eyes from her plate. The light in the garden had faded into early dusk and the windows were as dark as her thoughts. She stroked Katy's hand.

"Miss Etta?" she asked timidly. "Who is Regan Carr?"

Miss Etta didn't answer at once. She was watching The Box, hoping for a summons.

"Regan Carr," she said finally, "is a Herald in spite of her name and her yellow hair. She got that hair from her father. Her mother was second cousin to Mr. Hurst. She's an orphan. It's only right that she should come here." She paused, and when she spoke again there was a new authority in her voice. "You girls ought to get back upstairs. Somebody may want something and Mundy can't see to everything."

The Crains bobbed their heads in agreement. They hurried from the room, anxious to be useful and wanted. When they were safely out of ear-shot, they told each other that they were worried about Regan Carr. She hadn't had her tea.

When Regan followed Mrs. Mundy out of the kitchen she dreaded every step of the way. Mrs. Mundy's angular figure moved lightly and firmly, accompanied by the assured rustle of silk petticoats. Her own feet stumbled, from nervousness and doubt, from confusion and grief. The treasured letter in her purse gave her no comfort now, promised no happy future. That future was lying dead— what had Miss Etta said?—dead in the front parlor. It was no more than a face on a satin pillow. Her face. Miss Etta had said that too.

Her hand slipped on the waxed stair railing and she caught
her breath in a sob. She hoped Mrs. Mundy hadn't heard,
but she had. She turned and spoke over her shoulder.

"Don't let Miss May see you crying. She has enough to
contend with as it is."

They came out into a butler's pantry. A man bending
over a tray of glasses gave them a long, measuring look, but
he didn't speak. Beyond the pantry was a small passage
that led to the main hall. The dining room and conservatory
filled that end of the house. The former was dark and
empty, but amber shaded lamps burned in the conservatory
and people dressed in dark clothes stood about in groups,
drinking wine. One of those people, a woman, laughed
when they passed the open, glass doors, a low pleased
laugh as if someone had paid her a whispered compliment.

They turned down the main hall toward the front of the
house. Am I the only one who's sorry? she wondered.

She tried to identify the rooms they passed, but she had
been too young before. All she could remember was richness, and a feeling of peace; the richness was still there but
the peace was gone. Only her mother's wistful recollection
charted the closed doors, the library, the middle parlor, the
music room, the front parlor. She walked behind Mrs.
Mundy with bent head.

"Wait here," Mrs. Mundy said.

They had come to the foot of a broad flight of stairs, curving up on the right. Straight ahead was the Italian door, its
inner surface blandly mute. On the left was the front parlor.

People were moving in and out like visitors to an art
gallery, in orderly lines, not talking, not looking at each
other, moving with exaggerated caution as if the accidental
contact of sleeve with sleeve, skirt with skirt, was something
not to be borne.

"If you want to go in there," Mrs. Mundy whispered,
"this is a good time."

Regan shook her head. Mrs. Mundy smiled faintly.

"You've let Miss Etta frighten you," she said. "She's a
little crazy, you know. Nothing bad, nothing to be locked

up for, just simple in her mind. You needn't be afraid to go in. He looks all right. It was sudden and peaceful, he never knew what happened. Why don't you go in for a minute while I prepare Miss May? It'll save time."

Regan heard herself reply. It didn't sound like her own voice. "I have plenty of time," she said.

Mrs. Mundy looked blank. "Well, then—" She turned to the stairs. "Wait on that bench. I'll call you when I'm ready." She moved up the curving stairs, making no sound on the thick red carpeting. Only the whisper of silk grew fainter as she met the shadows above and became one of them.

A bald man with an old, friendly face and lively eyes left his station by the parlor door and approached the bench on tiptoe. He bent to look at the huddled figure. "Member of the family, honey?" he whispered.

"Y-yes."

"I knew it. Herald, not Beauregard. I know that bone structure." He leaned against the newel post and smiled. "I ought to know it. I did the old gentleman and Mr. Max's wife and the young girl. She was the first one. I helped my father with that job. I was young myself then. Pretty little thing she was too. Kind of upset me. They all went the same way. Sudden. Runs in the family."

She listened helplessly to his rambling, good-natured voice. She wanted to stop him, to tell him to go away, but she knew he wouldn't understand. His feelings would be hurt. He was such a gay old man, so eager and friendly. She had known at once what he must be. His fine black clothes and glistening linen were as professional as an actor's greasepaint. In his place, she'd want to talk too.

He'd probably been in that room all day, that dim room filled with flickering candle-light. It was cold in there. She could feel the cold creeping out, see it pushing against the portières, gently, experimentally, until it found the open space near the floor. The heavy fringe stirred for a moment and then fell back into place. She dragged her gaze away. The old man was smiling down at her.

"You are—" she began mechanically.

"Sheffy and Son," he chuckled. "I could give you my card here and now but that wouldn't look nice, would it? Anyway, you don't look like you need me. Little more flesh and you'll be fine. Sheffy and Son. I'm the son. They call me Young Sheffy. My dear old dad passed over twelve years ago. Now you got my pedigree all straight you better tell me yours. Where do you fit in the shebang, honey?"

"Mr. Hurst Herald was my mother's cousin."

"You don't say! Now that would be a branch I never met. Mama come along for the final rites?"

"She's dead too." Futility engulfed her again. "My mother died last month. My father died a long time ago." Her voice started to rise and she choked it back. "Don't Beauregards ever die?"

Young Sheffy put a clean, wrinkled hand on her shoulder. "There now, you're all upset. It's natural, but it'll pass. Believe me, it'll pass. I always tell the bereaved that. Of course Beauregards die! But only when their time comes. Like everybody else they go when their time comes. With some families it comes soon, with others it comes late. I've made a study of it and I know. Sometimes I can tell the doctor in charge that he don't have to worry. You take the Heralds, now. If the Heralds can get through their twenties, they're good till sixty. Get through the twenties, good till sixty, or thereabouts. After that it's touch and go. That's been my experience. Now Beauregards are different. They're good till eighty or ninety. Barring violence, of course. Like thrown from a horse in a barbed-wire fence. Funny thing."

She didn't answer. She was thinking. She was saying to herself—if Mrs. Mundy doesn't come soon I'll run away. I'll run, run, run—

Young Sheffy embraced the newel post and watched with approval while his assistant at the door dealt expertly with a newly arrived floral piece.

"More orchids. That makes eight tributes in orchids alone. Very fine, very appropriate. He was a good man.

Yessir, it's a funny thing. The Beauregards are old family, bred out, you might say. According to nature they ought to be weak. But are they? Nossir. Tough as nails. And the Heralds are new, been in this country only fifty years or so. Peasant stock to begin with, too, so they ought to be tough. And are they? Nossir. They are not. Go in the twenties, go at sixty, poof! Crack up like old china." He looked down into the young face turned from his. "I talk too much," he said regretfully. "Pay me no mind. What's your name, honey?"

"Carr. Regan Carr."

"Irish father. That's good, that's right. Like to see the blood mixed well." He looked as if he would go on forever but a whisper came from the top of the stairs. He touched her shoulder. "Mrs. Mundy wants you. I expect you're going up to see Miss May. You give Miss May my compliments, will you? Brave little woman."

She brushed by him wordlessly and ran up the stairs.

Mrs. Mundy led her down another hall. It smelled faintly of invisible wood fires and flowers. The flowers had a garden fragrance, unlike those in the room downstairs. Perhaps because they were in a warm place. Mrs. Mundy knocked on a door, opened it and stood back. Cousin May's room. They went in.

"My dear child," a voice said.

Two people, a man and a woman, sat close together on a sofa at one side of the fire. Cousin May sat alone on the other side, wrapped in pale pink shawls. There were pink lights everywhere, and pink roses.

Cousin May was old, Regan knew that. Older than Hurst, nearly seventy, she thought. But the white hair curled youthfully about her soft face and foamed and frothed into curls above her jeweled ears. Her round cheeks quivered as she held out her hand.

Regan advanced, full of pity when she saw how each step forward robbed Cousin May without mercy. When she reached the outstretched hand she found an old, old woman, hiding under a shell of pink powder.

Cousin May's voice was strong and full. "My dear child," she said again. "How dreadful this must be for you."

Regan blinked back sudden tears. "I didn't know. I'm so sorry. I didn't know until they told me downstairs."

Cousin May's hand, ringed with pearls, stroked hers. It felt dry and hot. "Sit here, on this little stool at my feet. I think it was made for a child like you. Take off your hat."

Regan pulled the old brown felt from her head and held it in her lap.

"Pretty," Cousin May said. "Very, very pretty. You look like the rest of them."

The man and woman on the sofa coughed like children calling attention to themselves.

"My sister Rosalie," Cousin May said. "And my brother Henry. Do you remember them, Regan? They remember you."

Regan smiled apologetically. Rosalie and Henry Beauregard returned unwinking stares. "I don't think I do," she said. "I was very young then and we were here such a short while. But I'm glad to see you now." She smiled again. The pair on the sofa examined her thoughtfully before they inclined their heads.

"So long ago," Cousin May sighed. "Such a happy, happy time. I can hardly remember those days myself. How old were you, Regan?"

"Six, I think."

Mrs. Mundy spoke from the door. "Not much more than a baby then. I wasn't here myself that time. I'd gone over to the farm for a few days."

"I know." Cousin May's eyes looked far away, as if she were traveling back across the water to her old home.

Mrs. Mundy rustled over to her chair and needlessly adjusted the shawls. "Don't talk too much," she counseled. "Tomorrow you'll need your strength. You must save yourself. I'm going down now and see about dinner." She paused. "Miss Regan, will she—"

"Yes indeed," Cousin May said warmly. "Of course she will. She'll stay with us just as long as she wants to. Just as long as we can make her happy. We'll give her a nice room all to herself, won't we, Mrs. Mundy?" It was half question, half order.

"Then I'll have to open one up. Mr. Max has the red room, Mr. Fray has the tapestry, and you know Miss Rosalie and Mr. Henry have the other two on this floor. That leaves only the—"

"You'll manage," Cousin May said gently. "And I'm sure Miss Regan understands our situation. So much distress and so many extra people. And it isn't as if we'd known she was coming." She stroked Regan's hand again. "But we mustn't talk about that, must we, Mrs. Mundy? Will you send Katy up with fresh tea for Miss Rosalie and Mr. Henry? They'll have it in their rooms."

Mrs. Mundy hesitated. "Shall I take Miss Regan with me?"

"No indeed. Poor Hurst's little cousin! We're going to have a nice talk and be great friends. I'll send her down to you later." She waved gaily to the couple on the sofa. It was a brave, bright gesture and it stirred Regan to admiration. "You two dears run along now. Come back and talk to me after dinner."

Mrs. Mundy left, trailed by the Beauregards. The Beauregards moved heavily and reluctantly. At the door they looked back, their full lips pursed into pouts.

"More tea," Mrs. Mundy reminded them. "With frosted cakes." They moved quickly then and the door closed behind them.

Cousin May gave Regan a deprecating smile. "I know I spoil them. My little brother and sister. But I can't help it. Now, tell me all about yourself!"

Regan hugged her knees and looked into the fire. It was going to be all right after all. Cousin May was kind, full of consideration even though her heart was breaking. Even Mrs. Mundy was more friendly now, and soon someone would be making up a bed for her to sleep in. Perhaps one of those nice old women in the kitchen. Jenny and Katy.

Of course it was going to be all right. Downstairs she

had been frightened; Young Sheffy's babbling talk, the hostile reception in the kitchen, the wreath on the door when she'd been looking for a smiling face. She had nothing to worry about, she told herself. Everything would be all right when she explained to Cousin May how Hurst had sent for her. No wonder they had been surprised and confused. An unexpected guest and the house full of people. Unexpected and almost unknown. Unexpected.

Cousin May said, "Did you hear me, dear?"

Regan flushed. "I was thinking. This must be very hard for you, having me walk in without warning. But you see I didn't know."

"You should have been notified. Fray's carelessness. It would have saved you that long, tiresome trip. But no, I forget. You'd already started, hadn't you?"

"Yes. You see, I wrote Cousin Hurst when my mother died last month and he told me to come here as soon as I got things settled. He was very kind. He and Max and Fray are the only people I have left. Had left," she corrected herself gently. "He said I could be his daughter." She looked hopefully for confirmation.

"How like poor Hurst," Cousin May sighed. "So extravagant when his sympathies were touched. I've known him to promise the most extraordinary things one minute and forget all about them the next." She caressed Regan's shoulder. "You say that was a month ago?"

Regan faltered. "Y-yes. I don't know why he didn't tell you."

"He wasn't himself, even then. He wasn't well. He'd had several attacks but I didn't tell his brothers. I didn't want to worry them. How did he get in touch with you, Regan? By letter? Or was it a telegram? Or perhaps he phoned?"

"He wrote."

"Ah, that explains it. Such a wretched letter writer. So confusing always. Jumping from one subject to another, almost incoherent at times. You probably misunderstood, my dear, and no wonder. I often did myself. Did he say anything about his illness?"

Regan went over the letter in her mind. She knew it word for word but she was trying to relive the night it came. There had been something odd, not in the words themselves but in the way they'd made her feel. A hot, breathless night; she'd walked home from her job at the library at nine o'clock, through noisy, sweltering streets, and climbed up to the small flat she had shared with her mother. The letter was under the door. She'd opened it with shaking hands, afraid of conventional sympathy and an offer of money. But it had been an answer to dreams. He'd said he wanted her, needed her. There was no mistake about that. He'd said—'Come as quickly as you can.' But standing there in the close, hot room she'd felt that he was saying even more than that. There was something between the lines that plead with her. She'd read the letter again and again, looking for a message that she couldn't find. Then she'd told herself she was imagining things. It was no more than an affectionate invitation from a man who must have known what loneliness was like. That was all. After she'd bathed and had her supper she couldn't remember why she had been disturbed. She couldn't remember now.

Mechanically, she fumbled with the clasp of her purse. The letter was in there. She'd let Cousin May read it. He'd said nothing about illness.

"Did he?" Cousin May's voice was suddenly sharp. "Did he tell you?"

Regan looked up, her hands still on the clasp. Cousin May's bright blue eyes, deep in the powdered flesh, were watching her hands. She folded them over the purse, suddenly ashamed of its shabbiness. The lining was torn. She didn't want Cousin May to see that.

"No," she said. "He didn't talk about himself at all."

Cousin May laughed softly. "You funny child. I always have to speak to you twice. Little dreamer, always wandering off, thinking silly thoughts. Do you have the letter with you?"

The bright blue eyes didn't meet hers even then. They were following the movements of her hands as they twisted and turned the worn clasp. Someone came down the hall and paused for a second outside the door. Regan heard the steps move on.

"Never mind," Cousin May said. "It isn't important. It's just that everything he said or wrote is precious to me now. He was so quiet; too quiet, too self-contained. But I know he was happy. He loved his little family. He gave us everything."

Regan thought of Max and Fray, Hurst's own brothers. Max was the oldest. She remembered him vaguely, a tall, thin man who said little. Fray had been away that summer when she and her mother had come to the house. He would be—she counted rapidly—he would be thirty-seven now. Not married, and too many girls, her mother had said.

Max and Fray were here somewhere, somewhere in the house. She remembered the woman laughing in the conservatory. Was Fray in there too, drinking wine and forgetting the cold front parlor?

"I haven't seen Fray," she said. "Or Max," she added quickly.

"They came this morning. Fray from the farm, he lives there now, and Max from New York. You'll see them later. But not tonight, I think. You're tired, my dear. Now don't apologize, I know. A nice tray in your room, and early to bed, that's what you need most. I shan't go down to dinner myself and I don't really feel that Max and Fray are good company for a young girl, such gloomy, silent men. Now Henry is great fun, you'll enjoy Henry. But there's no hurry. Tonight we'll all rest."

"I heard somebody laughing when I came up. I wondered who it was."

"Laughing? Where?"

"In the conservatory. It wasn't anything." She saw at once that she'd said the wrong thing. "Some caller, I guess. A woman."

"Miss Etta Luders? A little old woman, very untidy?"

"I didn't see. But it wasn't Miss Etta. She was in the kitchen."

Cousin May smiled faintly. "We'll hope the dear old creature stays there . . . Was Miss Etta here when you came with your mother so long ago? My poor memory—"

"I don't think so. I don't remember."

Cousin May bent down and pinched her cheek. "You don't remember anything, do you? Such a little thing you were, and such a wool-gatherer. So much imagination too, so bad for you. But then I expect you've outgrown that." She touched the curls at her temples and frowned. "My poor head. Dear child, I know you'll understand."

It was dismissal. Regan stood up, clutching her hat and purse, uncertain of her next move. But it was decided for her.

"Mrs. Mundy says you have a suitcase. That's all you brought, isn't it?"

"There's my trunk, too. I sent it by express. I thought—" Again the old, disturbing doubt. "All my things are in it. I thought I'd need them."

"Oh well, we'll take care of that when the time comes. We won't think about that now."

The small gilt clock on the mantel chimed faintly. Cousin May patted her eyes with a lacy handkerchief. "If we could only turn that back. Turn it back to yesterday. I found him, you know. Last night. He was lying on the white rug in front of the fire in his sitting room. I'll never get over it, never. I'm not strong. I know I look amazingly well but I'm really not strong." She smoothed the soft pink wool that covered her knees. "Did your mother tell you about the others?"

Regan's blank eyes were answer enough.

"I see that she didn't. She was a Herald and they never talk about themselves. The others died here too. Suddenly, without warning. If I were superstitious that might frighten me. All Heralds, and they came here for their holidays every year. And quite right that they should, after all it's their old home. But they died . . . You aren't superstitious, are you?"

"No," Regan said slowly. She was remembering what Young Sheffy had said. There had been three before Hurst. Hurst was the fourth. If they got by their twenties they were good until sixty. Was that why Cousin May had wanted to know her age? Twenty-two. She was twenty-two. Eight more years before . . . She told herself she was being absurd.

"I'll go now, Cousin May," she said.

"That's my good girl. Run down to Mrs. Mundy and arrange about your dinner. And later on, if anything disturbs you, or you feel lonely, come straight to me. You'll find me here whenever you need me. Have you something black to wear tomorrow?"

Tomorrow? The funeral? All she could say was—"I didn't know."

"Never mind. We'll arrange something. Perhaps though, well, never mind. We'll see how we feel in the morning. Do you know your way downstairs, my dear? Or shall I ring for someone to show you?"

"I know the way," Regan said.

She closed the door quietly behind her and leaned against it. She told herself that she had a headache too, but she could find no name for the sudden despair that filled her heart.

There were dim lights at intervals along the hall, and closed doors. There were other people behind those doors, Fray, Max, and the Beauregards. She had only to reach out a hand and someone would answer her knock. Heralds and Beauregards, they'd open their doors and look blank when they saw her there. The Beauregards would know who she was but Max and Fray might not. She'd have to explain all over again about her mother, about Hurst's letter. They'd look at her as Cousin May had done: kindly, puzzled, incredulous looks. They'd tell her politely that Hurst was impulsive, generous, and forgetful. No, she couldn't go through that again.

The kitchen. That was where she belonged. She turned right, toward the front stairs. At the top of the flight she looked down. Young Sheffy was still there, pacing back and forth. She saw the portières move as people went in and out of the front parlor. Did they move because people brushed against them, or was it the creeping cold? All at once she knew she couldn't go down that way. She didn't want to see that swaying fringe. She couldn't face Young Sheffy with his happy, whispering voice and his clean, wrinkled hands that knew the Herald bone structure. There must be back stairs somewhere. She turned again and retraced her steps down the broad upper hall.

Near the end of the hall she came to a short, branching passage. It was dark, but a faint light at the far end showed a narrow stairway going down. She had started toward it when she saw a figure moving toward her, hugging the wall. It had materialized out of the shadows. For a minute she knew panic, then she heard a faint, chirping scream. It was one of the maids, as frightened as she had been. Katy or Jenny.

"Katy?"

"Jenny, Miss." Jenny had flattened herself against the wall and her sad old face was smiling. "I come out of the linen closet back there and you give me a turn, you did. You've come the wrong way, dearie. Your stairs is back up front."

"I know, but I didn't want to pass all those people. This way leads to the kitchen, doesn't it?"

"Kitchen? Why, yes, if that's where you want to go. But there's no need. If you want something I can get it for you."

"No. No, thanks. I only want to tell Mrs. Mundy about my dinner. I'm not having it with the others, but in my room. I'm—I'm tired. And my suitcase is down there, and—"

"Don't you fret about that. Your dinner's all arranged for. Mrs. Mundy's seeing to it herself. And Katy's got your suitcase this minute, unpacking and putting away." She drew nearer. "You like champagne?" she whispered.

"Do I like—?" For one wonderful moment she wanted to laugh. Jenny's face, close to hers, belonged to a benevolent goblin.

"A beautiful bottle," Jenny went on. "Mr. Fray just sent it up to Miss Etta. You go in, I'll show you the way, and get a nice glass for yourself. There's plenty, and Miss Etta don't know when to stop when she gets started. You come along."

She led the way back to the main hall and down to a row of closed doors that stood in a line across the end. She knocked on the first door. "This was Mr. Herald's suite. Miss Etta's in the sitting room now, taking things hard." She opened the door and urged Regan gently forward. "Enjoy yourself while you can," she whispered. "We're dead a long time."

It was a small room, smaller than the one she had just left. There were worn Persian rugs on the floor, red leather chairs, and books halfway up the walls. There were more books on an open desk, flat, thin books in irregular stacks that looked as if someone had been called away in the middle of reading them. Hurst's collection of Dresden and crystal gleamed behind the glass doors of plain wooden cabinets.

There was only one light, a tall candelabrum in the center of a round table. Miss Etta sat at the table, fussing with a wine cooler. She was completely transformed.

"You're an answer to prayer," she said earnestly. "I thought it was Fray but you'll do just as well. You're nice and tall, aren't you?"

For the second time in a few minutes, Regan wanted to laugh. "Taller than you, but that's no record. What's nice about being tall? And what's this about prayer?"

Miss Etta gave the bottle a twirl and jerked her head backward. "There's a picture of a man behind me," she said. "Left of the fireplace, dark corner, and too high for me to reach even if I dared. Turn the ugly devil to the wall, will you, lamb? The old fellow, with the decorations."

Regan looked. "You mean Bismarck?"

Miss Etta screamed hoarsely. "Don't talk about him, turn him! I know what's going to happen and you don't. A little wine for my nerves and he follows me around with his eyes."

Wonderful, Regan thought. Wonderful and certainly crazy, but nice. She turned the picture, an old engraving in the grand manner, and came back. Miss Etta had covered her face, temporarily.

"All done?" Miss Etta asked in a muffled voice.

"Yes."

Miss Etta uncovered and sat up with assurance and dignity. "How many people in this house have told you I'm crazy? Don't answer, I know. Everybody. I'm not. And what's between me and old B. has nothing to do with the drink, either. It's a feud."

Regan put her elbows on the table and rested her chin in her hands. Her headache was gone; she was in another world, ridiculous and human, the same world that understood disobedient ghosts and gave them their freedom. She smiled gratefully at the old woman.

"Tell me all about it," she coaxed. "What kind of feud?"

"The ordinary kind. Grudge bearing. He has it in for me, that's all. Wouldn't you think a man of his age, dead too, would let bygones be bygones? The old devil. And I was very young at the time."

Regan added and subtracted silently. Miss Etta might have known Bismarck at that. Or she might be telling a tall tale. She looked as if she could. The bows and furbelows, strategically plastered on a meager façade, showed that Miss Etta knew the value of overstatement. But whatever it was, she was working a miracle. A gentle warmth filled the room. It was almost tangible. There was comfort even in the shadows.

"Tell me," she said again. "How young were you, and where did you meet—old B.?"

"Meet him! I never met him! This is on another plane entirely. I was eighteen when it began. It began the year I was eighteen and the Herald family gave me a trip to Europe. They thought it would be nice for me to see the old country again. I was only six when I came over . . . Are you going to believe any of this?"

"Of course I am!"

"That's right. It's gospel truth. Well, they gave me the trip but I didn't go. I mean I went, but not where they sent me. I up and changed the tickets when I got to New York, eighteen, mind you, all by myself and sheltered like a flower. I changed the tickets and went to England." She paused. "Aren't you going to scream? This is the place for it. I said I went to England—deliberately!"

"Was that so very terrible?"

"Terrible? It was a scandal. Not to the Heralds, of course. They were always broadminded. They just laughed. But it made my own people furious. They said I had disgraced myself. They carried on. They said they didn't know what old B. would think. Well I soon found out what old B. thought. He's had it in for me ever since. Tried to kill the ivy on the south wall that I stole from Kenilworth castle. I stole a little root and hid it in my hat. Nursed it like a baby on the boat coming home. You ought to see it now, I bet it breaks his evil heart. Five years ago he sent a blight but nothing happened. I beat it off with a smudge pot. You wouldn't think a man would bear a grudge beyond the grave, now would you?"

"No I wouldn't," Regan said. "Have you ever talked it over with—a doctor?"

"Doctor!" Miss Etta groped happily in the cooler. "Doctor my foot! Last fall I had typhoid fever and the doctor couldn't figure how I got it. Said it must have come from a bad oyster. I knew it was B. This fall I had influenza. Tries to kill me every fall, he knows how I like Christmas. But I'm tough . . . Here, ready now. Nice and cold." She filled two goblets. "How did you know I was in here?

You couldn't smell it, for pity's sake, so you must have heard the ice."

"Jenny brought me."

Miss Etta nodded approval. "They're good girls but the dust in this room is a sin. Drink up." She took a hesitating sip, choked in a refined manner and patted her thin chest. This pantomime, indicating a virginal experience, was instantly replaced by an honest wink. "I act like that because when I was young it was expected of a girl. Never lost the habit." She drained her goblet and refilled it. "It used to make Hurst laugh. Every month when I came for my check he'd have me in here and send for a bottle. And he'd have the picture all turned before I came in. He understood."

Regan said, "I know." She looked at Miss Etta with affection. Miss Etta was like herself. "I know," she said again. "I understand too."

Miss Etta had not expected sympathy and kindness. She thought they were gone forever. Her voice faltered before she went on. "We—we used to sit here and talk. We used to talk for hours. We made the world over, we made it over better and more fun." A film came over the small, vague eyes. "If he had to go, why didn't he wait until today? He knew I was coming today. He liked me. No matter what I did he liked me. I drink too much, and I tell lies, but he didn't care. He said we all did the things we had to do." Her voice faded and her hands opened and shut helplessly. For a long time she looked deep into the heart of something that only she could see; her eyes closed and the tired old body sagged into the warm embrace of memory.

Regan sat silent, watching with pity. Her own glass stood untouched. Miss Etta's glass had been emptied and refilled three times and now it held only the soft red glow of firelight. But the wine had turned its kindest trick. Miss Etta was bowed over the table, her dyed head resting on her folded arms.

The quiet room was like a harbor with a place for anyone who came. She and Miss Etta, years and worlds apart, had found it.

"If I could only stay in here," she whispered. "If I could only sleep in here tonight. They say he died in here, on that white rug, but it must have been peaceful because the room is full of peace. He could be sitting here, over in that dark chair, watching us, listening to us, smiling at us."

She looked about the dim room; the single candelabrum made a pool of light about the table and the silver bucket. She hadn't noticed the dust before. It was everywhere. Had they neglected him? Had he sat in that big chair with its telltale hollows and looked helplessly at the gray film that covered his treasures? No, he would never do that. Even if he were ill, he'd get up and ring the bell with good-natured fury.

She got up herself and moved soundlessly across the soft rugs, touching the old things, trying to remember if she had ever heard their story. The bedroom door stood open to darkness and she passed it by. The black marble mantel arched over a dying fire; the onyx clock, like a Greek temple with gold pillars, called the seconds in a whisper as they came and went. She remembered the clock. Its crystal face was blurred with dust and she traced her initials on the surface. They stood out sharply, as if they had been etched: R.C. It was a silly thing to do, she told herself, silly and thoughtless, and it might make trouble for Jenny and Katy.

She had raised her hand again, this time to erase the initials, when she heard the door open behind her. It was Fray.

She knew him at once. He was like Hurst in the old days, as she remembered him, like the picture that had always stood on her mother's dressing table. The same dark brooding look was there, but in Hurst it had been overlaid with tenderness.

There was no tenderness, no softness in Fray's face as he stood in the doorway, his dark eyes taking in the contents of the room, piece by piece. He ought to have a falcon on his wrist, she thought.

She stood without moving, waiting for him to see her. Or acknowledge her. He did neither. He crossed to the table and touched Miss Etta's shoulder, and the ridiculous feather boa fell to the floor. He replaced it carefully, frowning, and turned his attention to the wine glasses. He moved them about, as if he were undecided about something. His hands were long and white, with strong, slender fingers. Black and white. Black clothes, black tie, black hair.

She was sure then that he hadn't seen her; or perhaps he had taken her for one of the maids. An automaton, able to take orders but not geared to conversation. The fire was almost out and the room was dim except for the single pool of light. Then she knew she was wrong.

"Regan?" He spoke without looking up.

"Yes. You're Fray, aren't you?"

"That's a safe guess. Obviously I can't be Max—or Henry."

"You could be Hurst," she said. "That's how I knew." She spoke across the room, clutching her hat and purse, looking even younger than her very young twenty-two.

"Come over here and sit down." He drew two chairs to the table.

She looked doubtfully at Miss Etta's bowed body. "Won't Miss Etta—?"

"Etta's all right." Some warmth crept into his voice. "Etta's one of the wise ones. She knows exactly what she wants, goes after it, and gets it. I've just come from my brother's wife. What do you call her?"

"Cousin May. My mother always called her that."

"Of course . . . May tells me Hurst wrote you, asking you to come here. Do you mind telling me when that was?"

Here it was again. They didn't believe her. She drew a deep breath. "It was several weeks ago, when my mother died. He told me he wanted me. He told me this was my home." It seemed to her that she had said those same words

a dozen times in the last hour. Now they were old and lifeless and it was hard to believe they had ever been anything
else. But she had the letter, she had the proof. She tightened
her hold on the purse. "He said he was sorry about my
mother, too."

He felt the rebuke. She saw as much in his eyes.

"Go easy on us, Regan. We've all taken a wallop and
we're edgy. To tell the truth, I'd forgotten your existence
but I'm glad you came as you did . . . Did Hurst write
often?"

"Several times a year. At Christmas, times like that."

"That's like him. I'm afraid Max and I never had his
loyalty. He kept in touch with everyone who shared his
blood. You look like us. But where did you get the yellow
hair?"

"My father."

"Oh yes . . . Hurst told us nothing about your mother's
death. Even May didn't know. I suppose he wanted to arrange everything himself, plan your future and so on. He
always wanted a daughter."

"That's what he wrote! That's why I came! He sounded
lonely. But I don't want to stay, not now, not the way
things are. I've confused everyone by coming. As soon as
I've had some rest, I'll go home. I had a job at home and
they'll be glad to have me back again. I'm not helpless!"
She was afraid that sounded rude so she added, lamely, "I
couldn't sleep on the bus."

He shook his head, smiling. "Of course you're not going
back. I want you here and May wants you. You'll have to
give us a trial, at least. That's only fair. And we're sorry
about your mother even if we haven't said so."

He looked like Hurst when he smiled and she found herself smiling in return. That was surprising. I'm going to
like him, she thought. I don't want to, but I can't help it.

He was watching her. "What are you thinking?" he asked.

"Nothing." She flushed.

"Keep it up, it's very becoming." His eyes traveled to
the cluttered desk, the untidy bookshelves. "I've got to go

over all that stuff in the next few days. Ledgers, diaries, letters. Read and check. How would you like to help me?"

"If you think I can." She tried to make her voice sound doubtful.

"Sold! We'll have ourselves a time! Now what about that letter you got from Hurst? Do you mind letting me see it?"

First Cousin May, now Fray. It began to look as if everyone in the house wanted to read that letter. But that was natural. Anything that Hurst had planned or written would have a value.

"Hurst meant a lot to me," Fray said softly. "I think your letter is the last he wrote."

She turned the purse over and over in her hands, embarrassed and undecided. Fray wouldn't notice the shabby lining. Men didn't notice things like that. But her mother's gold beads and thirty hoarded dollars were in the envelope with the letter. The beads were good, she wasn't shamed of them, but the money was in old, eloquent bills that said too much about dark little shops on mean, small streets. She fumbled with the clasp, watching his face, trying to make up her mind.

Miss Etta stirred in her sleep and moaned. She raised one hand against an unhappy dream, and let it fall. The empty goblet rolled silently across the table and crashed to the floor.

Fray jumped, looked down at the old, dyed head, and laughed without sound. But his face and voice had altered when he turned to her again. "Well?" he asked.

She answered automatically. "I haven't got it," she said slowly. "I didn't think anybody would want to see it." She couldn't remember what she had said before, down in the kitchen, in Cousin May's room. She didn't know why she was lying now. "I didn't keep it," she went on steadily, "because I expected to see him." She watched for a sign that he didn't believe her, for any sign. But she couldn't tell what he was thinking.

"Forget it," he said lightly. "I was being sentimental and

that's always half-witted. And don't look so tragic. What's wrong, was that your glass that broke?"

"No. I didn't touch mine. I didn't want any."

"Teetotaler? You and Etta won't have much in common." His eyes were moving about the room again. When they came to the picture with its face to the wall he laughed out loud. "Did you do that?"

"Yes. She asked me to." He's forgotten about the letter already, she thought. "She told me about old B. And the ivy."

"Really? Then she loves you. You're going to be pals. Next time she'll tell you about the peacock feathers. That's her masterpiece, to date . . . Here, this won't do, you're making me forget what I really came for. Katy says your room is ready. She's taken your bag up. The floor above this to the rear. Directly over this room. The door's open, you can't miss it. Better get along, she's waiting for you."

He walked to the door and held it open.

When the door closed again she stopped and listened, but the wood was thick and no sound came through. When she reached the front stairs she climbed steadily up, not looking back.

In Hurst Herald's sitting room Fray emptied the full glass into the cooler together with the wine remaining in the bottle, and poured the whole into the bathroom basin. He went back to the table and sat there, watching Miss Etta. Miss Etta slept on.

Chapter Three

THE top floor hall was dark but a door stood open at the
far end. Light streamed out. A bent, white-capped
woman, smoothing the bed, turned with a smile when Regan
entered.

"There now," she said. "If I didn't forget to turn the
lights on out there! I didn't think about you not knowing
your way. The dark made you nervous, didn't it, Miss?"

"A little." Regan smiled back. "This time it's Katy, isn't
it?"

"Yes, Miss. You'll soon get used to telling us apart, although we do look alike. It's easy when you know how."
She touched a gnarled finger to her chin. "I have the mole.
Jenny is three years my senior but I have the mole." It was
a distinction, her eyes said, like a talent for playing the
piano. She took the hat and purse from Regan's hand and
laid them on the closet shelf. "You'll see I've put your
clothes away, and I've given you an extra eiderdown. These
nights surprise you sometimes. It's being so close to the
water." She gave the room a sad, appraising look. "It's
clean, I'll say that for it, and the view's nice in good weather,
but you ought to have a bigger one. But the big ones are
all taken. There's a bath next door. And if you're lonesome for home just remember there's the rest of us up front."

Lonesome for home. Regan's heart warmed. "You and
Jenny?"

"Yes, Miss. And the Mundys. These rooms at the back
are for extras, single folks, odd people, and so on. At least

that's what I'm told." She lowered her voice. "I gave you real linen sheets but you needn't mention it."

"Thank you." She wanted to keep Katy there. Katy was like the country women who sometimes came to the library on Saturday afternoons and shyly whispered their requests for a nice book, a pretty book, something with love in it.

"Katy," Regan began, but Katy had crossed to the hot air grate set into the wall and was banging and rattling the lever with daring insolence. Mrs. Mundy was miles away in the kitchen.

"Supposed to give out heat," Katy said boldly, "but what you get is soot and damp. Chimney's no good on this side. No good at all. I know more about chimneys than Santa Claus." She covered her mouth with her hand and doubled up silently at her own wit.

She's trying to cheer me up, Regan told herself; she's trying to make me feel at home. She too laughed silently and Katy glowed.

"Tell me something you'd like," Katy begged, "and I'll get it for you. You just tell me something!"

"Stay and talk to me a while," Regan said. "I'd like that. I'd like to talk to someone about things, about Mr. Herald. I haven't been told very much."

Katy sobered instantly. "Oh I couldn't, Miss! I hardly knew Mr. Herald, you might say. He was lovely but Jenny and me, we haven't been here very long." She threw a furtive look down the dark hall and her eyes came back to the figure huddled at the foot of the bed. She burst out: "You're so little! You're so little to be up here by yourself! It's all right for Jenny and me, we've lived our lives, but you haven't hardly begun!" She seized an armful of dust covers and scurried to the door. "I been up here too long already. They'll be wondering. I'll bring your dinner as soon as I can, you must be hungry. No tea or nothing." With that she was gone.

Regan followed to the door. She saw Katy's dim figure duck into a passage identical with the one on the floor below. Back stairs, she decided; they'll do for me too. She closed the door and stood against it, surveying the room. Plain wicker and maple furniture, plain cream walls, plain net curtains and braided rug. Better than she had at home, but cold, cold. She went to the window and looked out. There was nothing to see, only the night pressing close. It was like a curtain in a theater, soft but impenetrable, hiding the actors and the scene until the play was ready to begin. But there was nothing to hide out there. She knew the darkness would dissolve into an innocent garden if she turned out the lights in the room behind her. But she wanted the lights.

She pressed her forehead against the glass. The old magnolias and the holly trees would be green and glossy if she could see them, but the pink crêpe myrtles would be brittle and brown. The water was there too. She thought of raising the window and leaning out. She could hear the water then, and smell the clean, salt wind, but Cousin May wouldn't like her to do that and the neighbors might think it strange and talk about it. Then she remembered there were no near neighbors. A whole block of garden she had told herself proudly only a little while ago. Now it was an empty wilderness. She could even jump from the window and no one would see her body fall. Unless it fell by the kitchen windows. Unless the kitchen shades were up.

Something light and almost soundless pattered against the glass. She recoiled, then laughed shakily. It was nothing but rain, a small, warning handful. She leaned against the glass again and waited for the storm. She was still there when Mundy came in without knocking.

He was the man she had seen arranging glasses in the pantry. He introduced himself in a soft voice while he unfolded a portable table and placed her dinner tray. She was used to helping people and she tried to help him, but after a few attempts she knew it was the wrong thing to do. He conveyed that silently.

"I expected Katy," she finally said.

"Katy has the dining room this evening, "Mundy answered. He stepped back. "Mrs. Mundy says will you send her word, please, if you have everything you need? She has given you broiled chicken, but if you prefer a chop—"

"Oh no. Everything's fine. Thank you . . . Will Katy come up for the tray?"

"I couldn't say. When you've finished, will you place both table and tray in the hall, please? They will be collected later."

He drew the blinds at the windows and left her with a quick, backward look. There was speculation in his eyes, and she saw it. He thinks I'm going to cry, she said to herself. She smiled steadily, hoping he would turn around, but he didn't.

She ate slowly, purposely consuming time with the food. If she took long enough perhaps Katy would come for the table before she put it in the hall. Then they could talk. Talking to Fray and Cousin May had told her nothing. She'd ask about Hurst. Katy could tell her how he had looked.

Halfway through the meal she found herself shivering. Even the food had grown too cold for enjoyment. The melted butter on the chicken had congealed into a brown, lacy pattern on her plate. She moved the table over to the hot air grating but Katy had been right about that. There was no heat. Little puffs of air, smelling of damp, blew into her face. She moved back to the center of the room and hung her coat over her shoulders. The coffee, when she came to it, was hot; it was in a thermos jug. She cradled the steaming cup between her hands and held it to her cheek.

It was eight o'clock when she finished. The storm had come and the rain struck at the windows with an importunate hiss. It sounded like an invitation to come, or go, but there was no place to go. Cousin May's warm, rose-colored room was on the floor below but she couldn't go there again. Not until she was sent for. And the dusty little room that had been Hurst's was warm too, but Miss Etta might be there. She wondered what Fray had done with Miss Etta.

She undressed quickly and got into the old gray blanket robe that had been her mother's. It was ugly and shapeless but clean and carefully mended. She knew the fragile cloth on her dinner tray had cost ten times as much. Her bedroom slippers made her smile, as they always did. Gray plush, with toes shaped like rabbit heads. Black wool eyes, pink noses, whiskers; long ears of plush that she always tripped over. She dragged the ears into a standing position because that was a part of the ritual. They flopped back. Four dollars' worth of ears. She must have been crazy when she bought them.

The bath was next door, Katy had said. A hot bath, then bed. She'd go to sleep at once; she was already nodding. And in the morning the sun would be shining.

She put the table in the hall and found the bath. It was warm in there and scented with extravagant soap and salts, much too good for Katy's single folks and odd people. Katy must have raided the downstairs rooms.

She managed to use three quarters of an hour and when she came out into the hall again the table was gone. The hall stretched dimly to the front of the house; there was a faint glow at the entrance to the passage that led to the back stairs. She listened for footsteps, for opening and closing doors, for voices, but there was no sound. That was strange. A house full of people and silence. Three women in the kitchen, Mundy somewhere, Cousin May, Max, Fray, Rosalie and Henry Beauregard, Young Sheffy and his assistants, and the dark stream of callers moving between the front door and the front parlor. It was still early and the callers would be coming and going for at least another hour. But, she reminded herself, they were not the kind who rang the doorbell. The door opened for them.

She moved quietly through the shadows, up the hall to the head of the main stairs, and looked down the stair-well. Light came up, and the deep red carpeting glowed. The tops of peoples' heads—heads with hair, bald, glistening heads, heads with dark hats—moved back and forth below. Here was sound at last, comforting and human. A low murmur

rose and fell but it was not the murmur of articulate speech.
It was the sound that drifts out into the vestibule of a
crowded church, the rustle of good clothes, the subdued
clearing of dry throats; it was thoughts, unspoken, rising
and falling in a dozen minds.

She drew back and returned the way she had come. Her
room was so cold that she wore the ugly gray robe to bed.

The clock on the bed table ticked softly and the wind
joined the rain at the windows; she was too tired to listen.
It was warm under the blankets and the robe, and she fell
asleep.

Downstairs the callers came and went. At eleven o'clock
Young Sheffy, on unobtrusive duty in the front parlor,
knew from long experience that there would be no more.
He was alone in the big room. He touched the cold, waxen
cheeks with a disciplined finger, found that everything was
as it should be, and moved softly about the room, snuffing
out all but three candles, adjusting the windows, humming
to himself. His two assistants waited for him in the hall
and they left the house together.

The conservatory was dark and empty. Mundy washed
the last of the port glasses in his pantry and Mrs. Mundy
and the Crains tidied up the kitchen and banked the fire
in the coal range. They went upstairs with dragging feet
and joined Mundy. Together they checked bolts and locks,
moving silently from door to window, window to door, not
speaking. Half an hour later they were in their own beds.

The fire in Cousin May's sitting room curled brightly
around fresh logs and she still sat before it, wrapped in
shawls. The Beauregards nodded on the sofa, overcome by
heat, too much food, and dreams of the future.

Although nothing had been said about an increased allowance they had been promised fur coats for the funeral: an
almost new Persian for Rosalie and Hurst's mink-lined
broadcloth for Henry. Henry looked forward to the mink-
lined coat. He had no qualms about wearing another man's
clothes to his funeral and he didn't see how Max and Fray
could object. Max had his own handsome coat, and this

one was too old-fashioned for Fray. It was the wrong size, too. Henry frowned when he thought of the size, but not for long. It might be a little tight around the middle, a little long in the body, but he needn't button it. He was satisfied when he decided that he needn't button it. He saw himself standing beside the grave, his eyes full of tears, the broadcloth turned negligently back to show the fur. People would ask who he was. There were so many strangers in the county now, rich upstarts from New York and Pittsburgh; they wouldn't know he was a Beauregard. He'd talk to the strangers when everything was over, move from group to group, shaking hands, whispering his identity. He belched with pleasure. That roast goose had been rich.

Rosalie's dreams had no form. She played with the beads around her neck and sometimes held them up to the light.

Cousin May stirred and raised her eyes. "Bedtime for you, my dears." She got to her feet, the soft shawls slipping to the floor, and walked with them to the door. "Don't get up until you're called, darlings. Everything will be so confused and heartbreaking, and you must have a good, long rest." She kissed them both and they returned beaming smiles as they waddled up the hall to their own rooms.

Regan moved restlessly in her sleep and gradually woke. The robe was too heavy now. She turned on the light beside the bed and sat up. Two o'clock. She listened. The wind and the rain had stopped; the room was icy and the air was stale and thick. She'd been afraid to open a window before. If she opened one now and let the clean air in—

She turned off the light and padded across the room. The window opened soundlessly. That was better, much better. She could hear the lapping water of the bay and smell the good, salt air. She didn't want to go back to bed. The eiderdown was light and warm. She wrapped it about her shoulders and knelt on the floor, elbows on the sill.

The garden was full of mist. It coiled up from the sodden grass like spirals of smoke and met the fog that rolled in from the bay. In spite of the fog she could see the trees standing in orderly rows along the drive, in landscaped groups around the old stable and down by the water's edge. She knew it was the old stable because she could see the squat, square tower. The tower was invisible from the lower windows because the trees were too thick, but up here the garden could be read like a map. Even against the dark sky, even through the shifting fog, the tower and the trees stood out.

The blackest trees were a circle of cypresses down by the water. Years ago they had been black in the noonday sun; she vaguely remembered that. She had liked them then because they were different and strange; they were different and strange now, but they were disquieting too. She looked away, trying to find the hollies that had always held enchantment in their prickly depths, but her eyes came back to the cypress ring. The still, black circle held her fast; she could see nothing else. She dug into her mind, exploring, turning the years over, wondering why she felt the way she did. She was unaccountably afraid of the road she was traveling. It was both alien and familiar.

Then, suddenly, she found a reason for her fear and it was simple and satisfactory. The trees had made her think of a picture she had once seen in the principal's office in grade school. You went to the principal's office when your marks were low and the picture hung behind the principal's head. It was called The Island of the Dead, or something like that. Cypresses and water. Even the sound of lapping water fitted in, even the feeling of foreboding. Funny, she thought; that was a long time ago. That was the third grade. Why do I remember it now?

She looked again. The pointed cypresses were blacker and the lapping water sounded nearer. One tree rose from the center of the circle, taller than the others, bleak and bare. It's dead, she thought; it's dead, and they ought to cut it down. As she looked, the lonely tree slowly dominated the garden.

She turned away from it, concentrating on the stable tower to the left, on the straight trim lines that marked the driveway on the right, but each time her eyes returned to the dead tree. "I'm tired," she whispered. "I don't know what I'm thinking or seeing."

The bare tree pointed to the sky and the fog rolled in from the bay and made a shroud. "I don't know what I'm thinking," she repeated dully.

She left the window and went back to bed but although her eyes were aching and heavy they would not close. They moved from the open window with its silent, swaying curtain to the closed door leading into the hall, back and forth, back and forth. "The tree is dead," she whispered. "Why do I keep thinking that?" The curtain blew inward, until it was like a horizontal net spread to catch a falling body. Dead, she said to herself, dead.

The portières in the front parlor had moved like that, but with less power. Hurst was dead too, the beloved Hurst who always remembered his own. And she had refused to look at him. She had come a long way to answer the summons of a living man, and she had refused to look at him because he was dead. Or because she was afraid. I know what's wrong with me, she told herself; that dead tree is my conscience. Instantly, she knew what she had to do.

She turned the light on long enough to read the time. Quarter of three. She'd go down there now while the house was asleep, down the back stairs, two flights to the ground floor. A few minutes to get there and return, and then a quiet heart until morning. Robe, slippers, a paper book of matches, and she was ready.

The door made no sound when she opened it. She turned right in the hall and groped her way along the passage to the dim night light at the head of the back stairs. The stairs were not as wide as those in the front; they curved sharply and there were walls on each side. It was like climbing down a well. After the first few steps the light was useless and she moved cautiously, with both hands on the enclosing walls. She thought of Mundy toiling up in that darkness, with dinner tray and folding table. There must be other lights but she didn't know where they were.

Suddenly her right hand left the wall and plunged into

a deep, hollow space. At the same time the stairs made a sharp turn and she nearly fell. She steadied herself against the other wall and felt for the matches in her pocket; her hand shook as she held up the flickering light. The hollow space was a deep niche cut into the wall, and it was empty.

She'd seen that kind of niche before, in other old houses. It had always been filled with something, statuary, artificial vines, even books, but she knew it wasn't meant for those things. Its original purpose had nothing to do with decoration. It was a coffin niche. In old houses where the stairways turned sharply there was always a niche to hold one end of the coffin as it was carried down and around the bend.

The front stairs were wide and open, with gracious curves, and there were no niches there. But back here they were needed. If servants died, this would be the way they'd leave. Servants on the top floor. Servants and odd people who lived on the top floor. The match burnt her fingers and she dropped it.

She reached the second floor, a small, square landing, and a second dim light. The rabbit slippers made no sound and the long, clumsy robe trailed silently in her wake. Down the last flight to the first floor. There was light coming up and she could see every step of the way. Another niche, empty as the first, another sharp turn, and she was in Mundy's neat pantry. She made her way to the wide front hall, thickly carpeted and warm. The dining room, the dark conservatory, the closed doors that had been closed before; she passed them all as she went forward.

Young Sheffy had left a burning lamp on a table near the red portières. She waited only long enough to draw a deep breath before she went in. The walk across the polished floor seemed endless. It was like walking between two walls of flowers, like walking down the aisle of a greenhouse. At the end of the aisle she came to a cleared space, lighted by three candles. There were no watchers. She was alone.

She studied the closed eyes and pale, folded lips. There was nothing there that she remembered. No sunburned man

in white linen with a red scarf wrapped around his brown
throat; no brown hair crinkling, no brown eyes full of
confidence, smiling down into hers while he told impossible
tales with happy endings. She could look down at him now
but he couldn't look up.

She tried to return one of those confiding smiles, as a
debtor repays gold with gold; she twisted her mouth the
way he had twisted his, and shrugged an entreating shoulder.
That was the way he had shrugged when he asked her to
believe. The candles flickered in the draft and threw a
shadow on his face and that was all. She whispered her own
version of a happy ending to an impossible tale. "It's going
to be all right," she said.

Then she left him.

Closed doors, conservatory, dining room, pantry, and up
the winding stairs that grew darker as she ascended. Turn
at the first niche and on up to the second floor. The landing,
the faint light, and up again. The second floor was behind
her; ahead was the last dark flight. She had reached the
second niche when she heard a door close softly. A door
somewhere above.

Someone was coming down the upper passage, quickly,
lightly, sure of foot, coming toward the stairs. Mundy?
Mrs. Mundy? She stepped up into the niche; it received
her body easily; it was deep enough, wide enough, tall
enough. She held her breath and waited. A light clicked on
above and threw a shadow around the bend, a towering
shadow with arms and legs. Mundy. He had heard her and
was coming to investigate. She remembered his small, appraising eyes. What could she say to him? She shrank into
the dim oval. With luck he wouldn't see her.

The black shape plunged downward like a rolling ava-
lanche, swallowing the walls, the stairs, and her own arms
that she had instinctively thrust forward; then it dissolved
into nothing. Fray rounded the bend with the light behind
him. He was in dinner clothes.

He stopped short. "Who is that?"

"Regan," she whispered.

He stood on the step above the niche. "Exactly what are you doing there?"

"I went down to see Hurst." The words sounded thin and foolish and so did her voice. He won't believe that, she thought.

He slouched against the wall, hands in the pockets of his jacket. "At this hour? Why? Did you think he wasn't there?"

"No!" she answered in a low, furious whisper. Suddenly she hated him, because she was shabby and unkempt and he looked as if he were waiting for an orchestra to play again. "No," she repeated. "I went because I'd refused to go before. I kept thinking about it and I couldn't sleep. So I got up and went down there."

"Jitters. Why didn't you call me? I'd have gone with you."

"I didn't know where you were and I didn't think you'd care anyway. You don't look as if you cared now."

"I know. I can't seem to grieve like Henry. He's turning out a perfect job. His hands wobble, his lips tremble, he has trouble with his soup. It runs down his chin. Now some people might call that messy but I think it's very impressive. He cries too. I hope you didn't wake the old boy up, he's downright exhausted."

"I haven't waked anybody up. I couldn't if I tried. Everybody's sleeping too well. I think I'm the only person in this house who's really sorry! Now if you'll get out of the way, I'd like to go up to my room!"

"Worked yourself into a nice little act, haven't you? Almost as good as Henry's. But if you don't mind my saying so, you're not dressed for it."

She tried to step down but he barred the way with a firm arm. "Wait. It's all right. I'm glad you went down there but the next time you feel like prowling you'd better come to me first. I'm in the west room, second floor front. You don't want Mundy taking pot shots at your shadow, do you? Now come out of that. It wasn't meant to stand in."

"I know."

"Well, come on. I'll take you back to your room. I've just come from there, or near there. You have a new neighbor, Miss Etta. But she won't give you any trouble. She's out cold."

"That isn't funny, and it's your fault. You ought to be ashamed. You could have stopped her if you'd wanted to."

"You don't know what you're talking about. Come along."

He stood against the wall and let her pass. Then he followed, switching on lights she hadn't known were there. When he walked beside her she saw that his eyes were tired and his face was white.

Outside her door he said, "I'll wait here until you tell me you're in bed. In to stay."

She went in and his voice followed. "I like your little fur feet," he said.

She closed the door firmly.

He leaned against it and listened. After a minute he called, "All right?" There was no answer. He straightened up and moved on to a door on the other side of the bath. He listened there too, seemed satisfied, and went back the way he had come, turning off lights and frowning at his own thoughts.

The room was full of gray light when Regan woke to the sound of knocking. One of the Crains was edging through the door, a breakfast tray in her hands and a long black coat over one arm. Katy, with the mole.

"A terrible day," Katy said with satisfaction. She put her burdens on table and chair and went over to close the window. The rain was falling with quiet insistence. "Bad weather for mourners. Nine o'clock, Miss."

"Nine!" Regan stared at the clock. "And I wanted to come down to breakfast!"

"We got orders about that. Mr. Fray. He said to let you sleep. Here." She carried the tray to the bed. "You stay where you are. The room's cold and the food'll warm you up. And I'm to call your attention to this coat, please. You're to wear it to the funeral. Mrs. Herald says to tell you she got it for Miss Rosalie but it didn't fit."

That was a lie and Katy knew it. It was a whopping big lie and it wasn't her own, but she had to tell it just the same. Mrs. Herald had sent Jenny up to the attic for the coat the night before, that's what. It was in an old trunk with initials painted on the side. C.H., they said. Jenny had been told to sponge and press the coat and they'd both been told to say it had been meant for Miss Rosalie but didn't fit. The chances were Miss Rosalie had never set her eyes on it. And even if she had she couldn't wear it in a million years; too fat. And since when, for pity's sake, did C.H. stand for Rosalie Beauregard. That coat had belonged to Mrs. Max Herald. Claudine her name was, poor soul, and she'd died the day she bought it. Mrs. Mundy had said so, looking as if she'd like to bite her tongue out afterwards.

Katy sighed. Another sin to confess before she could make her next communion. That made three, counting greed for cheese and envy of Miss Etta. Greed and envy were old offenders, she wasn't worried about them. It was the lie about the coat that weighed heavy. But surely the good Lord knew that a job was a job and everybody knew how funny rich people were about old clothes and poor relations. She clutched at one truthful straw and held her soul above water. "See?" she said. "It's never been worn."

Regan looked at the coat and then at Katy. Somebody was playing a joke. It had to be a joke. She touched the braided scrolls and jet buttons with fascinated, incredulous fingers. "Katy! It came out of the Ark!" She started to laugh but the look on Katy's face stopped her. Katy's eyes were full of urgent pleading. She was trying to say something without words.

"Do I have to wear it, Katy?"

"It'll only be for an hour or so, Miss. And it isn't as if you were going among strangers who'd be likely to notice. You can wear your little blue dress underneath and that'll make you feel better. I told Mrs. Herald you had a nice black hat in your suitcase." She waited anxiously for this to be accepted.

"Thank you, Katy. You can tell Mrs. Herald it's all right. But don't overdo it!" Katy flushed and retired to the hot air grating where she noisily resumed her feud of the night before. She banged and rattled the grating as if her life depended on it, or as if she wanted to stop the conversation where it was.

Regan poured her coffee and drank it slowly. The poor thing was embarrassed, she thought. She was afraid I'd hurt Cousin May's feelings and didn't like to say so.

"Katy, did Mrs. Herald say anything else?"

"Yes, Miss. I'm to tell you that the funeral's at eleven-thirty. But if you don't feel up to going, why nobody cares to press you. That's what I'm to tell you."

She thought she understood about the coat then. It wasn't a joke, it was a tactful move. It was meant to call attention to the shortcomings of her own wardrobe and keep her out of sight at the same time. But that was crude and it didn't sound like Cousin May. Well, she told herself, whatever it is, it isn't going to work.

"I'm going," she said to Katy. "You can tell Mrs. Herald and everybody else. I'm going."

Katy nodded. "That's proper, that's right," she approved. "It don't matter what you wear when you're young. And there won't be any service in the house and no church at all. Those who wish to pay their respects will meet in the main hall at eleven-fifteen and drive out to the graveyard. That don't include Jenny and me because we're new and somebody has to see to the lunch. The doctor's coming. He's a fusty boots." Katy was frankly enjoying her temporary escape from the Mundys' watchful eyes. She abandoned the gating with a small kick.

"You should have had the room on the other side of the bath. It's nice and warm in there, but that Miss Etta!" She gave Regan a look that was like a whisper. "She's going to stay on a bit, did you know that? Mr. Fray said so. Told Mrs. Mundy himself this morning. Says Miss Etta needs a

change and he wants her here until he goes back to the farm.
Will you care for that, Miss?"

"I haven't anything to do with it, Katy. I'm only a visitor
too."

"Oh." Katy's face fell. "Jenny and I, we were hoping
you'd stay for good. We were saying we could look after
you. We know how. There was a young lady in one of
the places where we worked before so we know what's
required." She was begging, coming closer to the head of
the bed, smoothing the covers as she came. "You eat all
those biscuits. That's good country butter and I put it on
with a free hand . . . We offered to look after Miss Etta
but it wasn't accepted."

"You can look after me as long as I'm here, Katy. I love
having you around."

Katy's relief expressed itself in a small spasm. She fluttered
like a lame bird reaching for a fat worm and pounced on
Miss Etta as a likely substitute.

"That Miss Etta! She won't wash, not properly! Cologne
instead of water and all that paint. If she's going to stay
here like one of the family somebody'll have to keep an eye
on her. And she talks too much. Lies, like. Many's the
time I've heard Mrs. Herald say that a person listening to
Miss Etta might think there was something wrong with the
rest of us. Did anybody ever tell you Miss Etta is sort of
crazy?"

Regan hesitated. There was a legend building up around
Miss Etta but whether it was old or new she couldn't tell.
Four people had emphasized Miss Etta's craziness, Mrs.
Mundy, Cousin May, Fray and Katy. And Miss Etta
herself had made no small contribution. She looked at the
coat again. She was running Miss Etta a close second for
blue ribbon in the misfit class.

"Almost everybody has managed to tell me something,"
she said. "But I like her. She's old, that's all, and she likes
the things she makes up better than the things that happen.
I don't blame her. I'd probably do the same thing in her
place. And we have a lot in common. We both loved Mr.

Hurst and we're both outsiders now . . . Where does Miss Etta live?"

"She's got a little flat on the other side of town, the bad side, but she only stays there in summer. By rights she ought to be in Baltimore with her niece this minute. I don't know what's got into Mr. Fray, keeping her here. She takes things too. You know, helps herself to things that strike her fancy. Nothing valuable, I'll say that for her, but little things, like a magpie. Let Miss Etta find a broken cup and she hides it away until she's ready to leave. They ought to search her bundles, Mrs. Mundy told Mr. Fray so, but he said let her alone." Katy lowered her voice to a whisper. "Got herself under the influence on purpose last night. That comes of giving her the run of the cellar. But Mr. Fray says let her alone. He's like Mr. Hurst in some ways. Soft with queer people and children."

There was no censure in Katy's voice, only the old, sinful envy. Miss Etta was lucky like Mrs. Mundy. Still she oughtn't complain. It was fine to have the bits left over in the wine glasses. You let the glasses stand in a warm place and the drops on the sides ran down to the bottom. Sometimes you got a good swallow. It warmed the stomach.

Regan studied the childish old face, puckered with the effort to say and do the right things. Katy had the mind of a precocious baby. She saw nothing but the color and shape of things but she had been shrewd enough about Miss Etta. Regan put her next question carefully.

"Katy, who took care of Mr. Hurst's rooms?"

Katy's hopscotch attention had jumped happily to the window. She was looking down into the garden, chirping with pleasure. "That Mr. Fray," she said. "Prowling in the rain, no hat, no coat, no gumshoes. He'll be down with something sure's you're born. What did you say, Miss?"

Regan repeated her question. It sounded bald and crude the second time but she knew Katy wouldn't notice that. "I was just wondering," she added.

"Why I did," Katy said. "That is I did until two weeks ago or thereabouts. That was when he said he didn't want to

be disturbed. Didn't want me coming in and out and said
he'd do for himself a bit. I think he was beginning to feel
bad then and wanted to be left alone. So I gave him a car-
pet sweeper and a nice dust rag and let him be. Jenny says
the place was a living sight when she went in yesterday but
Mr. Fray don't want anything touched yet." Fear and in-
security struck at Katy again. "Have you heard any complaints, Miss?"

"Oh no, that isn't what I meant. I meant that whoever
looked after his rooms could tell me all about him. I want
to know everything, what he said, what he did, what he
looked like. I was very young when I was here before but
I never forgot him. He wasn't like a relation. He was more
of an—"

"An ideal, like?" offered Katy.

"That's it. So, I want to know what his life was like before he died. I can't talk to the others. They're strangers,
even Mr. Max and Mr. Fray. You and Jenny," she smiled
up at Katy, "you and Jenny are like old friends already."
She patted the edge of the bed invitingly. "I wish you'd
talk to me, Katy."

Katy lowered her old body with a sigh of pleasure but
she saw the clock at the same time. "Mercy!" She scrambled
to her feet and scuttled over to the door. "Now I got
trouble coming sure's you're born! Half-past! You leave
that tray right there. I've got to tell Mrs. Herald that
you're going to the funeral and I've got to open oysters for
lunch, the nasty dirty things all over mud. I hope you like
'em." She vanished in a tempest of worried sighs and pattering feet.

Regan bathed and dressed slowly. She stood at the window where Katy had been but there was no sign of Fray in
the dripping garden. The fog still clung to the cypress trees
and the dead tree rose above it. The dead tree. She looked
again, amazed at what she saw.

It wasn't a dead tree after all. It was a thin wooden spire,
pointing upward like a finger. She saw it as she would have

heard a clap of thunder on a clear day. It was so familiar that it hurt and yet she had forgotten its existence until that moment. That's the pavilion, she marveled. The pavilion's down there. She stood at the window, brushing her hair, wondering why she had forgotten that heavenly place.

The pavilion had been the best part of her visit before. It was a small, circular building, at least that was how she remembered it. It was a summerhouse of one room, weatherproof, with a fireplace for chilly days and little round windows. The side that faced the water was open, with screens to let in the air and sun and shutters that rolled down at night. How could she have forgotten the pavilion!

Hurst used to do his accounts there, and write his letters, and every afternoon at five he had entertained a lady with orange sherbet. She could see and taste the orange sherbet as if it had been yesterday. She left the window abruptly.

I won't go there, she told herself; that would be too much. I won't go there, she repeated; even thinking about it hurts. I can't bear to think about it and I don't know why. But in spite of herself she looked again, over her shoulder. The spire was more than ever like a beckoning finger. I won't go, she said, I won't go. But she knew that she would.

She buttoned the despised coat over her blue jumper, carefully avoiding the mirror, and put on her black hat and gloves. Hurst's letter, the gold beads and the thirty dollars were in her purse. She looked at the envelope a long time before she locked it in her suitcase.

The door on the other side of the bath was open when she went out into the hall. She called, "Miss Etta?" There was no answer, and she went to the door and looked in. The room looked as if it had been accurately shelled by guerrillas. Miss Etta, she decided, was waiting in the main hall.

They were all there when she went down, Cousin May, Max, Fray, the Beauregards, Miss Etta and the Mundys. Miss Etta was physically keeping in the background. She had evidently figured that her proper place among the mourners was several paces in advance of the Mundys and a good yard behind the Beauregards. But her cologne recognized no boundary.

Regan stood alone until Mrs. Mundy rustled to her side. "Mrs. Herald would like to speak to you."

Cousin May's gloved hand drew her close. "So sweet," she murmured. "So unaffected and sweet. Do talk to Max, like a good child. I can't do a thing with him. He's grieving terribly, terribly. If he seems odd, you mustn't notice. Not himself, you know, not himself at all." She touched the arm of the tall man whose face was resolutely turned from the parlor door. "Here's the little Carr girl, Max. She came last night, such a surprise, so providential and so sad."

Miss Etta moved in silently, head forward. Her cologne met Cousin May's Attar of Roses and her eyes met Cousin May's cool stare. Both went down to defeat. She retired hastily.

Regan had recognized Max at once. He was an older Hurst, gaunt and beautiful, white instead of brown. He made no attempt to hide the pain in his eyes. He's another one like me, she thought; the only other one. She put out her hand but he didn't see it. They stood side by side, not speaking.

The Beauregards, flushed with anticipation, sat together on the carved bench and their plump hands in new black gloves smoothed their unaccustomed fur and broadcloth. Fray was at the front door, talking in a low voice to Young Sheffy. The Mundys, decorous in black sleevebands, kept correctly to the rear. The smell of flowers still drifted through the portières but there was no investigating cold to stir the fringe. It was warm everywhere, too warm.

Young Sheffy opened the front door and beckoned soberly to the silent group. Cousin May, austere and composed, moved forward, followed by the Beauregards. A flurry of rain blew in at the door and spattered Young Sheffy's fine clothes. He brushed futilely with one hand and beckoned again with the other. Fray took Max's arm and they left together, Fray with a firm, arrogant stride, Max with a dragging limp. Miss Etta went next, with the Mundys at her heels.

The first two cars drove off. The third, designated for Miss Etta and the Mundys, waited.

"Come here, honey," Young Sheffy called jovially. No need to beckon or whisper now. "You want to ride with that lot or me? Thought I'd give you a choice. I start a little later, got to see to the remains, but my car always gets there first. I know all the short cuts. What'll it be, them or me?"

"Them. I'll go with them."

He waved her on with a smile.

There was a silent readjustment when she got in the car. Mundy went in front with the driver and she took his place by the window.

Afterwards she could remember almost nothing about the drive. No one spoke to her. She saw the rain falling in vague and empty streets. Now and then a lone pedestrian stared as they passed and on the outskirts of the town where the whitewashed houses leaned together for support an old colored man took off his cap and bowed.

She knew when they reached the open country because the road was full of ruts and they ran between sodden fields. At last they turned in at a pair of iron gates, tall, dripping, flaked with rust. A swinging sign, clacking against its standard, said *Memorial Park*. A bell began to toll, too quickly, as if someone had forgotten it until that minute and had flung himself at the dangling rope. Almost at once the bell slowed down into a melancholy rhythm. She saw what had happened. The door to the gatehouse was open and a man in shirtsleeves, with a half-eaten sandwich in one hand, was clinging to the rope as if he were drowning. For one embarrassed second his eyes met hers. He was laughing at himself. The car moved on.

After that there was nothing she wanted to remember. A small marquee, insecure in the wind, a semi-circle of people, some of them strangers; raw, red earth inadequately covered with a rug of artificial grass; no words, only the sound of shuffling feet. A short distance away two young Negroes leaned patiently on their shovels, unmindful of the rain, and close to the freshly turned earth a marble angel with brooding wings bent to the ground. The fluted wings were chipped and the beseeching hands were crumbling. She heard a voice behind her say: "Altar marble. I told him it wouldn't do but he knew better!" She didn't know who spoke and she didn't care.

The circle of people shifted and broke into black segments; someone took her arm.

"Come along," Fray said. "That was a mistake before. You were to ride with Max and me." She followed him to the car where Max was waiting.

She sat between them on the ride home. Max was quiet; he said very little and only moved when the swaying car threw him helplessly against her shoulder. Fray was restless and irritated.

"I didn't know it was going to be like that or I'd have done something," Fray said.

"What?" Max asked.

"You know what I mean. There should have been prayers, or something. We could have been dogs burying a bone!" He talked straight ahead, staring at the red neck of Young Sheffy's driver. "But May said he wanted it that way. She said he had a premonition and told her how he wanted it several days ago . . . But that wasn't like him, it wasn't like him at all! He was sentimental about birth and death, you know that. There should have been one hymn at least, one of the old ones, von Weber, something like that. You know, Max!"

"Too late," Max said.

"Yes. Too late . . . And the lot's a disgrace. Ivy needs trimming, marble needs cleaning. Who's supposed to take care of that?"

"We pay for perpetual care."

"Perpetual! That's the damndest word I ever heard used in this connection. It's all my fault, I suppose. I live nearest. I should have come over more often. He must have been failing for some time. That poor, crumbling angel, that tells the story. He loved that angel, he used to go out there once a week, just to look at it. He acted as if it were—oh, what's the use!"

"Exactly. No use. Forget it."

"I can't. I don't want to. When things don't make sense I want to know why."

"Leave it alone, Fray."

They were ignoring her and she was glad of it. She was free to listen and put things together in her own way.

Fray said, "The last time I saw him was—wait—four months ago. He looked all right then, too thin perhaps, but all right. When did you see him last?"

She waited for Max's answer. She wanted to know, too.

"What about you, Max?" Fray repeated. "When did you see him last, or talk to him?"

"A month ago. I called him from New York and said I was coming down. He said not to come." Max's voice dropped suddenly.

They both turned to look at him. He was leaning back against the cushions and his eyes were closed. "It's all right," he said faintly, "I'm tired, that's all. And I'm old." He forced himself to sit erect. "I don't like rain, I hate to get up before noon and I think I've caught cold. Add sixty years to all that and you have a crotchety result."

"Sixty," scoffed Fray. "A wonderful age!"

"An incredible age, viewed from the vantage-ground of thirty-seven and twenty-two. I think I'll lie down after lunch."

"Do!" Fray was both relieved and solicitous. "Don't apologize to anybody. Do as you like. I'll look after Regan, if she'll let me." He turned to her abruptly. "If you've said as much as a single word I haven't heard it. You don't talk much, do you?"

"Yes," she said easily. "When people talk to me."

He laughed. "She wears little fur rabbits on her feet," he said to Max. "She doesn't drink champagne and she prowls at night."

"That's enough, Fray," Max said. He went on mildly. "Is Dr. Poole any good?"

"Hurst must have thought so."

They turned into the maple-lined street and entered the grounds by the long, straight drive.

"Do you think I might be excused from lunch?" Max murmured. "I'm not hungry."

"Better make an effort," Fray advised. "Everybody'll be there. Poole, too."

There were two cars leaving as they drew up to the veranda. Theirs was the last to return. Once in the house she was alone again. Max and Fray went down the hall without another word. She watched while Fray unlocked one of the closed doors. The library, she decided.

They had gone ahead without looking back, without removing their coats. They've forgotten me already, she told herself. Nobody remembers me for more than one minute at a time. I can't make them notice me when they don't want to. I can't make them want me around. Max doesn't even look at me. She unfastened the ugly black coat and hung it on her arm. I don't even know if I'm to lunch with them or have a tray again.

She started up the broad front stairs, thinking of Cousin May. I'll talk to her, she decided; I'll ask her what she wants me to do.

Cousin May's door was closed but Mrs. Mundy opened it to her knock.

"Mrs. Herald was asking about you," she said. "I was on my way to give you a message. There's a family lunch at one and Mrs. Herald would like you to join them. You'll have to excuse her now. She's upset."

"I know," Regan said. The door was slowly closing. "Is there anything I can do?"

"Do?" Mrs. Mundy looked as if she didn't understand. She took the coat from Regan's arm with an air of finalty. "No, there's nothing." The door closed.

The breakfast tray was gone when she reached her room

and the bed was made. She stood at the window and watched the bay through the gaps in the trees. It was as gray as the sky, and as still. The pavilion spire was black against the gray. The old tide of remembrance washed over the new disquiet and receded. I won't go there, she said, over and over. I won't go. I can't.

She listened for Miss Etta's return but no one came to that part of the house. At a few minutes before one she started downstairs. The gong rang when she reached the first floor.

They were all at the table when she reached the dining room. That was a bad beginning and she knew it. Nine faces turned when she came to the door, nine pairs of eyes watched her hesitate before she entered; Cousin May at the head of the long table, Max at the foot, the Beauregards on one side with a strange man, Fray and Miss Etta on the other side with an empty chair next to Fray. Mundy and Jenny at the sideboard. All silent, all watching. She was sure the gong had rung only once, when she was already in the hall. They must have started before that, forgotten her again. No, not forgotten. There was the empty chair next to Fray.

"Dreaming again?" Cousin May asked. "Or weren't you hungry, dear? You must eat, you know. We can't have you ill. Now come along quickly, we've been waiting."

She moved to her place, murmuring an apology. Max, at the foot of the table, was on her right, Fray on her left. Fray smiled a welcome but Max looked down at his plate. Mundy hurried over to her side with the air of someone called away from vital statistics to put out a cat. He drew out her chair, but not quite far enough. By that time she wanted only one thing, to seat herself without further attention. She tried to slip into the narrow space but the prankish league of inanimate things had marked her for its own. Her belt buckle tangled in the lace cloth. Fray's hand reached for her water goblet as it toppled, but he was too late.

"My fault," he said to the table at large. "I never know

when to let things alone." He gave the words an odd emphasis, as if they were a challenge.

She wanted to thank him but Mundy was between them, slipping a folded napkin under the damp cloth, refilling her glass.

She ate slowly and carefully because her hands were shaking and it was some time before she trusted herself to raise her eyes. Then she saw that Fray had finished his oysters and was watching Henry with a look of awe. She watched too, covertly.

Henry had sent for a battalion of condiments, catsup, lemon, horseradish, tabasco, Worchestershire. Such behavior was treason to a gourmet but not to Henry. He squeezed, shook and poured until his plate was swimming. He had drawn the corners of his mouth into a set design of grief but he saluted each vanishing oyster with a rich, wet smack of his full lips.

She hoped desperately that Fray would remember his manners and say nothing. She wondered if Cousin May had noticed and saw that she had. Cousin May was talking brightly to her guest but her eyes were on Henry. Miss Etta, virtuously eating oysters plain, laughed out loud.

Fray turned to Regan. "I dredged every one of those in person," he whispered. "I should have fallen overboard first."

. Henry voiced a dignified complaint. "I heard that, Fray. I heard Etta laugh at me, too. Considering what we've all been through, I call it unseemly."

Fray ignored him. "May, I don't think Regan has met Dr. Poole."

They were looking at her now. Henry was forgotten. That was better, easier for everyone. Fray knew how to do the right thing.

Cousin May made a little gesture of distress. "Forgive me, Dr. Poole. I'm not usually so remiss. This charming child is one of the remote Heralds. A cousin of poor Hurst's, far removed. Regan Carr, Dr. Poole."

Dr. Poole challenged Regan's existence over his gold-rimmed glasses. "This is a melancholy occasion," he told her severely. "How do you do."

She returned his bow, wondering how the ebullient Hurst had ever tolerated the little man. Dr. Poole looked as if he had been tossed from a tree by embittered owl parents, and the abundance of his gold jewelry, the rich perfection of his fine clothes said clearly that they'd live to rue the day. But he had forgotten to smooth his feathers. His hair stood on end.

There was a long silence while Mundy removed the plates and Jenny carried them to the dumbwaiter. The faintly creaking cable announced the coming of the second course. Regan studied the centerpiece of white lilies because the others were doing that. The lilies looked out of place; they looked as if they belonged on a sheaf of fern. She turned away from them with a small shudder.

Miss Etta, whose mind was skipping along the same path, had no such reserves.

"Came too late for the funeral," she said clearly, and there was no mistaking her subject. She pointed a horny finger. "Didn't they come too late for the funeral, May?" When she got no answer she leaned across the table and snapped off a blossom. "Souvenir," she said to no one as she tucked it in her blouse.

"Fried chicken, Dr. Poole?" Cousin May said gaily. "Our own chicken, from our own farm. Oh dear, I still think of it as our farm. I keep forgetting it belongs to Fray. Fried chicken from Fray's farm, Dr. Poole?"

Max spoke for the first time. "Perhaps Dr. Poole will take some wine?" Cousin May's smile embraced Max. "Dear Max, thank you! What a splendid suggestion. Will you order? This dreadful weather and all that standing about in the rain, I'm sure we all need a little something. And Dr. Poole most certainly! We can't have you coming down with a chill, Dr. Poole! You're much too valuable!"

Henry, who had been watching Jenny's progress around the table with a large platter of chicken, coughed abjectly. "That's a very sound idea," he approved. "It's what I call a sensible precaution. We'll all be the better for it. I got my feet wet, didn't I, Rosie? I forgot to wear overshoes. I don't think I have any. Have I, Rosie?"

After a pause for thought, Rosalie shook her head.

Why doesn't she talk? Regan wondered; I've never heard her say a word; she smiles sometimes but she never talks. She sent a smile across the table herself, coaxing and friendly, but Rosalie was hunting out the largest piece of breast.

Max called Mundy over and ordered wine. Fray also gave an order. "Max," he said, "this bottle is for you. You're to drink it yourself. My brother," he went on, addressing Dr. Poole, "has a legitimate chill."

"They come on quick for some people, don't they?" Miss Etta marveled. "But I never get one . . . I drink for the hell of it."

Regan waited for an outburst but none came. Miss Etta settled back with a satisfied look.

The wine was served and the meal progressed. Cousin May talked softly to Dr. Poole. Max ate sparingly. His face was flushed and his eyes were heavy. Regan watched him uneasily. He ought to be in bed, she thought. He's really ill. She watched them all.

Fray gave his attention to Miss Etta. She was restless, peering up and down the table as if she were daring herself to do something. After one strangled scream of laughter that made Mundy and Jenny jump, she huddled in her chair as if it were a shell. But her bright eyes always came back to Henry.

Rosalie was also watching Henry. She devoured her food with her face turned to his. Sometimes her fork met her cheek instead of her mouth. She had a foolish, confused look but Henry, deep in his own affairs, didn't see it. He was contriving, by a system of dignified but covert signals, to keep his wine glass filled, working on Mundy and Jenny in turn. When he swayed toward Rosalie for the second time Fray spoke quietly. "Easy does it, Henry," he said.

Cousin May turned sharply. "What was that, Fray?"

"Just giving Henry a bit of advice," Fray said. "That's a

deceptive wine. You don't get that kind in Philadelphia, do you, old man?"

Henry agreed earnestly. "No I don't. And I need it. My blood's thin. It's a condition. May understands my condition, don't you May?"

May turned to Fray. "Of course. Henry knows quite well what he's doing. He's a connoisseur, Henry is. You didn't know us in the old days, Fray, you never saw our dear father's cellar. I know very little about such things myself, not very womanly I've always thought, but I believe our claret was considered unusual. You remember our claret, don't you, Dr. Poole?"

"This isn't claret," Fray said mildly. "I was giving Henry a friendly tip, that's all. Forget it."

"Of course I will, Fray dear." Cousin May was gracious. "But I do hope we haven't embarrassed poor Henry. These personal discussions are so awkward and misleading. Mundy, fill Mr. Henry's glass. I declare he looks quite pale, and no wonder." She addressed herself to Max with an air that neatly banished Fray to a corner with his face to the wall. "Henry was devoted to poor Hurst, he was here when he died, and today has been a dreadful strain. You great, husky Heralds can't understand that. I do believe I'll have another glass myself. I'm chilled to the bone. Here, Jenny . . . Regan, are you quite happy, my dear? You are? Splendid! Max?"

"Thank you," Max said. "I'm very well taken care of." He smiled at his sister-in-law.

"Max!" She laughed as if she had made a discovery. "I should say you are! That huge bottle, all to yourself, you wicked man!" She recalled Fray from exile with delight. "There, you see, Fray? Max is the one to worry about, not poor Henry who's only had one little glass!"

Miss Etta spoke loudly. "He's had seven."

In the silence that followed an ugly little current ran around the table. It was almost audible and clearly visible. It suspended moving hands, stiffened relaxed figures, and widened Rosalie's frightened eyes. Regan suddenly knew it had been there all the time, waiting. She could even trace its source. She looked from Cousin May to Max.

"Really, Max," Cousin May said. "I do think—"

"Etta!" Max calmly reproved the old woman.

"Bad girl," Fray said. "Where are your manners? . . . You know our Etta, May." He talked easily over Miss Etta's unbowed head. "Crazy as a bedbug and madly in love with the sound of her own voice. And don't worry about Max. He has an enviable reputation. He also has a cold and his bottle is a medicinal dose. He's going to lie down right after lunch."

"Then he really—oh, I'm so sorry! I didn't understand! Dear Max, you must let me send you something from my little store of drugs. We simply can't let anything happen to you!"

"Nothing will," Max said.

"Dr. Poole, do prescribe something, won't you? Is aspirin good? Oh dear, I'm so helpless in the face of illness. If you'll just tell me what Max should have I'll send Regan down to Mayer's. You'll do that for Cousin May, won't you, dear? Just to the corner drugstore? So good for you to make yourself useful."

"Yes, Cousin May."

Dr. Poole, frowning importantly, wrote a prescription with a fountain pen encrusted with gold.

"How fortunate that you should be here, Dr. Poole," Cousin May sighed. "In these days—to have someone who is absolutely trustworthy! Mrs. Mundy will take this to Mr. Mayer and little Regan will call for it later."

The current was subsiding, Cousin May had turned it with a deft hand. Max now held the center of the stage and Henry was retired to a merciful oblivion.

Regan was sorry for Henry. His gross body and aging face were funny and pathetic at the same time. She sent a quick look in his direction and as quickly looked away. Oblivion was what Henry wanted. The others may have forgotten him but he had not forgotten himself. His eyes were measuring the distance between his empty glass and Rosalie's full one, and he was smiling.

The meal resumed its former pace. Mundy and Jenny removed the plates and served dessert. Cousin May and Dr. Poole talked together in gratified tones, Fray and Miss Etta whispered like children, Rosalie devoured her compote of fruit and Henry captured his ninth glass. His face was purple and he mumbled to himself.

Why doesn't somebody do something? Regan wondered. Why doesn't Cousin May stop him? She must know what he's doing. Everybody knows. Is she afraid of him?

She turned to Max. He looked like Hurst; perhaps he had some of Hurst's authority and tact. Perhaps if he spoke to Henry in the right way, let Henry know that he was being watched . . . But one look at Max told her how hopeless that was. Max was staring at the centerpiece of lilies as if they had a dark and special meaning for him alone. Still he must have felt her steady gaze because he turned in his chair as if she had spoken, and smiled. It wasn't much of a smile, it touched the corners of his mouth and left his eyes as somber as they were before, but it was more than he had ever given her.

"You're going to be all right, aren't you?" she said to him. "You'll tell me if there's anything I can do to make you comfortable?"

He nodded.

Then it happened, the one thing she had been afraid of. Mundy, on his way to join Jenny at the coffee table, ignored one of Henry's signals. A glimmer of the truth flared in one corner of Henry's fuddled brain and spread. He glared belligerently up and down the table and saw that he was ostracized. His lips moved silently. So they thought he couldn't hold his drink, did they? Well, they were wrong. He was a gentleman, he was a Beauregard, and Max Herald, sitting in Hurst's chair as if he owned the place, was no better than a common immigrant weaned on black bread and beer. Smiling at that girl who was a Herald too. Smiling because they had all the money and thought they were somebody. Smiling because they had the Beauregard land. Smiling at him. He'd show them. He'd give them something to think about. He'd done it before and he could do it again.

He tipped back his chair and tried to reach a full bottle on the sideboard. Mundy, over at the coffee table, hurried forward, followed by Jenny. They were too late. Henry crashed to the floor.

Cousin May looked slowly from face to face and saw the sudden preoccupation of all but Rosalie and Dr. Poole. Dr. Poole helped Mundy and Jenny lead the sobbing Henry from the room. Rosalie sat rigid, her mouth open and fear in her eyes. Fray talked softly to Regan. Max stared at the lilies, frowning with concentration and Miss Etta folded her napkin into a variety of shapes and hummed.

None of them stopped what they were doing. Cousin May covered her face for an instant and her skin was yellow under the coating of powder. Jenny re-entered the room alone and took her place beside the coffee table.

"Coffee, everyone?" Cousin May asked.

Chapter Four

THE clock shaped like a little Greek temple struck four. Fray collected the scattered papers, folded them and returned them to their envelope.

"That's that," he said to Regan. "Now you know where you stand and you ought be very pleased with yourself. Aren't you?"

"I don't know. I haven't had time to think." They were at the round table in Hurst's sitting room. The dust was still thick over everything. A key lay on the table between them, clean and shining, and she moved it back and forth as if she were gaining time. "What's this for?"

"This door. I'm keeping the rooms locked, too much personal stuff lying around." He walked to the mantel and returned. "What's the matter with you? Don't you like what you've just heard?"

"I suppose so. Of course I do. I guess I still don't believe it, that's all."

"You'll get used to it in time. Well, this settles everything, doesn't it? Can you think of one good reason for not staying on now?"

"Yes, a very good one. You'll be going home soon and I don't want to stay here alone. It isn't—right."

Fray tapped the envelope. He didn't look at her. "You heard what I read, didn't you? It's perfectly right. Hurst said this was your home and he knew what he was doing when he wrote that. Yours to live in as long as the house stands. Come on, tell the truth, don't you and May get along?"

"I hardly know Cousin May," she said carefully. "No, it isn't that . . . Does Cousin May want to know how long I'm staying?"

"She hasn't even mentioned your name. I'm asking you because I want to know, myself. Don't forget you more or less agreed to help me with Hurst's papers."

"I know I did, but—"

He looked at her then. "But you're going to back out. What's wrong? What happened to make you change your mind? Aren't we making you comfortable?" He spoke carelessly, without emphasis, but she felt him waiting for her answer with an interest that was out of proportion.

"It hasn't anything to do with comfort," she said. "And I don't know what's wrong, maybe nothing. I simply feel that I don't belong, I don't fit in, and that's all there is to it. You and the Crains are the only people here who seem to want me and there's only one room in the house where—" She stopped short. "I'm like Young Sheffy, I talk too much."

"Go on," he said.

"No. You'll laugh."

"Go on before I wring your neck. There's only one room in the house where—what?"

She drew a deep breath. "I might as well get it over with," she said. "And I don't really care whether you laugh or not. It's this room. It's queer."

"There's nothing queer about it. It happens to be very nice."

"That's what I mean, that's why I say it's queer. It's the only one I feel right in." She waited for his ridicule and braced herself to fight back. To her surprise, he didn't laugh. Instead, his shoulders slumped as if he had shed a great weight. That was out of proportion too.

She traced a pattern on the dusty table and went on. "It's shabby, it hasn't been aired, and it isn't even clean, but when I'm here I feel right . . . Is that because Hurst lived here?"

"Maybe. Maybe something would get over to a susceptible person. But don't go droopy on me. How many times have you been in here, anyway? On this visit, I mean?"

"This is the second time. You know that as well as I do. I was in here yesterday with Miss Etta."

"Sure, sure. You and Etta and old B. Did you feel right yesterday too?"

"You're making fun of me, Fray!"

"I'm doing nothing of the sort. Don't be such an egoist." He took a cigarette. "Tell me something else. I've been wondering about those initials on the clock. They could mean several things but I suspect they mean Regan Carr. Do they?"

She colored. "Every time I do something silly it shows."

"I'm glad it does. It looks kind of cute. It also looks as if Hurst spent his last days in a pigpen. That's hard to understand, isn't it?"

"I know," she agreed quickly. "I wondered about that too. I asked about it. I couldn't understand because I remember him as being so fastidious."

"He was. So you wondered, and went around asking questions. You don't care what toes you tread on, do you? Well, what did you find out?"

"He said the maids disturbed him. He didn't want them coming in and out. Katy told me. He said he'd rather look after the rooms himself so she left him alone. I suppose he was ill then, and nobody noticed. He'd never tell anybody about a thing like that. People like Hurst never do."

"Don't they? . . . Now wait, we're getting away from the original subject and I think you're doing it on purpose. What about that promise to help me? I want you. I'm asking you as a favor."

"Why?" She heard the eagerness in her own voice and suddenly remembered a childhood phrase. I'm begging for sugar, she told herself. "I mean you're so vague," she said in an offhand manner. "You haven't really told me anything. You're so vague."

"I want you to help me and there's nothing vague about it. We'll work on Hurst's letters, diaries and so on, and decide what to keep for the family archives. You know the kind of thing I mean, paste all the nice stuff in a scrapbook, dun the guys who owed him money, bury the skeletons when nobody's looking. We'll have fun. Don't you like to read other people's mail?"

That would be all right, she told herself. That was good enough. And he looked and sounded as if he really wanted her. It wasn't much, but it was good enough. "Well, if you're not just being tactful—"

"Me! You're hired!"

"But I want to be kept busy," she insisted. "I want something definite to do. And you've got to promise you won't go off and leave me alone. You don't know what it's been like, even in this short time. Nobody to talk to. I—don't like being alone."

"You won't be alone from now on, not with Henry in the house. I suspect you're due for what Henry will certainly call a "rush." When he gets the word that Hurst left you ten thousand a year he'll try to take you down to Mayer's for a soda. On your money."

Ten thousand. She'd forgotten that part of it, honestly forgotten. Ten thousand a year when she'd never had more than twenty-five a week. She laughed. "You won't believe this, but I'd forgotten the money part."

"I know. I saw the gleam in your eye when you began to remember. Very sordid. What are you going to do with it?"

"I don't know."

"I do. Go crazy with new clothes. And as a special favor to me please burn up that toga you wore to the funeral. When poor Max saw you he nearly collapsed."

"That wasn't mine! You know I'd never buy a thing like that! I didn't have any black so Cousin May lent it to me."

"May? Never in this world. May doesn't keep a handkerchief from one season to the next and that coat was about twenty years old."

"It wasn't hers. It was Rosalie's."

"Not Rosalie's either. Wrong size, too expensive, and twenty years ago our little Rosie wasn't even—never mind." He looked at the clock and compared it with his watch.

"Rosalie wasn't even—what?" she asked.

"Nothing. Rosalie didn't have clothes like that, that's all. Now I've got to get back and see Max."

He wants to change the subject, she told herself. Or he wants to get away. I'll show him that I understand. "Of course," she said. "How is Max?"

"He'll be all right if he keeps warm and does what he's told. The real problem child is Henry."

Poor old Henry. She recalled the greedy hands and eyes, heard the wheedling, whining voice.

Fray went on. "By the way, you'd better make up your mind that you didn't notice anything odd about Henry at lunch. Henry was and is a model of good deportment and a fine Southern gentleman. Anything you think you saw or heard was simply a bad old mirage with sound effects."

She stared. "He was as drunk as a lord."

"Oh no, my girl, you're wrong. Henry doesn't drink, that's official. I'm telling you because you haven't been around long enough to know. Henry positively doesn't drink. Sometimes he takes a spoonful of brandy in a glass of water for his heartburn, his palpitations, or a little number that he calls his stomach stoppage. A spoonful of brandy, that's all. In a glass of water. Remember that."

"Oh." She was suddenly enjoying herself. "Which one did he have today?"

"I haven't heard, but I will. Probably all three. It was bad today. The poor fool used to time his seizures with May's trips to town but today he went hog wild. He got some good news. Hurst left him three thousand a year and I'm almost sorry. Henry should have twenty-five cents, in pennies, every Saturday night, no more."

Fray was right. Henry shouldn't have money of his own. He shouldn't live alone, either. "Why don't Henry and Rosalie live with Cousin May?" she asked. "There's plenty of room and she seems very fond of them."

Fray laughed. "She dotes on them. They're Beauregards. But they're better off in Philadelphia where nobody knows them. The Beauregards were big shots around here at one time and May wants to keep the legend bright and sweet. Can't do that with Rosie and Henry on the loose. So she gives them a small allowance, just enough to live on, and our loss is Philadelphia's gain."

"But Rosalie! She must be fifty and she's so babyish and helpless. How in the world does she manage Henry when they're at home?"

"She doesn't. May pays an old colored woman to look after them both. Nobody's supposed to know that but Hurst found out and told me. And don't worry about Rosie. Sometimes she cuts up but she'll be a good girl while she's here. She's afraid of Max, always has been. I don't know why. But as long as Max can stare her down she'll behave. I sort of like the old thing."

"So do I." She remembered how Rosalie's frightened eyes had looked from Henry to Max. Henry, fat, mottled, babbling. Max, thin, white, silent. "Does Rosalie ever talk?" she asked.

"Constantly, for twenty-four hours straight about twice a year. You won't see any of that though. If it should happen here Mrs. Mundy will take her for a nice, long walk." He stood up. "Jenny's sitting with Max and it's my turn to take over. That means I close up here. You run along and amuse yourself, and if you get bored stick to old Etta. She's a wholesome devil."

"I've got to call for that prescription and maybe I'll take a walk. It isn't raining now." She followed him to the door. "Fray?"

"What?"

"I went to the back garden after lunch, down by the shore. I tried the door to the pavilion but it was locked. Who has the key?"

"I have . . . There's nothing in the pavilion. Nobody ever went there but Hurst. It was his private domain and I mean to keep it that way. Even May understands that."

"But I'd like to go inside. Only for a few minutes. I have a reason."

He turned so quickly that he struck her shoulder. "Reason?" His voice was sharp and his eyes were full of suspicion. "What reason?"

She drew back. "Don't look at me like that," she said slowly. "You looked at me as if I were trying to get away with something."

"Sorry." He was instantly contrite. "Got the jitters. I didn't mean a thing, not a thing. I was only wondering why you wanted to see the place. I didn't even know you knew about it."

"Of course I knew about it. I've been wanting to go there ever since I came. It's the first thing I thought of." She corrected herself at once, with a look of surprise. "That's wrong. Why in the world did I say that? I didn't remember the pavilion at all." She went on slowly and carefully, thinking her way. "I'd forgotten it entirely until this morning, forgotten it existed. When I saw the spire from my window last night I thought it was a dead tree. But this morning I saw it again in the daylight and knew what it was. That was when I remembered how I used to go there with Hurst. That's why I want to go there again."

"Sorry," he repeated. "So you used to go there with Hurst? . . . What did you do?"

She didn't answer at once. She put one hand to her head, unconsciously, and frowned. "We played games and ate." Her voice was almost a whisper.

"Cutthroat Lotto and chocolate ice cream?"

"Up Jenkins and orange sherbet."

"Go on," he urged. "I'm beginning to like this." He watched her closely.

"When I was here before," she said, "we went out there every afternoon at five o'clock, and we played games and ate sherbet. I guess that's all. But I want to go there again. When I first saw the spire I didn't want to go, but now I do." She was embarrassed and distressed for no reason. "Does that make any sense?"

"Not a scrap. What did you and Hurst talk about? You must have talked."

"Talk about? Food, I guess. That sounds ridiculous but

food is all I can remember. And whether or not it was gambling for me to keep the quarter when I won Up Jenkins." She gave a small, self-conscious laugh. "This is silly. I've drawn a complete blank about those times. I know we must have done other things, talked about other things, but all I can remember is the food and the quarter! What does that make me?"

"A kind of cad . . . Well, we'll see. We'll think about it. The pavilion's pretty shabby now and you might be happier if you didn't go there again. But we can talk about that later."

He closed and locked the door behind them and she left him standing in the hall when she went upstairs for her coat. There was a note from Mrs. Mundy on the chest. "Please bring the medicine to me in the kitchen when you have it. Paid for."

She went downstairs the back way, wanting to avoid a chance meeting with Henry, or even Rosalie. Mundy, counting table linen in the pantry, dropped his work and hurried down the hall ahead of her.

"I'll let you out, Miss," he said.

She wanted to tell him not to bother but his sudden deference gave her a new feeling of importance. She told herself that Mundy had heard about the ten thousand, but she didn't care. It was nice to have doors opened for any reason, nice to receive servile little bows. Last night seemed far, far away. She walked down the path to the gate, hands deep in pockets, hatless. A fine mist began to fall.

Last night belonged to another world. The dead tree, frightening at first, was only the old pavilion spire. Hurst was gone but there was comfort in the fact that she hadn't seen him ill. He was away from her as he had been for years, but still close. Closer. Sometimes she felt as if he stood beside her but she wasn't afraid. And then there was Fray.

She kicked the sodden leaves with deep contentment and strolled on. The wide street was deserted. The lamps blinked slowly into life although it was not yet twilight.

Gray sky, yellow lamps, yellow trees. The grass in the gardens across the street was a bright, wet green. She gave the other houses an appraising look that held a shameless and cheerful condescension. They were fine, big houses but the one she had just left was finer. The finest house, the biggest garden . . . She walked slowly toward the corner where a jumble of light marked the shops and the trolleys screamed around the curving tracks. The lamps in the drugstore window made the old familiar pattern on the brick pavement. "I'm glad I'm staying," she whispered. "Everything feels right now."

Mr. Mayer was expecting her. He was the white-coated man she had seen the day before. He came forward, smiling, the prescription in his hand. "Here you are," he said. "And you tell Max I said he ought to be ashamed. You tell him to behave himself."

She stared. "Behave?" She decided that she didn't like the way he smiled. "What do you mean?"

Mr. Mayer elaborated hastily. "Nothing. I wasn't talking in particular, I was just talking in general. Max isn't so young any more and he's got to take care of himself. That's all I mean. That's all." His mild, round face flushed. "That's all," he said again. He fussed with a row of bottles and made himself look busy. "Will there be anything else?"

"Some aspirin," she said mechanically. It wouldn't be wasted. She could use it herself. She wanted time to frame another question. Max? Behave?

But before she could speak the door opened to admit another customer. Mr. Mayer pushed the aspirin across the counter and bustled over to the tobacco stand. She stood where she was, frowning, waiting for him to return. She hadn't paid for the aspirin. Small towners, she told herself angrily. Gossipy old men were as bad as old women. She knew exactly what had happened, she told herself she could hear and see the whole thing. A tradesman at the kitchen door, Jenny's gasping account of Henry's ill-timed celebration at lunch, what this one had said, what that one had done, and the garbled result traveling from mouth to mouth down

the street until it reached Mr. Mayer on the corner. Mouth
to mouth and house to house, and by the time it reached Mr.
Mayer Henry had turned into Max. Because Max had openly
had a bottle of his own and needed a prescription. She
shrugged. It was infuriating but better left alone. Later,
when Max was well, she'd tell him. Maybe she could make
him laugh.

A voice hailed her from the front of the store.

"Why hello, honey, I didn't know that was you!" It was
Young Sheffy. He was filling his pipe and chuckling. "No
hat, no umbrella. My, my. Going home now?"

"Yes," she said, moving over to the counter. She smiled
coolly when she paid Mr. Mayer for the aspirin.

"Then I'm taking you," Young Sheffy announced. He
opened the door and unfurled a large umbrella. He chuckled
again. "You must have a lot of faith in sulfa."

She reluctantly measured her step to his slow trot.
"Sulfa?"

"Sure enough. Rain. No hat. Pneumonia. Sulfa. See?"

"Oh. But I never take cold." She tried to increase her
pace but he held her arm. There were people on the street
now, coming home from work. The lighted trolleys clanged
around the bend, stopped, and rumbled on. Newsboys, a
chestnut man with a glowing brazier, an old woman selling
penny Hallowe'en masks. The old woman held the masks
up to her face, one by one, and laughed when she took them
away.

"I like this time of day," Young Sheffy said. "I like to feel
life going on around me. What are you hurrying for,
honey? Walk slow, that's the way to live long."

"I ought to—they expect—"

"Nobody expects you to kill yourself for a box of pills.
Look over there. That's my little place next door to the
church. Now what were we talking about? Oh yes, sulfa.
Fine thing in its way but it won't keep a fool from dying.
Nossir. Science can't help a fool. I've made a study of it
and I know. Charley Mayer can tell you the same thing.

Fool gets a cold out of pure carelessness, tries to cure himself and gets worse. Calls the doctor too late and gets me too soon. You ought to wear a hat."

"I will," she said helplessly.

Light came on behind the stained glass windows of the church. It looked like a toy from a child's Christmas garden.

"Pretty," Young Sheffy said. "Getting ready for choir practice. That's a nice, wholesome way to spend an evening. Maybe you'd like that. No, I guess you wouldn't. Too old in there, all of them. I don't know why young folks don't go to church these days. Movies now, that's where they go, and very nice too, but it don't prepare you for the other life. You can't begin to prepare too soon. I know . . . there I go, talking too much again and you just fresh from a funeral. Pay me no mind."

She shivered, although it wasn't cold. The lights on the passing motor cars and the patches of deep shadow under the trees were playing tricks with the wrinkled, smiling face so close to hers. One second the face was there and then it was gone. It gleamed, pink and wet, in a brilliant sweep of light, so close that she could count the false, pearly teeth. Then it dissolved in darkness. It came and went, over and over again, a face without a body.

She tried once more to quicken her pace. "Mr. Sheffy, I've got to hurry. They're waiting for me."

"Be there in a minute. You just tell Miss May you were with me. You tell her I brought you home safe. You'll have no trouble. How's Miss May bearing her trials?"

"She's all right, thank you. Everybody's all right," she added defiantly.

"Sure enough," Young Sheffy agreed. "You can always count on Miss May to do the proper thing. That Miss Luders now, she's a different type. A very unpredictable person. I looked to see her throw herself in the open grave this morning but she didn't." There was a note of wistful regret in his voice. "People used to do a lot of that in the old days. You hardly ever see it now."

They had reached the gate and Regan stopped thankfully. "Please don't come any farther, Mr. Sheffy. I'll run the rest of the way and it isn't raining much now."

"You take my umbrella, honey. I'm a healthy old fellow, I don't need it."

"No, thanks. I'll run." She closed the gate between them and fled. Once she looked back and saw that he was still standing there. He stood as if he were waiting for something.

She went the way she had gone the day before, around the house to the back door. The kitchen curtains hadn't been drawn and when she passed the windows she saw them at the table drinking tea. Mrs. Mundy, Miss Etta, Jenny and Katy. The door was unlocked and she entered without knocking.

"You're soaking wet," Miss Etta accused her joyfully. "Take that coat off and hang it near the stove. You need hot tea with a drop of something but I'd like to see you get the something."

Mrs. Mundy took the coat silently and spread it over a chair. When she came back to the table she poured a cup of tea. "You were a long time," she said.

"I'm sorry. I met Mr. Sheffy and he wanted to talk."

Jenny and Katy shook their heads. Their eyes told her that they knew Young Sheffy and his talk.

"Has anybody been asking for me?" Regan went on.

"No," Mrs. Mundy said. "But when you didn't come back right away I was afraid something might have happened. I didn't know you were dawdling. I thought you might have been lost, or met with an accident. Lots of accidents on that corner. Too many. But now that you're here there's nothing to worry about. What did Mr. Mayer have to say?"

"Nothing." She saw Mrs. Mundy watching her and thought she knew why. Mrs. Mundy's next words told her she was right.

"He's an old gossip," Mrs. Mundy said. "They both are, he and Young Sheffy. Mayer on one corner and Sheffy on the other. You wouldn't know your own mother when they got through with her . . . Did he say anything about the Heralds?"

"Why?" Regan asked evenly. She knew then what had happened. Mundy had regaled Mrs. Mundy with his version of what had taken place at lunch and she had passed it on to Mr. Mayer. Mentioning no names, of course, but pulling down the corners of her mouth, lifting her eyebrows, and letting Mr. Mayer draw his own conclusions. Max's prescription, Max's bottle that Fray had called a medicinal dose. That had done it. Poor Max. "Why?" she asked again. "What could he tell me that I don't know?"

"Not a thing, I guess." Mrs. Mundy shrugged. "But he's Herald crazy. They lent him some money once when the business was in trouble, years ago and he talks about it like it was yesterday. He has Heralds on the brain."

She wondered if she'd misjudged Mr. Mayer. "I think that's nice," she said.

The Crains nodded in agreement. There it was again, the Heralds helping people and they had come too late. They looked at Regan, almost as shabby as themselves, her bright hair curling from the walk in the rain. Jenny's eyes spoke to Katy's. The young lady was a Herald. She'd inherited a lot of money, too. Maybe she'd inherited more than that, like a heart and feelings. She was kind. Hadn't they talked about her kindness when they were alone, even when they'd thought she was poor? Maybe she'd take a little place of her own now, and ask them to come with her. They'd work their fingers to the bone for such a place and glad to do it. No more setting the alarm an hour too soon so if you overslept you still had a chance; no more walking brisk and smart so nobody'd know your bones ached; no more answering the bell every time The Box made that terrible sound, praying it was only somebody wanting a cup of tea or a clean handkerchief, not somebody saying—"I've been thinking that the stairs are too much for you."

They looked at Regan soberly. She saw the look and thought they were like two old dogs, half-blind, rheumatic, useless, but eager to prove their worth in love. She smiled and held out her cup, and Jenny's hand trembled as she re-filled it.

They sat in silence around the spread table, each woman busy with her own thoughts.

The Box whirred, the red light blinked, the little hand spun crazily. Jenny and Katy got to their feet and hurried across to the stairs, getting in each other's way, sending appealing little looks over their shoulders.

"Come back," Mrs. Mundy said calmly. "You didn't even look to see who rang."

Jenny flushed. "Excuse me. But one of us'll take it. One of us'll be glad to go." She hastened to The Box and peered up at the dial.

"I can see it from way over here," Mrs. Mundy said. "It's Mr. Max's room. Mr. Fray will be wanting to know if the medicine has come. I'll go." She looked at Regan. "Where is it?"

She only calls me Miss when I'm upstairs with the others, Regan noted. "It's in my coat pocket," she said.

"Don't disturb yourself," Mrs. Mundy said. "I can find it. You finish your tea." She collected the package and rustled quietly up the stairs. Jenny and Katy returned to the table. They didn't look at each other.

"Wants to do everything herself," Miss Etta said to nobody. "Too much ambition. I'd like to tell her what ambition did to Napoleon . . . What are you doing down here, Regan? It's all right for me but not for you. You belong in the parlor . . . Worth money now," she said to the Crains.

The Crains beamed their congratulations.

"I went in to see Max," Miss Etta went on. "Nothing but a cold in the head, at least that's what he said. I wanted to stay but Fray put me out. Do you know what I think?" She turned to the Crains. "Don't listen to this part. It's personal."

The Crains turned their heads and managed to look as if they were miles away. Miss Etta continued. "I think Max is grieving over that funeral. That was the worst funeral I ever attended. Nothing to it, no style, no gumption. We did better with a dead oysterman that washed up on our beach in 1910 and we didn't even know his name. What do you think?"

"They say Hurst wanted it that way," Regan said

"Never! Never in this world! Hurst was like royalty. He liked show. Nothing fancy, but good, substantial show. If they'd let me run things you'd have seen something." She recalled the Crains with a small, chirping whistle. "You can listen now, girls. This part is educational. Some years ago I had the pleasure of attending the late King Edward's funeral. You know the one I mean, little beard and all the friends. I had a beautiful position right on the curb so I know how things are done. Everybody in deepest black, long veils to hide the features, music that would break your heart. I cried myself sick. Things always happen to me."

"One of the lucky ones," Jenny murmured to Katy.

"But Miss Etta," Regan said carefully, "you were only eighteen when you went to England and King Edward—"

"This was the second time. The second time was much later. This time I went to see what you-know-who would do if I picked a few little seedpods in that Hathaway girl's garden. But I never found out. After that funeral I didn't have the heart to steal seeds. So I went to Paris. That's a cheerful place." Her small eyes moved expectantly from face to face. "It won't do anybody any good to ask me about Paris but I don't mind mentioning one small thing. I was walking behind two peacocks out at Fontainebleau and a couple of feathers came off in my hand." She looked narrowly at Regan. "Don't blame me if you don't believe that. I can show you the feathers."

Regan laughed and reached for a cake. The Crains laughed too, and took cakes for themselves. The room was warm, filled with the smell of good food cooking on the range, the lazy tick of the clock, the comfort of being indoors on a wet day. Maybe I do belong upstairs, Regan thought, but I like it here.

The Box gave off another angry whirr, the light came on, the little hand went twice around the dial before it stopped. "You'd think that thing had a disposition," Miss Etta said. "Sounds to me like somebody's mad."

Jenny scurried over and read the summons. "Mrs. Herald!" she gasped. She ran for the stairs. "Maybe Mr. Max—"

"I'll go up with you," Regan said quickly. "There may be something I can do." But when she reached the second floor she wasn't needed. Fray met her at the door of Max's room and told her in a whisper that Max had gone to sleep. She had started up to her own room when Jenny called her urgently.

"Mrs. Herald would like to see you," Jenny said primly. "Got the blues," she whispered.

Cousin May was sitting by the fire, alone. A foolish, flimsy bed jacket, obviously Rosalie's, lay on the sofa. Cousin May saw her looking at it.

"Poor little Rosie has a headache," Cousin May said. "I've tucked her up for a nice nap in my own bed . . . Come closer, dear. You look quite pale."

"Do I?" She went to the dressing table and bent to the mirror. The table was a great carved piece, festooned with flowers and figures, and the huge, round mirror was like nothing she had ever seen before. Her delighted fingers traced the sentimental promise that framed the glass. There, a plump and dimpled Cupid, lolling in ribbons and roses, eternally pulled the beard of an anguished Father Time.

"How perfectly lovely!" she said.

"One of dear Hurst's little gifts," Cousin May said. "Very old and rather sweet, I think. Such a pleasing little story, I like to look at it."

"It's wonderful." Regan abandoned the Cupid and studied her face. She was flushed from the walk in the rain, from the heat in the kitchen. "There must be magic in it too," she said. "I look rouged and I'm not. I haven't even got any rouge."

Cousin May reproved her gently. "When I said you were

pale, dear child, you were. That color is too sudden to be right. You must be very, very careful. I don't think I could bear it if you were to be ill too."

"I won't be," Regan assured her. "I never am." She took her old place on the footstool. "I wish you'd give me something to do, Cousin May."

"Nonsense! Just having you here is a comfort. And you've helped me so much today. My day of great sorrow. Your sorrow too, my dear, I don't forget that. But no one can say that I haven't always done the best for that sweet companion of so many years. That is my comfort now." She closed her eyes.

Regan said nothing. She was seeing the weather-stained angel with its crumbling fingers, the rug of artificial grass, the grinning man clinging to the bell. She was seeing Max. "Cousin May," she asked, "why does Max limp?"

Cousin May studied her hands as they played with the fringe of her pink shawl. "That's a painful subject, Regan. I should have thought your mother—but no. They never talk."

Regan knew who they were. The Heralds. Cousin May had said that before. "I was only wondering. I'm not curious. Please don't tell me if you'd rather not."

"Funny, odd child! It isn't my story, you know. It's one of the Herald tragedies. Those poor, unfortunate people! They seem always to be paying for some—shall I say sin? No, that's too strong. For some old, strange weakness. And they've no one but themselves to blame. The Heralds always idolized their women. Mothers, wives, sisters, they pampered and spoiled them out of all proportion. And one by one they lost them, too soon and tragically. Almost as if it were a judgment, I think. That is what happened to Max."

"I didn't know. Poor Max." She began to understand his grim silence.

"Yes, poor Max. That unhappy creature was desperately in love with his wife. He was hurt, this is what I was told, my dear, he was hurt while trying to save her life. It was all very odd, and never fully explained, but the authorities called it an accident. Nobody saw anything happen and we have only Max's word for it. He was, of course, quite incoherent."

Cousin May looked deep into the gray eyes raised to hers. She touched Regan's cheek. "Oh dear, so like them all, how I pray you will escape—I even wonder if it's wise to tell you this! So upsetting, but you really ought to know . . . Max had gone out for the evening, alone, and when he returned he was limping badly and looked quite dreadful. He told us an amazing story. He said he had heard Claudine calling him. He had been walking up the path from the gate and heard her calling, down by the water. He'd gone to investigate, he said, and slipped through one of the dock boards. Of course she wasn't there. But there was no doubt about the leg injury, he was bleeding horribly, and we knew a board was loose although we never did find it again. But we didn't worry then. We thought he was imagining things. He was quite childish where Claudine was concerned. We told him plainly that she was safe in bed, and we thought she was. I'd seen her go up myself, more than a hour before, and we finally convinced him. So he and Hurst talked for a while and then Max went to his room. We heard him shout, I'll never forget that shout, and that was when we discovered she wasn't there . . . In the morning we found her body under the dock, wedged between the piling stakes."

"How awful, awful."

"Yes. Too awful. And quite a mystery. What was she doing down there at midnight, alone? If she was alone . . . Hurst was frantic. I try so hard not to think of that night. Try not to think of little Claudine. She was a Herald too, you know, a second cousin. They'd come here to spend a holiday, come back to their dear old home to rest and be happy. Then it happened, as it always does. That dreadful, dreadful fate. Home to die."

Regan drew closer to the fire. Her hands were icy. "It doesn't seem fair," she said. "The trouble always comes to you. It doesn't seem fair that Herald trouble should come to you."

"Sweet of you to say that, dear. And so, so true." She laughed ruefully. "When Heralds and Beauregards come together something always happens. It's quite like a book. When I first saw Hurst and learned his name I was actually frightened. He came stamping into our old home one day, as if he owned it already, and asked us to lend him a horse. His own had gone lame. I looked at him as if he were a ghost because, you see, he was repeating history. Years before, during the War Between the States, another Herald, a Bavarian observer with the Union Army, came to us in the same way. I was brought up on the story. The first Herald took two of our finest horses instead of one, took them as if we should have been honored to oblige. Of course he paid for them, but that wasn't the point. And then, years later, Hurst came. I think he must have looked the same as the other. When I told him about it he said the man was an ancestor. He laughed. He thought it was amusing and romantic." Cousin May shuddered lightly. "But we'll have no more of this old, sad talk. Life, we must remember, is a measure to be filled, not a cup to be drained! Now tell me how it feels to be rich!"

"Good!"

"And how are you going to spend your little fortune? In travel? I hope so. So good for young people to see the world and they tell me South America is charming." Her voice quickened suddenly. "Why do you look like that, Regan? What have I said that's odd?"

Regan retreated hastily from a mental picture of Fray condemning the toga to the flames. "I'm sorry," she said. "I was thinking about clothes. I haven't very many." She stumbled on. "And I haven't thanked you for lending me the coat. I—I think I'll get a new one, for one thing."

Cousin May looked at her sharply. "I thought the coat did very well, and so did Henry. A young girl should be unobtrusive, you know. And I should think twice about spending money foolishly. I'm sure you have a trunkful of pretty, girlish things."

"My trunk hasn't come and there's nothing pretty in it.

Just old things that I couldn't bear to throw away, and books and old letters. People always forget that my mother and I were poor."

"I see, I understand, dear . . . But why does a chit like you save letters?"

"They're Hurst's." She said it simply, as if it explained everything.

They sat on in silence, watching the fire. Cousin May braided the fringe of her shawl.

"Do you know that I'm going to help Fray?" Regan asked. "He's collecting Hurst's personal papers and things like that. Some of them ought to be destroyed, he said, and some kept. I'm to help. I'll like that."

Cousin May laughed. "Fray had better get back to the farm and his own personal papers! There's work enough there but he doesn't seem to realize that. Bad, lazy old Fray. He's simply looking for an excuse to stay on here. He can't resist a new face. Don't let him fool you, he's completely unreliable . . . And when was all this decided? You sound very definite."

"I don't know when he decided. But he's collecting the diaries and things. I think he wants to keep some of them."

Cousin May looked bewildered. "How utterly fantastic! What does he think he's— I simply refuse to give it another thought! . . . And now will you do me a favor, dear? Dine in your room tonight. A nice tray. So dull for you I know, but such a help to us all. And early to bed and a fine, long sleep. I'm sure you need it."

It was nearly eight when she finished her lonely dinner. She put the tray in the hall and went downstairs to the library. She wanted a book, there was nothing to read in her room, but the library door was locked. There was only one thing left to do, go back to the cold and cheerless room, write a letter to the only girl at home who was her friend, and go to bed. And she wasn't sleepy.

But by the time she was settled in bed with tablet and fountain pen her eyes were heavy. She wrapped the old gray robe about her shoulders and tried to write. It was no good. She'd had too little sleep the night before, too much to think about during the day and, added to that, her head was aching. She put pen and paper aside, raised the window a few inches, and opened the door. There was a doorstop shaped like a sleeping kitten and she pushed it into place. I may hear Miss Etta come up, she thought, or Jenny and Katy. Even the Mundys. It was comforting to think of other people coming up the stairs to bed. She turned out the light and fell asleep almost at once.

At first the curtains stirred lightly at the windows but as the hours went by the wind increased. It sucked angrily at the net, dragging it out into the night, returning it with a sigh. The linen blind rattled against the upper glass like an urgent hand on the panel of a door. She turned restlessly, and slept on. The eiderdown slipped inch by inch over the side of the bed and dropped soundlessly to the floor.

Little by little the cold crept under the covers and she struggled awake. She sat upright, staring at the curtains; a bitter wind was blowing in from the bay. She stumbled out of bed and crossed to the window. I'll hear about this in the morning, she promised herself; I've probably frozen everybody in the house to death. She closed the window and went back to bed but she couldn't sleep.

Her head still ached and even her bones felt cold. The eiderdown, pulled back into place, gave no warmth. Lying there in the dark she could think of only one thing, the warm kitchen with its comforting, old-fashioned stove. There'd be a kettle on the back of the stove. Tea, hot tea. The box of aspirin was in her coat pocket and the coat was down there too. Tea and aspirin.

She turned on the light and looked at the clock. A quarter of four. In two more hours the servants would be up, but she told herself she couldn't wait. Her teeth were chattering as she got into robe and slippers. It's my home now, she reminded herself. There's no reason in the world why I can't make tea if I want to.

The hall was cold too, even the back stairs. As she felt

her way down, the cold came creeping up to meet her.
Somebody else has left a door open, she thought. But all
the doors she saw were closed. The second floor was like
an ice house, dim and frigid. She hurried on.

The kitchen, when she reached it, was like a haven. She
turned on a light and found her coat still on the chair where
Mrs. Mundy had put it. She took the aspirin from the
pocket and went over to the stove to warm her hands. A
pot of soup simmered gently at the back, and she eyed it
longingly. Soup instead of tea. A big bowl.

She was smiling when she sat down at the table with a
steaming bowl before her. My home, she repeated; my
home now, where I can do whatever I like. There was no
sound but the clink of her spoon against the china, the low
crackle of burning coal, the soft, slow ticking of the clock.
And then The Box spoke.

She stared at the blinking red light, at the little, spinning
hand. Who? At four o'clock in the morning, who? She
crossed to The Box slowly, her eyes never moving from the
little hand and the unfamiliar letters on the dial. The red
light blinked again. Who? And not only who—why?
The kitchen was supposed to be empty. Why did someone
ring a bell that sounded only in an empty room? She read
the fine white letters on the dial. Two Front East. The
little hand clung to the letters, quivering. She tried not to
think about the other hand that was pressing, pressing, holding the little one there. Two Front East. Henry?

No, not Henry. He was in one of the middle rooms.
Two Front East. She knew that location, she could see the
closed door of that room. It was an end door in a row of
three, but that was all she could remember. Her mind refused to go on. It stood in one place like the little hand,
quivering, pointing, silent. Then the little hand clicked, and
after one long second dropped back to the foot of the dial.

Something clicked in her own mind. She felt the answer
gathering, a half-remembered word here, a gesture there,
all coming together, joining each other, ready to spring.

Fray standing in a doorway, a closed door behind him, Fray smiling down at her and saying—Max!

She could never remember how she got up the stairs but suddenly she was there, outside Max's door, turning the knob, recoiling from the blast of air and the smell of alcohol. She groped frantically for a light switch and found one. A crystal chandelier blazed down.

Max was half in and half out of a bed that stood between two open windows. He was drenched to the skin. The discarded sheets and blankets trailed to the floor and there was an empty bottle on the rug beside one limp, dangling arm. She closed the windows and tried to drag him back into bed. He was slight but a dead weight. His breathing had an ugly, rasping sound. She thought he was dying. He looked dead. All precaution left her and she cried—"Fray!"

Almost before the word had left her mouth she heard footsteps on the stairs, pounding up from the floor below. Doors opened along the hall outside but she neither saw nor heard them. Fray materialized like magic, bareheaded, his yellow slicker wet with rain. He took Max in his arms and laid him on the bed, dragging up the covers, smoothing the blankets, silent, white-faced. His hands shook as he pulled the blankets up around the shrunken body.

"Regan!" Cousin May stood in the doorway with Rosalie and the Mundys looking over her shoulder. Katy and Jenny crept forward, their sparse gray hair strained back from their terrified faces. Someone in a plaid dressing gown padded slowly up the hall. Henry. Regan stared dumbly.

"Regan!" Cousin May said again.

Fray answered for her, without turning. His face was bent over his brother's, his lips were almost touching Max's cheek. "One of you fill hot water bottles. Call Poole. May, come in and close the door. The rest of you go back to your rooms."

The group divided. The door closed as Cousin May came in alone.

"Max," Fray whispered. "Try to answer me. One word, anything. Try."

The old man lay motionless while three pairs of eyes watched and waited. Slowly his own eyes opened. He looked at Fray as if he were struggling back from a far place.

Cousin May walked to a chair and sat down heavily. "Now I suppose one of you will give me a version of this," she said. "I won't pretend to be surprised, I've been expecting something of the sort, I've been waiting for it to happen. But I'd like to hear the story you plan to tell Dr. Poole. You have one ready, of course?"

She spoke directly to Fray. He didn't answer. He looked as if he hadn't heard. His hand rested lightly on Max's forehead.

"You made a very sad mistake when you sent for Regan instead of me," she went on. "I've been trying to protect her. I think you really must be mad."

Fray turned at that. "Mad?"

"What else can I think? Subjecting a young girl to this sort of thing! And she's completely useless. Why didn't you call Mrs. Mundy if you needed assistance?"

"I didn't send for anyone and Regan's not here to assist. She's here because she found him like this herself. Didn't you, Regan?"

"Yes," she whispered.

"But what—how—"

"That's what I'm going to find out." Fray's voice was mild. "Don't worry, May. We'll have a story to tell Poole and it will be good enough. Regan, what happened? Go on, what happened?"

She told them both, looking from one intent face to the other. She told about the wind and the cold, about her headache, and the aspirin down in the kitchen. When she finished she added, "It was cold on the second floor too. Awfully cold. I know now that it came from this room but when the bell rang in the kitchen I thought perhaps Henry—"

"Henry!" Cousin May flushed. "Henry's been decently asleep in his own bed since ten o'clock! I don't know what you mean! Still, it's all very clear to me. Max found himself—in difficulties, and rang the bell. He can thank you and Providence that it was heard."

"Go on, Regan," Fray said.

"That's all. These windows were open and the rain was blowing in. And Max had thrown the covers off. He looked dead and I thought he was. I called Fray."

"Called Fray?" Cousin May frowned at the yellow slicker spotted with rain. "And where was Fray, please? I distinctly heard him go to his room at nine o'clock. And that's where he should have been all evening, there or here. His own brother—"

"I came back from dinner at nine," Fray said. "Max was perfectly well then. Sleeping lightly, but sleeping, and no temperature. I left instructions with Mrs. Mundy to give him another sedative in a hot toddy at ten and I went out again. I was coming in when I saw the lights go on in this room. And I heard Regan call."

Cousin May smiled faintly. The empty bottle had rolled under the bed but her quick eyes found it. "Don't tell Dr. Poole about the toddy, Fray, until you dispose of the real evidence. No one knows better than I how painful the truth can sometimes be, but you'd better tell it if you want the correct treatment."

"I don't know what the truth is, May."

"You don't know? I don't understand you, Fray! I never have. You know as well as I do that Max is deplorably drunk and if pneumonia develops it will be no more or less than suicide."

"But he isn't dead," Fray said. "Not yet. Not this time."

"He wanted to be, oh, he wanted to be!" Her lips trembled. "His grief was more than he could bear. I can sympathize with that, I know what grief can do. But I do think—today of all days—to hurt me so—to bring this new trouble—" She closed her eyes as if she were shutting out her thoughts. "When I think of the things people will say!"

"Don't think of them." Fray was too urbane. Regan watched and listened, unbelieving. He was silky, false, frightening. He looks as if he were going to snap his fingers, she told herself, snap them with the sharp sound of a closing trap. She watched while he took one of Max's arms from beneath the covers and rubbed it gently. The gesture didn't match his face.

"Poole will be here soon," Fray said. "I think you'd both better leave. And hurry that hot water." He gave his orders as if he were speaking to the Mundys.

Out in the hall Cousin May put her arm around Regan. "Don't distress yourself, my child. You did all you could but it was hopeless from the start. Next time, and I pray heaven there won't be a next time, call me . . . You did tell the truth, didn't you, dear? It all happened exactly as you said?"

"Of course it did! What else could have happened? And what possible reason could I have for not telling you?"

"I don't know. My poor old head hurts me so! I don't know what to do or say. People running all over the house at odd hours, none of you where you should have been. And the dreadful, dreadful part of it all will be the talk. They'll rake up all those old, sad stories and I can't bear it. We've always been so careful, we Beauregards. Never a whisper of—anything."

They had reached her door. Mrs. Mundy came up the hall with steaming jugs of hot water. Katy and Jenny followed with arms full of bankets and rubber bottles. Mrs. Mundy said, "Dr. Poole is coming up the drive, Miss May. Mundy is waiting for him at the door."

"Thank you, thank you. And please stay in the room with the doctor, Mrs. Mundy. Give him all the help you can. He'll want to know about the toddy and you must tell him plainly that you made it yourself." She opened her door and went in without another word.

Regan climbed the back stairs to her own room. It was

nearly four-thirty. She left the door open and the light burning and got into bed. Jenny and Katy would see the light when they came up and perhaps one of them would tell her what the doctor said.

She watched the hands of the little clock on the table beside her bed, and counted the minutes. She had never done such a thing before. At twenty-two, a minute doesn't exist and an hour is sometimes long enough for drinking a soda. Two days ago time came and went invisibly, leaving no trace of having been; now it paraded like a mannequin before an unsophisticated audience, mincing, arrogant, flat-faced.

She leaned on her elbow and watched the minute hand. It posed interminably on the same black second and conceded nothing. She watched with dismay until she saw it tremble, and jump two seconds with a little, mocking purr. She watched for a long time, waiting for each small jump, listening for footsteps in the hall.

It was quarter after five when she heard someone coming. She knew it was Fray. He went to Miss Etta's door and stood there; then he stood in her own.

"I want to come in," he said. "May I?"

She nodded. "Max?"

He closed the door behind him and pulled a chair up to the bed. "Max is all right. I don't know why and neither does Poole. He'll be in bed for a week instead of a day and he'll have to go south to recuperate, but that's all. According to the rules he ought to have pneumonia but he's stronger than he looks. That's the joker."

"Joker?"

He ignored that. "I suppose you think I was heartless, going off and leaving him alone."

"I do. I'd have stayed with him if you'd asked me. I wanted to, you know."

"I didn't think it was necessary. I had a dinner engagement that was fairly important and Max encouraged me to keep it. He was all right when I came back so I went out a second time. That was important too."

"You've already told us about your comings and goings," she said. "But I'm glad to know about Max."

He looked at the ceiling. "What did you do after I left you this afternoon?"

She told him about calling for the prescription. She was tempted to repeat Mr. Mayer's warning but something told her not to. It looked now as if Mr. Mayer had known what he was talking about. She didn't want to believe that but there it was.

"Very interesting," he said. "Very exciting." He transferred his attention to the bed table. "What have you been doing? Writing a letter?"

That sounded like a useless, time-killing question but his eyes were speculative. "Yes," she answered. "To a girl back home. What's wrong with writing letters?"

"Nothing. It's pretty work. What are you telling the girl back home?"

"Not about Max, if that's what you mean. I'd just started, you can see that."

"You're going to be a shrew when you grow up . . . I like the idea of girls writing to each other. You'll have lots to tell her, won't you? Pages and pages, all about me. But don't forget to mail it. I want the world to know how wonderful I am. Get it off today."

He's acting like this because he's worried about Max and doesn't want me to know it, she thought. "All right. But there's no hurry."

"No," he agreed. "But it's always a good idea to let people know you've arrived. Manners." He walked to the window, came back and sat down again. "You were going to say something else when you mentioned the prescription. What was it?"

"Nothing. Do you like Mr. Mayer?"

"He's a nice old guy." He waited, then went on. "There was nothing wrong with that medicine, by the way. I thought you might like to know because you had it in your possession for quite a while."

The words struck her like physical blows. "What did you say?"

He repeated it. "That's the first thing I asked Poole. It was the smart thing to ask. Don't be dumb, Regan. Who'd be in a jam if Max had died? You."

"Fray! I think Cousin May's right! You're crazy. You're stark, staring mad! Why would I—"

"I know, I know. Forget it. Nothing happened and everybody's lucky. Almost everybody. No pneumonia, sleeping pills okay, toddy okay. The toddy was good Maryland rye. All on the up and up. Max simply kicked the covers off and let himself get rained on. He woke up, saw what had happened, and managed to ring the bell. Too sick to think straight, no voice to shout with." He grinned. "No pneumonia," he repeated.

She pushed back a growing uneasiness. He was talking around something again, approaching and retreating, watching her face for a sign that she was following. She huddled in the old, gray robe. "Why do you keep saying pneumonia? You sound like Young Sheffy."

He jumped at that. "What's that about Young Sheffy?"

"He says odd things, that's all. The first time I met him he said he knew all about my bones. Herald bones."

"Yes. He knows them all right. What else did he say?"

"I met him in the drugstore this afternoon and we shared his umbrella because it was raining and I wasn't wearing a hat. He had a good time warning me about pneumonia. I don't like him. I don't like the way he talks about anything."

"He's harmless. Gets a little ghoulish in bad weather, maybe. Always counts his coffins when he sees people running around hatless. We've known him for years and he knows us, very well."

"So he said." She went on, carefully. "He said he knew them all, your father, your little sister, Max's wife, Hurst."

"And almost Max. Yes, that's Young Sheffy's record. A nice foundation for a cozy friendship, don't you think?"

She let him light a cigarette before she spoke again. "Cousin May told me about Max's wife."

The match burned down to his fingers. "May? How did the conversation get around to that?"

"I asked about Max's limp . . . Was she pretty?"

"Claudine? Very pretty. A fragile piece of porcelain from Vienna. Pink, white, and gold." He snapped the match across the room. "Never heard about her before?"

"No. I don't know anything about your little sister, either. Except that she was young."

"She was very young. She was fourteen. If she were living she'd be fifty now. I keep forgetting that she'd be fifty." His voice grew thin and he spoke as if he were a long way off. "Her name was Carlotta Maria and she had two long braids of yellow hair. So they never called her Carlotta Maria, they called her Gretel. She was fourteen when she shot herself. Accidentally."

If he heard her gasp, he gave no sign. "Then there's my father. You want to know about him too, don't you? My father died of pneumonia, in the same room Max has now, under almost identical circumstances. Not very original of Max, was it? You'd think he'd shy away from being a carbon copy, wouldn't you? But maybe he forgot."

He was grinning again, and snapping his fingers lightly. He looked as if he had forgotten the little sister with yellow braids. "I'm going now and let you get some sleep. Don't get up until you feel like it and when you do, come down to Hurst's old rooms." He flicked a hand along her cheek and left her.

Chapter Five

COUSIN MAY was trying hard to hide her irritation. She entered the room preceded by Mrs. Mundy and flanked by Jenny and Katy, announced by the rustle of Mrs. Mundy's silk and the subdued clank of the Crains' scrubbing pails. Fray and Regan, bending over a card table in front of the fire, looked up.

"Well, May?" Fray got to his feet. "Have you come to help us?"

Cousin May smiled firmly. "No, my dear. Although you do look like two nice children with painting books and paper dolls. You almost tempt me. Such a charming pose for little Regan but you, dear boy, look quite absurd. Now you've played long enough. Jenny, you may begin in the bedroom."

Fray leaned against the mantel. "Jenny has been thrown out of here twice before, twice in fifteen minutes, to be exact. I'd hate to have to do it again."

"But Fray! You can't possibly be serious! Please! It isn't fair to poor Hurst's memory. Do go somewhere else like a good boy. You're disrupting the whole household!"

"I am?" He was amazed. "Why?"

"Because these rooms must be cleaned, goosey! Do be reasonable. I'll open the small parlor for you, much, much more suitable. This place is dreadful to look at and I'm sure it must be depressing."

"We like it, don't we, Regan?" Fray said.

Regan, openly appealed to, colored with embarrassment. She had forgotten to rise when Cousin May entered and

97

now she struggled to her feet hastily and awkwardly. The flimsy table rocked; papers and books slid to the floor in a slow, deliberate cascade.

"I don't know—it doesn't matter," she managed to say. She tried desperately to stem the flow of falling books.

"Jenny, Katy!" Cousin May's bright voice directed the Crains to their knees. They groped feverishly and silently in the disorder, helping each other, sending anxious looks up into the faces above them.

"You see!" Cousin May was triumphant. "That ridiculous table, absolutely useless. Now let's have no more nonsense. If you still insist, you may come back tomorrow, but do run along now."

"Why all the rush?"

"Rush? Are you blind? Dust over everything, ashes on the floor! It's appalling. What will cunning little Regan think? That Hurst lived like a savage? Really Fray, she shouldn't have come here in the first place. So unsuitable, so thoughtless of you. I couldn't believe it when I heard you'd brought her here. Sometimes I think you really try to make my life difficult, you wretched boy. And this is the very first chance we've had to straighten things out."

"Straighten things out after we've finished, May. We won't bother you. We'll keep the door closed and what you can't see won't hurt you."

"Fray! The door stays open! A young girl, it's not nice! And such a bad atmosphere. And little Regan has that ugly pallor again, I'm sure she feels upset. I know I do."

"Little Regan isn't upset at all. Or maybe she is. We'll ask her. Want to move down to the small parlor, Regan, or do you want to stay here?"

She answered quietly. "I'd like to stay here."

"See? My round, May. Now don't be cross. Regan likes this room. She said so. She loves clutter and she isn't superstitious about death. I think she'd like to live in here, wouldn't you Regan?" He laughed. "Tell your Cousin May you like the room so much that you had to sign your initials on the clock."

Cousin May saw the clock for the first time. She said nothing, but Mrs. Mundy came forward and removed the tracing with her handkerchief.

"I'm sorry," Regan said. "I did that without thinking."

"It's quite all right my dear, and you may stay in here as long as you like. We'll forget that I asked you such a little favor." She dismissed the gaping Crains with a gesture and Mrs. Mundy followed them out. She watched them leave and when the door closed she turned with a light shrug. "I give up, my dears. It's only a small matter after all. But if I'd known you were going to de difficult I'd have come alone. So awkward having the Crains present." Her jeweled fingers explored the books and papers on the table. "Do let me see this work that is so important it makes young people forget their manners. Diaries! How extraordinary! I haven't seen these for years! You're reading them, Fray?"

"Right."

"But I don't understand! Surely they are—private!"

"Sure they are. And I think they'll be fascinating. Hurst kept them from the age of six and he wrote better then than I do now. I thought I'd look them over, maybe put them in order for eventual binding."

"How smug of you Fray, and how boring. Why do you do it?"

"Call it a labor of love. Yes, that's it, a labor of love. I saw too little of Hurst in his last years and this is one way I can see him again. It's a kind of sentimental journey into the past, for my own good. I want to know what he thought about, what he looked forward to with pleasure and looked back on with pain . . . I sound like a ham actor, don't I?"

"You sound like yourself, you foolish boy." Cousin May viewed the disordered table with distaste. "They look horrid, filthy. Where in the world did you find them?"

"Bookshelves."

"Oh Fray! Never! Some of them, yes. But the mildew, the damp! This one looks as if it had been buried!"

"That one practically was. It's an early one that I found in the pavilion. The weather and the rats got it before I did but I think it's readable . . . And here's the latest." He rifled the pages of a thin book bound in limp red leather. "He began this one last year and it ends the morning of the day he died."

There was a pause while Cousin May fumbled for a handkerchief. Her mouth worked pitifully when she spoke. "I'd like to read it, please," she said. "So did I see too little of him at the last. But I'm afraid."

"What are you afraid of?" Fray asked.

She visibly gathered strength, and the words rushed out. "I'm afraid of what he may have written! He wasn't himself, Fray! I couldn't bring myself to tell you and Max. He was moody and depressed. Even the Mundys noticed it and they knew him so well. He wasn't my old, gay Hurst, gallant and full of life. Sometimes he didn't speak for days, not to me, not to anyone. Sometimes—I was afraid he'd kill himself!"

"But he didn't, my dear May. We all know that. He didn't."

Regan heard their words against the dragging undercurrent of her own thoughts. Why were they talking like that? Of course he hadn't killed himself. Why did Cousin May even suggest it? Why did Fray take the trouble to deny it? She saw them facing each other across the table, poised and assured, looking into each other's eyes, talking steadily. It was all wrong, it was out of place, it didn't make sense. It was like turning too many pages of a book by mistake; the characters were the same but the action was wrong. She heard Fray's smooth voice repeating what he had said before and she forced herself to listen.

"Yes, we know. His heart, Poole said. He probably hated that, and brooded about it. It must have given him some dark days and nights and he may have written things he didn't mean. But if he did, I'll understand. Don't worry about that. I'll know he wasn't responsible."

"Dear Fray." Cousin May reached for his hand. "I believe you do understand. So sorry I was cross before. I didn't understand how unselfish your little plan was. Of

course you're to go right ahead with it! But grant poor May
just one small favor. Let me read the last one. You have the
others, the real Hurst; let me have the last one for a little
while. I want to see it. I dread it, oh you don't know how I
dread it, but I'll be brave . . . I think it will help me."

"Did you know he was writing it?"

"I knew he was writing something but he was dreadfully
secretive. I hate to say this to his own brother, but he was
suspicious of everyone, even of me. I begged him to have
you and Max here for a visit but he refused. Some days I
hardly saw him at all. He locked himself in this room, he
wouldn't let the maids come in to clean. I didn't want you
to know about the locked room but little Regan spoiled
that for me. Scrawling her initials in the dust. A sweet,
cunning trick, my dear, but rather childish. Poor Hurst!
Living, eating, sleeping in squalor. You know that wasn't
like him."

Regan spoke softly. "I know."

Cousin May turned an astonished look. "You know? My
dear child, you know what?"

"About not letting the maids in. Katy told me."

"Poor Katy. She was so confused. We all were. He
said and did such odd things." She held out a supplicating
hand. "Let me have the last book, Fray. I'll give it back to
you tonight."

He didn't see the hand. He was turning the limp, red
book over and over, smoothing it between his palms. He
didn't open it. He smoothed, fondled and caressed the soft
leather. It could have been something alive. "Later," he
said. "I want to read it myself first."

"Fray! But surely I—"

"Much better if we do it my way," he said. "Much better
for all of us." His quick, confiding smile went from one
face to the other. "Hurst thought he was writing for his
own eyes, remember."

"But Fray—his own wife—"

"Makes no difference. Wives, brothers, he wasn't thinking of us. He didn't know that a few days after his death

we'd be pawing around in his private life. Reading his little secrets. Or did he?" Fray's smile grew. "Or did he?"

What in the world is he talking about? Regan asked herself. He had flipped his senseless question into the air like a burned out cigarette and he wasn't even watching to see where it fell. She saw her own confusion repeated in Cousin May's eyes. Cousin May's face had reddened under the pink powder.

"You have an odd way of putting things, Fray," she said. "You sound as if I were the one who planned to—paw. And what do you mean by 'did he?'"

"Just an idea that hit me all of a sudden. I wonder if I got a bull's-eye?" He opened the limp book and read a page quickly and silently before he went on. "I wonder which kind he was?" he said thoughtfully. "You know some people have a sneaking hope that their diaries will be read. That's what they write them for. Some do it to be plain nasty and some because it's the only way they can say what they honestly think. That last lot are pretty pitiful but the first are nuts. Not crazy, just nuts. I know. I've read plenty."

"Fray!" Cousin May was horrified. "You can't possibly mean—"

"I don't mean anything. I'm simply telling you I'm a diary expert. The things I've read! The things people write out of pure devilment! Wonderful! They like to paint themselves as beautiful, misunderstood saints or black-hearted hounds, and if they bit a little girl at the age of twelve and broke off a tooth they say it was kicked out in a fit of temper by a Sunday School superintendent. Pages and pages, sometimes with locks on them. And the keeper of the diary is pretty sure some member of the family, like you or me, will bust the lock, read, and have a tantrum. He doesn't care if he's dead when that happens. Dead or alive, there's no thrill like knocking the loved ones for a loop."

Cousin May's lips trembled. "How wicked, wicked of you! You're suggesting things about your own flesh and blood! You frighten me!" Her bright eyes clouded and grew dark. "Fray, Fray, if you only hadn't said that. You've made me think, and I don't want to think. If there should be anything like that in Hurst's—no, I can't believe it! But we all know he—he wasn't himself, we all know that."

Fray laid an affectionate arm across her shoulders. "I was kidding," he said. "Don't worry. Hurst won't fool me, he never did." He propelled her gently to the door. "You run along now. Look, I've scandalized Regan too. I'll square myself with her and then we'll get to work. I'll keep you posted."

Cousin May hesitated on the threshold. "You will? You really will?"

"Sure. Now run along. Why don't you look in on Max? Etta's with him now and I imagine he's more than ready for a clean break."

"Max!" Cousin May shivered. "That's another thing I'll never understand. Max, of all people, to behave as he did at a time like this! All he had to do was ask for what he wanted. I'd have given it to him gladly and I'd have stayed with him too, and taken care of him. He nearly died—suppose he had died!"

"But he didn't—this time." Fray closed the door gently.

"Well," he said to Regan, "where do we go from here?"

Regan, back in her chair, silently watched his approach. He doesn't know what to say to me, she thought; he wants me to start something, to give him a lead. She waited until he sat down. "I don't know where we go," she said, "but I think you do." She folded her hands on the cluttered table. "What are you hiding from me, Fray? Why did you talk like that to Cousin May? Something's wrong. What is it?"

"Nothing's wrong. You're just sore about that little scene. I didn't show proper respect, did I? Only teasing, and she knows it."

She went on as if he hadn't answered. "What's wrong? What's wrong with everybody here?"

"Everybody here is fine. You're dramatizing yourself, that's all. Big, dark house, beautiful young girl, crêpe on the door . . . Or have you really got something on your mind?"

She saw him waiting for her answer. He looked as if he were bracing himself. It didn't make sense. Nothing made sense. She shrugged, hopelessly. "What's the use?" Her voice rose in spite of herself. "I'm going home! I'm tired of situations I don't understand! Words that don't mean what they say! Everybody talks to me and then watches to see what I'll do! I don't even know what I'm expected to do!"

"That's too deep for me. I don't get it."

"You're doing it now, just as I said! You're looking at me as if you were calculating! You're stringing words together, any words, as if you were marking time, waiting for something to happen! Cousin May does it too. Everybody does it. What are you waiting for?"

His hand went out to the stack of books with a gesture that was almost protective. She didn't see it. She continued.

"I don't know why you talked to Cousin May the way you did but I do know it wasn't teasing. You were trying to hurt her, through Hurst. You made up all that talk about diaries, I could feel you making it up as you went along."

"Good," he applauded. "I was afraid you didn't have any sense. Anything else?"

"Yes! Why are you staying here? Why don't you go back to the farm? And don't tell me about the diaries again. You dug them up because you wanted an excuse to stay here yourself and you're using them now because you want to keep me here too. I don't know why, but you do!" He'll hate me now, she thought. He'll hate me.

"Sure," he said. "Sure." He was smiling but his eyes were sober. "Sure I want you here, Regan."

"Why?"

"Better believe this, it's on the level. I want you because I'm trying to take Hurst's place. I want to see you started in the right direction before I go home."

She weighed that. "Maybe," she said. "But that isn't all of it. All the time you've been talking and smiling you've been listening too. Listening to me and to something else. I'm not stupid. I know something's wrong. What do you expect to hear when you look like that?"

"The years, like great black oxen." He laughed again, shortly. "You're a queer one."

"Go on, laugh," she said. "Everybody laughs in this house. Everybody eats and drinks and laughs, and all the time I can feel something else underneath."

"So help me, Regan, you sound like Henry warming up for a stoppage. Listen to me. What you feel underneath is simply grief. Grief and fatigue."

"Maybe some of it is but not all. There's something else too, something that moves around, as if it were following me. It's down in the kitchen and it's up in my room, even when I'm there alone. It keeps me awake at night, makes me see things wrong. It made me think the pavilion spire was a dead tree." Misery and desperation crept into her voice. "Following and reaching. Two things seem to be reaching from different directions. One wants to hold me here and the other wants me to go."

Fray spoke softly. "You say you're wakeful at night. That's the answer. You haven't had enough sleep."

"That's not the answer. And Cousin May is worried too. She tries to be kind but there's something on her mind, worrying and nagging. I think she feels the same thing I do."

"You're right, there. She does. You must remember that May's been through a bad time. Consider your own feelings when you heard that Hurst was dead, and then consider May. She was his wife, she lived with him day after day, year after year, and she—found him. Doesn't that explain May?"

"Well." She tried to be convinced. "Well, I suppose—"

He went on easily. "It explains all of us, everything. Even Henry and Max. Even Etta. And here's something else. A gentle tip. Try keeping in the background for the next few days. Don't hang around poor May too much. When a southern lady tries to run away from her seventieth birthday she doesn't want to bark her shins on anything in the twenties. Get it?"

"Fray! That's silly!"

"Sure it is. Now you sound more like yourself and it's

about time." He stacked the small books and put them aside. The red book he kept under his hand. "What say we start? Or do you want to argue some more?"

"We'll start. What do you want me to do, Fray?"

"I don't know yet. We'll find that out as we go along. Maybe I'll read you a list of dates to copy down. Dates and names. Or maybe I won't. Maybe I'll just read to you and ask you what you think."

"Think about what?"

"About Hurst. This is straight. I neglected Hurst this last year. I was busy with my own life and I thought he was busy with his. I talked to him on the phone several times and offered to run over here for week-ends, but he always discouraged me. That was out of character but I didn't question it then. I simply stayed away. Now I think there was something wrong and if there was I want to know it. Maybe this book will tell me."

"Then Cousin May is right?" She didn't want to believe that but his face told her it was true.

"I think she is."

"But what have I to do with that? Where do I come in?"

"Woman's intuition! Also, he wrote you. He asked you to come here." He spaced the words carefully, with quiet emphasis. "You, not me, not Max. You. Why did he want you?"

"I don't know." The letter again. She'd almost forgotten it. He'd asked about the letter the day she came, and so had Cousin May. They'd both wanted to see it. She remembered their insistence, their wordless disbelief, their smiling implication that she'd misunderstood, that Hurst hadn't really wanted her.

"What are you thinking?" Fray asked.

"There was a letter Fray, just as I told you. And he did want me."

"I'm sure of that. But you lied, didn't you, when you said you hadn't kept it?"

"Yes. I don't know why I did that. But it's the only letter I ever had that seemed to be all mine. I hid it in the side pocket of my suitcase. My mother's gold beads are there too. You want to read it, don't you?"

"You're making things very easy for me, Regan. Yes, I want to read it very much. Do you mind?"

"No, I don't mind now but I did before. I was angry before. I thought you were making fun of me." She rose. "I'll get it."

He had reached for a cigarette when he heard her say, "Why, hello."

He turned quickly. The door was open. He hadn't heard it open, he'd been too engrossed. One of the maids was halfway in the room, blinking, hesitating, twisting her hands. "Well?" he asked. His voice was sharp but he softened it almost at once. "Well?" he repeated.

"Lunch, sir. Lunch, Miss. I didn't like to interrupt but Mrs. Herald said—"

"It's all right. Thank you . . . Which one are you, I never know."

"Katy, sir." Katy's gnarled finger crept to the identifying mole. She nodded and smiled. "Katy."

"Coming right away, Katy," he said. To Regan, "Don't bother now. After lunch."

Katy stood back to let them pass. She followed them with her eyes, still smiling. She was thinking that they made a handsome couple, him so dark and her so fair. And now they both had money too. Like what you read about. And writing letters to each other and hiding them like in an oak tree you might say. And giving each other presents already. Gold beads, was it? She must tell Jenny and Mrs. Mundy. A wedding would be lovely now. Well, that's the way it went. After a funeral a wedding.

When Katy reached the kitchen her head was high and proud because she fancied herself in a nurse's cap, with streamers.

Cousin May was late for lunch. She came in after they were seated, full of apologies. She'd been talking to Dr. Poole on the telephone. She and Dr. Poole were both pleased with Max's progress. Everything was simply splen-

did, except poor Henry. Henry was paying for his interrupted sleep. "I'm trying to keep him in bed," she told
Fray. "He hates it, he's always been so active, but I tell him
he must conserve his strength. I need him now as I never
did before. He and Rosalie are all I have left."

"You have me," Fray said. "What would you do without me, May? No, don't tell me!" They smiled at each
other. Cousin May shook her head playfully.

That's what he calls teasing, Regan thought, and she
doesn't like it although she pretends she does. She's trying
to make this lunch run smoothly, not like yesterday's, and
it's working. It's nothing like yesterday's; we could be another family, in another house, living in another year. Maybe
because there are so few of us at the table, maybe because
Henry isn't here.

There were only Cousin May, Fray, Miss Etta, Rosalie
and herself. Rosalie's face was wreathed in tremulous smiles.
There was a new blue ribbon in her hair and a new bracelet
on her fat wrist. The newness was a matter of possession
not age. The ribbon was faded and looked as if it had been
torn from the top of an old, elaborate candy box, and the
bracelet was a child's affair of seashells strung on tarnished
gilt cord. Rosalie patted the ribbon and the shells. She loved
them so much that Mundy stood unnoticed at her elbow and
finally served her himself.

Even Miss Etta was subdued. Her manner was humble
and deferential, even to Fray, and she had a washed look
that was oddly appealing. She ate neatly and quietly and
kept her eyes on her plate most of the time. The old fox,
Regan thought; she knows exactly what she's doing and so
do I. She knows she overreached herself yesterday and she's
afraid she'll have to eat in the kitchen again. So she's trying
to behave. And she's had a bath.

Regan smiled at Miss Etta, a confidential smile, and received a bland look in return. It was the kind of look that
stays on the face of an abandoned doll. She was relieved
when Miss Etta rapidly closed one eye and bared her teeth.

Cousin May and Fray talked about farm matters, comparing the two regimes with an equal exchange of compliments. Rosalie silently counted the shells in her bracelet and Miss Etta ate with the painstaking manners of a child whose program includes the possibility of two desserts. The serenity continued through coffee. Even Cousin May looked happy when they left the table.

Out in the hall Fray whispered to Regan. "Skip up the back stairs and get the letter. Then meet me in Hurst's room. I'm going to stop and check on Max."

The first thing that frightened her was the suitcase. It was unlocked. She groped blindly in the side pocket. Her only thought then was for the gold beads and the money. In her eyes the beads had the value of emeralds and the thirty dollars, hoarded over many months, was worth more than the income she had heard about and only half believed in. When she found them both exactly where she remembered putting them, she reached confidently for the letter. It wasn't there. She told herself that she had put it with the other things, she could almost see herself doing it. But she could almost see herself locking the suitcase too. She turned over the small heap of mended stockings and odds and ends that even Katy had decided were too shabby for proper unpacking, and tried to recall the last few minutes before she had joined the others for the funeral. She saw herself tucking the beads in the corner of the pocket, pinning the money in the envelope where it still was, slipping the letter—Her hand touched a folded paper. It was the letter, not in the side pocket but under the stockings. I probably did that myself, she said, when I lost my head about the money and the beads. She closed the suitcase, took the frail key from her pocket and experimentally turned the lock. The key made a complete rotation. That's what I did before, she decided; I turned it all the way and it didn't lock. It never was any good anyway.

She went down to Hurst's room and waited for Fray. She wouldn't tell him about the suitcase. He'd think she was unreliable.

When he came in he said, "Get it?"

"Here." She held it out. "You'll give it back to me, won't you?"

"I'm not sure that I even want it—yet. Read it to me."

"Now?"

"Yes. Go on."

She read, breaking in now and then with explanations that he accepted gravely. Reading aloud was not the same as reading to herself. She noticed for the first time that some of the phrasing was odd, even a little foreign.

"'Dear Regan: You are not to worry about the future or about anything. (He meant my mother. I'd written him that she had died.) I am almost inclined to call your present situation a providential one for me because it simplifies a plan I have been making in my mind. I am thinking of you so much these last few weeks and wishing you were here with me. So because I am always a good, good boy, my wish is coming true. You remember how I made you a magic wand? Well now I have made one for myself, a fine peeled stick, and I have waved it three times and you are going to appear, pop! Like a genie out of a bottle. And of course you will give me my wish which is that you will come at once and live with me here forever after. Will you do that please? Come as quickly as you can. Because I want to talk to you again. It is a long time since I last did that. As for material things, which are always important too, I can promise you security and happiness I hope, not always just talk. Also important is that I need you. We will say that I need you because I need a daughter. Will you do this for Hurst? I am enclosing a check to cover the traveling expenses. You see I am very sure! (I used the check to pay bills, doctors, medicine and things. I knew he wouldn't care.) I remember the old days as if they were yesterday. Do you? Even if you don't remember now I am sure that you will when I show you some of my old treasures again, the good, fine things that you used to admire. You were such a little child in those days but such a wise one. You always understood whatever I told you and you were very obedient. Perhaps I should say you were amenable to suggestion. I wonder how much you will recall of our funny games if we try to play them again? Don't write to me when you are coming, little one. I want to see you walking up the path to the door, like a good surprise, and I will hurry down to meet you. But come soon. Yours, Hurst.'"

She folded the letter and put it on the table between them. "Does that help?" she asked.

He cleared his throat before answering. "I don't know. What do you think?"

"I think there was something wrong," she said slowly. "It's not in the words, it's a kind of feeling I get."

"Maybe you get that feeling from me, unconsciously, because I told you I was looking for something. Or because you've been listening to May."

"No. I had it before I saw you. I had it when I read the letter at home. I've got it now."

"Don't overdo the woman's intuition stuff because you know it's expected of you. What have you got?"

She didn't answer. Her eyes were traveling from the clean clock to the dusty cabinets and tables, to the furry rolls of lint under the chairs. "Seeing things?" he asked.

"Yes . . . Hurst didn't live in here."

He waited before he said, "Guessing?"

"No. I've kept house and I know what I'm talking about. No one has lived in here for at least two weeks."

He lit a cigarette. "You heard what May said, didn't you? And Katy? Of course he lived in here. He died in here. What are you getting at?"

She looked around the room again, frowning. "It's all wrong. He'd never live like this. He'd send Katy away because she bothered him, but he'd keep the place in order. I think he sent her away and locked the door because he didn't want anyone to know he was going somewhere else."

"You're fascinating me! Have you figured where he went?"

"No. It's a big house. Lots of the rooms are closed up. Even the library. He could have slept in there."

"Well he didn't. I locked the library myself because I was running down these diaries and thought some of them might be there. They weren't. It's open now."

He unfolded the letter and studied the closely written page. Finally he said: "Suppose you are right? Suppose he didn't live in here? Where does that knowledge take you? and," he paused, "are you sure you want to go that way?"

"I don't understand that, Fray."

"If Hurst went to all that trouble to make people think he was living in here when actually he was somewhere else, then he was deliberately hiding out. And when a man like Hurst hides out it means he's frightened, or crazy, or what? If you try to pick up his trail you may find yourself embarrassed. See?"

"It was your idea in the first place, not mine! You asked me to help you, I didn't offer!"

"That was before I saw this letter."

"What does that mean?"

He smoothed the paper on the table. "Listen to this, Regan. 'I remember the old days as if they were yesterday. Do you? Even if you don't remember now I am sure that you will when I show you some of my old treasures again, the good, fine things that you used to admire. You were such a little child in those days but such a wise one. You always understood whatever I told you and you were very obedient. Perhaps I should say you were amenable to suggestion. I wonder how much you will recall of our funny games if we try to play them again?' . . . Does any of that make any sense to you?"

"N-no."

"Think. What does he mean by 'amenable to suggestion'?"

"I don't know." She frowned again, and pressed one hand to her head.

"What are the old treasures?"

"I don't know. I suppose he means the old things in the cabinets. I remember them of course."

"What about the funny games?"

"Up Jenkins maybe. And waving a magic stick when you wanted something. Of course he always arranged the magic ahead of time so when you waved the stick your wish came true. Once he waved it in front of a holly tree and I found a doll in the branches. A small doll, hatching for Christmas, he said." Her voice was almost inaudible when she asked, "Is that important?"

"Perhaps." He was noncommittal. "But we won't think about it now . . . What's the matter?"

She was pressing her temples with both hands. "Headache," she said vaguely. "I never had headaches before and now I have them all the time. There's no sense to it. Go on, Fray, we can't stop now."

"Yes we can. We've done enough. I've got to drive out into the country to see a man and you're coming along."

"I don't feel like dressing."

"Listen." He shook her gently from the chair. "The man we're calling on will never see eighty again. Warm coat and a hat. I'll meet you downstairs."

She followed him to the door. "Have you got the letter?"

"Sure. Pocket."

Ten minutes later they were on the road heading for the open country. They drove along the water, on a shell road lined with tall pines. The clean air brought color to her face and the heeadache vanished. She didn't see Fray's sidelong scrutiny.

"Nice country," he said, "but crazy. I love it . . . Ever hear about the little town across the bay from here? You can't see it, but it's there."

"No, what about it?"

"Back in the old days when we were British, the king sent an admiral over to say hello to the little town. The town got all steamed up over the honor and decided to fire a salute when the admiral hove in sight. So they ran up the flags of welcome, dusted off the cannon, and let him have it. Right in the middle. Killed him."

"I don't believe it."

"Neither do I but that's what they say. Nice country

but crazy. I know a guy who takes all the trophies in the regattas because he butters the bottom of his boat with fifty pounds of the best creamery. You can believe that one because I provide the butter." He turned off the bay road into the woods and followed a cart track. They bumped over the sandy ruts.

"You'll like this man we're going to see," Fray said. "I'd forgotten all about him until last night. The friend I dined with happened to mention his name. Retired doctor."

"The one we're going to see?"

"Yes. Used to live across the water . . . He looked after Hurst for years."

"Oh."

The cart track joined a broad, smooth road. This was farm land, cultivated to the last blade of imported grass. Flat, rich fields swept down to the road and distant groves of trees hid all but the chimneys of old, restored houses. "This is the neck of the woods where the Rolls Royce mates with the mule," Fray said. "Here we are."

They stopped before a small, red brick house buried in trees and unfashionably close to the highway. She followed him up the path between rows of overgrown boxwood. He rapped smartly on the white painted door and spoke to the woman who opened it.

"Dr. Slocum? Please tell him it's Fray Herald."

She stepped back. "You don't have to tell me it's Fray. I've got eyes. Come on in."

"Miss Maggie! Shet mah mouf Ah didn't know yuh! Who's taking you to the Bachelors Cotillion or am I too late?"

"You'll always be too late for me," she said. She slammed the door and herded them down the small, perfect hall. "Who's your girl?"

"She's my cousin, Regan Carr. Regan, this is Miss Maggie Slocum, the doctor's sister. She used to be the toast of seven counties, now it's eight."

Miss Maggie bowed like a duchess and opened a door at

the end of the hall. "Go on in. Tell me what you want to drink and I'll bring you tea." She left them abruptly and they heard her talking to herself as she disappeared. She was saying, "I wish I hadn't used the rum for the hard sauce."

Dr. Slocum sat by his fire. He was small and frail, bald and benign. That he was pleased was immediately evident. He raised both arms in a gesture of disbelief and greeting and his soft, slow voice was like a benediction at evensong. What he said was, " 'Let me live in my house by the side of the road and be a friend of man.' And what I'll get is tramps. Did you run out of gas? I haven't got any. I'm overdrawn at the bank too."

"It's wonderful to be loved like this," Fray said. "Do you mind if we sit down? This is my cousin, Regan Carr."

"You've lived long enough in this county to know what happens when cousins marry. How do you do, my dear. Try the sofa."

She liked Dr. Slocum. She liked the way he made no apology for not getting up, assuming she had wits enough to see the crutch against his chair.

"You know Hurst is dead, don't you?" Fray said at once. "You can still read, I suppose, and you still have a few pennies for a newspaper. Why didn't you come to the funeral?"

"I don't go anywhere now on account of my leg. Even when I'm not invited."

"Like that, eh?" Fray stretched his hands to the fire. "I wish I could afford to burn apple wood. Not many people showed up. It was all very sudden. Private, too. Largely family. Poor Hurst." He talked as if he didn't care.

"Poor Hurst," agreed Dr. Slocum. "What did you come here for, Fray? Not to tell me Hurst is dead. You know I knew that. Not to call him poor Hurst to my face, either. I knew that too."

"Did you? I wondered . . . When did you see him last?"

"Professionally I haven't seen him for five years. That's

when I gave up practice and came back here to live. This is my Mama's old home," he said to Regan. "I used to practice across the bay."

"What about socially?" Fray insisted gently. "You and Hurst used to run around together, didn't you? Didn't you sort of take him under your disreputable wing at one time?"

"That was a long time ago. I took him on his first formal round of New Year's calls when he was sixteen. Promised his father I'd learn him how much eggnog a man could be expected to carry without cackling. May Beauregard stopped all that when they were married. I had to make the rounds myself then and in later years I was a pitiful sight. What are you trying to find out, Fray?"

"How Hurst was, mentally and physically. Now you know."

"Physically sound five years ago except for a slight heart condition. It could have gotten worse. It could. Mentally —well I wouldn't make any guesses on that. That never was my line of work."

"When was the last time you saw him?"

"This year, this fall, early in September. I had to go up to Baltimore to see my oculist. Borrowed a car from one of my filthy rich neighbors and had myself driven up in style. Oculist on Charles Street, and it was a nice day and my leg felt pretty good so I hobbled along a block or so, taking in the girls. Outside Purnell's, looking in the window, I saw Hurst. He looked like sin."

"Say anything?"

"Certainly. He said a lot of nothing. Thought he might buy a few of Purnell's hunting prints, he said. Thought it was warm for September, he said. Never felt better in his life, he said. And all the time he was leaning up against the window like he was afraid he'd fall. I thought young Roby would come out of the store and drag him in."

Regan looked at Fray and saw his mouth contract.

"Nothing else?"

"That's all. I know when I'm not wanted and that was one

of those times. I went on back to my swell car. I didn't even ask him to come to see me. I knew he wouldn't."

The door opened and Miss Maggie entered with a loaded tea tray. She put it on a table before the fire and stalked out, wordless.

"She's been listening at the door so she knows this is private talk," the doctor said. "That's why she's acting like a servant. Very diplomatic woman." He looked at Regan. "Pour, will you, honey?"

She did. They accepted the cups she handed them and paid her no attention. They acted as if she weren't there, so she sat back in the cushions and listened.

"Who looks after you, Dr. Slocum?" Fray asked. "Poole?"

"I look after myself, thank you. It's my leg that's wrong, not my head. I don't know Poole. I hear he's good. The women think so. The women all have him."

"Hurst had him too."

"I know. But Poole's all right. I guess May called him in . . . How's May?"

"About as you'd expect. Max is under the weather now but he's getting along . . . You looked after the Beauregards years ago, didn't you?"

"When they still had the old farm, yes. Rosie and Henry turn up for the funeral?"

"They were there when he died. They don't change much. Older, that's all. Fatter. Doctor, wasn't there some trouble once about—"

Dr. Slocum slapped his knee, winced, mouthed a long, flowing sentence soundlessly, and relaxed. "So that's what you came for!"

"No. No, not entirely. Just taking the air and found ourselves in your neighborhood. But I've been thinking a lot about little Rosalie these last days. She sits across the table from me and fiddles with her jewelry like a kid."

"That's what Rosie is, Fray." Dr. Slocum was mildly chiding. "You've always known that. You ought to make allowances. Rosie never got the hang of growing up, the poor benighted creature."

Fray nodded. "I've heard things, of course, even noticed a few when I was a kid myself, but it's all pretty vague. Nobody ever says anything. You know how May is about her family. Beauregards are perfect. Beauregards never fall down, they're always pushed. I'd like to do something for Rosalie but I don't know how to go about it. What do you think?"

"You can't do anything. You better forget all about it. Old Beauregard spent plenty of money on Rosie when she was young and Hurst did the same thing later. No cure. No nothing. She's happy when you leave her alone. So's everybody when you come right down to it. She's not so crazy when you look at it that way."

"What's her trouble? What caused it? They must have a name for it."

"They didn't have names for those things when they were doctoring Rosie. Maybe they got one now, or would have, if they could get hold of her again and put her through the works. But that won't happen. They did it once, some years ago, and it wasn't any good. It was what you might call bad."

"Tell me."

"What do you want to know for?"

Regan saw them measure each other; their eyes met and locked and the old doctor moved first.

"All right," he said carelessly. "That's old bones anyway. And I don't know much. When Rosie was about thirty they sent her away to one of those rest homes. You knew that."

"I knew she disappeared for a time but nothing much was said. I was away at school then."

"Well, they had to send her away. She was going downhill too fast and I guess they were afraid people would start talking openly. When Rosie was a youngster and got the shakes, everybody looked the other way. And if somebody was bold enough to speak of it, the Beauregards just said

Rosie was growing too fast. But this time they had to do something, and they did. The rest home worked fine. She got along like a house afire, no more shakes, no more hiding under the bed which is a mean thing to watch in a grown woman. Everybody was as pleased as Punch. Why they even got her to playing lawn tennis and croquet, things like that. So they patted themselves on the back and figured— say, is it all right to talk like this in front of the young lady?"

"She's my confederate. Go on."

"Well, so they just about figured Rosie was going to be all right. Not that she ever had been, you know; she'd always been twitchy, but they thought they had it nailed down. They thought it was one of those, well, you know. Take a nervous child to start with and maybe somebody frightened her once. Maybe somebody said something and didn't explain it enough, and it stuck in her muddled little head and she buried it deep. Then adolescence comes along and, well, you know. So the rest home people aimed to dig the thing up, whatever it was, and talk her out of it, when bang—she got worse."

"What happened?" Fray set his cup down carefully. "Somebody come to call on her?"

"Think you're smart, don't you? No, nobody called. She didn't see anybody the whole time she was there except the other rest cures, and she got along fine with them. No, it was something silly, no point to it that anybody could see and therefore nothing to get a grip on. They had a storm one afternoon, a little feller. Just wind, and not much of that, but it set Rosie off. She didn't mind the wind, they said. She sat in her window and watched people running around the grounds chasing their hats and dragging in the chairs. She was laughing and enjoying herself, they said. Then a branch from a tree blew past the window, not a big branch, mind you, just an overgrown twig you might say. But she let out a howl fit to wake the dead and was out of her head for two days. Nobody could handle her after that. May and Henry had to come and take her away. Feller that ran the home called me in later and told me about it. He knew I'd been a neighbor and wanted me to tell him where he'd missed the bus. I couldn't tell him anything. I only swabbed throats for the Beauregards. They wouldn't trust me with anything else . . . Didn't you ever hear any of this before?"

"A little, not much. Hurst didn't talk, in deference to May, I suppose. Max more or less put me wise when I was a kid, no details, just that Rosalie was nervous and mustn't be teased. I think he only told me as much as he did because he wanted me to be nice to her. I was inclined to howl when she made her rare appearances. All that fat, and those eyes. I wish I knew how to be nice to her now. Sometimes she looks desperately unhappy."

"Sometimes we all do, if you catch us with the guard down. Leave her alone. She has her own world and on the whole it's better than some I could mention."

Fray stood up. "Thanks," he said. Regan stood up too; she didn't want to leave the small book-lined room and the old doctor's compassionate voice.

"Don't go," Dr. Slocum said. "Stay for dinner. We've got wild ducks."

"So have we, and they're higher than kites. No, I've got to get back to Max. He's in bed with a cold and Regan is worn out even though she doesn't know it. Thanks again for everything."

The doctor eyed him thoughtfully. "You don't look fit to burst with happiness yourself, in spite of your flip tongue. What are you doing these days?"

"Killing time." He laughed when he said it. He laughed all the way to the door. They let themselves out. Miss Maggie was nowhere in sight.

"Poor Rosalie," Regan said when they were in the car.

"Oh, I don't know."

He whistled under his breath all the way home and she didn't try to talk. Dusk had fallen and he drove erratically, sometimes missing the ditch by a few inches. Once she said, "Do look where you're going, Fray!"

"I am," was all he answered.

That night she dined alone again. Mundy explained, when she came down in answer to the gong, that Mrs. Herald, Miss Rosalie and Mr. Henry had gone up to town unexpectedly, and that Mr. Fray was with Mr. Max. "A business matter in town," he said. "Something to do with Mr. Henry's inheritance. They will have dinner there and return early."

She didn't ask about Miss Etta. With Cousin May out of the way there was no telling what Miss Etta might be doing.

After dinner she went to her room and finished the letter she had begun. Her trunk had come while she was out and she unpacked and put away the few things it held. Schoolbooks, some of her mother's clothes, Hurst's letters. They were the semi-annual letters that had come on Christmases and birthdays, short, affectionate little notes that said little. She read them again and wondered for the first time why they said so little. The last letter, the one Fray had, might have been written by a different person.

At ten o'clock she went down to the library to get a book. She ran her finger along a row of novels, looking for something familiar and loved. Eugene Sue, *The Prince of India*, *The Virginian*, James Lane Allen, *No. 5 John Street*, *The Prisoner of Zenda*. She took down *The Prisoner of Zenda*. The edges were worn and someone had liked it so much that it opened by itself. She looked at the yellowing page and read: 'God sometimes makes the wrong man king.'

I remember that part, she told herself. That's one of the places where I always cried. For no reason, the old uneasiness returned. She blamed it on the gloomy, unaired room, on the empty halls that lay ahead. She tucked *The Prisoner of Zenda*, with its familiar red cover, under her arm. It seemed like a good idea to cry over a book again. She started up the front stairs, wondering if Cousin May had returned.

She had. The door was open and the sound of voices came out into the hall. "Cousin May?" She stood in the doorway. "I'm on my way to bed and I thought I'd say goodnight."

"Come in!" Cousin May was at the carved dressing table, creaming her face. Rosalie sat beside her on the long bench, happily turning her head right and left as Mrs. Mundy

brushed and combed her straight, scant hair. Jenny and Katy
stood by with a pot of hot chocolate and cups and saucers.

"I do hope you weren't lonely," Cousin May said. "But
we simply had to run away for a bit. Business, tiresome old
business. Mrs. Mundy went to tell you but you weren't to
be found. Naughty!"

"I went driving with Fray. You mustn't ever think about
my being alone, Cousin May. I don't mind . . . It's nice in
here."

Cousin May smiled into the Cupid mirror. "My little
nest."

Miss Etta ambled in silently and stood watching. She
looked rumpled, vague, and half asleep. Nobody spoke to
her. Her nose twitched when she smelled the hot chocolate.

"I'm ready when you are, Mrs. Mundy," Cousin May said.
She wiped away the cream and examined her face. "Where
did you and Fray go, dear?"

"I don't know the name of the road. It runs along the
water. Then we went inland and stopped to call on a friend
of Fray's. Dr. Slocum." That was the wrong thing to say
but she knew it too late.

"Dr. Slocum! Not for diagnosis, I hope! Old Slocum has
been retired for years and some people think he waited much
too long." She laughed at her reflection in the glass and
touched her curls delicately. But Hurst was fond of him.
One of those old relationships that men cling to. So silly. I
suppose that's why Fray called."

"Yes," Regan said. "That's what Fray said. He said Dr.
Slocum was a family friend." Her eyes went to Rosalie as
she remembered the old man's gentle defense.

Mrs. Mundy combed Rosalie's hair into a child's topknot
and turned to Cousin May's thick, soft curls. Rosalie accepted chocolate from the Crains with fumbling, eager
hands.

"Dr. Slocum used to look after us," Cousin May said.
"Years ago and for very simple things. We thought he was a
little too modern, too ready to experiment with new and un-
tried methods. Quite dangerous, I think. He read dreadful

books in foreign languages, all about slums and free clinics
and horrible diseases. Such a sad waste of time I always
said. Heaven only knows what he hoped to gain. That kind
of knowledge had no place in our quiet, gentle lives . . .
Come dear, kiss me goodnight. And all of you good people
go now. So, so tired."

Regan bent over the lacy shoulder and touched her lips to
the plump withered cheek. There was a slow, measured
rustle behind her, as if small creatures moved through tall,
dry grass. She looked ahead, straight into the mirror.

The others were closing in, framing Cousin May's face
and her own. They were creeping forward as if they were
bewitched. The Crains, with ashen skins and staring eyes;
Rosalie, open-mouthed; Mrs. Mundy, a face in granite; Miss
Etta, a satyr. They stooped to the level of the dimpled Cupid
and the writhing Father Time, all silent, old and ugly.
Cousin May's eyes met hers in one long look before they
slowly closed.

She drew back, making herself small. She backed away
until she was in the center of the room. Somebody sighed.
She thought it was Rosalie.

"Goodnight, dear child," Cousin May said.

Chapter Six

MISS ETTA waylaid Regan in the lower hall after breakfast. Her mouth was buttery and she looked happy. "There's something to be said for eating with servants," she volunteered. "You get your food hot and plentiful. Good morning. I'll bet you didn't have a squab on toast."

"For breakfast? No, I didn't. And I think it sounds heathenish."

"Oh I don't know. Those heathens knew a thing or two about eating. But that's not what I want to talk about. Can't we go off somewhere alone? Just the two of us?"

"I'm afraid not." Regan tried to sound regretful. "Fray's waiting for me upstairs. I'm late now, I overslept. Can't it wait, Miss Etta?"

"As far as I'm concerned it can. I've got all the time in the world but how about you? When did you say you were going home?"

"I didn't say I was. I don't know."

"Now where do you suppose I got that idea? Maybe I'm as crazy as May says I am. Are you sure you didn't tell me you were going home in a day or so?"

"No, I'm sure I didn't. I told Fray I wanted to go but I changed my mind." She moved on up the hall with Miss Etta trotting at her side. "Can't you tell me what it was you wanted?"

"Glue."

"What?"

"Glue, for mercy's sake, mucilage! I've got a little going-away present for you but I have to fix it up first. That's what I want the glue for. Have you got any?"

It was a waste of breath to tell Miss Etta again that she wasn't going anywhere for a long time but she could settle the glue problem. "I haven't any but there may be some in the library desk. And thank you for wanting to give me a present." One of the broken cups from the kitchen whatnot, if the stories about Miss Etta were true. "You can keep it for me until I'm ready to leave, can't you?"

"That's what I intend to do. No use letting everybody in the house know I'm giving things away. They'll all want something, so don't tell . . . Max was worse last night, did you know that?"

"No! Why didn't you say so right away? Why didn't Fray—"

"Fray didn't tell anybody, not even me, his dearest friend. I found out by what you might call accident. I just happened to be coming upstairs after a little midnight snack and I just happened to see Fray go into Max's room. I waited, but he didn't come out. Then I went in. I didn't want to startle them by knocking."

They had reached the stairs and Regan stopped. "How was Max then?"

"Terrible. Like death. Not talking, just looking at Fray. Fray had his hands on Max's shoulders and it looked to me like he was holding the poor man down. He sent me away of course. One of these days people are going to call me and call me, and I won't come. I tried the door again this morning but it was locked. Find out what happened, will you?"

"I'll try." She was uneasy. Miss Etta's little eyes were relishing something. "Where are you going now, Miss Etta?"

"Out to look at my ivy. They can't kill us." She minced out the front door.

Regan found Fray waiting in Hurst's room. The card table was cleared of everything but a stack of books, the red one on top. The dust was gone and the furniture gleamed.

"We've had company," Fray announced. "Katy with
the mole. She looked so hangdog and begged me to let her
in. To please the madam, she said. So I did, but to please
Katy. What are you frowning about?"

"Miss Etta says Max was worse last night."

"He's all right now."

"Is he? Miss Etta says you had to struggle with him . . .
She says you locked his door."

"And so I did. I suppose we'll read all about it in the
paper tomorrow. I locked him in because he's reached the
stage where he wants to wander." She thought he looked
annoyed. "Etta! Etta could write like Charles Dickens if
she could write."

"Somebody told her I was going away. Did you?"

"Certainly not." The annoyance deepened. "I wonder—
oh, forget it! She made that one up too. Come along and sit
down and stop looking like Katy." He pulled a chair up to
the table and took one opposite. "I've gone over some of this
stuff. Do you mind?"

"You know I don't. Does it—do you feel any clearer
about things now?"

"What I feel isn't important. You're the test tube in this
case. Now listen. I'm going to read from these diaries.
Better for me to do the reading because I noticed how the
phrasing in the letter nearly threw you. When Hurst was
touched, or moved, he ran wild with the verbs. All right?"

"Of course." She put her elbows on the table, chin in
hands. "Go on."

"I'm going to do it the wrong way, too, beginning with the
last, which is the present, and going back to the earlier ones.
You'll soon see why." He threw a quick look over his
shoulder. The door was closed. "Secrets," he grinned, but
the grin was unconvincing.

He turned to a page in the limp, red book. "So. This is
dated two months ago. I'll read it without comment.

    " I am filled with horror. Nothing in all the world
can be darker than my thoughts. In the last few days

my life has turned in to a mockery. The things that I believed in and lived by are gone and in their place I see a dim and ugly signpost that dares me to look ahead into a hopeless future and tells me it is not wise or safe to look back.

I have tried to convince myself that I am going mad. How else, after so many years, could I suddenly have these thoughts? I try to convince myself that only a slow-growing madness could bring me to this state. It is as if an army had assembled itself in secrecy and attacked without warning. Can that happen to a man's mind? Is there a form of madness that grows through the years, waiting for a time to strike? Or have I come upon a truth that has been hiding in the dark, gathering strength, waiting for me to be old and tired and receptive?

Last night I went to the pavilion and it was not a wise thing to do. The water spoke to me, the trees spoke, and I answered them in my head. The words they used were bitter words and the thoughts they gave me were bitter thoughts. It will be better for me if I am mad, better for all of us, because then the things I think are delusions and that is a happier outlook.

In the pavilion I moved from chair to chair, from corner to corner, always trying to get away from the voices that spoke. And, such is the nature of man, always trying to hear them again. I built up the fire until I thought I should suffocate. The firelight and the lamplight are my friends. They fill the room, they eat up the shadows, they take away the secret of the darkest corner. But they have no sound. The water and the trees still spoke and I still heard. So I played myself some music on the small piano but that was an effort and I played badly. Even if I am mad I do not have to listen to bad playing so I tried the record machine. It was better. I could drown the voices, send them away. All but one. One little one, it would not go. The water and the trees were gone but one small voice remained. I have told myself, if this is to continue I must know why. I must see a doctor. But a doctor will ask me questions. No, I cannot tell this to a doctor yet. First I must know more myself. I must know more. I must watch. I must examine the years, I must examine each small thing as a man does when he plans to build a good house. Like a good builder I must go back into the records. If I find that everything is clear then I shall know that I am the one to be watched, not the other.

If I am to be watched, that is not a thing one asks of one's own family. It is not a thing one tells them about. I will find my own solution. Will I go for a long swim in the bay and be drowned? No, Fray and Max would not believe that. They know me too well. Even May would not believe that. I must think of something better. Perhaps I will go away, but where? Who will take care of me, a stranger? Will I knock at the door of some unworldly sanctuary and ask the brothers there to take me in?

But perhaps I shall not have to go. Perhaps the voices tell me right. If that is true then I am also doomed, but in a different way. But I must know, for all our sakes, and soon. The little voice that cries above the others would like to rest. Sometimes it calls Max and sometimes Hurst. But almost always it calls Hurst.' "

Regan sat quiet while he closed the book and covered it with his hands.

"Well?" he asked.

"What little voice?"

"Can't you guess?"

"No. It's dreadful. I can't think . . . What did he think he heard?"

"He thought he heard Carlotta Maria."

"Gretel," she amended softly.

"Yes." He selected another book from the pile at his elbow. His face was empty of expression and his hands were firm and steady. He might have been checking household accounts, tracking down a defaulting butcher, but she felt his racing pulse as tangibly as if she held her fingers to his wrist.

He went on. "Now I know why he wouldn't let me come to see him. Do you remember what he said about going back into the records?"

She nodded.

"That's our job. We'll follow his trail and see where it takes us. Do you understand?"

"I think so. But he must have been ill, Fray! He must have been. Otherwise none of it makes sense to me. What do you think started those—delusions?"

"We'll find out. He wasn't sure himself. You got that, didn't you? He wasn't sure of anything. He was being ridden by something, but whatever it was it could be reduced to one of two things. Either he was mad or he wasn't. He wanted to find out. If he'd been given a choice he would have chosen madness."

She rubbed her damp palms with a handkerchief. Even her forehead was wet.

"Does your head ache again?" he asked. "Want to quit or go on?"

"Go on, I'm all right, go on!"

He opened the second book, a small black one, worn and shabby. "This one was written thirty-six years ago. Thirty-six. Hurst was twenty-three then. I looked into this one too while I was waiting. The first entries tell nothing we haven't always known. He was getting ready to be married. He'd taken over this house, my father's house. My father, my sister and I were going north to live with Max. My mother was dead, she died when I was born, but you knew that . . . There were guests here for the wedding, not many because old Beauregard had died a month before and everything was to be quiet. So the guests were family people only. Not our family, we're the last of it, but Rosalie, Henry, and a few ancient Beauregards, all dead now, and my father, Gretel, Max and Etta. I was an infant. Max was twenty-four then, not married. He didn't marry until much later and that's another story. The Mundys were here too. May brought them over from the farm. They were young, newly married themselves, and anxious to please. I'm setting this up because I want to save time and give you the picture. There's only one interesting thing about it. Of all those people, probably sixteen in all, Rosalie, Henry, May, Max, Etta and the

Mundys are still living. And they're all in this house now."

She had followed every word. It was all new. Her people, her family. But what did he mean when he said that the living people were all in the house now? Why did he call that interesting? Something told her not to ask, to wait. "I've never heard about the wedding," she said.

"How could you? Your mother was a little girl then and she lived miles away. And this was to be a very, very quiet affair, because of old Beauregard. Now, here is Hurst's account of the day before the wedding. I'm starting with that because I think it's a good place to begin the title clearing.

" 'Morning: Ever since daybreak there has been the most heavenly activity! Even the sky is heavenly; such blue I have rarely seen. Max says my condition paints things in the style of Murillo and he says that is very, very bad. For myself I wouldn't know. It is with difficulty that I remember even how to spell the man's name. Once I saw such a sky before, when I was twelve and Max and I were at Capri. We stood at the top of a high place looking down into the sea. The ruins of a villa, old Tiberius I think, were beside us. There were little roofless rooms still marked by crumpling walls. We walked in the little rooms, carpeted with cyclamen and violets and open to the blue sky. Max said they were bedrooms. Already he knew such things, and how romantic it was to a couple of gaping schoolboys! I have that same blue sky overhead this morning and how much I wish I had one of those rooms for my sweet May. This is not a nice way to talk I think!

The cooking that goes on in this house today is on a scale to please father. He has actually had ladles in his hands and if he continues to sample and taste he will be fit for nothing. I meet the Beauregards, the visiting ones, in halls and passages and they are always sniffing the air. It smells good. I am bending over backward to be kind to these new relatives because I think they do not like me too much. Henry and Rosalie I know well of course but the aunts and uncles are strange to me in many ways. I notice a lack of grace, in thought as well as deportment, so odd I think, considering that I am the upstart and they are of the good old breeding. But perhaps only an upstart would think such a thing and write it down on paper. Oh well, it is my private paper, for me only. Now there is someone calling under my window! A lady!

Later: Gretel, the little witch! She was imitating May's voice and laughed when I put out my head like a hungry colt. She wanted nothing, only to tease, but I went down just the same and played a game of croquet with her and Rosalie. I let them win. I am a smart one! They are of the same age and I hope will be friends. Gretel is like a little mother with Rosalie. Poor Rosie, she is so uncertain of herself and Gretel is so the opposite. I am sad when I look at Rosie and I think Gretel is too for she makes things easy when they are together. I have seen her push Rosie's croquet ball close to the wicket when Rosie was not looking and be so thunderstruck with big, wide eyes when Rosie got it through. It is a nice child that thinks to do such things by itself. If Rosie were mine I would send her away to a good school. It is unfortunate but sometimes it is better for a child to see less of its family. Henry is not very understanding and old Beauregard was without tenderness. We will see what we can do later. . . . The young girl that May has brought here to be a personal maid has just told me that lunch is ready. It will be a good lunch. Father has cornered the terrapin market.' "

Fray looked up. "Getting a picture?"
"Yes. This is Hurst. That other—that other wasn't."
"I know what you mean. Ready to go on?

" 'Later still: The gifts arrive in a continuous stream. I have been helping May to sort them out. The old family friends in New York have sent such handsome things. I think May is a trifle awed so I tell her it is only what she deserves. At the farm things were not going well for years and this display of unlimited money must bruise a little. May is sensitive and I am glad

because I do not like hard women. I wonder what she
will say when I give her the pearls tonight! I will cut
my own throat before I tell her what they cost! But I
have already told her that I am making Henry the man-
ager of the farm and she is so pleased. But they are not
good managers, the Beauregards, and that is why they
lost the farm in the first place. We shall see how it
goes. Much better for them that I was the one to buy
the place because I am in the family now, or will be,
so it is still the same as theirs. That is what I tell May.

At lunch there is much excitement when a man from
the Express Company arrives with a package for Father.
It is a small package and it is insured and marked for
the most extravagant care in handling. Max and I are
agog. We tell each other silently that father has done
some mad and wonderful thing, that he has bought at
least the eye of an idol. And Father looks at us as if he
has been decorated or has made a million dollars. Father
knows what is in the package because he sings one of
the old songs while he is cutting the string and breaking the seal. No one breathes for a minute and then—
the treasure is revealed. It is herbs for the Mai Wine!
Some of his cronies in New York have turned the
world upside down to get them for him. They have
come from Europe on the fastest boat, in the icebox. I
have not heard of a prettier compliment but I must tell
Father not to be so pleased, not to show his pleasure so
much. For those who do not understand such things a
few herbs are nothing. They do not know how difficult
it is to get them.

Henry has made a very gallant gesture in my behalf.
He has given me his father's guns. Several of them are
truly beautiful and I long for the time when I may handle and examine them at leisure. Gretel has already
begged to try a small one but I have told her she must
wait until another time when Rosie is not here. Rosie
has a great love for guns, it is like a fascination, but the
poor child is too unsteady for such things. At home she
was forbidden to enter the gunroom, so we shall avoid
all temptation here. I have put the guns in the pavilion.

It is four o'clock and I shall lie down for a while because Max tells me it is the thing to do. I must ask him

how he knows so much! There is a small dinner this evening with a few old friends coming in and Father has ordered out the best we have. It should be imposing. I tell him too imposing but that is his pleasure. He is very proud of his life that he has made himself, and why not? Gretel has a new frock for the wedding, the color of the sky, and she has tried it on until I tell her she is ugly in it and blue is not her color. She is an angel in it of course. We wish her mother could see her. She is pinning up her braids in a crown, by very special permission, and I have ordered her a small bouquet. And because it is a great day and it is foolish to wait until she is eighteen, we have given her our mother's own pearls. She is a peacock, showing them to everyone, and wearing them with her old Peter Thompson.' "

"Fray, are you cold?"
"Yes." He built up the fire. He moved quietly, as if someone were sleeping.
"Ready?" he asked.
"Yes."

" 'Midnight. This is my wedding day. We will be married as we planned because May and I have talked it over and we must let nothing keep us apart now. May will help me to forget.

The guests have gone home. They left us almost at once which was a great kindness—how kind people are —and sometime today the clergyman will marry us with no one but Father and Max to see. Henry has taken Rosie home; she is in a pitiful state and can tell us almost nothing. Only one voice is raised in this big house. Our Fray knows he has lost something and he is inconsolable. I hear him now. Can a baby know such things or do I imagine that? I have read this over and what I read only brings more pain. In my own hand I have written about that blue frock.

Sometime I must face this and that time is now, I think. In a few hours I will stand with May in the small parlor, not in the large one as we had planned. The flowers are still there and we will let them stay because now they have another purpose to serve. I will face this because in a few hours my new life will begin and there must be no shadows in my heart and mind. Some shadow there will always be but for the coming weeks I must be free to make May happy and content with her choice and not think of myself at all. So I will put it all down in my little book and not read it again until I am older and wiser.

At four o'clock I went to my bed but not to sleep. The sun was outside my windows and once I saw a red-bird. All was quiet in the house. All were resting for the dinner except the little girls who were too full of excitement. This we know because the young servant of May's was ironing in the kitchen and she has told how she saw the children walking to the pavilion with their arms around each other as I have often seen them myself. I did not ask any more. I know too well how they looked. They have a little game that is always played when they walk together. It is a little game that Gretel has invented to give her friend pleasure. Poor Rosie, so little hair, so short and thin, and Gretel with so much. They walk slowly, with their arms about each other's waists, and Gretel puts her cheek so close to Rosie's, with one long braid arranged on Rosie's shoulder. I have seen them this way and it has always made me smile because Rosie is so happy to have a braid and swings it with her hand as if it is her own.

The servant finishes her work and goes upstairs and there is no one at any window to see what happens. I am lying on my bed watching how the sun makes a pattern on the ceiling and thinking my own good thoughts when there is a shot. I am at the window at once and although I do not know for a certainty where the shot has come from, I remember with horror that Henry's guns are in the pavilion.

I hear people coming from rooms, doors opening and cries. I join the others in a rush for the garden because they all think as I do. There is much confusion, much crying, it is hard to say who has arrived there first. We tell it to the coroner and he agrees that it is impossible to know much. The pavilion when we reach it is a place of chaos. We hear poor Rosie's voice before we are there, screaming as if she is tortured. But she is all right, only frightened out of her wits. It is our Gretel.

Gretel is lying on the floor and she is shot dead, with blood coming from her heart and making a dark round mark on her Peter Thompson frock. She looks so gallant in that little frock, like a young boy who has died defending a ship. There is nothing to do.

One of the guns is beside her. Rosie is able to speak only a few words and she is mercifully taken away by May. Later we put things together and it is very little. We think it goes like this. The children are looking at the guns Henry has given me. That is forbidden to Rosie and she says she did not touch them. I believe her. So it must be Gretel who holds one of the guns in her hand and I think she is showing off a little. We have taken her to the theater on birthdays and Christmas and she is fond of long, fine speeches and acting. So I think she is acting then, for Rosie. There is a leafy branch lying on the pavilion steps, a small branch from a syringa bush, and I think perhaps it was a part of Birnam Wood that came to Dunsinane.

That is all we know. Rosie says only that she was frightened. That they both were frightened. That may be true of poor Rosie because she has little stamina, but Gretel is not frightened by anything. That is the story. They were frightened and Gretel lost control. I ask myself what could frighten two little girls on a happy afternoon in spring?

There is a stain on the pavilion floor. I have covered it with a rug. Max says we will plane it away. I do not know if I will allow that. I do know that I cannot enter that place now.' "

"What are you thinking, Regan?"

"I don't know. I don't want to think now . . . Is there much more?"

"Not much. Not much more." He turned a few pages slowly. "It ends very soon and after that there's nothing but the usual stuff, rain today, fishing tomorrow, a trip to town to buy a present for May. We might as well go on. We'll clean this up now and call it a day.

" 'Yesterday I was married. We have decided on a trip to New Orleans, May has never been there and she thinks a change will help us to be happy. Max has arranged the transportation and we leave tomorrow. Max has arranged everything.

This afternoon we will take Gretel to the cemetery, just the three of us, father, Max and I. May is too distressed. I do not want her to come. I have ordered a monument from Barcini. I have seen it before in his workshop and it is a beautiful thing, an angel. They all tell me it is the wrong kind of marble and will not last. It is altar marble, for a church indoors. But the sculpture is so fine, the mood so delicate, with tenderness in every line. It is what I want.

Later: We have returned. Father is in bed. He is bitter and resentful and he will be ill if he does not discipline himself. But I can tell him nothing. He refuses to listen. At the cemetery he was a man of stone.

We did not care for black horses and plumes for Gretel so we took her in the pony cart which is what she always liked. The pony is too fat and lazy because she has always overfed him but it is odd that today he has behaved well. He was not lazy, but quiet and well-mannered. Max drove the cart and father and I sat with Gretel on the seat across from us. We took no flowers but the small bouquet which was ordered for the wedding party. I kept it safely in the ice chest. Gretel wore her pale blue frock and was an angel indeed.' "

Fray closed the book and laid it aside. She handed him the box of cigarettes because he seemed to want them and didn't know it.

"Don't you smoke, Regan?"

"Not often."

"This is one of the times." He gave her a cigarette and she took it mechanically.

"Fray? How could he hear her voice, the small voice he wrote about? It was Rosalie who screamed."

"He didn't hear it. He got to thinking that she may have called him. It was an obsession, that's all."

She thought that over. After thirty-six years could an unhappy memory turn into an obsession? After thirty-six normal years could it suddenly turn a man from sanity to madness? "Is all this as new to you as it is to me?" she asked carefully.

"Practically. I've always known the general story but no details. Rosie was never mentioned. Now it begins to look as if much of Rosie's trouble dates from that day. When I was about five they told me I had a little sister who shot herself accidentally. That's all."

"Yes. That seems to be all."

He looked at the fire, burning low again. When he spoke his voice was dry. "If I had a Bible here, Regan, and asked you in a wrath of God voice to put your hand on it and swear that you really do think that's all—would you do it?"

"No," she said.

"I wondered. Why? Isn't everything open and aboveboard?"

"It looks that way."

"Then why?"

"I don't know. Rosalie said they were frightened. How could they be? I feel the way Hurst did. A warm, sunny afternoon and two little girls looking forward to a big dinner and a wedding. What could frighten them?"

"Maybe we'll never know. Rosie couldn't tell anyone then and she certainly can't now. She's still frightened. She'll always be frightened. Remember Slocum's story about the falling branch?"

"That's what I'm thinking about now. Fray, would every detail of that afternoon stay with Rosalie? Would such a small thing as a branch stay with her all this time? Or wasn't it a small thing?"

"They were playing some game. Hurst thought it was acting. Rosie was excitable. Yes, I think it would stay . . . Lunch pretty soon." He looked at the clock. "I think I'll run in and see Max. Etta says your trunk has come. Unpacked?"

"Yes."

"That's good. That makes you fairly permanent. Finish the letter to your little friend?"

"Yes . . . Why are you suddenly making conversation about nothing? Are you afraid I'll guess what you're really thinking?"

He laughed. "Don't get too smart for me, Regan . . . Listen, I've got an idea for us to play with after lunch. I want to talk something over with you. How about meeting in your room?"

"Why not here?"

"Too accessible. Your room's quiet and out of the way. If we turn Etta loose on Max we won't be interrupted."

"All right."

She went to her room to get ready for lunch. He's got something up his sleeve, she told herself. He doesn't believe in that accident and he doesn't believe we'll never know what happened. He's going to find out what happened if it's the last thing he does.

There were still a few minutes before the gong would ring so she stood at the window and looked at the pavilion spire. It meant other things now.

The day was clear and cool and the shrubbery around the cypress trees bent in the wind from the bay. The glossy laurel, the rhododendron and magnolias were easy to recognize but the others were dry and leafless and forlorn. They could be anything, but one of them was syringa. She wondered what syringa looked like in the spring. Did it have blossoms and were they sweet?

There was still time so she went down to the library and looked it up in the enclyclopedia. Syringa . . . 'Syringa— an ornamental shrub having cream-colored flowers resembling the orange blossom in form and fragrance. Also called mock-orange.' . . . Mock-orange. Mock. She was closing the book when someone came into the room.

"I used to do that," Henry said.

"Do what?" she asked politely.

"Look up words. You know, words." He rocked with

silent laughter when she colored. "Go ahead, don't mind me. I won't tell Fray."

She tried to ignore him. She saw that he was dressed in his best clothes. She didn't know that he was wearing everything of Hurst's that he could button. The fur-lined coat was over his arm. It was too heavy for the day but it had a rich, careless look.

"I'm going up to town," he went on. "A little business to transact. I'll have my lunch there, whenever I feel like it. Want to come?"

"No, thanks."

"We can do anything you like." He was eager. "I can take you to the Belvedere, that's where you see the kind of people you know. Or," he lowered his voice, "or I can take you to a little place where—well, never mind that! But I can! And you needn't think I haven't any money because I have! Look." He struggled with an inside pocket and pulled out an old-fashioned clasp purse. This apparently enraged him because he threw it into the fire. "No more of that!" he said. He finally produced a wallet, new and bulging. "Went to the bank yesterday. You got yours yet?"

"I'm in no hurry."

He interpreted this to suit himself. "Well I am! One o'clock!"

The lunch gong rang in even, measured strokes and he threw a conspirator's look over his shoulder as he made for the hall. "You haven't seen me," he whispered hoarsely. She heard the front door close a few seconds later. He had cut it fine. Cousin May's steps sounded on the stairs.

She and Cousin May and Rosalie were alone at lunch. Fray was with Max.

"So faithful, I think," Cousin May said. "I'm sure there are other things Fray would rather do, but it's better to have someone with Max constantly. Poor Henry said he'd like to help but something came up and he had to go out. An old friend sent for him, I think. He has so many old friends and they always keep in touch. That's right, isn't it, Rosie dear?"

Rosalie nodded. After a long pause she pursed her lips
and said, "Yes."

That single word, so clearly spoken, had the impact of a
bomb. Mundy literally wiped the amazement from his face
and Cousin May blushed like a girl and patted Rosalie's
cheek.

"Miss Rosalie would like more shrimp," Cousin May said
happily. "They're so good today, aren't they? This air gives
us a splendid appetite!"

Regan had been afraid to look at Rosalie before; both compassion and fear had made her self-conscious. She was certain that her new knowledge was reflected in her eyes and
she didn't want Rosalie to guess. But now when she smiled
across the table she saw that she needn't have worried.
Rosalie was in her own private heaven, devouring a second
portion of curried shrimps.

Even Cousin May had forgotten Regan was there.
Rosalie's mysterious decision to speak so much as one word
had temporarily wiped Mundy and Regan from the face of
the earth. Mundy, dropping a salad plate in his excitement,
went unreprimanded, and even the absent Henry profited.
He was not mentioned again or missed.

Cousin May talked happily to Rosalie and was content
with acquiescent nods and smiles. Rosalie ate steadily, her
plump hands rising and falling from plate to mouth like pis-
ton rods. Regan watched her as long as she could.

Rosalie looked any age above the fifty she actually was.
Her small, child's mouth was too soft and her eyes could
have belonged to anyone or anything, even to a trapped
animal. She tried to picture Rosalie at fourteen, walking
across the smooth grass, caressing the yellow braid that was
hers for a little while. No wonder Hurst could hear a small
voice crying thirty-six years later. You didn't have to be
crazy to hear that. She could hear it herself.

After lunch Cousin May announced that she was going
out. "I owe it to myself," she explained. "And I owe it to
Hurst. He'd want me to go out, to drive a bit, to see people.

He was so opposed to outward signs of grief. He used to tell me all his little thoughts and now I have them for guidance." She arranged with Mundy for the car. "And Rosie will be quite happy by herself," she told Regan. "We have a small piece of needlepoint and it's so good for us to make pretty things."

Back in her room, Regan watched the car leave the old stable and disappear around the drive. It was a maroon limousine, high and elegant, dated like the rest of the house. When it was out of sight she straightened the already immaculate room and wondered why Fray had chosen it for the talk he wanted. Now that Henry and Cousin May were both away and Rosalie was busy with her needlepoint, they could talk anywhere. There was only Miss Etta to interrupt and she was no problem. You simply told Miss Etta to go away and she went.

She returned to the window and watched the sunlight on the water. There were sailboats out because the wind was brisk. She watched them dipping in the wind; one of them came near the shore and she could see the Star mark on the canvas.

Outside in the hall she heard Fray laugh. He was not laughing to himself but with someone. It was the kind of laugh you use when you want to encourage a shy child beyond the first line of Humpty Dumpty. She knew instantly, and with a sinking heart, who was with him. He can't do that, she told herself with panic, he can't; he'll frighten her and it isn't fair. She stood where she was, helpless and angry, watching the open door.

Fray came in smiling, with Rosalie's arm in his. He held a plate of sliced cake in his free hand, held it at arm's length while he bent his head and talked softly. Rosalie's eyes were on the cake and she stumbled in spite of his firm grasp.

"A dozen eggs in it," Fray was saying. "Jenny told me so herself. And that stuff between the layers is whipped cream. Real cream, so help me, straight from the farm. And the chocolate is French—you know how good that is. Mrs.

Mundy's going to be as mad as hops but I don't care. I felt like a party and I'm going to have a party. And what's a party without Rosalie? Huh?"

"Yes, yes, yes," Rosalie said.

"Say hello to Regan," he went on.

"Hello," Rosalie said.

He led her to a wicker armchair and drew up a small table. On this he placed the cake, carefully out of reach. Regan watched silently. He hadn't looked at her once. He's ashamed, she thought, and he should be. It's like coaxing a stray dog with poisoned meat.

"Fray," she said in a low, furious whisper. "You can't do this!"

"Find yourself a chair," he said. "The mice are going to play."

"Mice?" quavered Rosalie.

"I call Regan a mouse," he explained hastily, "because she acts like one. Timid and silly, not like us. And," his roving eyes spied the rabbit slippers under the bed, "and she wears rabbits on her feet!" He snatched them up and placed them in Rosalie's hands. "Look. Pretty?"

Rosalie nodded. She stroked them gently and her lips parted in a slow, pleased smile. "Mine now?"

"No. Regan's. But I'll get you some tomorrow, cross my heart. And you can play with these now if you want to. Regan won't care."

Rosalie gave him a long, understanding look. "Tomorrow you'll forget." She bent over and tried to reach her own scuffed oxfords but it was too great an effort. "Help me," she begged, looking up.

Regan turned her head when Fray went down on his knees to unlace Rosalie's shoes. It wasn't a thing she could watch. They made a pretty picture, full of gallantry and trust, but she could see the specter in the background.

"It's just a lend," Fray said. "Not a give. Just a lend, for a little while, and then we'll give them back again. After the party we'll give them back. And honestly I'll get you some of your own tomorrow. I do forget some things but I won't forget this."

"Won't forget," Rosalie agreed.

Regan heard Fray get up, and she turned. He drew two chairs to the table and took one himself. Rosalie stared at the slippers. They watched her discover that the rabbit ears would flop if she swung her feet.

Fray touched Rosalie's arm and spoke slowly and clearly. "Hurst never forgot anything. You remember Hurst, don't you?"

Regan waited for Rosalie's answer. What if she refused to talk, or talked on and on until they couldn't stop her? What if this turned into one of the bad times and she had to be walked for miles until she was exhausted? If that happened, Cousin May— She tried to signal Fray but he ignored her.

"Hurst," Fray repeated distinctly. "We all remember Hurst, don't we? No, Rosie dear, no cake yet. Not until you tell me how well you remember Hurst."

"I remember Hurst very well," Rosalie said dutifully. She drew a deep breath. "We all remember his kindness and we pray for him. He was a good man."

"That's beautiful, Rosie. Who taught you to say that?"

"May . . . Now?"

"Yes. Take the big piece. Ouch, where's your hankie? Here, Regan, get me a couple of yours. And sit down." He said the latter under his breath.

Rosalie beamed as Fray dabbed at her mouth. She pursed her lips, trustingly. "I'm glad I came," she said.

"Fray, please." Regan touched his arm. "I don't want to stay."

He answered in a rapid undertone. "For the last time I tell you to sit down. This is all right. Don't say anything, just follow me."

She took the third chair because there was nothing else she could do.

Fray broke off a small piece of cake and ate it with noisy

relish. "Do you remember my tenth birthday, Rosie? We had a big party here then. You and Henry both came. You were older than I was but we all had a good time. Remember the ice cream? All done up in fancy little nests. That was spun sugar. It was good, too."

"It was good," Rosalie said.

"Then we had a Fourth of July party the next year. You came to that one too, didn't you? Funny thing, Rosie, I don't remember very much about that party but I bet you do. You were always good at remembering things. Tell Regan about it." Rosalie looked blank and he pressed her gently. "Wasn't there something about a dog? Regan would like to hear about that. Wouldn't you, Regan?"

Regan nodded. She saw what he was doing. He was building Rosalie up, feeding her, grooming her, taking her over the small jumps as he would a green colt, winning her favor, giving her confidence in herself. Then, when she was ready, he'd raise the bars bit by bit until they were where he'd wanted them all along. And then—

"There was a dog," Rosalie said to Regan. "Henry didn't like it."

"Sure enough!" Fray was delighted. "Rosie, you're wonderful. That was a terrible dog. Max and I brought it down with us from New York. Max and my father and I lived in New York then. Hurst and May lived here. You and Henry lived at the farm."

"At the farm. Henry and I lived at the farm."

"That's right. And what did we eat at the Fourth of July party, Rosie? What was the ice cream like then?"

"Like red cannon crackers with little flags on top!"

"Bless my soul, so it was. And we had real fireworks too, after it got dark. Colored lights along the water and in the trees, skyrockets and Roman candles. I nearly blew my hand off. Remember that? It hurt."

Rosalie's face clouded. "Poor Fray. It hurt."

"Oh not very much, though. Not as much as I pretended. I yelled like a stuck pig because I wanted to be fussed over.

Here, Rosie, more cake." He edged the plate closer. "We had good parties then, didn't we?"

Rosalie took her second slice after careful investigation. "Yes."

Fray looked thoughtful. "The next big party was when Max got married. When Max got married. A wedding."

Regan heard the change in his voice, so light, so subtle that if she hadn't known the route he was following she would have missed it.

He went on. "But I didn't have a good time at the wedding, did you, Rosie?"

Rosalie's face puckered with her effort to remember. For a moment she looked as if she might cry. Then she said, "Claudine?"

"Sure! Claudine! The pretty girl Max married. Everybody was very sad and I never knew why. All the women had long faces and I never knew why. Do you know why, Rosie?"

Rosalie separated the layers of cake and weighed a piece in each hand. "Who wore a blue dress?" she asked suddenly.

This is it, Regan thought. He's getting it. She leaned forward in spite of herself.

"Claudine did," Fray said easily. "She wore a lot of blue. Rosie! I just remembered something! You didn't see that wedding after all, did you? You hurt your ankle and they put you to bed. You hurt your ankle, didn't you? You were running and you hurt your ankle."

"I hurt my ankle," Rosalie repeated. Her eyes filled and he went on quickly.

"You didn't miss a thing, Rosie. It was all very dull and they went away as soon as it was over. And I went back to New York with my father. That was the last big party we had and it wasn't any fun. We were too grown up. When everybody was young," he emphasized, "when everybody was young the parties were better. When I was a baby they had wonderful parties but of course I never went to them. And poor Regan here, she's never been to a real party at all."

Rosalie's attention wavered and focused on Regan. "Poor Regan," she mourned gently, "you mustn't care."

The small, kind smile and the well-bred, empty voice were almost beyond bearing. Regan forced a smile of her own. It was as much as she dared. If she spoke she might tear down all that Fray had built; he would never forgive her for that. But she wanted to put her arms around the fat, dumpy figure and lead Rosalie away. She didn't want Rosalie to go where Fray was leading her.

"Why don't you tell Regan about the parties you had when you were little?" Fray urged. "Tell her about the farm, and coming across the bay in a big boat to see us here. Regan doesn't know about things like that. She's always lived in a city and she's an orphan."

"I'm an orphan," Rosalie said. "I haven't any parents and May is my father and mother."

"Yes, she is. But you had a father for a long time, Rosie. I know your mother died when you were very, very young, but you had a nice, big farm to live on and a father. I didn't know him but there's a portrait of him over at the farm. He looks very clever."

"Very clever. He was very clever. He was a good father. He never whipped me."

Regan straightened in her chair and saw that Fray had done the same. He relaxed at once but not before she saw the confusion in his eyes. He looked as if he had opened the door to the wrong room and didn't know how he had come there.

"Never whipped you?" he repeated. "I should hope not! What a silly thing to say, Rosie!"

It was anything but silly and Regan knew it. She saw that Fray also knew. It was the first original, uncued and unaccountable thing Rosalie had said.

"I never heard of such a thing," he went on. "Whipping boys is all right, they often need it. But little girls. People don't do that, Rosie!"

Rosalie corrected him soberly. "Some people do." She looked at him as if he were very young and in need of instruction that only she could give. She was proud of her sudden prominence but she was nervous, too. One hand, lying on the table, opened and closed. "Some people do," she said again. She looked over her shoulder, furtively.

He touched her arm and her eyes wavered and met his. "You know so much, Rosie." He was humble and admiring. "You can tell me so many things I never knew before. That whipping business, for instance. I can see that you know all about that. I think it's very interesting, too. How do you know so much? Did you have a little friend who was whipped?"

"I was never whipped," Rosalie repeated. Her hand went to her throat and stayed there.

"Of course you weren't. You were a good child, Rosie, everybody knows that . . . But did you know some little girl who wasn't? Some other little girl?"

"No. I never knew anyone. We never knew people like that. But I know all about whippings."

"You read about them in a story, maybe. I know those old stories. Very sad, some of them." His face was wet but he went on steadily. "Unhappy stories, that make you cry. They used to make me cry. Did someone read you a sad story, Rosie dear?"

"No. I was told. I'll tell you." Suddenly, and without warning, her head snapped back and her lips curled in a wide, false smile. Words came from her mouth in a thin, searing hiss. "Children are like little animals. As the twig is bent the tree's inclined."

Under their astounded eyes she changed into another person. Her body shifted from side to side, settled, and grew strong. There was power in the thick, white neck and her fat fingers drummed the table with intolerable patience. The same fingers that fondled the shell bracelet and tore the cake apart now drummed on the table like steel hammers. She sat back in the chair, head forward, chin lowered, drumming the table and measuring Fray through half-closed eyes. She was arrogant, despotic, implacable, and she held all the cards. Fray was something small and helpless and she was not Rosalie.

She spoke to him in a high, clear voice that had no resemblance to her own, and unconsciously he drew back. She looked at him as if he were on his knees.

"Whip you, my dear child?" She laughed silently. "Don't be absurd. Do you think I want every Tom, Dick and Harry on the place to hear you screaming? No, there will be no whipping. I have a better plan, a wiser, saner, more civilized plan. I call it discipline, not punishment. Discipline. Do you understand? Get up! Stand up! Don't cringe, you little goose! Now listen. When you stand before me with a hanging head and tell me you have forgotten to close the door, forgotten to learn your Bible verse, forgotten to wash your face and hands, then I must do something to make you remember. You see the wisdom in that, I trust? It does no good to tell me that you're sorry. Sorry is a cheap and lazy word and tomorrow you will use it again. I know your little mind, my child, I read it like a book. Without me, you would grow into a fool.

"And that must never happen, you know that. You must be forced into remembering, made to think. And I prefer to do it without violence—if that is possible. I am not a savage, my dear. So, every morning when you wake you will hear me reminding you. Reminding you, that's all. You will hear me—like this."

Rosalie's fingers reached across the table and fastened on something that wasn't there. They wrapped themselves around an invisible object and gripped it until the knuckles were white.

The others watched, almost without breathing. They followed the arc of her steady arm as it swung high, they saw the satisfaction in her eyes as she swept the invisible weapon through the air and brought it down to the table with a silent crash.

"You will hear me reminding you like this," she said. "I will never strike you, you may not even see me, but you will

hear that sound and know that I am near. I will strike the
steps as I come up the stairs, one by one." The plump arm
rose and fell again. "I will strike the walls as I come down
the hall, the steps, the walls, the door to your room. You
will imagine that I am coming for you and you will ask
yourself what you have done. That is the point I want to
make. You will not have done anything wrong, not then.
You will not have had the time. But you will ask yourself
questions, and you will remember the things you now take
pleasure in forgetting. You will wonder if I will—open the
door!"

The flailing arm rose and fell for the last time and was
still. Rosalie sagged in the chair. When she raised her eyes
again they saw she had come to the end of the dim old road
she had been traveling.

She looked from face to face with a vague, tremulous
smile. "Did you hear it? I did. On the steps, on the walls,
coming to the door. That's the leaves. The leaves do that.
They whistle through the air. Like this." Her hands returned for the unseen switch.

"Don't!" Regan's voice was shrill.

"I won't, Regan, I won't . . . But I was never whipped."
Her hand shook as she touched the rim of the cake plate. She
looked at Fray. "May I?"

He got up, wearily. "Come along, Rosie dear, Regan's
tired. We'll finish the cake in your room." His arm was
around her shoulder when he led her away.

Chapter Seven

THE brisk wind had gone, the sun had set, and early dusk filled the back garden. Instead of the wind a soft, sweet dampness blew across the grass, brushing her cheek and stirring the hair at her temples. It felt like a kiss in a dream, light, disturbing, and full of promise.

She drew a long, slow breath and wondered about the sudden fragrance. It was too late for flowers. The garden beds were brown and empty and the bushes rubbed their dry, bare stalks against the pavilion's walls. Yet the air that touched her cheek might have blown across a garden. She wrapped her arms about her knees and leaned against the pavilion door. There was sand on the pavilion steps. There had always been sand on those steps. She remembered that now.

She had come out alone because she wanted to forget the child Rosie. Fray had led a gray haired woman from her room but he had left behind a child who still cringed before a leafy switch that had whistled through the air more than forty years ago. He had come back later and told her that Rosie was all right. She'd been standing at the window, shivering, trying not to cry. He'd been angry.

"She's all right, I tell you," he'd said. "She's better than ever, she had a good time. She's forgotten all that stuff already. And she likes you, she said so. I think she confuses you with Gretel. Herald features, yellow hair, all that. She wants to know if you'll be her friend. She told me to ask you. She wants you to be her best friend, with emphasis on best. Can you bear it?"

"Can I bear it! I can do more than that! She breaks my heart." Then she'd asked the question. "Fray, I know she was talking about herself and that someone used to threaten her with a switch with leaves on it, but—who was it?"

"Papa. Pronounced Papah. Papah Beauregard. I got that much out of her before she went back to the shell bracelet. He was a pious stinker. Poor Rosie wasn't clever, as May was, or handsome, as Henry was, if you can make yourself believe that about Henry. She was nothing but a shy, dreamy, ungifted kid and she didn't glitter to advantage in the Beauregard showcase. Apparently that got under his skin and fed the nasty little fungus he cultivated instead of a heart. He seems to have enjoyed baiting Rosie. It probably started with plain and simple baiting and moved up gradually to fancy, bloodless torture. A medieval sort of guy. He drove her nuts, of course. He must have been a maniac himself."

She'd put her second question carefully, "Was there a wind that day?"

"What day? Oh, I get you. Birnam Wood. No, I don't think so. There couldn't have been. Not a strong one, anyway. Not strong enough to tear off a branch of shrubbery, carry it around the pavilion and deposit it neatly on the steps. The steps face the water, you know, and the syringa grew on the side facing the house." He'd eyed her thoughtfully. "Don't think about it. Don't think about anything until I ask you to. Just play along with Rosie, be nice to everybody, and let me do all the head work . . . Are you going to feel like more reading tonight?"

"Yes, I want to get it over. I want to get it over and then forget it."

"After dinner then. The usual place, Hurst's room."

He'd left her, and she'd come out alone to the pavilion. She couldn't stay away.

Somewhere in the deepening dusk a dry bush rustled. She huddled against the barred and bolted door and listened. The bush was quiet. Down on the beach the small waves crept in, ending their journey with a little rush, expending themselves with a sigh.

The shore line curved away to her left, bit deeply into the mainland and swung out into a promontory. She saw the promontory like a rock, rising above the black water, standing against the dark blue sky. One by one a string of lights blinked on along its length, threading their way from the mainland out into the bay. When they reached the end they formed squares and rectangles, like little houses of light.

She watched them as if they could tell her something. She had seen them before, in that same place, glowing in the summer night, but there had been more of them then and they had risen like golden towers to the stars and looped across the sky. And their reflection had lain on the water like a net.

The soft air found her cheek again and drifted away. She heard it in the rustle of dry bushes, in the docile chatter of magnolia leaves; then it returned with a small rush, like the waves on the shore, and she began to remember. The sounds, the smells, the night itself, were turning time back.

Long ago the wind had brought music. The lights on the promontory had leaped and circled and the wind had carried music across the water to the pavilion. It had been faint, and sometimes it had drifted away altogether, but she had wanted to go where it was. Hurst had explained.

There was an amusement park on the end of the promontory. It was called Golden City. She'd thought it was the most beautiful name she had ever heard. The music came from the Flying Horses. She didn't know what that meant so he'd described the Flying Horses in detail. She'd corrected him. At home they were called Merry-Go-Round.

They didn't go to Golden City that night, or any night, although he'd promised. He'd said it was too late and far past bedtime. Some other night, he'd said. Then to make up for her disappointment he'd carried her out to the dock and they'd climbed down into the launch and sat there, watching the lights. The launch was tied up and the rope was wet and full of seaweed. She'd told him it looked like long hair.

He had been very quiet, quieter than she was, and she'd stolen looks at his calm face. She could remember now that his hand was cool on her bare arm and that his eyes were somber. She could even remember the words he had used, and the little accent that sometimes broke through.

Funny, she thought. After all these years the things we said and did are coming back. Not in bits and pieces, but whole and complete. Perhaps the pavilion brings them back.

She had studied his face and asked him what he was thinking, and he'd said he was thinking a foolish thought. "I have thought of a new name for Golden City," he'd said.

"But I like Golden City," she'd said firmly.

"So do I. It sounds like The Promised Land. It looks like The Promised Land, too. And for us it is inaccessible."

She had looked again at the tip of the promontory, far away and shining in the night, sending its light up to the stars and down into the smooth, dark water. It was both wonderful and sad. She had rested her head against his arm and they had looked across the water while the wind whispered around them.

"Stella Maris," he had said under his breath.

She had repeated it, wondering. "Stella Maris?"

"Star of the Sea." For a while he'd said nothing more, then, "I told you it was a foolish thought."

Perhaps it was. It had meant nothing then and it still meant nothing. But then, as now, it had touched something in her heart.

She tried to recapture the rest of that night and it seemed to her that the past and the present had somehow come together in a miraculous fashion. The small wind was the same, the sound of the water was the same, even the air had slipped back to summer. Only Golden City was gone. The strings of light were thin and pale, as if the years had drained their life away.

What had they done after they'd climbed into the boat? It

had been late then, long past bedtime, he'd said. Had someone come after her? Had someone scolded? That was it.
Someone had come.

They were sitting in the boat when they heard someone
enter the pavilion. They'd heard the scrape of shoes on the
sandy steps and seen a light go on inside. Hurst had stiffened suddenly.

"Stay here," he'd whispered. "You won't be afraid?"

"No," she'd whispered in return. It was going to be another game, she'd thought. He'd kissed her briefly.

"They want you to go to bed but we will fool them.
Wait for me, very, very quiet, and I will come back." He'd
swung lightly to the dock and disappeared in the shadows.
She'd watched him reappear on the strip of lawn before the
pavilion, a blur of white against the cypress ring. The light
in the pavilion glimmered through the trees.

She'd waited for what seemed a long time. Even now she
didn't know how long. She tried to account for those
minutes, pairing them with the parallel things she did remember; things like the lapping water, the moth that had
flown too close, the bird that had stirred in its sleep and
frightened her with a shrill cry. But it was useless. Time
stayed in the past, only the shadows and the sounds returned.
She drew one foot along the sandy step and heard the old
warning again. That was the way to go back. Minute by
minute, piece by piece, one thing after another. The scraping footfall on the sandy step, the sudden gleam of light.
Someone had entered the pavilion and lighted a lamp. He
had turned his head quickly and she had felt the tension
in his arm. Then he had kissed her, told her to wait, and
gone to investigate.

Then she was alone in the boat. Then—was that when
the bird had cried?

No, the bird had come later. First the water against the
boat, then the moth, then the bird. Then voices.

The voices had started in whispers but one of them grew
louder and rose and fell in a toneless wave. The Flying
Horses over in Golden City sent their muted invitation

across the water and she'd wanted to listen, but the voice in the pavilion was too loud.

She saw herself as she was then, crouched in one corner of the boat, turning her head from the enchantment across the water to the single light on the dark shore. She heard his voice again, raised for the first time, pleading. She'd been sure he was pleading for her, for one more hour in the summer night. She hadn't wanted him to do that, not if it meant a scolding for him. She would tell him so. And she'd tell the other person, too. She'd explain that it was all her fault, that she'd begged and teased. He was not to be scolded because of her.

She saw herself groping along the wet flooring of the boat. She was afraid to stand up because the boat rocked. She saw herself climbing up the little ladder to the dock. The rungs were wet and the dock was slippery, and she fell. The next day there was a stain on her white frock and she couldn't remember how it had come there. That had made her mother angry. Her mother had thought she was lying. When she'd said she couldn't remember, nobody believed her. But she could remember now. It must have been the fall.

The fall had frightened her too; the bird, the fall, the moth and the voices. The dock had stretched ahead, unsteady, long and narrow, and suddenly the water was too close, too dark. She had tried to walk slowly and carefully but the boat drifted against the dock and the boards trembled under her feet. She had dropped to her hands and knees and crept forward, longing for the safety of Hurst's arms. Her small legs were trembling when she reached the lawn and ran toward the pavilion.

She was trembling now. Her head throbbed and her hands were wet. What had he said when she came to the pavilion door? She couldn't remember. Had he scolded or laughed? Was he pleased or angry because she had disobeyed, even to come and help him?

She turned and pressed one hand against the door, touching the unyielding wood, the iron bolt, the new, round lock to which there was only one key. She couldn't even remember if the door had been open or closed then. She couldn't remember the other person at all. Only the voices. For a minute she thought she heard them again.

A footstep sounded on the grass. Someone with a lighted cigarette was walking toward her from the direction of the driveway. Fray?

"Who are you sitting there?" a thin, wavering voice asked. Henry.

He sounds queer, she thought. He's been up to something. "It's only me, Henry," she said. She was glad to see him. He was real.

He sat beside her on the steps. "What are you doing out here in the dark. What made you come out here?" The waver had gone from his voice. He spoke in a whisper and it was more compelling than a shout.

He doesn't sound like himself, she thought. I must have frightened him. "I'm not doing anything, Henry," she answered. "Just sitting, that's all."

"That won't do." The whisper was softer and stronger. "You've been trying to get inside the pavilion, haven't you? Why? Who put you up to that? Tell me."

"Henry! You don't know what you're talking about!"

"That's no answer. Nobody comes here. We don't like people to come here. Nobody's been inside the place for years, except Hurst. Now you come, in the dark, all by yourself. What for?"

"I came because I wanted to look at the water," she said patiently. She wanted to say it was none of his business but she knew he couldn't take rebuffs. "I'm going in soon, it's getting cold." When he didn't answer, she said, "What's the matter with you all of a sudden? Didn't you have a good time in town?"

After a moment he laughed, quietly at first, but soon his thoughts required a lustier expression and he brayed. The old Henry was back.

"Hush," he admonished her. "We're too noisy," He dug into his pockets one after the other, his gross body heaving from side to side until he found what he was looking for. "I had a good time, all right, no thanks to you," he said. "Here, have one of these." He held his palm close to her face. "Have a couple."

She peered at the small paper packet lying on the creased flesh. When she hesitated, he shook out a few red pellets and put them in his mouth.

"What are they?" she asked.

"A candy confection." He laughed again. "They sweeten the breath. I call them alibis. Go on, eat a couple."

"I don't need an alibi, thanks." She expected a whimper at that but none came. She felt him watching her closely.

He shifted his position, shuffled his feet and cleared his throat. "Regan?"

"What?"

"Come on and eat a couple, will you? Will you like a good girl? Come on and eat a couple, they won't kill you." He was wheedling. He was almost too much like himself. He was the old Henry underscored. She wondered, vaguely, if he was shrewder than he seemed, if the whining, childish behavior was a careful act designed to save him from responsibilities. His voice ran on, disarming and plaintive. "Come on, they're good, honest they are. Just sugar and spices and things like that. If you eat a couple they'll be on your breath too." He waited. "For God's sake, don't you know anything! Don't you know about gin!"

"Yes, I know." She took a few and let them dissolve in her mouth.

"Not bad, are they?" he asked.

"Not for you. But I didn't have any fun before." She knew he didn't like that because he put six more inches between them, drawing the precious fur coat with him. I've hurt his feelings, she thought; I'd better do something about it. "Henry?"

He grunted. "If you go blabbing to May I'll fix you . . . I'll find out something about you and I'll tell."

"Don't be silly, there's nothing to blab about. Look, Henry. What are those lights over on the promontory?"

"Oyster house. Crab house in summer, oyster house in winter."

"For packing and shipping?"

"What else?" His voice pitied her ignorance. "When a catch comes in after dark they work fast to get it out. Big market in New York. Lots of money in it but dirty work. I don't know anybody over there, not my kind, so if you want to go you'll have to ask somebody else. Fray knows them all." He laughed shortly. "Fray."

"I wasn't thinking about going. It used to be an amusement park, didn't it?"

"Sure." He was surprised. "How do you know about that? You never went over there, you were too young. Who told you about that place?"

"Hurst." She wondered where Henry had been that night when she and Hurst had watched the lights from the boat. When someone had come to the pavilion— He and Rosalie had been visitors then. Cousin May had said so.

"Golden City!" Henry laughed. "Gone but not forgotten! Rest in peace!"

She touched his arm. "Tell me about it, Henry. I always wanted to go. Did you go?"

"Did I!" Something new crept into his voice. It sounded like longing. "It was some place! They used to run excursion boats down from Baltimore, all kinds of people, factory girls and people like that. Moonlight sails, they used to call them. I used to go over there whenever I could get away. From the time I was fifteen until they closed the place ten years ago I used to go over. They used to have everything. They don't have places like that any more."

"I used to watch the lights across the water," she said.

He didn't hear her. He was back in Golden City, a boy of fifteen, a young man, a not so young man, an aging Lothario, too fat, too short of breath, strutting up and down the sandy little streets. He was smelling the molasses popcorn balls, the hot sausages, the cold beer, the violet talcum powder that turned to paste on warm, white necks.

"They had a Midway," he said. "Little shows, games of

chance, fortune tellers. I had my fortune told every time
I went. She was good, too, that woman was. She told me
the same thing every time. I'd even wear different clothes,
on purpose, and talk and act different, but I never fooled
her. She told me the same thing every time."

The thin voice trailed off and ended in a sigh. He leaned
against the bolted door as she had done, and watched the
distant lights. She wanted to help him. She didn't know
what he was thinking, or seeing, but she knew he was looking for lost hours. Like herself. He was vulgar, stupid,
tricky, but she wanted to help him because she knew how
he felt.

"What did she tell you, Henry?"

"Who?" He sounded startled.

"The fortune teller."

He lit another cigarette and she saw that his eyes were
moist. "Fatima. That was her name, Fatima. Twelve
petticoats." Then he laughed and she knew the spell was
broken. "I know it was twelve. I counted them once."
He counted them again, on his fingers, and raised his arms
in a curving gesture. He wanted the gesture to say things
he didn't dare put into words but it only said he was clumsy
and old. "I'm almost sixty," he whined. "Damn it, I keep
forgetting I'm almost sixty!"

"Go on, Henry," she said. "What did she tell you? You
can remember that, can't you?"

"Of course I can remember! Do you think I'm crazy?
She told me I was going to be rich and popular with the girls.
She told me I could do anything, anything, because I had
determination and will power . . . And I have. She was
right. I can do anything."

"I know," she said.

"What do you mean by that?" His voice dropped again.

"I mean exactly what I said." She hurried on. "I know
you can do anything. I've watched you."

"Oh."

She changed the subject easily. "Henry, you were here
when I came to visit years ago, weren't you?"

"Everybody knows that. There's no secret about that."

"And Rosalie, and who else?"

"What do you want to know for? What's that to you all of a sudden?"

"Please, Henry. I'm only trying to bring back the best time in my life. I've been thinking about that time but I can't remember all the people who were here."

He answered slowly. "Max was here, and people kept dropping in, callers and so on. I don't know. I didn't have much time for people."

"You sound as if something had happened," she said carelessly.

"Something did. Rosie and I left the farm for good after you went home." His voice sharpened. "You knew that! Fray told you about that, you can't fool me! You're just leading me on! What do you want to talk about that for? Why do you want to rake up all that stuff, making me out a fool? All I had was bad luck. Bad luck, that's all. If I'd been a damn peasant, born in a muddy ditch, I'd have made a go of it. The hell with it, I say, the hell with it!" He swore like a little boy with a piece of chalk in his hands.

"I don't know anything about it," she said mildly. "I don't even know what you're talking about. I was only asking about you and Rosalie, and that summer. I remember now that somebody said you moved away from the farm. Maybe Miss Etta—"

"What? What did she say? Etta! She's a liar. She's an ugly old woman that I wouldn't have in my kitchen. I wouldn't let her carry slops to the pigs. What did she say?"

"I'm not sure that she said anything. But she talks a lot and she may have been the one who told me. Somebody said you'd managed the farm for Hurst and then you gave it up and moved to Philadelphia."

"Right! Right! I managed the Beauregard farm for Hurst Herald. Right. That's what I did. I got up at daybreak like a cowman, and tramped around in the mud. I sat up all night with sick horses because the Heralds believe in sitting up with sick horses. Two vets on hand but a representative of the landed gentry had to be there too. The landed gentry were the Heralds who had money in six banks and the representative was a Beauregard with empty pockets. Me. Why should I take that? Why? I had to get away once in a while, I couldn't stand it. I had to have a little fun, I was human. I was human, that's all . . . Then in comes master Fray, twenty-two he was then, a fresh young kid. He takes over, he's the boss. The very first day young master Fray walks out in the fields in his nice new boots, the drought breaks. The wheat grows two inches, the hens lay double eggs, the cows give cream. Money, money, money . . . So Rosie and I went away."

In someone else it would have sounded funny. If Fray had talked like that she would have laughed. But Henry's voice was bleak and bitter and it was oddly controlled. There was courage behind it, the kind of courage a man hoards against the day when another man's back will be turned. If he hated me, I'd be afraid, she told herself. But I'd never let him know I knew. That would be worse.

"I think you're lucky," she said. "You don't belong on a farm. You're cosmopolitan."

"I don't belong on a farm as a laborer!" He was partly mollified. "But it's my land. I don't care who lives on it now, it's mine! Ours. We've always had it. Hurst should have given it back to me. When he bought the place and married May he should have signed it over to me. I told him so too, told him straight out. If it had been mine, all mine, things might have been different."

"Maybe you'll get it back one day."

He didn't pounce on that as she thought he would. He didn't rush in with a list of his qualifications, his plans, his grievances. There was a long pause before he spoke. Then, "Think so?"

That was all. He might have been saying that tomorrow would be another day. Not a red letter day, an ordinary day. It was a quick change, too quick. It left her wondering.

He struggled to his feet and steadied himself against the

door. "Come along, we'd better go back to the house. Getting late, getting cold." He wrapped the coat around himself like a cape, with the lining on the outside even though there was no one to impress. She followed him silently.

"Look," he said as they turned the corner of the pavilion, "why don't you tell May I've been out here with you all the time? She'll like that."

"Even so, I don't see why I should. What's the point?"

"All right, don't then. But it wouldn't kill you to give that impression. It wouldn't cost you anything. You'd do it if you were a sport."

He tried to keep a few steps ahead of her. He's reminding himself that he's a Beauregard, she decided. He's putting space between a Beauregard and a Herald. That kind of pride is like a disease. Poor Henry. She almost felt a twinge of sympathy when the pride literally fell. A root in the path threw him against her and he had to grip her arm to keep from falling. Without thinking, she drew away.

"You're a prude," he said. "Serve you right if I tell everybody you sneaked away and met me in town this afternoon."

"Better not," she advised. "Fray knows where I was and so does Rosalie."

"Rosie? What do you mean? You been talking to Rosie?"

She didn't answer. She was ahead now and he had to walk fast to keep up with her.

"You been talking to Rosie?" he repeated. "You been bothering her, trying to get things out of her?"

"I haven't been bothering anybody. Fray and Rosalie came to my room this afternoon. I didn't ask them to. They brought a cake. We talked for a while and Rosalie told us about the farm." After she'd spoken she wanted to take the words back. She tried to remember what Fray had said about Rosalie's party. Was it a secret? Hardly, because the Crains knew about the cake. And Rosalie would boast about the rabbit slippers. She might even wear them to dinner. She was too busy with her own thoughts to notice that Henry was silent.

She saw Rosalie as she had been that afternoon, a fat woman with graying hair, comfortably settled against the cretonne cushions of a wicker chair, swinging her feet like a child. She saw her in the same chair, wearing the same ridiculous slippers, dominating the room, tearing the nerves of her audience to shreds. She heard the invisible switch cut through the air.

Fray said Rosalie had already forgotten that part of the afternoon. Was that because Rosilie was mad? Could she forget the ugly things and remember only the good? Was that a compensation for madness? Forget, remember, remember, forget.

Was she like that too? Was she deliberately hiding in a safe little world padded with the recollection of Hurst's love? Did she cling to the safe hours that held magic wands, Up Jenkins and orange sherbet, the way Rosalie clung to her beads and bows and food, because they stood between her and something she wanted to forget? Rosalie had learned the trick of forgetting ugliness except at rare intervals. Had she learned that trick too?

She could remember Golden City across the water, she could retrace her steps along the slippery dock, the strip of lawn, straight up to the pavilion door and no farther. Did that mean she had closed the pavilion door in her mind? That night when she stood at her window and saw the spire for the first time in many years, her mind and eyes had refused to recognize it. Was that a key? She counted the things she could remember, Up Jenkins, orange sherbet, the boat, the light through the trees, the footstep on the sandy step, the voices—

"What are you mumbling about?" Henry asked. They were passing the lighted kitchen windows and she saw his face clearly. He was grinning with sudden good humor. "May says you're below par and she's right. No self-control, no stamina. Talking to yourself! What's the matter with you? I'm here. Talk to me."

She tried to think of something to say but he didn't wait for it.

"Look, Regan," he coaxed, "I'm not such a bad chap. You and I could enjoy each other's company if you weren't so stiff." He made his voice soft. "Look. If I take your arm when we go in the house, will you pull away and act silly?"

"No," she said with quiet desperation. "I won't pull away."

"Well, well!" He was enchanted. He slipped an arm through hers and stared obliquely all the rest of the way.

They turned into the path that led to the front door. Henry had his own key. He dropped her arm reluctantly when he fished it out. It was a bright, new key and apparently the sight and feel of it made up for the temporary loss of human contact. He unlocked the door with a flourish. This is the first time he's ever done that, she told herself.

Someone was playing the piano in the music room. Henry's spirits soared higher. "May," he whispered. "She's feeling good. This is my lucky day."

The music tinkled down the hall. Cousin May was playing Narcissus.

"Come on," Henry said. "She's feeling good. It's a pretty piece, too. She likes people to watch her. She crosses her wrists in it. It's graceful."

She followed him into the room and it was like walking into a lithograph. Candles burned on piano and mantel. Cousin May, in trailing gray lace, gave them a quick, bright smile, uncrossed her wrists with delicate precision, and went back to the beginning. Fray lounged on a gilt sofa, his head resting on pink silk pillows, his long legs stretched before him. A fire burned in the grate.

Rosalie overflowed an Ottoman on one side of the fire. She was stabbing a needle in and out of a rumpled piece of canvas and she had hung a rope of crimson wool about her neck. On the other side of the fire Miss Etta, cannily draped in a lace fichu, had taken the pose of Whistler's Mother and was keeping it.

Regan stared at Miss Etta. She was a cheering sight but she invited speculation. She looked as if she might have done something dreadful, as yet undiscovered, and had set the scene for a convincing denial. Or, she might be planning to do something dreadful and hoped her present attitude would lull the household into giving her a clear field. She was deep in reverie, on the surface.

Cousin May brought *Narcissus* to a tinkling close and spun around on the piano stool. "There, that's done! And here you are, safe and sound! We've all been wondering but none of us dared ask! So naughty of you both to stay away and you've missed your tea but I suppose you weren't thinking of food! Regan, how very pretty this evening! Henry, you funny, funny boy, you're actually blushing!"

Fray dragged in his legs as if he were reeling in a line. His lips moved silently.

Cousin May continued. "Everything is working out so well, all the little strains and worries gone. But then I knew they would. And Rosie had a happy afternoon, all thanks to you, dear Regan. She told me all about it and that pleases me so much. Rosie's quite another person, aren't you, Rosie? So light and gay, so full of fun tonight. But we mustn't have too much excitement, we're not very strong, you know. Better ask poor Cousin May the next time, Regan. So glad to help with all your little plans."

Henry lumbered over to the piano and patted Cousin May's shoulder. "The music sounded nice, May. Do you know what it said to me? When I opened the door and heard you at the piano, it said—home." He didn't brush a hand across his eyes but the gesture was in his voice. "Do you suppose we could have a little more, May? If you aren't too tired?"

"Henry! Dear boy!" She faced the keyboard again and spoke over her shoulder. "What shall it be, one of the old ones?"

"Anything you like, May." He gave her a nostalgic smile, tiptoed across the room and chose a chair. He leaned his head against the cushions, composed himself for listening, and saw Miss Etta for the first time. His jaw dropped but he recovered instantly. But from time to time he sent covert and puzzled looks in her direction.

"I know!" Cousin May said. "I know the very thing!"
She opened an enameled box that stood on the piano and
took from it two ribbon bracelets sewn with little bells.
She muffled the bells with her hands while she fastened the
bracelets on her wrists. "Dear Rosie's favorite composition.
Mine too. I'm afraid I'm old-fashioned, I love the simple
tunes the best."

Rosalie had been staring at Regan, smiling broadly and
beckoning. At the sound of her name she turned to Cousin
May.

"Me?" she asked.

"Yes, darling . . . Do sit down, Regan. So disturbing to
have you standing. There, next to Fray . . . Yes, Rosie
darling, tell the others what I'm going to play. You know
it, see the little bells? It has two names, remember? Two
names. *A Winter Fancy*, or—"

"Or, *What Do the Bells Say?*" Rosalie cried triumphantly.

"See! See, Henry? See, Fray? Isn't she marvelous!"
Cousin May blew Rosalie a kiss and the bells spoke pre-
maturely.

Rosalie's eyes followed the prancing white fingers and
her head kept time to the music. The needlepoint was forgotten. It lay on the floor, crushed down by one scuffed
oxford. Regan saw with relief that it was an oxford. So
Fray had retrieved the rabbit slippers after all; she'd been
sure that he couldn't. She'd made up her mind to give
them to Rosalie, to save tears and trouble. Maybe she'd
give them to her anyway. She watched Rosalie's nodding
head and held her own severely still.

She looked at them all, one after the other, while the
music pattered on in a series of little runs and flourishes and
the bells tinkled in its wake. Henry listened with closed
eyes, the picture of a man engulfed in memories. Fray
stared at Miss Etta with an intensity that dared her to stare
back. Miss Etta concentrated on the fire.

Regan's eyes went back to Rosalie, and she was suddenly
overwhelmed with an almost unendurable despair. It came
down like a black cloud and covered her physically. It was

so real that she thought it must be visible. She drew back in a corner of the sofa because she thought the others would surely see. Rosalie drew her like a magnet, and she looked again. There was a contagious rhythm in the nodding, grizzled head. When she felt her own head begin to nod she unobtrusively raised both hands to her face and held them like a vise. If anyone noticed she'd say she had a toothache.

I've got to talk to somebody, she thought. I've got to tell somebody that something is wrong. But I don't know what to tell. I'm thinking the way Hurst thought, I'm thinking the way Hurst did in the diary. I'm beginning to think I heard voices tonight too, and that's wrong. I couldn't have. There was nobody there. I must be sick, I'm imagining things, I must be sick. Hurst was sick and he imagined things and I'm a Herald and I've got to be careful or I'll die the way he did. Is there something the matter with the Heralds? Is that why Fray wants to read the diaries? Does he draw blanks when he tries to remember things, does he hear voices as Hurst and I did? Is he wondering about us as I am?

She counted the Heralds in the house, herself, Fray, Max. Miss Etta? That could be. Nobody ever said anything, but it could be. Would Max tell her the truth if she asked him? But that was no good. Fray kept Max's door locked. She made a small sound when she remembered that.

She felt Fray turn and saw him watching her. "What's wrong?" he whispered.

"Nothing. Can I see Max tonight?"

"No visitors. Don't worry, he's all right. Maybe tomorrow. What are you trying to cover up with the cinnamon?"

His smile was so normal, his whispering voice so warm and friendly that she felt as if a clean wind had swept through the room.

"Covering Henry," she said. "But I want to see Max. I've got to."

"S-sh," hissed Henry. He glared and shook a finger. "S-sh."

"Talk to you later," Fray said.

The music tinkled to a close, Cousin May lifted her hands from the keys and shook them lightly. The bells rang on alone until she stilled them with a quick movement of crossed hands.

"Home again!" Cousin May said.

Miss Etta sat up straight. "What?" she barked.

"Home again. After a drive through the winter wonderland, our sleigh has brought us back to our own fireside."

Down the hall the dinner gong sounded.

"Nice timing," Fray said.

Rosalie was quiet through dinner. She was preoccupied, but not with food or ornament. She ate little and smiled when people spoke, regardless of what they said. She looked sleepy and contented and her face was curiously young.

Henry clung to his role of man of affairs returned from a grueling day in the city. He reviewed the past twenty-four hours with pleasure. Fatima's prophecies were coming true and he hadn't raised a hand to help them along, either. Money, girls, determination, will power, they were all coming along. He didn't have to do anything, not any more. Everything was falling into his lap. He asked for a bottle of wine and got it without trouble. Even that didn't surprise him.

After the first glass benevolence entered his body and soul. His eyes grew tender as they moved from face to face and he rebuilt his life. He made every woman at the table dependent on him for every mouthful she ate, every stitch she wore. But he was only too glad to provide. His eyes said so.

"Tired, my poor Henry?" Cousin May asked.

He denied this with wan playfulness, and reflected. Gad, yes, he was tired, but she must never know. She must never know the sordid hurly-burly of his days, she must never see the ugly side of life. He appraised the jewels on her hands with silent pleasure. Fine, fire, and no more than she deserved. In the last minute she had become his wife.

He looked at Regan, too quiet, too pale. The little orphan

daughter of an old and trusted employee. His ward. He pursed his lips and smiled. A little surprise for Regan, a warm fur coat, an ocean voyage, he'd plan it all and say nothing until he gave her the tickets. That would bring the roses back.

His eyes traveled on to Miss Etta. His adoring and doting old—His world crashed. She was looking at him as if he had been talking out loud.

The dream had been real while it lasted. Now it was gone. She had snatched it away with her grinning, rouged mouth and her small pig's eyes. He'd fix her. He'd fix her and nobody would ever find out. Nobody ever laughed at him and got away with it. He stared coldly, thinking, planning. Why was she dressed up like that? She'd dressed herself up to look like somebody. What for? Who was it? It was somebody he knew. It was familiar and unpleasant. He tried to remember but his mind refused to function. His eyes raked her mercilessly, from the scrap of lace on her hennaed head to the trailing fichu that narrowly missed her plate, looking for something to complain about. His voice pounced.

"May!" he thundered. "Look at Etta! You look at her! She's got something that doesn't belong to her! She's been taking things again!"

They all jumped when he began to speak. Regan turned instinctively to Fray who was sitting in Max's chair. She waited for him to intervene but he was openly having a good time.

Henry's pointing finger abandoned Miss Etta in favor of Fray. "That's right, turn against me when all I'm trying to do is save you trouble! You bring a common thief into the house and it isn't even your house! It's May's now, it's May's!"

Cousin May signalled to Mundy and Jenny and they left the room. "'What a great pity," she said when they were out of hearing, "what a very great pity. Henry, you are not to distress yourself on my account. Fray, will you take charge, please? I haven't the heart."

Miss Etta projected her lower lip and took up her own defense. "Little old piece of lace that wasn't fit for the Good Will Bag," she muttered distinctly. She grappled with the fichu and wrenched it from her thin neck. Her chest was bare.

"Put that back," Fray said. He waited while she tied the long ends under her chin, deliberately taking her time, purposely making herself ridiculous. She looked warily from face to face, hoping to catch a furtive smile that she could turn to her own advantage. But only Rosalie was pleased.

"Fray." Cousin May's voice held a warning.

He didn't need the warning. He was watching Miss Etta with an inward look, no longer amused.

"Come on, Etta," he said. "We'll clear this up right away. Where did you get that—whatever it is?"

She tried looking arch, but it got her nowhere. She tried tears, exemplified by a frenzied agitation of eyelids, but they wouldn't come. She fell back on hurt feelings and forgiveness.

"I just happened to run across it," she said gently. "I happened to run across it and I said to myself I'll rinse this out and press it up and go from door to door until I find the person it belongs to."

"She's lying," Henry said with satisfaction. "I knew she would, I've been waiting for it. She's taking you in, May, she's trying to throw you off the track with that stuff around her neck. That's not it, that's not what I meant. She's got a bulge on the left. You look at that bulge on the left, May. It's not natural on Etta." He backed his chair away from the table. "I don't mind looking myself. I want to see justice done."

Cousin May said, "Keep your seat, Henry. Fray?"

"Dig it out, Etta," Fray said.

Miss Etta sent a slow, challenging look around the table. It said everything or nothing.

"Etta!" Fray spoke sharply.

She sighed, plunged one claw into the depths of her blouse and brought her plunder to light. It was a pitiful haul judged by value and usefulness, a tangled piece of knitting, once baby blue in color, now faded, dusty and shapeless. It might have been the beginning of a sweater, an afghan or a shawl, but the hands that once held the needles had been unskilled. Even Henry saw that. He shifted his gaze to Cousin May.

"That's not yours, is it?" he asked uneasily.

"No." Cousin May's voice was a reflection of Henry's. "Put it away, Etta."

Miss Etta perversely displayed her treasure. She looked at no one. "There! I never thought the day would come when I'd be publicly stripped for a bit of old wool. Lying in a corner of the attic, full of moths, and I thought it might be good for something, like a present for Rosalie. I thought she'd like to take it apart and put it together again."

Rosalie's hands reached across the table. "Now!" she demanded.

"Might as well." Miss Etta put the wool in the eager hands. "That is if nobody's going to claim it. And I'll also be much obliged if everybody takes a good look at this collar. It came out of the attic too. In a corner with a pile of trash, all covered up with rags and paper like you do when you want to hide something, or forget something. Or don't dare throw something away. But if the owner wants it back all she has to do is step up and claim it. All she has to do is come right out and say it's hers." She waited.

Cousin May spoke quietly. "You may keep it, Etta. And go to your room, please. Take the knitting with you, too."

"No!" Rosalie said. "No!"

"I'm not keeping anything that people can still use," Miss Etta said. "I only want things people are through with." The spiteful old voice droned on.

She's dragging this out on purpose, Regan thought. They're all embarrassed and she knows it.

"I'm no thief," Miss Etta persisted. "I'll be glad to give

it back to the rightful owner. After I've rinsed it out of
course. It needs a good rinsing, it smells funny. Kind of
salty . . . Well, I'm waiting."

Regan saw that Fray was waiting too. He studied the blue
wool in Rosalie's fat hands. He studied Cousin May's calm,
white face and Henry's baffled eyes.

"Well, Henry?" he asked. "Anything to say or suggest?"
Henry shook his head.

"May?"

Cousin May broke into sudden laughter. It rang down the
table like the little bells in Rosalie's favorite composition.
It made Rosalie laugh too. Even Henry, after a bewildered
survey that turned his head in amazement from one sister to
the other, opened his mouth in a wide, confused smile.

Cousin May held a handkerchief to her lips and struggled
with merriment. "Wait," she begged, "wait!" She touched
her eyes with the scrap of fine linen and composed herself.
"This is dreadful, dreadful. I'm so ashamed. I didn't mean
to laugh, not really, but I couldn't help it. It's Etta!" She
appealed to Fray. "We must do something, we really must.
Do you know what she's done? I couldn't believe my eyes
until this minute. It's just come over me. She's found poor
Claudine's things, you know, the things she wore that night.
That knitting, too. She was working on that."

Miss Etta rose from her chair and stood before them,
smoothing the lace at her neck. She rearranged it, fluted it,
and flicked at invisible dust. Then she said, "I'll go now."

They watched her leave and something like a sigh swept
through the room. The candles flickered. Fray's fork
dropped to the floor with a clatter and he picked it up and
stared at it stupidly.

"Don't use that," Cousin May said. "Mundy will bring
you another." She rang the bell and Mundy and Jenny returned. Dinner went on.

Cousin May wanted to walk in the grounds. She looked
tired and plead for company. Henry and Fray had disappeared, but not together, and Rosalie had gone to her room

hugging the pale blue wool. Regan looked at the clock. It was nine, and Fray would be waiting. She wanted to talk to Fray but Cousin May was gently insistent.

They walked down the path to the gate and Cousin May leaned heavily on her arm. Miss Etta wasn't mentioned but Regan knew she filled both their minds. She wondered uneasily about the present Miss Etta had promised her.

"Are you happy here, my child?" Cousin May asked. "I want you to be, you know. Such a grave responsibility, a young girl in the house. And so unfortunate that I don't see more of you. I should dearly love a nice, long talk. But—youth calls to youth!" She sighed. "Did you and Henry have a pleasant walk?"

"We didn't walk. We met on the pavilion steps. We talked for a while, that's all."

"Sweet! Was it an—appointment?"

"Oh no. I went out there alone. He just happened to come along."

"Alone?" Cousin May sighed again. "How very odd, my dear, and please understand me when I say—unwholesome. So dark out there, so gloomy and depressing. Not the kind of thing for you at all."

Regan said nothing. Something told her that Cousin May would stop talking if she asked questions, and she wanted her to talk. Perhaps Cousin May knew the answer to the things she'd been asking herself.

"I haven't offended you, dear?"

"Oh no, please go on. I want you to talk to me. I want your—advice."

Cousin May gave her arm a gentle squeeze. "Such a good, good child, but such a sad little voice! I sometimes wonder if we made a mistake when we encouraged you to stay with us. We have so little to offer, how I wish we had more! I like to think of you surrounded by a bevy of young girls, gay, happy, free from care. That's what your life should be . . . Have you ever considered a return to school? Some nice, modern school where they teach domestic science, costume design, clever, practical things like that?

In New York? I think you'd love New York. A little apartment of your own. You can afford it now, you know."

They were getting away from the things she wanted to hear. She carefully turned the conversation back.

"I know. But I can't plan anything now, not until Fray and I finish our job. It isn't important, of course, but it's interesting." That sounded flat but it was an entering wedge.

"Fray," Cousin May said decisively, "is having trouble with his conscience. That's the answer to all this ridiculous activity. He knows he neglected Hurst and now he's deceiving himself into thinking he can atone. Atone! By reading diaries! I declare, I sometimes lose patience! The Heralds have always been self-deceivers. I believe it's called escape, or some such word. When things go wrong they look for a reason outside themselves. And they always manage to find one. Even my poor Hurst—He worried me so! . . . You say the diaries are interesting? Fray promised to keep me posted but he hasn't said a word. So like him. What are you reading now? The butcher's bills? The pedigree of a new herd?"

They had made the trip to the gate and back and Cousin May hesitated at the foot of the veranda steps. The branching path that led to the back garden and the water wound off to the right.

"This way," Cousin May said. They took the path. "You haven't answered, dear. Didn't you hear me or are you being secretive?"

"I didn't want to hurt you. We've been reading about the wedding."

"Wedding? Whose wedding?"

"Yours. I'm sorry! It must be dreadful to remember, I didn't want to say anything about it. I didn't even want to read about it but Fray thought we should. Anything that concerns Hurst is important to us."

"I see. Yes, I see what you mean. And I imagine Hurst wrote entertainingly. Quite like a novel. So much imagination . . . I didn't know he kept a record of such things.

That old, unwholesome attitude again! Hoarding the ugly things. I suppose he wrote about the accident?"

"Yes. But he wasn't hoarding ugly things. He was putting down the things he wanted to remember, the good things too. He wrote about the way you looked and how he felt about you." The cypress ring loomed ahead in the darkness. She'd been going to say something about Gretel but the sight of the trees stopped her. Time for that later.

"Sweet! You're so like them, so like them all." Cousin May's soft voice was faintly chiding. "So sentimental, moody, unpractical. You must fight against it. That's why I disapprove of your association with Fray. And those foolish diaries! So bad for your nerves. See, you're trembling! Even thinking about them makes you tremble! Poor old Hurst and his little troubles. So bad, so bad for everyone."

"No," Regan said defensively. "I'm cold, that's all. It's the bay wind. It comes in my room, too. After dark. It always blows after dark." They had reached the pavilion. The bare bushes rattled their dry stalks and the wind cried in the cypress trees. "After dark the whole places changes," she added slowly. "I don't like it down here at night."

"No?" Cousin May said. She halted. "Hear the wind and the water. They almost speak . . . If it distresses you, why did you come before, alone? Did you have a reason?"

This was the time. This was her opportunity. She answered carefully. "Hurst and I used to come here at night. For a special treat he'd bring me down to look at the stars and the lights at Golden City. I suppose I thought I could bring him back for a few minutes if I came alone."

"Bring him back! My poor child, you are completely mad. All this living in the past, believe me, it must stop at once. Do you want to make yourself ill, really ill?"

"Nothing Hurst ever said or did can hurt me," she answered. "He was the one who was hurt."

There was a long pause filled by the wind and the water. When Cousin May spoke again her voice was monotonous.

"Control yourself, Regan . . . How do you know what Hurst was?"

"I know by the things I remember and the things I've been reading. He was sensitive, he lived only for the people he loved, and when tragedy struck him he kept it to himself. I didn't know his heart had been broken until I read his diary."

Cousin May snapped a twig from a crackling bush and broke it into small pieces. "His heart," she said softly.

Regan went on. "The little sister they called Gretel, that nearly killed him. If it hadn't been for you, I think he would have died too. He never got over that, never. She was always close to him, even in this last year. He used to hear her voice."

"Extraordinary! But I'm not surprised. I saw the way he was going . . . Did he actually write that? Did you read it in black and white?"

"Yes. He sat in here, in the pavilion, and heard her voice. He tried to drown it out with music but it wouldn't go."

Cousin May touched the damp, dark wall that rose beside her. "This should have been destroyed," she said. "I should have insisted. I should have done it myself . . . Heard a voice! Doesn't that tell you anything, Regan? Doesn't that prove he had reached the end? I'm ashamed and frightened that you can even repeat such things. If anyone should hear you—"

"No one will. I won't talk about it. I can't, not to anyone but you." She looked over the dark water. The lights on the promontory went out, one by one. "But I believe everything he says. I can't help it. I have to. Maybe it's because we have the same blood, I don't know. But I do know he heard her. I can understand that. When I was out here by myself I heard voices too."

"Regan!"

"I heard them. In the pavilion. Not a child's voice, his. His and another one, quarreling."

She felt Cousin May's hands on her shoulders, strong and steady, turning her about. Cousin May's face was close to hers. The Attar of Roses was heavy, sweet and familiar.

"There was no one here," Cousin May said. "There couldn't have been. There has been no one here for months. If you heard voices they came from a passing boat. Sound carries on the water, even a whisper carries. You must believe that, you must. Otherwise—"

Cousin May's arms went around her and tightened. It was like being locked in a padded room, a padded cupboard that had no light or air, no space. Cousin May's voice was husky with emotion.

"Such a tiny thing," she said. "Little Regan, the youngest of them all, the only girl that's left. You must be good, you understand, you must be careful."

"Cousin May—"

"You must tell yourself that you heard a boat on the water. The people in the boat were talking and the voices carried to shore. You see how I'm trying to help you? You see?"

I'm frightening her, Regan thought. I mustn't do that. She's so old and it isn't fair. It's the Heralds bringing trouble again. "Of course it was a boat," she said. "I'm sure of it now." Will she believe that? she wondered.

"Quite sure? Absolutely sure, dear child? We can't have this happen again. And you mustn't talk about it, you know. People are so unkind, they draw such odd conclusions, make strange comparisons. You haven't talked to Fray?"

"No. To no one. I've been silly, Cousin May. Let's forget it."

"Splendid, splendid, that's my wise girl! But we must be certain. Perhaps we should talk things over, so helpful to talk things over, so relieving. Perhaps you'd better tell poor Cousin May about those funny voices, and after that we'll both forget the whole thing. We'll both laugh about it." Cousin May laughed in anticipation. "Come, you heard actual words, of course, whole sentences, sounds? This is really thrilling! I'm almost ashamed to talk so but I must."

Regan said nothing. There was nothing she could say. Much better to pretend the boat explained it all. Much better than ridicule.

"You're making me wait for an answer, dear, and you're

pulling away. So cold and unaffectionate, so unnatural. Surely you're not afraid of me? Not of me?"

Afraid? That was an odd thing to say. She hadn't even thought of fear. When she was alone, yes, but not when her own people were around her. "No," she said quickly. "I'm sorry, but I was thinking. There's nothing to worry about, Cousin May. I'm all right now. I was probably half asleep before, and a boat went by, and—I can't imagine why I didn't think of that myself. It's all right."

"You're sure?" The hands were on her shoulders, digging into her flesh. "You must be sure, for my sake. You must be convinced."

"I am! Honestly I am! Cousin May—"

"Yes, yes—"

"You're hurting me."

The hands dropped with a contrite gesture. "My dear child, I'm so sorry. Forgive me." A light kiss brushed Regan's cheek. "You disturbed me more than I care to admit."

Once more they both waited and once more there was nothing to say. They faced each other in the dark, both silent. Far out on the water a passing speed boat sent its muffled roar to shore. It came like a confirmation.

Instinctively they turned back to the house. The fog was coming in and the mist was rising. "You'll go to bed at once, dear," Cousin May said. "You must have a fine, long sleep. No talking, no reading in bed, sleep."

"Yes, Cousin May." Each lie was easier than the one before. Fray was waiting in Hurst's room and Hurst's room was directly under her own. The back stairs.

There was a dim light in the kitchen. As they passed the windows they saw a figure pressed against the glass, hands shielding eyes, looking out.

"My good Mundy," Cousin May said. Even as she spoke, Mrs. Mundy disappeared.

When they entered the hall Mrs. Mundy hurried forward to meet them, breathing heavily because she had run up the stairs. She touched her hands to Cousin May's hair, scolding and tender, as if the older woman were her child.

"You're damp," she said. "Miss May, you shouldn't do this. You're not strong. You come along to bed with me." She gave Regan an accusing look. "Night air is dangerous. You ought to know that, Miss Regan."

She went to her own room at once and waited a few minutes before joining Fray. She wondered whether or not to tell him about the last half-hour, and decided against it. If she told a little, she'd have to tell all. She'd have to tell about the night Hurst left her in the boat. So far, so good. But what would he think when she said she'd heard the same voices again? Coming from behind a locked door? Would he agree with Cousin May? "You are completely mad, my dear child." No, she didn't want to be told that again.

She opened the door to the sitting room, making no sound. Fray was bent over the card table, reading the red leather book. He didn't hear her until she spoke.

"You're late," he said. He looked at her closely. "Where have you been?"

"Walking." She took her place at the table. "Anything happen here?" He looked as if something had.

"Nothing new. The usual emotional gamut ran from floor to floor. Rosie didn't want to go to bed and Mrs. Mundy had to chase her up and down stairs before she caught her. I didn't know Rosie could sprint. Henry retired to his room with a copy of *The World's Great Love Letters* and I don't think he's brushing up for Etta."

"Miss Etta still sulking?"

"Sulking! She can't make up her mind whether to live or die. She says she's lost face. Look, drag out the intuition again, will you? Did you get a feeling that Etta knew exactly what she was doing at dinner?"

"Yes, I did," she said slowly. "I think she always knows, in a way. I think she likes to show people up. I don't think she has the wits to figure things out but she does have an instinct about hitting where it hurts. She doesn't like the Beauregards, does she?"

"They don't like her. That always works both ways. Why?"

"That business of the wool and Rosalie. I don't think Miss Etta knew they were Claudine's things when she first took them. I think she simply took them the way she takes food, and broken cups and so on. She may have caught on later. I think she staged the whole thing to humiliate Cousin May. She knew somebody would notice that bulge, she knew Rosalie would want the wool, and she knew Cousin May wouldn't want Rosalie to have it—publicly. When Rosalie gets hold of things like that she's dreadful to watch."

"Deliberately getting May's goat, eh?"

"Yes, because Cousin May snubs her and makes her eat in the kitchen sometimes. I wouldn't want Miss Etta to hate me."

"You're safe, she loves you. When I went up to her room to give her the devil she was tying up a package for you. A going-away present, she says. She's made up her mind that you're going away."

"I know she has. I've told her I'm not, but it's no use. What's the present like?"

"I got there too late to see. She was doing it up with what looked like an old corset string. Big, round package in tissue paper, with last year's Christmas seals still on it. She wanted to talk about herself. Said she'd never hold up her head again. I fixed that. She's holding it up, all right. Tilting it back." He illustrated.

She didn't laugh. "Not funny?" he asked. "Well, maybe not . . . Now we'll get serious. Why did you want to see Max?"

"That's natural, isn't it?"

"Not when you look at me as you did when you asked. You want to talk to Max about Hurst, don't you? Well, you can't. I won't have him bothered. Max isn't strong."

"Does he know what we're doing? Does he know about Hurst's—condition?"

"You sound like Henry. Max knows what we're doing and he approves. There's nothing to tell him now, you know that. Do we know anything now that we didn't know before? Or guess before?"

"No. But I was thinking about Rosalie, too. I was thinking about the switch."

"Rosalie is a Beauregard. Our business is with Heralds."

So he is wondering about us, she decided. He's wondering the same way I am but he won't admit it. If something is wrong I wonder which of us will see it first. Which of us will break first. I don't want him to be hurt. I don't care about myself. I'll do anything to keep him from being hurt.

She heard Fray's voice as if he were far away.

"Have you got anything on your mind, Regan? Got any troubles you want to shake?"

"No. Let's get on with what we came to do."

"Right." He opened the red book without another word.

Chapter Eight

FRAY said, "Dated September, this year." He read.

" 'I went up to town this afternoon because the weather was fine and I thought it would be good to see the streets full of people all very busy with their own lives. I thought it would be good to see other men's faces and hear their speech. More than anything I wanted to hear the speech of strangers. I was hoping that I would find in some small group one other man whose voice would tell me that he carries a burden too. But I have no success. I have looked from face to face for a sign that there are others like me but I found no one. I have seen happy faces, faces with silent, moving lips, but none like mine. The other lips moved because they were trying to remember the things they had promised to take home, the box of chocolates, the theater tickets, the perfume and powder that is so important and someone is waiting for. They did not move because they were trying to mouth the name of a murderer.

This afternoon I am looking in a window because I do not know what else to do and an old friend speaks to me. Old Slocum. I am fifty-nine years of age and he is surely eighty and I am ashamed when I see his face beside mine in the plate glass. I tell him I may purchase the pictures in the window and it is clear that he does not believe me. He is my oldest friend, I have known him since boyhood. He is well known to May, to her people and mine, and he is also a doctor. Superior in every way to the poor Poole May is so fond of. Surely,

I tell myself, this is my opportunity, this is made for me. He has been sent by fate. I will tell him my fears and he will say I can be wrong or right. I tell myself I will begin simply. I will say, "It is a fine day, my old friend, and we have not seen each other as we should. We will walk to the club together and have good drink and talk." So pleasant that would be, such an easy thing to say and do with the late sun low in the sky and an old friend at hand. We would sit in the window of the club and watch the sun go down. And soon would come the blue hour when people open their hearts to each other and if there is love between them it shows itself. Such an easy thing to say and do I told myself. But I could not speak. I reminded myself of his great age. He has done his work with honor and has earned his peace. If I told him what I think he would not sleep. Now I am glad that I left him there even though he thinks I am surly. He looked at me in a strange way. If he thinks I am surly that is all right.

Noon: Mrs. Mundy has brought a lunch to my room. I have asked to be served here because I am busy with accounts. That is what I tell them. I have even written in ledgers which are much in evidence. I do not need to write anything in ledgers. I am afraid I know too well what I can call mine.

There is a child who comes to my mind these days. Not Gretel because she is always with me but another child who is one of us also. I have not seen this other one for many years, not since she was very small with little legs that tried to keep in step with mine. Regan. We were very close to each other, hand in hand, and I think even closer than that. She was so young, a growing baby, but always she seemed to know what I was thinking. It was as if we heard the same tune. I have kept in touch with this child, not as much as I should have done, but who does that? And now when I come to this place in my life she is the one I turn to. Shall I admit to myself, even on this paper, that I need her for my own ends? That she is my one hope, my one proof? That she alone in all this world can help me? If she will.' "

Fray looked up. "A good place to stop, temporarily. What do you think now?"

"I'm afraid to think. I'm afraid of thinking something that isn't there."

"No, you won't do that . . . I've got a confession to make. I read this before you came in. I wanted to draw my own conclusions but I wanted yours, too. Unbiased. If you'd known I'd read it, you'd have closed your mind and relied on me. Well?"

"It all ties in with the letter he wrote, doesn't it?"

"No doubt about that. The key to his trouble is in that letter to you."

"Fray." Her voice shook. "He said—'trying to mouth the name of a murderer'."

"Easy, easy. That's not the way to help. Listen to this. I can quote, too. 'I remember the old days as if they were yesterday . . . You always understood whatever I told you and you were amenable to suggestion . . . How much will you recall of our funny games if we play them again?' Don't you get it, Regan? He wanted you to remember something."

"He was thinking about a murderer." She repeated it, thickly. "He was thinking about a murderer. I don't, I don't—"

"Stop that! Let me do the reasoning. He wanted you here because you were the proof of something. It was too important to write about, perhaps not safe to write about. You were, and are, a key, the only one he had. We've got to sift and sift until we come to something that rings a bell in your mind."

"Is that why you've been asking me about the games we played and what we talked about?"

"That's why. That's what he was getting at. Something you did together."

"But I've told you! I've told you everything! There was nothing, nothing at all! . . . Wait." She shivered.

"Take your time."

"I don't need time. There was something tonight."

"I thought so. I'm beginning to know you too well,

Regan. You can't fool me. Why did you go out tonight?"

"Let me tell it in my own way," she begged. "It began before tonight. When I saw the pavilion spire from my window that first night I thought it was a dead tree. Something made me refuse to recognize it. It hurt and terrified me. I didn't know why. Even when I knew it was the pavilion I hated and loved it at the same time. I didn't want to go there, and I wanted to go. I didn't even want to look at it and I kept going back to the window."

"Which feeling was stronger, Regan? Which won out?"

"I don't know if it was winning or losing. I went down there late this afternoon, at dusk. I went later, too."

"Alone?"

"The first time. I sat on the steps and looked at the water. We used to do that. That was one of the things. Then I began to remember. The air smelled as it did years ago. It wasn't just the salt and the damp; there was summer in it. I could smell flowers. And the lights on the promontory brought things back. We used to watch the lights and listen to the music over in Golden City and he called it Star of the Sea. I'd forgotten all of that until tonight. It had been wiped out and tonight it came back."

"Your head aches again, doesn't it?"

"Yes. It always does now, when I try to think."

"I know. That's all right. It'll pass . . . What else came back tonight?"

"I remembered sitting in a boat tied up to the dock. We were happy and we knew he'd be scolded for keeping me up but we didn't care. Then something happened. Something happened that night and it happened all over again tonight. It was like a—duplication. I remembered everything up to a certain point and then I began to forget."

"Go back to the old night, to the place where you begin to forget."

"We'd been in the pavilion and then we went out to the boat. We left the pavilion dark. He turned off the lights because we didn't want to be found. Then while we were in the boat someone turned the lights on again. We saw

them through the trees. And he went back to shore. He told
me to be very quiet and wait for him. I thought he was
going to tell the person in the pavilion that he was alone. I
thought he was going to tell whoever it was that I had gone
to bed. So I waited in the boat. I saw him go up to the
pavilion. I waited a long time, at least it seemed long, and
then I heard voices. His voice, low and pleading, and another one that I didn't know or recognize. I never did hear
any words, just voices, up and down, up and down. I began
to be frightened because I thought he was in trouble on my
account. So I got out of the boat and went to help him. I
thought he needed me. I fell down, I remember that, and
I ran up the slope to the pavilion door. The other voice
was loud and clear. I ran up to the door." She stopped.

"And that's where you draw the blank?"

"Yes. How do you know?"

"It fits. Someone wanted you to forget the rest of it and
saw to it that you did. Is tonight the first time you've remembered that?"

"Yes. It came back little by little as I sat on the pavilion
steps. But when I came to the last part, it didn't exist. It
was gone. Do you think I may have hurt myself when I
fell?" Her eyes said she wanted to believe that. "Could I
have been unconscious? That might explain it."

"No. A thing like that would have been public property.
There'd have been talk about a thing like that. Henry,
Rosie and Max were here then. I'd have heard about it my-
self. No. No accident. What about the next day?"

"Nothing. It must have been an ordinary day."

"And tonight it all came back for the first time. You ran
to the pavilion because you heard voices and thought Hurst
was in trouble." He was talking to himself, out loud.

"That's all." She lowered her voice. "Except that tonight
I heard the voices again."

He looked grave. "Did that frighten you?"

"Yes. I thought I was—"

"Don't say it. You aren't. Things like that happen. Minds

open and shut, and skip around like fleas. Nothing to worry about." He reached across the table and took her hand.

She closed her eyes. "Fray, was Hurst worrying about Gretel's death? Is that the trouble?"

"You weren't born then," he evaded. "If it were that, how could you fit in? We'll do this one step at a time. Henry was down there with you tonight. Did you talk to him?"

"Not about this."

"What about the second time? The time after dinner. Why did you go out again?"

"Cousin May wanted to walk and there was no one else to go with her . . . Fray, who was in the house when I came here before? Rosalie, Henry, Max, and who else?"

"That's all I think. And servants, a couple of colored women. I believe the Mundys were away. I know I was at camp and Etta was off on a rampage somewhere. Are you trying to identify the other voice?"

"I've got to! I know it's important!"

"Maybe it is. If that's what Hurst wanted you to remember, it is. But we don't know that. And all you can do is guess, and that's no good. We don't want guesses."

"I keep thinking it may have been—Gretel."

"Stop that!" He was angry. "You're talking like a lunatic! If that's the way your mind works I can't do much about it, but I do wish you'd listen to one thing. You say you thought Hurst was in trouble, that the other person had brought him trouble. If Gretel could return, do you think she'd do that?"

"I don't know, I don't know!"

"Well I do. And forget the voice. If it's worth anything it'll come back to you at the right time . . . What did you and May talk about?"

She knew she'd have to tell. When he looked at her like that, she had no secrets. "I told her, Fray. It slipped out before I knew it. I was so miserable!"

He wasn't angry and she was afraid he would be. "Did she laugh at you?" he asked.

"Not exactly. She said I was imagining things. But she wasn't pleased. She thinks I—make things up."

"Well, well."

"She said the voices came from a boat."

"She could be right at that." The clock on the mantel struck ten. "You want to go on with this, don't you?"

"I've got to! I feel as if there weren't a minute to lose!" She watched while he calmly turned a page in the red book. "You've read them all, haven't you? Read them to the end. You know what he was looking for and whether or not he found it. Tell me!"

"I've read them all but I haven't anything to tell you. Of course I know what he was looking for, and so do you. He said he was looking for the name of a murderer."

Under her breath she repeated the phrase Hurst had used. She knew she'd never forget it. 'Trying to mouth the name of a murderer'. Aloud she spoke one word. "Gretel's?"

He didn't answer.

She refused to give up. "I'm in this! I don't know how or why, but I am. You've got to tell me one thing, Fray. Now. I've got to know one thing. Did he find what he was looking for?"

"He didn't come to a conclusion on paper. But I know he came to one because he is dead." He bent over the table, the red book cradled in his arms. "We'll go on. I want to finish this period before we check back . . . Still September, a few days after he went up to town and saw Slocum on the street." He read.

" 'Morning: Mrs. Mundy brought me my breakfast at seven o'clock. Too early and I had asked not to be disturbed. But there was a misunderstanding. No one had told her.

I am sometimes ashamed of the feeling I have for Mrs. Mundy. For her husband also. They have done their work well for many years but I do not like them. She looks at me oddly. I remind myself that each time sorrow has struck us the Mundys have been in the house. How much have they observed in these long years?

Last night I am here at this table, staring at the pages of this book, when May comes in. She says she has heard me moving about. I do not remember moving about. I thought I was a figure of stone, in one place, for that is how I felt. But we cannot always know what we do.

May is hurt with me although she does not say so. She knows I am doing something that I will not share with her and she is hurt and confused. Before this we have always shared. But now I tell her to go away and leave me alone. If there were another way to do this I would do it. But this is the only way. I must make no mistakes. I must be alone no matter what is said of me in consequence. It is better so. It is better that no one should talk to me. I do not know how much my face tells.

So I have told May and the Mundys that I will live like a hermit until I finish some important work. I tell them it is a family matter and nothing to worry about. I do not know if May believes me but I think she does. She smiles at me. I also tell her that I will eat in here and if she will send the Crains to serve me I will be pleased. The Crains will give me no trouble. I must do something for the Crains very soon. A poor, frightened pair.

Today is old Etta's day but I do not want to talk to her, I cannot risk it. So I will give her the wine she loves and tell her I am busy with accounts in the pavilion.

The pavilion. Why have I not thought of that before? That is where I must go now. That is where I must live. It is mine, all mine, and if I go in the night and return in the early morning no one will know. There is only May to think of. Will she come to this room again and find that I have gone? If I lock the door will she know that I am not here? And will she ask me questions? I cannot tell her what I am doing, that would be fatal. I am not ready. I do not even know when I will be ready. Or if I will have the

strength to speak when the time comes. My mail is before me on the table and I have no mind to open it.
There is nothing I want to know of the world outside
these windows. Only one thing I want, to sleep in that
little house down by the water. There I will be free to
face this horror. It has come so quickly, it is full-
grown, monstrous, yet only in these last few days have
I seen it. Has it always been there, from the beginning,
invisible to me and to the others? Yes, to all the others
but one. I can almost believe that Father slowly came
to see what I see now, and that he was planning to speak
but did not have the time. But did not have the time.

How have I been living all these years? How have
I been so blind? I have always known that my life was
empty of some things but so is every man's. I ask myself what has suddenly opened my eyes.

It does no good to ask. Even now, today, I do not
know. But I think perhaps for years the truth has been
collecting in the back of my mind. The little words
and actions that a young and healthy man dismisses as
trivial, they do not always go away. They wait in a
dark corner for the man to grow old and sick. The
mind is always patient, it hoards like a miser. It can
afford to wait. It knows that when a man is old and
sick he takes an inventory of his life.

That is how it happened. I come to that age, I sift
the ashes of my life as all men do, and I find strange
bones.

Claudine. It is Claudine I must think of now. She
was the second one. Claudine has been gone so many
years but not so long as Gretel. I must forget Gretel
and think of Claudine.

It is only a few minutes since I wrote the above and
in that small time something has happened. Something
that I put away as a useless thought has returned, strong
and fresh, asking to be considered. It has come in a
strange way. I have written before that my mail has
come and I do not care to open it. That was true. But
my eyes returned to it a dozen times, in spite of myself,
and I pushed it aside. It is then that I see how one letter
separates itself from the rest and looks up at me. I

know that writing. It is Regan Carr's. Her mother is dead and she is alone. I have wanted her here but could not bring myself to ask. I have hoped to reach the end of this without her help. I have hoped that I would never see the day when I must take her before strangers, ask her those ugly questions, tell her she must answer truthfully, regardless of consequence. But right or wrong, no matter what the end, this decision is taken out of my hands. Something stronger than myself has placed her in my path again.

I will ask her to come here, writing the words very carefully. I will post the letter when I go for a walk and say nothing to anyone. I must plan ahead for every step of the way. First I must win her confidence again, then I must lead her back, over the years. I must discover how much she remembers. I must make her remember, and speak. But she must not be frightened and she must be closely watched.' "

Fray said, "The letter again. See? If you hadn't come across, I'd have torn your room apart. I had to have it."

"Somebody else felt the same way," she said.

"What!"

"When I went to get you the letter it wasn't where I'd put it. I thought I'd misplaced it myself but now I think somebody went through my things and found it." She told him about the faulty lock, her strained eyes searching his face. "Katy heard us talking but we didn't say much."

"You told me where the letter was," he said. "No, not Katy! I'd swear to that. Never Katy! She might talk about it in the kitchen but I don't see why she should. She didn't know it was important. No, not Katy. When did you put the letter in the suitcase?"

"On the day of the funeral."

"Plenty of opportunity." He was thoughtful. "It didn't say anything to the person who read it, otherwise it would have been destroyed. No, that's wrong. It may have said too much. If the reader had destroyed it you'd have started asking questions. And questions would have started talk.

Forget about that. Too late now anyway." His hand went across the table, he touched her locked fingers gently. "Hang on to yourself."

"He said"—her voice thickened and she cleared her throat —"he said I must be watched."

"What do you think I've been doing? Look back. What do you think I've been doing? Don't go out alone, that's all. Don't go anywhere alone. Stick to the rooms that have at least two more people in them . . . Know something? When you signed your initials on the clock it was more than a cute gesture. It tipped me off to the pavilion. I knew he couldn't have lived in all that mess so I went out to the pavilion to investigate. I have his keys. I found bed linen on the couch, tobacco, food. Apparently nobody ever guessed that he actually lived in his little house on the water. He must have come and gone like a wraith. The diaries were locked in a wall cabinet. Do you remember that cabinet?"

"I don't remember the inside of the pavilion at all. Not now. I thought I did, I was sure I did, but now when I try I can't—I can't—".

"Stop trying. This is not the time. We're not ready yet." His voice was gentle. "So, I found the diaries, all but one dated 1908-1909. That was the year of his meeting with May, his purchase of the farm, his marriage, Gretel. It was under the rug in front of this fireplace. I think that represents his last, conscious gesture."

Her eyes went to the white rug. She knew they were both seeing the same thing.

He went on. "But we've finished with that year, at least for a while. The next thing we want is an entry in 1926. Can you take it now? I think you can." He smiled encouragement.

"If you say so," she said quietly. "If you say so, I can."

He opened a smaller book, bound in black. "This is what we want. Claudine. Do you remember what he said? 'Claudine was the second' . . . One night in September, nineteen years ago, Claudine took a walk. Just as you did tonight. Out in the fog, down by the water." He read.

" 'Today I have distinguished myself. I have fallen overboard. I, who have been called a fish from infancy, have fallen overboard and come uncomfortably close to drowning. I record this so that my children will know I was not as perfect as I pretended to be. My children. Oh well, that is nothing. I will adopt an orphanage. So there is a board loose in the dock and I step on it and fall in. Mundy, who is serving tea on the slope, thinks at once that he must be a hero with his name in the papers and he comes in the water to help me. In his fine white coat and a teacup in his hand. I laugh and go down for what I am certain is the ninth time. May is always telling me I have nine lives like a cat and while I am bobbing up and down under the dock and hitting my head like a fool I am also counting. And almost I do not come up that time. That is because I have the helpful Mundy on my back and a rope of seaweed around my neck. This time I am drowning, I tell myself, and it is not the way I have planned my life at all. Drowning I do not mind if there is heroism attached and a fine spectacular backdrop. Off the Dalmatian coast I would drown with pleasure, off the Sorrentine peninsula I would sing a song as I counted my ninth life. But here! My own little bay, my own house behind the trees, my own dock hitting me in the head, my own flesh and blood in nice clean clothes laughing and drinking tea on a safe green slope.

It is clear that they think I am being funny, that it is all a little performance arranged by Mundy and me to brighten the tea hour. I tell myself in some fury that they will throw me a coin when it is over. I tell myself that the coin will be useful for my eyelids.

Only Mundy understands my predicament and in his helpfulness he nearly finishes me off. I know I am done for and resign myself and the next thing I know I am being saved. It is young Fray who finally sees that all is not well. He comes into the water with his new green scarf in his hand. He must love me. With his new green scarf he ropes me in.

I will have that board repaired tomorrow. Already Etta has experimented and nearly fallen overboard herself but her purpose was clear and promptly defeated.

Father himself walks out to the dock and tells her not to be a fool. We all know our Etta. And she knows us, too well. She knows that since we are children the one who meets misfortune in the water is warmed with a special brew.

I must also do something about the seaweed. It has never been so thick before. Like ropes. And under the dock the tide has washed deep holes. It was even over my head.

Rosie and Henry are with us now, as well as Fray, Max and Claudine. We are a houseful but not so many as we would like because there are always vacant places at the table and empty rooms. But perhaps one day—

I take much pleasure in my brothers now. In his looks, Fray is like someone who drives a gypsy wagon down a country lane with bolts of cotton lace and trinkets for the simple housewife; and who stands beneath a hedge at night and whistles softly while he waits. In his looks he is that. And I am afraid in his head also. Four schools in three years. Good schools! I have talked myself hoarse and Father and Max also. He only smiles at us. In history he is excellent because, I think, he enjoys the record of other men's foolishness, but in everything else he knows less than a puppy. And cares the same. Perhaps we did not punish him enough. After Gretel, it was hard to punish a child. Well, he is still young, and I have confidence in his heart. The heart was evident in that fine new scarf. The first day of wearing it, and he ruins it for me. Thirty-five dollars from Sulka's and who should know better than I who have just paid the bill!

And Max. Max is the miracle of us all. I looked at him this afternoon with wonder, remembering how he used to be. Always so reserved, always so pessimistic, always so dubious of happiness, afraid to take it or think about it. And now he is so soft he is almost ridiculous! I can bear to watch him without laughing only because I love him so much. Claudine, Claudine, Claudine. He brings her name into the conversation even when there is no place for it. If the sky looks like rain it reminds him of a day when Claudine forgot her umbrella, and he must tell us all about it. And if someone has arthritis,

and poor Father has, it is too bad of course but we
should have seen Claudine's uncle! It is good to see him
and hear him. He is married only one year. He waited
for marriage until he was forty, and some people say he
waited too long and is foolish in consequence. But I
like it. It is true that he puts her on a pedestal but that
is what we all do. She is so pretty. And now that she is
knitting with that nice blue wool we are all a little
crazy and spoil her sometimes. I have told May the
reason for the knitting and that we hope it is a little girl
because in this family we like little girls and she is
pleased also. I think I see a thoughtful look in her eyes.
I must make very, very sure that she does not think I am
envious of Max or that I am sorry the blue knitting is
not for us. Already I have tried to make it clear that I
do not give such things a second thought but I must do
so again because with a woman it is sometimes better to
over-emphasize. I will not have May unhappy.

Tonight Max goes to a conference. It is business, an
old friend is president of a little bank that is in trouble.
Max will talk him into a quiet frame of mind, tell him
what to do and write a big check also, if I know my
Max and I do. And after dinner I will play cards with
Rosie which is my good deed for the day. Rosie will
win each game because I am such a clever dealer. I
should work the boats. There is the gong. Dinner.

After dinner: A few minutes before I go to join
Rosie. I will finish the day's record now. I am writing
in my room because May and I have been talking pri-
vately with Max and Claudine. He wants to make a
new will and has said as much to Claudine and it has
made her cry. I come into the picture because I am
supposed to have a good head and I tell her that a new
will is the businesslike thing to do. Why is it that
women think a will is an invitation to sudden death? I
explain that Max only wishes to make provision for the
new baby. That is what I tell her. I tell myself that
Max is making an excuse to let himself go with sentimental language. I can see it now, that will! Like a
valentine. He will have it on parchment if possible,
with hand painted capital letters and a great deal of gold
like an old missal. "To my dear child," it will say.

Well, it hurts no one and pleases him and we have managed between us to stem the flow of tears. Claudine is
like a child herself; it is easy to make her believe anything. So tomorrow morning we go to a lawyer. Tonight we have had a gay dinner. Max and Claudine
have decided to return to New York tomorrow night.
Claudine is pale after her tears and Max is worried. He
will feel better if she is near her own doctor. Father
will return with them but Fray remains for another
week. For myself, I think Claudine looks very well although I know little of such things. I say as much to
May who tells me at once that I know nothing whatever. She says that Claudine is truly in a sad state and
that she herself is worried. I think such talk is a con-
spiracy among women to make men feel like savages.
I tell that to Max and he says he does not feel like a
savage at all. I must stop this and go down to the music
room because they are waiting for me.

Fray has gone up to Baltimore on some skylarking of
his own and Max has left for his meeting and I have
promised him I will keep an eagle eye on Claudine. He
tells me that she was sadly frightened when I went into
the water this afternoon. I must change that. She has
no experience of the water except a pleasure boat on the
Danube. So I will tell her that our bay is like a little
lake and I will swear to buy myself some waterwings
such as the five-year-olds wear. I even think she will
believe the waterwings. She is very childish and endear-
ing. I like a woman who believes things.

So I must stop this now. They are waiting for me.
May has promised us some music and that will be pleasant. She plays in the old-fashioned style, very feminine,
with graceful little touches of her own. It is not exactly
music perhaps, but it is pretty to watch. And Etta will
read her interminable Marlitt. She is asked to spend the
night because Claudine has taken a fancy to her. And
Henry, if I know him, wil make a great show of working on the farm accounts which will fool me not at all.
Father, I hope, will doze in the big chair by the fire.
That is how I like to see him because it means he is content. And Rosie—ah well, we must all do some penance
in this world. But it would be so much easier if Rosie

could remember that the Queen of Spades is not neces-
sarily the Old Maid. I go!' "

Fray lit a cigarette and inhaled deeply. He saw her lips
move and bent forward to hear what she said.
She said, "Will this be murder?"
"It won't look like it," he answered. "It won't sound like
it. You'll have to draw your own conclusions, as he did."
He read on.

" 'After: I look at that word again and again. After.
After what? After music with May, after cards with
Rosie, after talk and laughter with Claudine who gives
me a skein of wool to hold, after sending Claudine to
bed, after waiting for Max. After years of quiet and
repose once more the garden echoes to a shout.

It is better to move one step at a time, to think of
only one thing at a time. Better to recover the minutes, the small pieces of conversation, and put them all
together in a pattern. But I know that pattern so well.
I have been a part of it before.

This time I should have seen it forming but I was content and busy. That is how it happened before, I was
content and busy. This time, like the other, it gathered
itself together and exploded behind our backs. And I
blame myself for I have been remiss.

The last time it was the guns. I should have remembered the guns. The guns were important from the beginning. They were forbidden as playthings but I did
not lock them away. They were talked about, they
were handled and admired, they were given a promi-
nent place in everyone's mind. It was almost as if something were warning us—"Remember the guns. They
are accessible, they are dangerous. Remember the
guns."

This time it was the water. She was afraid of the
water. She said so. We told her she was foolish and she
cried a little and we teased her back into smiling. The
water. It was warning us then. It began to warn us in
the afternoon. It crept into the foreground, for no
apparent reason, like the guns. For the first time in my

adult life I go overboard with my clothes on. I think
now that it was no doing of my own. It was the water,
calling attention to itself.

She did not laugh with the others. She was frightened. Then the sudden talk of a new will. In her mind
she must have tied all things together, Max, the will,
death, water. That is why she left the house in the fog.
She was thinking of those four things and something,
I do not know what, drove her out.

I will write it all down for there are details to be
checked and statements to be made to the authorities.
Father has reminded me of this. That is odd. For me,
for Max, for even Fray to demand an investigation
would be natural. We are the younger ones, we are of
this world and Father is old and out of touch with material things. At least that is what we have always
thought. We have called him a dreamer and a senti-
mentalist but we were wrong.

Tonight Father is young and hard, younger and
harder than his sons. He is the one who takes me aside
and tells me to write down all I can remember. He
tells me to write the trivial things, the thoughts I have
had when someone has said this or that, the comings
and goings from the room, everything. I tell him that
is heartless and a waste of time and he says that nothing
is ever wasted. He gives me a veiled look that makes me
cold for a minute. Then he shakes his head as if he is
denying something to himself. I think it is bitterness
that makes him talk and look like that. A harmless
woman has died in his house without reason, or for a
reason that is not evident. He is like a man who has
been struck. I have not seen him look so before. Even
when it was Gretel he was not like this.

So I write things down as I did with Gretel but this
time it is different. With Gretel it was almost clear, not
to be understood perhaps, but almost. This time there is
no gun to touch and handle, to lock away in a cupboard
with regret and blasphemy. This time there is no explanation unless we accept the general one which is
that Claudine was not herself. That is not unusual they
tell me. Eccentric behavior is possible to women in
Claudine's condition. Even Etta tries to tell me that,

rubbing her head against my shoulder like a tired old horse. Etta has aged a hundred years tonight. She begs to be sent home at once. Always before she wants to stay and stay until I tell her she must go, that we need the room she is in, but tonight she wants to go and I cannot permit it. She must talk to the authorities again.

So I begin at the beginning which was perhaps nine o'clock. I come down from my room and find them all as I knew they would be. A small fire because there is a chill in the air, May, Henry, Rosie, Claudine, Etta, Father. Mundy brings a jug of mulled claret which he stands on the hearth to keep warm. Mrs. Mundy brings May a shawl. More and more she regards May as a little child and May likes to be thought so, I can see. I remember thinking it is odd that the capable, unchildish woman likes to be babied and the truly childish one, such as Claudine, pretends to be old and wise.

We are gay at Mundy's expense because he coughs a little and looks injured, so we will not forget to inquire after his health in consequence of his heroic afternoon plunge. We are solicitous and Father whispers that there will be a token of thanks in the monthly check. Mundy is at once happy.

What is next? There is so little, it is all so trivial, only a family that sits in a room together and talks and laughs. The Mundys go and after that we have the music and cards. And Father and Etta talk of Europe and of Etta's adventures which are not nearly so much in her imagination as they seem. But wait, I am ahead of myself. Before the cards, before everything, I am asked by Claudine to help with the blue wool. She does not need my help, she is being nice to me. So I help. Then because Rosie is restless I get out the cards and we play. Henry goes into the library with his farm accounts, very executive in manner, and looks at us as if we are noisy. I think we are a little noisy. Etta is full of giggles because Father reminds her of a railroad ticket-collector in Bavaria who tried to arrange a marriage between her and his son when she was only three years of age. Etta thinks she remembers the whole affair and screams with horror at the fate she has escaped. I write down a thing like this because perhaps it is not trivial.

For when Etta screams, she is only making fun of
course, Claudine is frightened. She is sitting with her
back to Etta, talking to May, and she flings up her
hands and cries out. But almost at once she apologizes.
She says she is startled, that is all. May talks to her
quietly and everything is calm again. But I notice that
Claudine is not entirely happy. She listens to May's soft
voice but she also looks about the room and at the clock
and the windows. So I myself look. The fog is coming
up, a heavy fog. It is white against the glass.

She is thinking of Max, I tell myself, out in the foggy
night, and she is wishing he were home. So I draw the
curtains and tell her I am reading her mind. She laughs,
but it is not a gay laugh. Then it is May, I think, who
says perhaps Claudine would like to go to bed. I do not
remember that too clearly. I was thinking such a thing
myself and wondering if the suggestion would be
gauche, so I do not know if I spoke also. Now I wish
that none of us had spoken or even thought.

So Claudine goes to bed. It is still early, ten-thirty,
but after she is gone there is a drop in talk and spirits.
Rosie is more restless than before. There is a small wind
and we can hear the trees. Rosie's voice is very high
and she complains that the night is bad. I am glad
Claudine is not with us to hear that. May takes Rosie
upstairs and soon Henry comes in from the library,
yawning and saying he is tired. He leaves us also and
we see him no more until later. Then Etta takes her
book and says she will read in bed. She takes also what
is left of the claret, a good pint, and I know it will be
wise to investigate before I retire myself. She does not
always remember to undress properly.

May returns, and Father and I sit quietly while she
plays for us. We close the doors so that no one will be
disturbed and she plays the things Father likes. But my
poor sweet May, she cannot play the music as it is
written. She must improvise, with little runs and
chords and trills. It is not Father's Brahms but we tell
her it is beautiful.

It is nearly midnight when Max returns. We do not
hear his key in the lock or his approach, because the
doors are still closed, but we see the door handles turn.

They turn slowly. We hurry to the door, not knowing what we will find, and he is there, pale and shaking. He tells us a story that makes us laugh to ourselves but we do not let him see that. Thank God.

He tells us he is walking up the path from the gate when he hears Claudine calling. That is what he tells us, looking about the room all the while, noting the blue wool on a chair and the empty claret mug on a small table beside it. He smiles then. We tell him she is safe in bed and he nods and finds a chair for himself. That is when we see he is limping, when he crosses the room to find a chair for himself, and we see that his trousers are wet and muddy. We are full of concern and we ask questions, and he tells us it is all a part of his adventure. We do not know then how badly he is hurt. We encourage him to talk because we think he has been frightening himself, and talking is like medicine at such times.

His story is this. He is walking up the path when he hears Claudine calling his name. He is startled at first but he tells himself that his mind is playing him a trick. He hears the voice a second time, clear but faint, and he is terrified. It comes, he thinks, from the direction of the dock, and he goes there at once, in the fog, running, calling her name in return. But when he reaches the water there is no one there. The fog is thick, he cannot see the dock, he can only feel the boards beneath his feet, but he runs out upon it and calls her name again because he does not known what else to do. He has forgotten the broken board and he slips through. He does not go into the water but hangs there, helpless and in pain.

We ask him why he makes no outcry and he says that he has no breath left and is beginning to feel like a fool. It is a long time before he can extricate himself, he does not know how long, and after that he sits on the pavilion steps until he is calm once more. He smiles when he tells us but we can see that he is still disturbed. We want to send for a doctor but he says his wounds are slight and of no importance. I think he is ashamed to tell a doctor what he has been doing, and May thinks as I do for she says so, outright, and he smiles again.

But I know my Max. I know that look in his eyes. He is not yet convinced. So I describe to him what we have been doing all evening and how Claudine has gone to bed long ago. I call him an old woman and he agrees, and he makes us promise that we will not tell Claudine how he is hurt. So we plan our story. We will tell her he has slipped on the path. In some places the flags are mossy, and tomorrow I will scrape them ostentatiously. That is what we plan.

Then we all four have a nightcap and go up to bed. We are quiet in deference to the others. I leave Father and Max in the hall outside their rooms, which are in the front of the house, and take May to her own door. I go down the hall to my rooms at the back. I tell myself I will read before sleeping and I will not disturb May because she is looking tired. Too much company, I tell myself. When we are all together, we Heralds, we make noise and excitement. I tell myself I will watch that in the future and be more careful.

I am walking softly down the hall making these promises and telling myself to see that Etta is properly covered and warm when I hear a shout. It comes from behind me, from one of the rooms at the front. I do not know which room but I know that death is here again.

After that I remember little. No detail. Movement, sound, confusion. It is like Gretel's time. Doors open, everyone is in the hall, crowding, pushing, asking questions. I can understand nothing that is said. I count the faces, the shifting figures, and only Fray is not there. No, that is wrong. Claudine is not there also. We know that Fray is in Baltimore but we do not know where Claudine is. Father tells us as we crowd around the door. Max is staring at the empty bed, the covers turned back, the small round hollow in the pillow. May, Rosie, Henry, Etta, the Mundys; only the colored maids are not in the hall. They live over the stable. Max touches the pillow. He is like a man in his sleep. It is May who takes a hand. She asks if Claudine's clothes are all there and for a minute no one moves and no one speaks. Then Etta goes to the big wardrobe and counts the dresses and the coats. She opens a box that is on a chair. There is a new coat in it, not yet worn. I learn afterward that Claudine has bought it that morning. Etta says nothing is gone but a dressing gown with a lace collar and slippers.

Max rushes from the room and Father and I follow. We go out into the night without a word to each other. There is no need to speak or to give directions. We are all thinking the same thought. The fog is still heavy and we blunder down the familiar paths like blind men in a strange country. Twice Max goes down, he is unable to help himself and we drag him to his feet and go on. I try to send Father back to the house and he refuses. I am afraid of what we will find.

We find nothing. There is the gaping hole in the dock but we expected that. We use cigar lighters, they are too small in the fog and are swallowed up but they show us the gaping hole. I do not remember if I have ever put the board back. Max does not remember either. He does not know if he displaced it himself or if it was already gone. Mundy comes down to us with lanterns and Henry drives the car from the stable and parks it on the slope. The headlights cleave the fog and for the first time we see the black water beneath us. It is smooth and quiet like black oil and it tells us nothing. The grass and the dock tell us nothing. There is not even a crumpled handkerchief on the grass, not even a small gold hairpin on the wet boards. Not a ripple on the black water.

We send Mundy for the doctor, for the policeman in the village, and I take our motor boat and cover the shoreline. The others search the beach. Nothing. Men come from the village, neighbors come, and all night we search. Fray returns and joins us. But the fog is our enemy from the start and it is dawn when we give up. We know it is dawn because our watches tell us so. It is still impossible to see the sky. It is a little lighter, that is all.

We talk everything over in the kitchen where we have coffee. Mrs. Mundy is crying as she serves us. We go over every minute of the night that has passed. We tell ourselves that Father and I were the only ones who were always there in the music room, in plain sight of

the door, and we saw and heard nothing. One by one
the others left to go upstairs but Father and I were always there. The others say the same. Upstairs and
downstairs no one has heard a sound.

We ask ourselves why. Claudine is a little woman but
she cannot float on air. She must walk, down the front
stairs, down the back stairs. If it was the front, Father,
May and I would have heard her. If it was the back,
she would pass other doors, Henry's and Rosalie's. We
heard nothing.

Then someone, I do not remember who, but someone
says we must not forget that we closed the door to the
music room. We discuss that. It is after May returned
to play for Father that we closed it.

We try to fix the time, the hour, even the minute.
The policeman from the village says it is the thing to
do. So we make a little list as best we can. We write
that Claudine went to bed at ten-thirty. Then May
takes poor Rosie up, perhaps ten minutes later. Then
Henry comes in and says goodnight and he too leaves
us. Then Etta. Then May returns. All of that takes less
than half an hour and no one, upstairs or down, has seen
or heard Claudine. It is a little before eleven, then, that
we close the door to the music room, and from eleven
o'clock until Max comes in we have nothing but a
blank. Even Max cannot tell us when he heard her call.
He tries to think but he cannot help us. It may have
been fifteen minutes after eleven when he entered the
front gate but he is not sure. He does not even know
how long he was at the dock.

Henry has a theory that Claudine went out to meet
someone by appointment and laid her plans well in advance. That is so like Henry, so pale in character and
black in thought. I am ready to knock him down but I
cannot do that with May's eyes watching me. Then
Etta, who has been talking to herself, says in a loud
voice that perhaps Claudine has never left the house at
all. Perhaps she is lying ill somewhere, unconscious.
For an instant we are struck dumb. Because of Max's
story, because he is sure he has heard her down by the
water, we have only thought to look there. As one per-

son we leave the kitchen and we go to each room in the
house. Rooms that I have not seen in years, I see again.
Gretel's, with white walls and curtained bed; with
shapeless dolls in a row on the window seat, with low
book shelves, with childish pictures from the Brothers
Grimm. My mother's room, closed as was Gretel's, but
still fragrant with something as if the life she lived there
is reluctant to leave. Those rooms are clean and orderly, someone has seen to that, and I later discover
that Max has arranged it all these years with Etta. In
all this time I have not known that. It is odd how little
a man knows of what passes in his own house.

We go into attics and storerooms, all to no avail.
Then it grows light outdoors, the sun comes through
the fog and the world is clean and fresh and new. Once
more we go down to the water, and this time we find
her. She is under the dock, between two of the stakes,
shrouded in seaweed.

Later: The authorities come from Baltimore and we
talk. I tell them what we know. I tell everything,
leaving out nothing. They ask questions. I tell them I
cannot understand what has happened at all. I tell them
she feared the water, that she had been frightened in the
afternoon when I went overboard. Then they tell me
there are two explanations. They speak kindly and with
sympathy. Two explanations, when we ourselves have
not even one. First, they say, she would never go to the
dock in the dead of night unless she was driven by
something stronger than fear for herself. I do not ask
them what they mean. I see what they are thinking. It
is in their eyes when they look at Max.

They ask him if he has called her on the telephone to
say that he is on the way home. They have noted the
phone beside her bed. They miss very little. I answer
for Max. I tell them we would all hear the phone ring.
It is an extension and there is one in every major bedroom in the house and in each room downstairs. They
seem satisfied but only for a moment. They ask if he
has arranged for her to meet him on the grounds, to
walk a little by the water before retiring. I laugh at
that. Max says nothing. He cannot. Walk on such a

night, I laugh. Wearing no more than a single gown of thin silk, a lace cap with ribbons, those foolish shoes with baby soles? I ask them if they think we are all crazy to listen to such talk. There are two of them, and they shrug their shoulders together like mechanical men.

Then I remember that they have said there could be two explanations. I ask for the second and I let my voice tell them how little I think of the first. They remind us of her secrecy, and say she could have killed herself.

There is nothing to answer. Father takes Max away and the others go to their rooms. Everyone goes but myself and Fray, and Fray is given his turn at the inquisition. He will not tell them where he was all evening. He will say nothing except that he was in Baltimore. Later he tells me. It is not much of a story, it is the usual one and so unoriginal that I believe him. He says he is protecting a lady.

So now it is all over. We have come to a conclusion that we must believe. It is the only one. If there were the smallest hint of a scandal, of a crime, those men from the city would fasten on it. They have done their best in their own way, and they have found nothing. The conclusion is death by drowning. "A tragic accident," they call it. The reason for such an accident is not apparent to me. One of the colored maids has another theory. She tells me it is the will of God. I see May nod her head in silent agreement.

I cannot believe that. Perhaps I have not gone to church enough and my understanding of God is not orthodox. Or perhaps I have no understanding at all. I do not know how a god arranges things. But I am a man, purposely made in the same image, and as such I am entitled to think. So I think that if I were the puppet master I would use more care in pulling the strings. And I think I would keep for myself some of the gifts I eagerly bestow on ordinary men. For it would almost seem as if the gods are too generous. They give compassion with a lavish hand, until there is none left for themselves.' "

Some minutes before Regan had drawn away from the table, and now when he closed the book she made a small motion of despair.

"You look as if you wanted to put space between us," he said.

"No," she answered. "Only between me and this house."

"But I thought you and I—never mind." She was too wretched to notice the disappointment in his voice. "Never mind," he went on. "You can go home very soon. Perhaps it's better that way."

"I'm beginning to be afraid," she said. "And I'm useless, I can't do anything about all this. Even if it means I'll never see you again, I want to go away."

"Don't be afraid. You can go—let's say the day after to-morrow. Is that all right?"

"All right."

"I'll arrange everything," he said lightly. "You're practically on the train. Notice I say train instead of bus? Drawing room, all to yourself, porters bowing and scraping. And on the level I'm sorry this has been rough on you. I had to keep you here, you can see that now. Hurst thought you were a key. I had to find out how much you knew of the—the—"

"Herald tragedies," she said.

"Herald tragedies? That's a neat phrase but it doesn't sound like you."

"It's what Cousin May calls them." She added, "Cousin May thinks they are a punishment for something."

"That's a new one. Did she happen to say why Gretel and Claudine rated that kind of punishment?"

"I think she meant the family, the family as a whole."

"Tribal curse, eh? What do you think of that?"

"I'm trying not to think anything. There's too much in those books that I haven't seen and you have. But there's one thing—"

"What?"

Her voice was almost inaudible. "Why didn't he confide

in you and Max? He loved you both but when you wanted to come here he told you to stay away. I think—"

"Go on," he said.

"All right. It sounds crazy, but I think he suspected one of you."

She might have been paying him a compliment. He looked pleased. "Good!" he said. "Now we're getting somewhere. But you can't really be thinking of me because I was exactly one year old when Gretel was shot. It's Max, isn't it? Max shot Gretel. Max held Claudine under the water when he said he was falling through the dock and sitting on the pavilion steps . . . Got a reason for thinking like that?"

"I don't think like that! Don't even say that!"

"But you must think something, Regan. Hurst did. And Hurst was counting on you."

He wants me to accuse somebody, she thought. He doesn't care who. He wants me to say a name, any name. He thinks I have a name hidden in my mind somewhere. Maybe that's what Hurst thought. I haven't, I haven't, I never did have.

"I don't know anything," she said. "I'm useless, I've told you that before, I'm useless. I don't know."

He went on, looking into the shadows behind her chair. "Everybody was here when Gretel died, including the Mundys and Etta. When Claudine's turn came we had the same cast. The same with my father, too. Hurst is the only one who managed to die with a different set-up. Max, Etta and I were miles away."

She said, "Miss Etta is a Herald, isn't she?"

His startled eyes came back to her face. "Etta! Now you're being fantastic! What are you trying to do?"

"Only what you want me to do. Give you a name you can use, the name Hurst was afraid to speak."

"That's nice headwork, but you can toss Etta out. Look at it this way. What could a child like Gretel and a young woman like Claudine have that Etta wanted? Not a thing. How could they stand in Etta's way? They couldn't. She adored them. Listen to this again. What did Gretel and

Claudine have? That's your key. If you can fit that in the right lock you've got the answer."

"There's another answer," she said soberly. "Maybe they were accidents. For years everybody thought they were. Hurst was sick, he said so himself. Maybe—" She dropped her voice to a whisper. "Has anybody ever called the Heralds mad?"

"Often," he said calmly. "That's the popular notion. But Hurst wasn't. And if you're thinking about yourself, stop it."

"How can I stop it! How can I help thinking like that! Tonight, out at the pavilion—"

"You're sane," he said. "Sane and loyal. That's why he wanted you. People take one look at you and believe whatever you say. That's a lucky break for all of us." He leaned forward. "That's why I wanted you, too. That's—one of the reasons . . . Regan, are you still afraid of the pavilion?"

"Yes." He was going to ask her to go there. To go through the door. I can't go, she told herself. Something is waiting for me in there. I can't go. But she knew she would do whatever he asked. She made only one effort in what she was almost afraid to call self-defense. "You told me not to go anywhere," she said. "Not even into a room unless there were at least two other people there."

"I'm the same as two." He took his raincoat from a chair and hung it over her shoulders. "Come along. You're my good girl."

She followed wordlessly. She had no choice. From the first morning when she recognized the spire, she had known that. He led the way down the back stairs, through the darkened kitchen, out into the garden. She took the lead there, turning without hesitation to the flagged walk that led to the water.

"There's nothing to be afraid of," he said. "You knew you'd have to do this sometime."

"Yes. I've been waiting for this." A few hours ago I was in a warm room filled with people, she told herself. I was listening to music. A few hours ago Miss Etta wore Claudine's lace collar and gave Claudine's blue wool to Rosalie. A few minutes ago I heard all about Claudine. Hurst and Miss Etta brought Claudine back to life again tonight. She died down here by the water and Gretel died here, too. Now I am going to the same place.

She tripped on the long raincoat. He took her arm.

"Careful," he said. "We can't use a flashlight, we don't want to be seen."

They rounded the pavilion and came to the steps. She heard the lapping water and the sandy scrape of his shoes as he went up to the door. The key in the new lock made no sound. Even the old bolt slipped quietly from its socket. He's oiled it, she thought. Or perhaps Hurst did that.

The door swung in. She heard him say, "One lamp will do for us. We don't want much light. Close the door and stand still until I get it on." She did as she was told.

The room was musty. She could smell tobacco, wood ashes and mold. She heard his steps on bare board and rug, and the faint click of a lamp chain striking against china or glass. Suddenly the room was filled with a soft light. She stood with her back against the door, holding her breath, looking from wall to wall, from ceiling to floor, from one piece of furniture to another.

He spoke to her from the middle of the room. He was standing beside the table that held the lamp.

"Well?" he asked.

She looked at the faded red curtains that covered the shuttered windows, at the small piano, at the fireplace where painted Hessian soldiers held all that was left of a burnt log, at the mantel filled with majolica and Dresden figures, at the hunting prints, the rack of riding whips, the shelves filled with silver trophies, the old, soft chairs, the bookcases, the wall cabinet.

"Well?" he asked again.

She sighed. "It hasn't changed," she said. She walked over to a chair by the dead fire and sat down. "I remember it now."

"Look again," he said. "Take your time. No change at all?"

"No." Her voice was weary. "Everything looks the same."

One of the majolica pieces on the mantel was a circle of grinning dwarfs whose uplifted hands held candles. He crossed the room and lit the candles one by one. "More light in this corner." He leaned against the mantel and studied her averted face. "Don't you want to look at me, Regan, or are you trying not to see something?"

"I'm trying to go back," she said. "That's why you brought me here, isn't it?"

"Yes, that's why I brought you here." He lit a cigarette. "This may be our only chance. I want you to forget me, forget Gretel and Claudine, forget everyone but yourself and Hurst. You didn't know Gretel and Claudine, you'd never even heard of them when you were here before, they don't belong in that part of your mind. They have nothing to do with the thing Hurst wanted you to remember. They can't have. See?"

"I see what you mean, but it doesn't work that way. They're in this room as much as you and I are."

"If that's the way it goes, all right. Do it your own way but take your time."

She leaned back in the chair and examined the room again. "Is that the wall cabinet that held the diaries?"

"Yes."

"It used to hold plates and silver."

"It still does. Go on."

She gave him a despairing look. "Something is happening to me. I feel as if I were drowning."

"That's partly because you hear the water. It's loud to-night. But you've got to go on, for your own sake as much as anything else. Coming to this house started something in your mind. You've got to go on, clear it up."

"I can't. There's nothing to go on with. Nothing comes back to me but—fear. That's all. It's useless."

"You're doing it the wrong way. Try it like this. This isn't October, this is summer, a warm summer night. You're not even in the pavilion, you're out in the boat, alone, in the dark." He was leaning forward, persuasive and soft-spoken. "You're frightened because you hear voices on the shore and you think Hurst is in trouble. You climb out of the boat like a good girl and run up the slope to the door. The pavilion door . . . The door was open?"

She sighed deeply. "I can see the light shining through on the grass."

"You stand in the open door and—"

Tears gathered and fell.

"You stand in the open door and someone speaks to you." She didn't know how closely he was watching her. She wasn't looking at him. She heard his voice like a voice in another room, reading from a book. She heard what he said but something came between them and robbed the words of personal significance. Something louder and stronger than speech was forcing him into the background. Her eyes were on the mantel with its orderly row of china figures. Her lips moved as she called them softly by name. The dwarf candlestick, the basket of red roses—

He spoke again. "Regan, listen to me."

"Yes, Fray." She sounded asleep.

He began all over again. "You were in the boat. It was dark, and the water was all around you." He reproduced the night as she had done it for him, leaving out nothing. He told her about the lights on the water, the lamplight through the trees, the smell of flowers. He even remembered the sandy scrape of shoes on the wooden steps. "The door was open," he said. "You stood in the doorway and someone spoke to you." He heard his own breath. "Who spoke to you, Regan?"

"No one."

"Why not?"

"No one knew I was there. I didn't make any noise."

"Did—they make any noise?"

"He had a whip."

He wanted to rush forward. Instead, he gripped the
mantel edge and forced himself to stay where he was.
"What was he doing with the whip?"

"He was looking at it. He held it in his hand. He stood
by the table, looking at it. I heard it, too."

"Heard?"

"Yes, I heard it. It cracked out, and crashed. It—"

One of the candles flickered and went out. She had been
watching the candles and when that happened she stiffened,
and turned a startled face to his. When she spoke, the drow-
siness had gone from her voice. "Fray! I'm talking like
Rosalie! You're doing the same thing to me that you did
to Rosalie. Don't!"

"It's all right, it's all right. You're not like Rosie, it's all
right. But you can't stop now, Regan, you can't. You know
what you were saying, don't you? There was a whip. You
saw it and heard it. What do you mean when you say you
heard it?"

Her eyes went back to the mantel. "Nothing. That's all.
That's the end."

"No, it isn't the end. You say he stood at the table with
the whip in his hand. You say 'he'. You don't give him a
name. Was it Hurst?"

"Of course it was Hurst!" Her voice began to rise before
she came to the end of the sentence. "It must have been
Hurst! I can't remember, but it must have been! This is
where he came. I saw him through the trees, walking across
the grass to the steps."

"That's fine. You saw Hurst." He went on as if it didn't
matter. "Did you see the other person too?"

"I don't know. I don't think so. I—"

He watched the struggle to remember. It was a battle
fought behind her eyes. It dug hollows in her white face
and dragged at the corners of her mouth. He watched in
silence, then— "That's enough. That'll do. Wash it out,
forget it."

"What did you say?" she asked vaguely. "What did you
say then?"

"I said forget it. We'll call it a night."

She had barely waited for his answer. She looked as if she had forgotten her own question. "That's queer," she said. She was talking to herself. "That's queer. I thought I saw something then."

"What's queer? Tell me, and I'll straighten it out."

"Light the candle again, Fray!"

He did so at once. "Still see it, whatever it is?" he asked easily.

"No, but it's queer. Just then, just for a second, I thought I saw or remembered something. I thought maybe the unlighted candle had played a kind of trick. But it isn't the candle, it's something else. It's—isn't there something missing up there?"

"On the mantel?"

"Yes." She laughed shakily, but her voice was full of relief. For the first time she sounded like herself. "This is getting beyond me. What can be wrong with a mantel full of ornaments!"

"Everything. I think they're terrible myself . . . What do you think is missing? An old favorite of yours?"

"No, I'm sure they're all there. That's the silly part. If they're all there, how can anything be gone?" She laughed again.

"I'll tell you what to do," he said. "Count them. You may be right, I don't know. That stuff has been here ever since I was a kid. Nothing added, nothing changed that I can see, but then I've been away a lot. Go on, count them."

She got up from the chair and touched each familiar piece, calling it by name. "The dwarfs, the pitcher shaped like a fish, the basket of red roses, the children in the swing." She touched the swing lightly and it moved back and forth. "The swing, the cornucopia of fruit, the sheaf of wheat, the little swans—"

There was a sandy scrape on the steps outside. Someone knocked at the door.

Fray held up his hand. "I'll do the talking," he whispered. He tilted the lamp shade, concentrating the light on the door. Then he opened the door with a single quick movement. Mundy stood on the top step, bareheaded, his collar turned up against the fog and mist.

The light was full on his face. He wore a coaxing look, as if he were prepared to flatter or cajole the pavilion's occupants. In another second that look was gone.

"I'm sorry, sir," he said. "I didn't know who was in here."

"And I'm sorry you had a disappointment. Do you mind telling me what you're doing out here at this hour?"

"I couldn't remember if I'd locked the stable, sir. I came out to see. I thought I heard voices and—I'm sorry, sir."

"Miss Carr hadn't seen the pavilion since she was a child. You remember that visit, Mundy?"

"No, sir." Mundy was sufficiently regretful, but no more. He was clearly feeling his way. The look of regret was immediately followed by one of polite interest. "My wife and I were over at the farm when Miss Carr came here before."

"So you were, so you were. Well, I brought Miss Carr down here tonight to have a look at her childhood playground. A last look. She's leaving us soon, in a day or two." He dropped the key to the door in a silver tray and it rang like a bell. "Put out the lights, will you? And never mind about locking up. I'll be responsible if anyone breaks in."

Chapter Nine

IT WAS after midnight when she reached her room. This time she closed her door and locked it. She told herself there was no reason for that. She was safe under her own roof. She told herself there was no reason for thinking that way, either. Of course she was safe. She undressed slowly and clumsily, struggling with the familiar belt and buttons as if she had never handled them before.

Miss Etta had been in her room while she was away. There was a package on the chest of drawers, a lopsided, shapeless mound of wrinkled tissue paper, pink corset string, and holiday seals. She tried to smile when she read the attached card. Its gilt injunction, "Do Not Open Til Christmas," had been canceled out with lipstick and "Bon Voyage" substituted. Miss Etta was right, she thought. She knew I was going soon but I didn't.

She turned out the light and sat by the open window, looking at the spire and the coiling fog. Her eyes closed and her head dropped forward but she straightened up and looked again. It was like the other time, the night when the spire had beckoned. She had to look, she couldn't do anything else.

She hardly knew what she was seeing. It was like watching a dream unfold. She thought she saw herself as a child, like a small ghost under the trees. She thought she saw herself and Fray, moving through the fog like people between two worlds. She thought she saw Henry. That was odd. Why should she see Henry.

He was walking across the grass, he came in and out of

the fog, he was walking and crouching and running with small steps. Henry. He disappeared behind the laurels and the rhododendrons, behind the dry, brittle bushes that had flowers in the spring. Sometimes called mock orange. Mock.

She left the window and crept into bed.

She tried to sleep but the wind was strong and the air was wet and cold. Each time she opened her eyes she saw the blowing curtains. Their rhythm was hypnotic. She tried to breathe in the same even rhythm. In and out, in and out. She tried it again and again, in and out, in and out. But still she was awake.

When the curtains blew in they made shadows on the ceiling. She tried to understand that but it was too difficult. The shadows moved across the ceiling and crept down the walls. They came and went like a lost procession trying to find a way out. Across the ceiling, down the walls, and back again. She watched them between sleeping and waking, wondering if they would go away if she closed the window. They became as real as people. They took on the shapes of people, they lengthened and broadened and grew arms and legs. After a while they were people.

They moved along the ceiling, down the walls, and drifted in a dim line across the floor at the foot of her bed. When they reached the foot of the bed they were people. They came and went, and each time they returned they were clearer in outline, firmer in step, with features that were recognizable. Not hair and eyes and mouth, but other features. She knew who they were.

It was no use telling herself that she was dreaming. She was awake, her own eyes were open, she touched them to make sure, and she knew where she was and what she was seeing. This is my mind working, she thought. This is what they call the eyes of the mind. My mind is showing me pictures, like a film. They have always been there and tonight something has brought them out, something like a developer.

One of the figures was Hurst and he had a strange, red welt on one cheek. He stood and looked at her silently, and raised a cautionary finger to his lips. He shook his head, he

was saying no to somebody. No to what? To whom? She
tried to sit upright but her body was too heavy. She could
nod her own head in agreement, that was all. She was glad
she could do that.

He stood there for what seemed a long time. His face was
so distinct that the red welt was clear against the tan. The
other figures were not as clear as this. They were like fog
but he was real. She recognized the jacket he wore, a white
linen with horn buttons. She remembered the buttons because they were carved with edelweiss. It didn't seem
strange that she could see the edelweiss in that dark room.
The mark on his cheek was the only strange thing. It was a
bright, burning red, it looked as if he had been struck by
something. She studied the mark and he stood without moving, as if he knew what she was doing and wanted to help her.
He was grave and unsmiling. Then she began to remember.
She had seen the mark before.

One morning, long before the others were up, he had
come into the room she shared with her mother and told her
he had been riding. He'd pointed to his cheek and made
grimaces. He'd told her he had struck himself with his own
whip. He had flicked it in the air and it had flicked back. An
Australian whip with boomerang ancestry, and he was going
to burn it up because it had hurt his pride and he never
wanted to see it again. And she was not to mention the red
mark, please; she was to pretend it was invisible. For the
sake of his pride, he'd said.

She'd laughed and her mother had said he had a way with
children and wasn't it a pity he had none of his own. She
remembered it now as if it were yesterday, the red welt and
the whip. She closed her eyes for a moment, to see if the
picture in her mind was as clear as the figure at the foot of
the bed. It was. But when she looked again he was gone.

The others returned, the dim shapes that had followed
him before.

This time I must be dreaming, she told herself. I never
did know these people, I never even saw them. I'm making
this part up because I've been hearing about them and I

know their stories. Because I've been down to the water and in the pavilion. This is a kind of hysteria and I've got to stop. I'm tired, my head aches, I see things even when my eyes are closed, I've got to stop. I didn't know any of these. I only see them now because I'm sorry for them. I've worked myself into a state of nerves. I'll be sick if I don't stop. A week ago I wouldn't have known these if I'd passed them on the street. I'd have known Hurst anywhere but I wouldn't have known these. I know them now because I've been reading the diaries and I know what they wore. I've only read about them and I'm letting something I've read get under my skin. I've got to stop. I'll be sick. I'll go to Dr. Poole. I'll ask Dr. Poole what's wrong with me. I'll ask him if the Heralds are mad.

The figures moved across the room, intent on some objective of their own. There were three of them. They didn't look at her as Hurst had done. They held their heads high as if they were listening and following.

One of them she didn't know. There was nothing in outline, in dress or manner to tell her who he was. She couldn't see his face, she only knew that he was old. The other two were women. One was no more than a shining coronet of braids and a pale blue dress. The yellow braids and the blue dress glowed as if they were lighted from within. All the rest was shadow.

The third was taller than the second and there was no character or color in her clothes. She was white, a vague, thin white like the fog. There was nothing to distinguish her from the fog except her gleaming bare arms and hands. They were like the arms and hands of a china doll. They were rosy and dimpled, with curling, tapering fingers. This one held something blue in her fine china hands.

She watched until the dim outlines faded into nothing. They melted away. The curtains blew in at the windows, the wavering shadows crept across the ceiling and down the walls. They were nothing but shadows. She watched until the rhythm of the curtains closed her eyes.

It seemed no more than a minute later when she opened

them again and saw that the room was filled with gray light.
The clock said nine-thirty. The door was closed and
locked as she had left it.

She tried not to think of Jenny or Katy climbing the stairs
with a heavy tray, unable to enter, carrying it back again.
But perhaps they hadn't come. Once before Fray had told
them to let her sleep. Perhaps he had told them this morning.

She dressed quickly, closing her mind to the dreams that
had haunted her sleep. She made herself believe they were
dreams, and thought about the pavilion instead. The pavilion
held no terrors now. She had been there, she had seen it, it
was nothing. It was an empty, abandoned shell. She went
over to the chest of drawers and brushed her hair, carefully
counting the strokes. Miss Etta's present was even more
ridiculous in the morning light. "Bon Voyage." She was
going away soon.

Fray had understood at once how much she wanted to go.
He had seen how hopeless his plan was. There was nothing
he could do, nothing either of them could do. Cousin May
was right, Hurst had been sick and irresponsible. Poor
Hurst.

She compared the early diaries with the last one. They
were as unrelated as the lives and thoughts of two people
living in opposite worlds. The early diaries were Hurst
himself, she could hear his voice on every page, but the last
one was the desperate cry of a stranger who admitted he
didn't know where his mind was taking him. Poor Hurst.
And now Fray himself was convinced. He knew now that
he didn't need her. Her treasured letter meant nothing. It
was a part of Hurst's last, sad days, like the day when he
walked the streets trying not to say the name of a murderer.
There was no murderer. There never had been. There was
nothing ugly buried in her mind, waiting for disinterment.
There was nothing in the pavilion but old furniture and old
memories. There was nothing in the house but tired and unhappy people. It was a house of illness and tragedy. Her
own house had been like that a month before. That's why

I've been thinking things and hearing things, she told herself. Atmosphere can do that. I read that somewhere. Atmosphere does strange things.

She looked at herself in the mirror and her hollow eyes stared back. She shrugged, and tried a derisive smile. It wasn't successful and she tried again. The second time was better. She gave her hair a final stroke and left the room as quickly as she dared. She was afraid to run. That would be the same as admitting something.

She went down the front stairs, deliberately taking her time. I'll apologize for being late, she promised herself. And if Jenny or Katy came with a tray I'll give them some money. I'll give them money anyhow, I have plenty now. I'll tip the servants when I leave, Mrs. Mundy, Mundy, the Crains. Little white envelopes sealed and marked, left on the chest of drawers like Miss Etta's present. Miss Carr tips very well. Miss Carr can come again.

The second floor hall showed closed doors, all but one, Max's. That door was ajar and a breakfast tray, cluttered with orange peel and egg shells stood on the hall floor. The faint whirr of a vacuum cleaner came from one of the rooms farther down. She went to Max's door and looked in. He was alone, lying on the big bed with the covers drawn to his chin. She went in, walking softly because she thought he was asleep.

She reminded herself that the door had been open, she hadn't forced her way in. It couldn't hurt Max, it couldn't hurt anyone if she sat there for a few minutes. She wouldn't speak unless he woke up and spoke to her first. If he was too ill to talk she'd go away. She'd be quiet and soothing, she wouldn't excite him. But she had to see him, to speak to him if possible, to make certain he was all right.

That's what she told herself. She sat in a chair beside the bed and tried to read the lines in his calm face. He looked more than ever like Hurst. His head on the fine linen pillow was like Hurst's head on the tufted satin. Like hers. That's what Miss Etta had said. Like hers. Fray had said something too, not about her but about Max. He'd said, 'Not this time.'

She tried to remember when he had said that and what he had meant. After a minute it came to her. Cousin May had said, 'Suppose Max had died?' And Fray had said, 'But he didn't. Not this time.'

She looked at the chiseled features. He had lost weight. His cheek bones were sharp, his eye sockets were circles of bone. Bone. Her bones. Young Sheffy had said, 'I know the bone structure. I ought to. I did them all . . . If they get through their twenties they're good 'til sixty.' Max was sixty. His door was kept locked. Fray kept his door locked. That was why. It was almost unbelievable but it must be so.

Max stirred and opened his eyes. He regarded her intently, as if he were making sure she was there. Then he smiled.

"Good morning. For a minute I thought you weren't real."

"Don't talk," she said. "Please don't talk if you're tired. The door was open and I came in just for a minute. I wanted to see you again."

"Oh, the door was open, was it? Well, we'll keep that a secret between us. Otherwise poor Katy—it was Katy, I suppose?"

"With the mole?" She smiled back at him.

"Ah, I knew there was something! Yes, a secret between us, otherwise poor Katy will pay out of all proportion. I'm not supposed to have visitors, you know. Young visitors." He laughed silently. "Ladies under seventy are forbidden."

"You've been very ill," she said soothingly. "You misjudge your own strength. They keep your door locked because it's best for you."

He looked at her for a long time before he answered. "So," he said. "Now tell me how you've been amusing yourself."

"The usual things," she said carefully. "Taking walks and reading. I'm going home in a day or two."

"That's too bad. Or is it good? Do you want to go?"

"Oh yes. It's the thing to do."

"That sounds very virtuous. 'The thing to do.' Almost too virtuous. Isn't this a sudden decision?"

"No," she said. She knew the truth would distress him.

She couldn't let that happen. She touched the shrunken shoulder under the blankets. "I'm glad I saw you, Max. You look like Hurst. Sometimes you sound like him, too."

"Sound?" he repeated. "My dear girl, how can you say that? I don't think I've said two words to you until today."

She thought she heard a faint amusement behind his words, as if he were laughing at her quietly, and it was confusing. She went on, feeling awkward and uncertain. "Is there anything I can do for you, Max, before I go?"

"Do for me? Haven't you already done enough? Fray tells me it was you who found me in that deplorable condition the other night. I believe I was slated for Young Sheffy's ministrations when you so happily snatched me back. I've never heard the whole story behind that and I've been doing some private wondering. What brought you to my door at that ungodly hour?"

She told him. "You were nearly dead. I thought you were. You didn't say a word."

"That's very gratifying . . . So I didn't talk to you? I've been afraid that I talked. People do, you know, when they're not themselves."

"No," she said firmly. "Not a word." She remembered the brandy bottle on the floor. He's ashamed, she told herself. He needn't be. He was too sick to realize what he was doing. He was only trying to get warm, to make himself sleep. She wanted to tell him not to worry about it but it seemed better to pretend ignorance. She tried to think of something else to talk about but everything that came to her mind had an unhappy connotation. The diaries, but Fray said he knew about them. The pavilion? That was too close to Claudine. Her own worry and distress? No again. He'd had trouble enough of his own, it wouldn't be fair. It must have been hard for him to come back to this house, she thought, to walk in and out of familiar rooms, to remember who sat here and who sat there. She looked down at the white face. He had closed his eyes again. I hope he finds peace, she told herself. He looks like a man who is driven by something, driven too hard in the wrong direction.

I ought to go, she thought. Someone may come in. But she sat on, thinking. In another twenty-four hours she'd be on her way home. Hurst had said this was her home but it hadn't turned out that way. The biggest garden, the finest lace curtains, the biggest house in town. She saw herself walking up the street, running the magic wand along the railings, scuffing the yellow leaves. She saw the white roses on the oaken door, she saw Fray's dark eyes looking down into hers. If only Fray—

Max's voice called her back. "You sighed then. Why?"

She flushed. "I didn't sleep very well last night." She seemed always to be saying that and it was always true.

"You look as if you needed more than sleep. Are you sure you haven't been—taking on too much?"

"Taking on too much?" she repeated.

"Yes. We Heralds are inclined that way. We take other people's lives into our own hands, make decisions, readjust. That course is sometimes dangerous, I think, don't you? But perhaps the word I want is foolhardy. Still, whatever it is, we do too much of it. So much that sometimes it looks like interference." He smiled again, gently. "Let sleeping dogs lie is an excellent maxim, unless you are stronger than the dog."

"I suppose so," she said doubtfully. She wondered if she had displeased him by coming in because the door was open. "Was it wrong for me to come in here because the door was open?" she asked. "Was that interference?"

"Not at all, I'm very glad you did. And now you're going away and we've not seen nearly enough of each other, not nearly enough. I don't even know what room they put you in."

"I'm upstairs, next to Miss Etta. It's quite comfortable," she assured him. "I've been quite all right. And before I go I'll ask Fray to bring me in to say good-by."

"You'll do nothing of the sort," he said kindly. "We'll see each other before that, I promise you."

She stood up. It seemed like the right time to go. He had closed his eyes once more and she was afraid she had tired

him. Outside, the hum of the vacuum cleaner had stopped.
Someone would be coming for his tray. If Cousin May
should see her—She was suddenly conscious of having done
something for which she might have to pay. Like Katy.
She looked down at the still figure. Max opened his eyes.

"I've got to get along," she said softly. Someone was
coming down the hall, stopping at the door. She caught a
glimpse of black uniform and white apron. "Good-by," she
whispered.

It was Jenny in the hall. Jenny looked aghast. "Did Katy
leave this door unlocked? Heaven help her, she's supposed
to lock it coming and going. He's a great one for wandering
and Mr. Fray don't like it." She closed the door and turned
the key.

"It's all right, Jenny. I only went in to say hello."

"Trouble last night," Jenny went on with relish. "I'm
not supposed to know about it but I've got wonderful hearing. Somebody walking around on our floor, somebody
walking around on this floor, way past midnight. Door on
this floor opened and shut twice, I heard it, but I didn't tell
Katy. She's a screamer. Somebody trying to walk quiet, but
I heard."

"Maybe Mr. Fray—"

"Maybe. Maybe, but I'm not saying anything. I'm only
saying that Mr. Fray don't walk like he's hiding something,
even past midnight . . . You missed your breakfast."

"Yes, but—"

"You go right down to the dining room and ring the bell
beside the dumbwaiter. Mundy'll take care of you."

Down in the dining room she looked at the bell for a
long time before she decided not to ring it. She knew too
much about the bell and The Box, the sudden, harsh whirr,
the blinking light, the little hand that spun around the dial,
the strained faces that turned to read the summons. Would
they hurry to the stairs if she rang? Yes, because they
wouldn't know who it was. And if Katy were in the kitchen
she'd run across the room to peer up at the dial and Mrs.
Mundy would say something about her eyes.

She left the dining room and went down to the kitchen. The kitchen was empty, too. There was a cup of coffee cooling on the table, and a crumpled newspaper that looked as if someone had hastily discarded it. Pots and kettles hissed on the stove and the cold water faucet flowed briskly over a basin of vegetables in the sink. The whole room had a look of sudden abandonment, as if its occupants had fled before an approaching disaster. The clock ticked on, the kettles hissed, the water ran noisily and wastefully over the basin of vegetables.

She stood at the table, touching the cold coffee cup, hearing the busy sounds of unhuman activity. She listened for voices in the pantry and cellar, for anything that proved the presence of living people, but there was nothing to hear but the clock, the running water and the kettles. An uneasy phrase ran through her mind: in the midst of life we are in death. The words uncoiled like a scroll of writing, not like a thought. She could see them. In the midst of life we are in death.

She pushed the kettles back and turned off the water. Her eyes went instinctively to The Box, as if it could tell her something, but the little hand was perversely still.

No sound of voices anywhere, no footsteps on the stairs. Had everyone gone but herself and Max and Jenny? She went to the window and looked out. There was a high wind and the leaves on the ground spiraled like waterspouts and flung themselves upward. The trees and bushes followed the way of the wind. They parted and closed, opened new vistas, revealed and concealed, all in one breath. That was how she saw the others before they were ready to be seen.

They were behind the shrubbery, between the laurels and the cypress ring, hatless, coatless, with the wind tearing at their skirts and whipping their hair. Mrs. Mundy, Miss Etta, Katy and Rosalie. Mrs. Mundy and Miss Etta had Rosalie by the arms, leading and dragging at the same time, while Katy ran ahead in little circles and wrung her hands. The laurels closed and the picture was gone.

She went to the door and stood there, wondering what to

do. The garden was noisy with the wind, the whirling leaves, the thrashing branches, but no other sound came from behind the laurels. She thought of Fray, of Mundy, even of Henry. Rosalie was too much for the three women. They fell back repeatedly before the impact of that plunging bulk.

That day at the sanitarium must have been like this, she thought; it must have looked and sounded like this. She took a step forward and the wind barred her progress like a great hand. She steadied herself against the door and tried again, but before she could take another step the figures came out into the open. They rounded the laurels and moved slowly across the grass, leaning against the wind. Katy led the way, throwing small, fearful looks over her shoulder.

Regan went back to the kitchen and waited. She poured a cup of coffee and sat at the table. Better to look as if she had just come down.

Through the window she saw Rosalie break away from the others and walk stolidly toward the kitchen alone. They made no effort to restrain her. There was something like relief in the droop of Miss Etta's shoulders but Mrs. Mundy regarded the stormy landscape as if that had been her original purpose.

Rosalie opened the door and slammed it violently behind her. She shook her head from side to side and blundered across the room like an animal in a strange pen, striking at the furniture that stood between her and the stairs. She saw nothing but the stairs.

Regan said, "Rosalie?"

Rosalie stopped short and turned. She struggled to come back from the place where her fears were taking her. Her face slowly broke into a wide, delighted smile. "I was looking for you," she said. "I was looking for you down by the water because you always go there."

"Not today," Regan said. "I don't like it down there today. I like it better in the house. You stay in the house with me."

"I was looking for you," Rosalie insisted. "What are you
doing here? This is the kitchen."

"I missed my breakfast so I'm having some coffee. Why
don't you have some, too?"

"Yes," Rosalie said. She came to the table, slowly, heavily,
still smiling. One fat hand went under Regan's chin and
pressed her head back, the other fastened on the nape of her
neck.

"Rosalie," Regan faltered. The white face was too close.
It came closer until she could see the brown flecks in the
pale blue eyes, the roots of the thin hair, the network of
fine wrinkles and tiny red veins that covered the flabby
cheeks. She tried to turn her head away but it was locked
fast. Rosalie's breath became her own, thick, hot, smother-
ing. "Rosie," she whispered. The hands fell.

"You didn't grow up but I did," Rosalie said wonderingly.

There were hurried steps on the flagstones and the door
opened. Mrs. Mundy slowed her pace when she entered.

"My, my," she said, "you just about walked my legs off,
Miss Rosie!" She went instantly to Rosalie and led her to a
rocking chair. "Poor old Mundy can't keep up with you.
Now then, after such a nice airing we'll all sit down and
have a little rest."

Rosalie accepted the chair and rocked evenly. "Coffee,"
she said. "Like Regan."

"If you'll wait a little while I'll make you a nice cup of
chocolate. Nice and rich, with heavy cream."

"Coffee."

Mrs. Mundy gave Regan a long look. "Will you go upstairs, please? Too many people. Upsetting." She didn't
wait for an answer but turned to Katy, still standing in the
doorway and staring at Rosalie with glazed eyes. "Bring
those kettles forward, I didn't leave them like that, and get
on with the vegetables. Miss Etta?" Miss Etta had taken a
chair at the table beside Regan. "Have you made your bed,
Miss Etta?"

"That's gratitude," Miss Etta said hoarsely. "After I've
run myself ragged. Had to yell for me, didn't you, had to

yell for me and Katy, two poor old women in their eighties, all because you couldn't run fast enought to catch a fifty year old girl."

"I want Etta," Rosalie said. She rocked evenly and quietly, stroking the arms of the chair with her fingers. Regan watched the fingers and saw that Mrs. Mundy was watching them too. Mrs. Mundy knows, she thought. She's waiting for the drumming to start.

"Etta will have coffee and so will Regan," Rosalie went on. "I want you to serve Etta and Regan."

Mrs. Mundy agreed with a smile. "If that's what you want you shall have it." She looked quickly from Rosalie to the stairs.

"May isn't up there," Rosalie said. "I know. She went out in the car with Henry. We're all by ourselves. They're going to buy a tombstone for Hurst. May and Henry have the money for it. Fray is out too. He went to see a friend. I heard him say so. Nobody thinks I hear but I hear everything. Sometimes my feelings are hurt when people talk about me as if I couldn't hear, but I always hear. I hear people making mistakes when they tell other people where they've been and where they're going and what they did in the night. I hear them telling things that are full of mistakes. I could contradict if I wanted to but that isn't nice. Where is Jenny?"

Mrs. Mundy answered rapidly. "Jenny's cleaning your room. She'll be down in a minute. Are you hungry enough for a piece of cold chicken? You've got room enough for a nice little wing, haven't you? Breakfast was a long time ago."

"Regan too. And Etta. Everybody sit down and eat. Nobody can see us. There's only an old man upstairs and he won't come down here. They keep the door locked. It's Max. They say he's sick in bed but he isn't. They keep the door locked so he can't get out. Once it was open a little way and I looked in. He wasn't in bed, he was walking up and down. I told May. She was afraid. I'm afraid too."

Dull red stained Mrs. Mundy's sallow cheeks. She put a

plate of food on the table before Rosalie. "There! You see
what you can do with that. It's all yours. Nobody else
wants any." She stood behind Rosalie's chair and her eyes
fought with Regan's.

Mrs. Mundy looked as if she wanted to speak and didn't
know how to begin. Her lips parted but she closed them
almost at once and something like defeat looked out of her
eyes. Her hands, resting on Rosalie's shoulders, said more.
They said that Rosalie was harmless, that Rosalie needed
protection, that Mrs. Mundy would give it with the last
breath in her body.

Regan saw and understood. How can I tell her that I
understand, she thought. She looks at me as if I were a thief,
as if I were robbing her. She's never tried to know me or
talk to me, she's hated me from the beginning, for no reason.
But almost before she finished the thought, she knew there
was a reason. Mrs. Mundy was a Beauregard, just as Miss
Etta was a Herald. She belonged to the Beauregards and
they to her. She would defend and lie for them, destroy
anything that came between them and happiness. Cousin
May, Rosalie and Henry were hers and she, Regan Carr,
was an outsider who had moved into the tribe.

Both of the Mundys were like that. She had watched
Mundy when he served Fray and Max. He was deft and
courteous but he acted as if he were under some compulsion.
He was like a conquered civilian forced to serve a successful foe. Henry acted the same way. It was because the
Beauregards had gone down in the world and the Heralds
had come up.

She tried to tell Mrs. Mundy that she understood. "How
long have you and Mr. Mundy been with the Beauregards?"
she asked.

Mrs. Mundy tried to conceal her surprise. "All our lives.
We were born in the tenant houses on the old farm."

"Then you're the same as one of the family, aren't you?
You belong with them more than I do."

Mrs. Mundy stared.

"I'm going away soon, Mrs. Mundy," Regan went on. "Did you know that?"

"Yes, I knew." Mrs. Mundy's eyes fell. She stroked Rosalie's shoulders.

Rosalie shrugged away from the protecting hands. "You take me with you," she said to Regan. "You take me with you when you go. We'll go together. I'm afraid here."

"Hush, hush," Mrs. Mundy whispered. "That's my good girl."

Miss Etta's voice whipped out. "Afraid? What have you got to be afraid of, Rosie? You're the queen bee around here. You've always been looked after and you always will be. Other people may have good looks and good sense but they die and you keep on living. You live on what the dead ones leave, you live on what rightfully belong to them. Afraid! That's a horse laugh, that is. Afraid! . . . If I was Regan Carr I'd be afraid all right!"

Mrs. Mundy's eyes glittered and she raised a warning hand. Rosalie gripped it, held it for a second and flung it aside. There were red streaks on the sallow skin where the fingers had been. A strangled cry came from the direction of the sink where Katy was working. Regan heard it but she didn't turn. She heard Miss Etta draw in her breath sharply.

Mrs. Mundy hid her hand between her armpit and breast and smiled faintly. "You're letting your tongue run away with you, Miss Etta. All I can say is you're not yourself."

Rosalie leaned across the table and spoke clearly. "I've got the right to everything I have. I've got the right. I've got the right to be afraid, too. I saw Max Herald in a room that wasn't locked and he was full of hate."

· Mrs. Mundy took the plump shoulders in her hands and gently drew Rosalie upright. "You come along with me for a nice walk," she whispered. "Maybe we can throw stones at the birds. A nice long walk, and we won't come back until we're good and ready. Just the two of us together, just the two of us."

Rosalie took Mrs. Mundy's hands in hers, forcing the

arms upward in a slow, powerful sweep. She held them parallel with her own, in a horizontal line, and the worn silk of her bodice stretched and split. Mrs. Mundy's face contracted but she smiled down at Rosalie.

"Last night somebody was walking," Rosalie said earnestly. "Walking down the hall and down the stairs. I looked out of my door but I was careful. I'm always careful. I have to be careful because I'm nervous and I'm a disgrace to my family. But I see and hear things that I don't tell anybody about. If I tell I'll be sent away to the rest home. I heard a man tell May that I should be sent away but May said no. She raised her voice loud and said no. May is my father and my mother, she told me so. Henry is my brother but he would have me sent away. He would have me given the name of crazy. He would take away the name of Beauregard and have me given the name of crazy. I am not crazy, Regan. But I know who is. I know by watching and listening. But I will never tell. Regan, do you know what a look of disgust is like?"

Regan knew she must have nodded because Rosalie gave a sober nod in return.

"So do I," Rosalie said. "That is how I am looked at. When I tell May she tells me to forget. May always tells me what to remember and what to forget. She is my father and my mother and I would be lost without her. She says so. If May is unhappy I will be unhappy. If May—" Rosalie's voice stopped in mid-air. The last words rose to the ceiling and hung there. She looked up, fearful, listening.

There were footsteps overhead, in the dining room. They were slow, labored, and almost visible as they crossed the rug and moved over the hardwood floor. No one in the kitchen spoke. The water dripped on the vegetables in the sink, the kettles bubbled on the stove, the clock ticked. Rosalie's hands tightened their grip and the rent in her bodice widened. The steps crossed the butler's pantry and moved down the stairs.

"Don't take my name away," Rosalie said to Regan. She dropped Mrs. Mundy's arms.

Jenny clumped down to the small landing, the breakfast tray in her hands. Her old face wrinkled with pleasure. "Well, don't you all look cozy," she said. "Real homelike. There's not enough of that these days as I'm always telling Katy. And I always say the kitchen's the nicest room in any house." She carried the tray to the sink and looked with disgust at the unfinished vegetables. "Behind in your work, my girl. Frittering your time. That's no way to show appreciation for a good home. Isn't that right, Mrs. Mundy? It surely is. You do that spinach over, I can see the grit. I've got good eyes, I have, and strong hands, and don't think you're too old to get what Paddy gave the drum."

Over her shoulder she said to Regan: "Mr. Fray just came in. He says if I saw you would you please come to Mr. Hurst's rooms."

Fray said: "Hello, I see Jenny found you. Where were you?"

"In the kitchen."

"Can't you find anything better to do than that?" He was making the diaries into a bundle. There were scissors, paper and string on the table beside him.

She said, "I talked to Max this morning."

"I know you did. I wondered if you'd tell me of your own accord. What else did you do?"

"I went down to the kitchen for some coffee." Her voice rose.

"And they gave you hemlock. That's what you sound like, anyway . . . Sit down and tell me what happened."

"They were all out in the garden with Rosalie. Mrs. Mundy, Katy, Miss Etta. All three of them, and she was stronger than they were!"

"Pretty bad?"

"Pretty awful."

"Take it easy," he said. "You knew about Rosie. You've seen Rosie in action before."

"Not like this. You've got to do something." She was afraid to speak above a whisper. The door was open and

she knew too well that her voice was treacherous. "She's
dangerous," she whispered. "She's stronger than anyone
in this house. She's mad, but her mind is stronger than the
sane ones. And she's afraid of somebody, that makes her
worse. She's afraid she's going to be locked up."

"She may be right at that. That should have been done
years ago but the Beauregards like to handle things their
own way. Don't worry about it, don't worry about anything. Everything's all over. We've reached the end." He
looked around the room as if he were seeing it for the first
or last time. "The end," he repeated.

She wet her lips. "The end of what?"

"The House of Usher. The house of cards. The house
built upon sand. Take your choice. Take the one that makes
the biggest noise in your imagination. This is it and it's going
to fall. Rumble, rumble, slow motion, c-r-a-s-h. The dust
rises and settles, the earth opens, and old bones reach
their bleached white fingers to the sun. Pretty, pretty. I've
been reading too many good books lately."

She drew back. He stretched his arms in a horizontal
line, like Rosalie's. "I'm half-dead myself," he said. "Do
you ever go into Etta's room?"

"Sometimes I look in." She had to clear her throat before
she could speak. "But she's never there."

"She doesn't keep her door locked then?"

She shook her head. He tightened the muscles of his
neck and shoulders and dropped his arms with a sigh.

"I'll give you a key," he said. "When you go up tonight,
keep an eye open for Etta. When she's safely tucked up,
give her time to drop off, then lock her in. She's been prowling lately. May doesn't like it and neither do I." He grinned.
"We don't want the old girl to break a leg. You've given
up prowling yourself, haven't you?"

"Yes."

"Right. And you locked your own door last night because I tried it this morning. It didn't do you much good,
did it? That's the great flaw in all locks. Things get in just

the same—because we take them with us." He reached across the table and tapped her cheek. "Poor Regan."

"Fray, what do you mean when you say we've reached the end. What does that really mean?"

"No more digging in the past. We've hit bottom." He picked up the diaries that were still unwrapped. "I went over to see Slocum this morning. He was asleep too, but I woke him up. He wants to borrow these and I think I'll let him."

"Then I'm not to hear any more?"

"No reason for it. There's a short entry in the last one that you might like to see for the sake of sentiment. And there's one about my father's death. But it's not important and I think you've had enough."

"I'd like to hear about your father. Do you remember when you said Max was a carbon copy? That's what you said."

"I know I did. But I still say you've had enough."

There's something in the part about his father that he doesn't want me to know, she thought. It can't have anything to do with me so it must have something to do with himself. Or with someone else close to me. He's trying to save me from something, trying to keep something from me. I won't let him. I want to know.

"I want to hear it, Fray," she said. "Please. It's my right."

The look he gave her was thoughtful and searching. "Yes, I suppose it is. But it won't tell you much, Regan. It won't tell you what it tells me." He selected the book from the others, wearily, and found the entry. "September 12, 1927.

" 'Two days ago Father died. He was going to Europe in a few weeks and wanted to see us all before he sailed. So he came here and we were happy to have him as always. He had completed all his arrangements and Max tells us that the night before they left New York he wrote many pages in a little notebook that he always carried. But we think he has destroyed the notes for we have not found them. Poor Father. Toward the end he

changed his mind as he did his linen, daily. His years
were heavy. He had his photograph taken also before
he came, very ferocious and gloomy, one for each of us.
Across the bottom of each one his crooked little writing says, "Farewell my dear child, your affec't Father."
It is clear to me now that he was not well but in the beginning I did not guess. I think he had a premonition
which he tried to conceal.

On the morning of his arrival he is very gay. He says
we will go to town, up to the Lexington Market, and
choose the dinner menu. It is foolishness, we have too
much of everything already, but we go. Some of the
old stall keepers are sons of his boyhood friends who
came to this country in the same year and even on the
same boat. He is well known to these men and he is
very good at remembering their little family jokes and
foolish legends. So he makes much laughter wherever
he goes and at the cheese stall he tells everybody within
hearing how the cheese man misbehaved in the usual
fashion at his christening in Zion Church. The cheese
man's wife is delighted.

I put this down because it is Father at his best, bringing out the simple little things that people forget about
themselves and love so much to have others remember.
It is altogether a triumphant morning for Father. But
on the way home he is very quiet and I think it is fatigue and his old distrust of the Atlantic Ocean.
Twenty times he has crossed, this is the twenty-first,
and he hates it. Also, I tell myself, he is homesick already.

He naps in the afternoon and when he wakes up he
wants to take a walk. He invites us all to come with
him, May, Max, Fray and myself, and he takes us to the
pavilion. For years he has refused to enter that place
but now he leads us there and we are surprised and
pleased. But we act as if it is nothing.

We watch the sun go down on the water and after a
time of silence he says we must all have a little talk before long, and he includes Henry. Because he is not
leaving for at least another week we say we are at his
service but there is no hurry. He says there is always

a hurry and too much time has passed already. I think
that makes little sense but his voice trembles and he
gives the words more than they have. I whisper to May
that the old gentleman is tired and we must humor him.
He hears the whisper and I am afraid he is hurt but he is
not. He looks at me with something in his eyes that I
cannot fathom.

And so we return to the house and we have dinner.
He is suddenly gay at dinner, too gay I think now, and
he makes poor Rosie laugh and tells Henry what he
will do when he gets to Paris. That makes Henry unhappy because he has never seen Paris. And when he
is unhappy he is full of complaints and drinks too much
and May is upset in consequence. I promise May that I
will see what I can do about a little trip for Henry. But
I do not like to think of Henry in Europe on his own.
Such reparations. After dinner Father is flushed and he
is sleepy and wakeful in turn. He sits by the fire and
says little, then all at once he talks rapidly and with too
much excitement. He says we must meet again in the
morning, when he is stronger. He says we must have a
conference about the past and the future.

So we look at each other and laugh and we tell him
he is thinking of his enemy the ocean. I myself try to
make him smile. I try even to make him angry, anything to break his mood. I tell him that people who fear
the water should stay away from it.

All at once I know it is the wrong thing to say. Of
all the words in the world I have said the wrong ones.
It is the look on May's face that reminds me. It is not
that I need to be reminded, I will never forget; it is
only that for the moment I have been careless in my
speech. The look on May's face tells us all what we
already know, that the next day is the anniversary of
Claudine's death. And I have brought that night into
our pleasant room by speaking a few thoughtless words.
"People who fear the water should stay away from it."

Father does not see May's face. Or Max's. Though
he looks at no one and stares into the fire we know he
has heard and where his thoughts are. Suddenly he
laughs, harshly. That is unlike him. He looks at each

238 THE PAVILION

one of us. He says, "That is interesting. That is very
profound. You will do well to study such contradic-
tions in behavior."

Max and Fray laugh at that. It is all they can do.
They call him Professor Herald. Soon they take him
to bed and I stay and talk with May and Henry
and Rosalie. Rosie does not talk of course. She plays a
little game of solitaire of her own invention in which
she wins a fabulous sum every five minutes.

Max and Fray return. They have made Father a
toddy on the spirit lamp in his room. He complains of a
cold but is well-covered, Max says. When we all go
up at eleven he is sleeping and we leave him without
worry or thought. The next morning he has pneumonia.

We find him drenched to the skin, burning with
fever and nearly dead. It rained in the night but we
knew the windows next to his bed were closed. Only
one window was open and that was on the far side of
the room. But when we find him in the morning they
are all open. It is the same as sleeping in a field.

He is wandering in his mind but it is easy to know
what has happened. He was hot with the fever and instead of calling us he tries to do things himself. He
opens the wrong windows and the damage is done. He
is like a drowning man. We send for a specialist from
Hopkins but nothing can be done. Not once during
that day or the next did he speak rationally. Sometimes he looked at us and we think he knew who we
were but that is all. Once when he looked at us I
thought I saw pity in his eyes. That is an odd thing to
see in the eyes of a dying man, pity for the living. At
the end he looked as if he were glad to go.'"

Fray closed the book. "You see," he said, "an old man
died in his own bed, surrounded by his children. Ready and
glad to go. That's what people pray for. He had it."

He wants me to think that, she told herself. He thinks
this one is worse than the others but he doesn't want me to
know that. He's worried, or frightened, and he doesn't want
me to ask questions. He's in a tight corner and he wants to

be there alone. He's being brusque and casual because he wants to make me stop thinking, but he can't make me stop. It's too late for that now. I won't let him know that I'm thinking. I'll be casual too.

"You look as if you'd been up all night," she said.

He brushed a hand over his face. "Maybe I forgot to shave. Yes, I forgot. Shirtsleeves to shirtsleeves in three generations. I got some money for you this morning."

"That's good."

"I'll get your ticket later. Talk to anybody today?"

"You know I did. I told me that."

"Oh sure." He looked out of the window at the tossing branches. "Bad weather, I don't like it myself. What are you going to do next?"

"Start packing."

"That's good, too."

Suddenly she knew she couldn't keep it up. Money, tickets, packing, that's good, too. It was all false and it was coming between them. Whatever the trouble was, she was a part of it. She couldn't stand aside and let him take it alone.

She said, abruptly, "Was there an empty bottle under your father's bed, too?"

If that struck, and she meant it to, he gave no sign. She waited for his answer while he selected and discarded cigarettes.

"I didn't get that," he said finally.

She said it again. "I saw the bottle under Max's bed. You told me he'd had a rye toddy, nothing else. But the brandy bottle was there, in plain sight, and Cousin May thought he was drunk. So did I, at first, but not now. Now I think the bottle was put there on purpose. I think somebody wanted to discredit Max. That's why I asked about your father. I wondered if the same person tried to discredit him too."

"How long have you thought this?"

"Since hearing what you just read. When we found Max that night you said he was a carbon copy of your father. That didn't mean anything then but it does now. Max was a carbon copy because the original worked. Did your father have a bottle too?"

"I've been thinking all the time that you'd missed that. Yes, he did. I found it and kept my mouth shut. I didn't catch on, then."

"So," she continued, "your father died and it was worth trying again, on Max. And Max was already sick, so it should have been easy. Even if the pneumonia failed, there were the empty bottles to start talk. Servants gossiping up and down the street, both men discredited. Your father and Max could say they'd never seen the bottles before but nobody'd believe them. This isn't their 'county,' that's the way people around here think, isn't it? Start that bottle story on its way and gossip would keep it going. I can hear it! 'Foreigners, drunk as lords, you can't believe a word they say!' Once you asked me what Gretel and Claudine had that anyone could want. Now I wonder what your father and Max had. They must have had something, or known something, or been on the verge of finding out something. That makes sense, doesn't it?"

The key to the door was on the table between them. He picked it up and weighed it in his hand. "Be careful, Regan. Be very careful."

"That's no answer," she said.

"It's the only one I can give you now."

She reached for the red diary, still unwrapped. "You said there was something else," she reminded him. "A short entry that I might read because of the sentiment. Is this the right book?"

"What? Oh yes." He looked at the clock. "Read it yourself, and hurry, will you? I've got to run."

"Run where?"

"Does that matter?" He was sharp. "To Slocum's, for one thing." He'd found the proper page for her while he was talking. "There. That's the last entry, he wrote that the day he died."

I've hurt him, she told herself. I've touched a raw place, I've hit on something. I don't know what I've done, but

I've done something . . . She started to read, softly, to herself.

"Louder," he said. "I can't hear you and I want to."

She read.

" 'My work is done. I have fitted all the pieces together. I have the answer. Today I have regretted that I sent for Regan. Now I think it is dangerous to bring a young girl into this. I have even gone to a public telephone and tried to reach her but there is no answer. So I think she is already on her way. That is fate again.

We will move slowly and cautiously when she comes. When she comes I will take her to the pavilion, for old times' sake. That is what I will tell her and the others. And when we have found each other again I will bring back the night I told her to forget. I will take her hands in mine as I did before but this time I will not say forget, forget, wash it out. This time I will say remember, remember.

I must gather together the same ones who were here the other times, Max, Fray, Henry, Rosalie, Etta. Henry and Rosalie came this morning, which is providential for me, and I will write to Max and Fray when I am ready. I will ask Slocum too. I cannot consider his age now. I need him. He will stand by and keep me going. I will tell him to bring his bag. We will need it perhaps. And he will know I am telling the truth because he knows each one of us and has had the training for this. It is odd how we used to say he wasted his time with those clinical books.

This is not for the police. There was never a weapon, only a sick mind. You cannot punish a sick mind but you can remove it from other opportunities. There must be no more opportunities.

We must make everything clear to the others who will disbelieve at first. We must show them how it began and how it progressed. The culminations we do not have to show. They are clearly marked with names and dates on marble.

I have written everything on a paper and the paper never leaves me. I will get a signature on the paper if possible. Slocum will stand by.

My Father. I know now why he looked with pity on the living. He knew. He was going to tell me but he had no time.

It is growing late and soon it will be dark. Regan is coming, perhaps tomorrow morning. I will go down to the fence and place a magic wand against the railing. She will find it and know that I am just the same as always. Maybe I am not the same today but soon I will be.' "

Fray wrapped the book and placed it with the others. "That's all, see you later." He stood up. "We've finished in here, I'm going to leave the key in the lock."

He gave the room a final survey. The fire burned briskly, the curio cabinets gleamed, even the colors in the faded Persians looked fresh and bright. It was a new room, clean, inviting, wholesome, a room to stay in, not to leave.

She didn't speak to him because there was nothing she trusted herself to say. She followed him to the door and stood by when he slipped the key into the lock. He turned it several times as if he liked the sound of the clear, strong click. She watched him go up the hall without looking back. Someone inside Max's room opened the door to his knock.

She returned to the room and studied it as he had done. The books on the shelves were orderly, the open desk looked as if it had never been used. The pigeonholes were filled with neat stacks of paper, the pens were new, there was ink in the silver well. Ready for a new occupant, she told herself. Everything is over. Whatever we were doing is done.

She wondered who would live there now. Henry? She ran her finger over the cabinets, the mantel, the little temple clock. They've been cleaning in here every day, she thought. Getting ready for Fray and me to leave, knowing we would leave. Does that mean anything? They knew Fray would go, but how did they know about me?

She folded the card table and put it behind the door, out of sight. Now I could never have been here, she thought.

She stood in the center of the room, making a silent farewell, but instead of the shining order she saw the old dust, the lighted candelabrum dripping wax, the wine glasses and the silver bucket. She saw Miss Etta's hennaed head bowed in sleep, the claw-like hand that rose and fell, the empty glass that rolled across the table. Go away from here, she told herself, go away at once.

It was then that she saw the Bismarck portrait, face to the wall as she had turned it herself. She turned it back, slowly, and it was heavier than she remembered. Then she went to the mantel and wiped the face of the clock. She knew that was a senseless thing to do, but it satisfied her. Like rain after a funeral, she thought, washing away the footprints of the newly dead. Washing all traces from the face of the earth.

She went to her room by the back stairs, down the narrow passage by the linen closet, up the winding flight. Daylight came in at the window on the landing and the coffin niche was nothing but a place for statuary.

Back in her room she went directly to the bed and dragged out the small steamer trunk that was under it. She dragged it to the center of the room and opened it. The stained and faded lining was torn. I'll get a new one later, she promised herself, I'll get everything new. New clothes, a new place to live, a new life. She took the suitcase from the closet and put it on the table. The same table she and Rosalie and Fray had sat around. The same table Rosalie had drummed with her fat, white fingers and struck with her invisible switch.

The peeled stick was still tucked under the strap. She tried to make a comparison between the peeled stick and Rosalie's leafy switch and she couldn't find one. But they were side by side in her mind.

I'll start putting things in the trunk, she thought. Anything. It'll be a start. I'll do it slowly and make the day go. I'll pack and unpack and take a lot of time and then I won't think about anything. She took Miss Etta's present from the chest and placed it in the bottom of the trunk. That's temporary, she reminded herself. It'll break if I leave it that way.

It feels breakable. But it's a beginning, anyway. If anyone comes it'll prove I'm going.

She sat in the big chair, Rosalie's chair, and looked at the package lying in the bottom of the trunk. It's the only thing . I'm taking away that I didn't bring, she said. She was still looking at it when Cousin May came in.

Chapter Ten

COUSIN MAY wore a small hat covered with violets and a spotted veil that deepened the blue of her eyes and added to the sheen of her white curls. Her fur coat was over her arm and she dropped it on the bed with a relieved little sigh.

"I'm exhausted," she said, "simply exhausted." She looked at the clock. "Nearly twelve! And I've been out since eight! What a lucky, lucky girl to be able to sleep late!" She laid her cheek against Regan's. "So sweet, so sweet," she murmured. "Do let me sit down for a moment. Those dreadful stairs . . . And what's this they tell me? They tell me you're leaving, dear!"

"I don't know who told you, Cousin May. I wanted to tell you myself."

"Don't apologize, don't think of it, I understand perfectly and I'm not one bit surprised. Dear child, I knew you wouldn't be happy here. Poor old Cousin May, not good for much these days, but she sometimes knows what's best! Such a sad house, so wrong for this little mouse, haven't I always said so, dear?"

"Yes, Cousin May."

"And to think this is the first time I've come to see you in your little room! So inexcusable, but the stairs! These poor old bones of mine. Perhaps a little elevator later on . . . When do you leave, my dear?"

"Tomorrow, I think."

"So soon, but then I mustn't scold. How I wish I were going away too. We'd all be better for a little change, all of

245

us. I said as much to my good Mundy. A little holiday way
from home, I said, to make us love it more. Bright new
scenes, bright new faces." She sighed. "I must plan a little
something for the rest of us, so much sadness in the old nest
now." Her quick eyes went around the room. "Dear child,
has it always been so cold in here?"

"That's all right, Cousin May. Would you like me to get
your coat?"

"No, no, I can only stay a minute, just a little peep to see
how things are coming on. Dear child, what can I do? Just
ask me anything, anything. Shall I send you one of the
Crains, for packing? Tell me what you want and it's yours."

"Nothing, thank you. There's very little to be done."

Cousin May stared at the open trunk. "Starting already,
busy little bee? You shame me! And Fray says he is leaving
too, and Max, in a very few days. So lonely in this great big
house with everybody gone!"

"Is Rosalie going too, Cousin May?"

"Rosie? Whatever made you think of Rosie? Oh dear,
I forgot. You and Rosie have become such friends, of course
you're interested. Yes, Rosie will be going soon and how I
shall miss her! But she's never quite happy away from her
own little place and the things she knows and loves. Dear
Rosie . . . Tomorrow, you say?"

"I think so. Fray's looking after my ticket."

Cousin May broke into a peal of laughter. "My dear little
girl, I'll sigh with relief when you see the end of Fray! I met
that young man this morning, much to his surprise. We both
left the house at the same time and I'm sure I don't know
where the wretched boy was going. He looked impossible,
like a dissolute rake, and I told him so, you may be sure of
that. I scolded him roundly! And I made him admit that all
that nonsense of locked doors and diaries was nothing more
than a scheme to keep you with him. You know his reputation, dreadful, dreadful." She pinched Regan's cheek. "But
I'm afraid you were a disappointment to him! Tell me,
weren't you a disappointment?"

"I'm afraid I was."

"Little parrot! Don't you ever say anything of your own? Always repeating, very sweet and childish, but you must try to express yourself in fine, strong words. We can't have people thinking that you aren't quite, that you can't—well, that doesn't matter now . . . So you think you were a disappointment to Fray? Oh dear, that must have been a blow to him! Were you a disappointment in the pavilion, too?"

"The pavilion?"

"Now, now my dear, don't look at me like that, I know perfectly well where you went last night. Do you think Cousin May is blind? Such a foolish, foolish thing for you to do, so bad for you in your highly nervous state. And the servants! Do you think they see nothing? Poor Mundy was quite upset when he told me, you gave him such a fright. He said you looked like death itself, he was really quite worried. You see? So awkward for me, how could I explain?"

"I'm sorry, Cousin May."

"Sorry? And you should be, you should be. Poor Mundy. I had to tell him something, I couldn't have him—thinking things. So I said that you were overwrought, and nervous, and that you imagined there were people in the pavilion, so distressing I told him. And I said that Fray had taken you there at my suggestion, to show you that the place was quite—normal. Fortunately, he believed me, no doubt he has noticed your odd, strained air . . . But the pavilion! Whatever possessed you, my dear, and I assure you possessed is the correct word!"

She tried to read Cousin May's smiling face. Cousin May was both angry and amused and her little suede shoes tapped the floor. She told herself to answer quickly, to say anything that came into her head. The real explanation would be no good, it would make things worse than they were.

"It was my fault that we went," she said. "I've wanted to go ever since I came. I knew I was leaving soon and last night seemed to be a good time. I only wanted to see it again, that's all."

"But at midnight! What an extraordinary excursion, I wish I'd gone myself! And what did you accomplish, my dear? Nothing much, I'm sure, nothing but a return of that terrible—nervousness. Do tell me, did you hear voices again?"

"No," she answered. "No, it was just a room."

Cousin May sighed. "Just a room. Yes, I could have saved you that, I could have saved you so much. All this time we've been living under the same roof, sharing the same sorrow, and I haven't been able to touch your heart, to win your confidence, not once. But it was always like that, even when you were a little thing, you always clung to Hurst and not to me. Do you remember that?"

"I'm afraid I don't. I'm afraid I only remember Hurst."

"Truly, my dear? I've often wondered. I tried so hard to read the thoughts in that muddled little head but it was useless. No one had your welfare more at heart but you always went your own way, and you still do, don't you? You still go your own way in spite of poor old Cousin May. Don't you, dear? Confess!"

"I don't know," she said helplessly. "I suppose so."

"Of course you do! I know, I know! Tell me, did you find many changes in the pavilion or don't you remember it that well?"

"I remembered most of it, I think I remembered all of it. I'm not sure." She groped for something impersonal to say, something that would sound natural and tell nothing. But her mind stood still. She saw the pavilion in the light of the table lamp, with the little dwarfs holding up their candles. Cousin May's bright eyes were like a bird's. They looked as if they knew everything. "I remembered the things on the mantel," she said.

"The old collections? Dear me, are they still there? I haven't been in the place for years, too tragic, too sad. Hurst didn't want me to distress myself, how wise he was. And I wanted him to have a little hideaway, a little castle of his own, so good for men to be alone sometimes. And he loved it, he loved it so! He even kept clothes and food out there!"

"I know." Hurst, taking the spoons for the sherbet out of

the cupboard, Hurst in a linen jacket with carved buttons. "Yes, I know. I've been thinking about that lately. I thought of it last night. He used to wear a jacket with carved buttons. I seem to remember that he kept it there. It was a riding jacket, wasn't it? I know he wore it one morning when he cut himself with a whip. He made me promise I'd never tell about that. But it doesn't matter now."

"No, it doesn't matter now."

"Funny, I haven't thought of that for years and now it's come back and it—sticks. I keep seeing the mark, it was dreadful, but he laughed about it and tried to make me laugh too."

Cousin May was thoughtful, tapping her gloved fingers on the rim of her fine suede bag. "I remember," she said. "But we mustn't talk about it, we mustn't even think about it, too sad, I want to cry. Poor Hurst, dear comrade! . . . Now tell me about your plans, your gay, happy plans. Oh to be twenty again! You're going back to the little library?"

"I suppose so. I don't want to decide that now."

"So wise of you, so foolish to make hurried decisions." Cousin May was earnest. "Think, plan ahead, examine the situation from all sides, allow for obstacles, for unexpected developments." She could have been talking to herself. "Take nothing for granted, then go ahead. You can't fail." She laughed. "Oh dear, I sound like an old fogy and I'm not at all, not really! I'm really quite frivolous and I'll prove it! I don't want you to go back to that horrid job, I don't, I don't! I want you to have a little fling instead! You've been so dismal here, it's quite, quite wrong. New York! A little holiday in dear New York! Lovely? And if you coaxed I do believe I'd join you! What do you say? Shall we run away, the two of us, and not say a word to a soul?"

"I could go later," Regan said doubtfully. "After my other plans are made. And I'd love to have you with me, Cousin May."

"Honor bright?" Cousin May's firm little hand reached out and took hers. "So sweet but so mournful, so little animation. I want to cheer you up, my dear, I want to make

you happy. Would you like a little present from Cousin
May, something to remember her by? Now don't protest,
don't say a word! A little present when you leave to make
you think of Cousin May."

Regan's eyes went to the open trunk and she smiled. "A
very little one is about all I have room for." She indicated
the bulky package. "Miss Etta."

"No!" Cousin May peered into the trunk. "How ex-
tremely forward and what an odd shape! Whatever can it
be? Not a cup and saucer surely, much too big! Poor Etta,
poor creature, I should feel sorry for the woman but I can't.
Just a little pinch, my dear, a little prodding. We really
must. It could be—anything!"

"I wish you'd open it," Regan said. "I'd feel much better."
She held out the package. "You do it; we won't tell her."

Cousin May sighed in agreement. "If you insist, if you
insist, and I'm sure you're being very wise. With Etta one
never knows. After that disgraceful exhibition at dinner I
really wonder if it wouldn't be better for all of us if Etta—
but no, I mustn't think of that, I mustn't think of it at all."
She held Miss Etta's offering at arm's length, with her head
on one side, smiling and frowning. "I'm almost afraid to
look, so enormous and no shape and so very, very light. I
can't imagine! Do you suppose she's been raiding the attics
again?"

"She hasn't said a word about it. She simply left it on the
chest. Open it, Cousin May."

"You're sure you don't mind, really sure? Of course we
won't be doing anything wrong. And I know you don't
want anything that's been stolen. I must do something about
Etta, I really must, although I don't like to think about it!"

She broke the seals with fastidious care and the present
emerged from layer upon layer of tissue paper and cotton
wadding. She held it up and they both stared wordlessly.

Miss Etta's bon voyage gift was a porcelain figure of a
young girl with flowers in her hair and hands. It was out of
place in the small, plain room, even out of place in Cousin
May's beautifully gloved fingers. It belonged in a museum

or in a cabinet, under lock and key. Regan caught her breath and looked at Cousin May. Cousin May's face was full of astonishment.

The figure was about ten inches high and it was faultless. The tiny hollows in the wrists and neck looked as if they had a pulse behind them. Blue flowers trailed from the curving fingers and fell from the smooth, yellow hair; the plain white dress hung close to the body that was clearly underneath.

Cousin May closed her eyes and murmured inaudibly.

"What is it?" Regan asked. "Where have I—what is it?"

Cousin May answered slowly. "It's one of Hurst's most treasured possessions. I haven't seen it for years." She shook her head in disbelief. "This is becoming monstrous. He used to talk to it, talk as if it could hear him and answer. He prized it above everything he owned. I don't understand how she, where she—" She placed the little figure on the table. "My hands are shaking, so ridiculous. I've been startled and shocked and I don't like that. This is too much." She touched her fingers to her temples. "I don't know what to do, this is too absurd, too awkward, challenging!"

Regan said nothing. She hardly heard. She bent down to the tiny, oval face and she thought it looked up, as if the two of them knew something no one else knew. Now I understand why people covet things and steal them, she told herself. I know why they steal pictures and jewels from museums, and hide them. I could steal this. I want it for myself, I don't want to give it up, I've never wanted anything so much. It's mine, it's always been mine.

She roused herself enough to say, "Has it a name, Cousin May?"

Cousin May was more composed and her voice was quiet and cool. "I lost my temper and I'm sorry, so silly and so useless. Of course it has no name. What a childish notion. It's a very expensive piece of bric-a-brac that I couldn't find after Hurst went, that's all. Etta, the wretched woman, probably knew where it was all the time and simply helped herself at the first opportunity. I'm surprised that she didn't try to sell it, I'm surprised that she didn't wrap it up in one of her horrid, greasy bundles and carry it out of the house!"

"I think I must have heard about it," Regan said softly. "When I was here before. It seems familiar." She touched the trailing blue flowers. "I may have even seen it, but if I did how could I ever forget? It's the most beautiful thing I ever saw. It looks alive. It even looks like—somebody."

"That's more of your nonsense, my dear. It's nothing more than a very clever piece of work. I don't suppose Etta told you anything about it?"

"No." Regan took the figure and held it between her palms. She was going to have to give it back, she knew that, but she wanted to own it for a minute. She thought the porcelain would be cold to her touch but it was almost warm. She made a protecting cup of her hands. "Where did he keep it?" she asked.

"He carried it about with him, here, there, everywhere, like a child with a rubber doll. He was quite mad about it." Her eyes looked as if she saw him, cradling the little figure in his arms. She made Regan see him too. Her voice was soft and distant and she looked as if she were distant in body as well. Her eyes strayed to the window that framed the pavilion spire.

"It was in the pavilion," Regan said, and her voice was as far away as Cousin May's. "In the pavilion," she said again. It wasn't a statement of fact but a suggestion she was making to herself.

"Don't mumble, dear. If you have anything to say, speak out. What was in the pavilion?"

"The little figure. I think I saw it there. I think it was on the mantel with the other things. Do I have to put it back?"

"Put it back?" Cousin May repeated. "Wait a minute, my dear, wait . . . Put it back, you say?"

"Yes!" She went on desperately, surprised at her own force. "I will if you want me to. I know Miss Etta had no right to take it and it isn't mine, but I want it! I want to keep it, I'll do anything to keep it! It looks like mine, it feels like mine, it's like finding something you'd given up for lost.

Isn't there some way I can buy it from the estate? I want it, Cousin May, I've got to have it!" I'm acting like a fool, she told herself, but I can't help it.

Cousin May was amused. "In another minute you'll burst into tears. How fortunate that no one sees and hears you. But at last you've made one sensible suggestion and I accept it with pleasure. You've saved me a lot of unnecessary worry. Of course it must go back, today, at once. I will arrange it."

"But can't I speak to Fray or Max? If I tell them I want to buy it—"

"I will speak to Fray myself, when he is in a better mood. And to Max, when he is able to concentrate. Now wait, let me plan."

Regan waited hopefully. Cousin May's fingers tapped the rim of her bag, her little slippers tapped the floor and kicked aimlessly at the empty trunk. The trunk gave off a hollow sound and she shuddered and drew back. "My poor, over-strained nerves, and I was beginning to feel so well again, so strong and sure! Sometimes I think the world conspires against me! And now this! Where did she—why did she—"

Regan's searching eyes met hers and she smiled brightly.

"Don't look so distressed, my dear," she said. "Poor old Cousin May lost her temper for a minute, so naughty and she's truly sorry, but we're quite happy again and all is straightened out. Do you know what Etta was trying to do? But of course you don't, you funny innocent. She was trying to make trouble with the inventories! The lawyers, the Heralds, checking over lists and asking what became of this and that! Haggling over a single silver spoon! That's what Etta was hoping for, that's what she wanted to enjoy! Hurst left his collection to Max and when this little figure is found missing, Etta will accuse you of taking it!"

"Oh no, Cousin May, that can't be right! She told everybody she was giving me a present. It wasn't a secret."

"My dear little goose, I know what I'm talking about and you don't. Etta thrives on discord and if she can make even a tiny tempest in a teapot she's perfectly happy. But it shan't happen this time, I won't have it, and they're not going to ask you silly questions and get you all upset. You won't suffer, I promise." She kicked the trunk again, almost playfully. "I'll have to do something about this. I'm afraid it's not strong enough, it looks as if it might fall apart." She rapped smartly on the wooden sides. "Flimsy. I wonder. Perhaps—"

Regan spoke uneasily. "But what about—"

"Oh yes! Poor Cousin May was wandering, wasn't she? Like you, so contagious, I must watch myself! Now you're not to worry another minute, my dear, it's all settled. We'll ignore Etta, we'll say nothing, we'll fool them all very cleverly. The little figure will return to the pavilion, where it belongs. The mantel you said? Good! Tonight, before dinner, when everyone is busy and occupied, you will go there quietly and replace it! That will take care of everything."

"But Fray knows it wasn't there last night. We looked at the mantel and I told him something was missing. When he sees it he'll wonder."

"But you'll be gone then, my girl, so why do you fret? I'll tell him he overlooked it, see how simple that is? Now smile, you foolish baby, a fine, big smile! There, that's much better! . . . Heavens, what's that?"

Cousin May had spied the peeled stick.

"Something I found, that's all. . . . Cousin May, I'd rather take the figure to Fray and tell him how I got it."

"No more of that, not another word! Cousin May knows best. Now we must plan for your departure. We must plan for the least trouble. Have you wired your little friends of your arrival."

"No. I have only one friend and she thinks I'm staying. We said good-by for good." She laughed ruefully at that. "She'll be more surprised to see me than not."

"Such fun." Cousin May laughed too. "I love surprises. I think we all do." She stood up and examined the trunk again, slowly, regretfully. "Too bad, really too bad, I'm afraid this is hopeless." She looked at the trunk a long time, smoothing her fine broadcloth and adjusting the violet hat.

Regan got to her feet. Cousin May came close and stroked her cheek. "You won't forget the little errand you have to do? And I'll see you later, my sweet." She saluted the porcelain figure with mock gravity and gathered up her coat. "So much to do in such a short time! I must fly!"

She stood at the window after Cousin May left, watching the water, turning back to look at the little figure on the table. It stood beside the suitcase and the peeled stick, incongruous and appealing. The shy, half-smiling lips looked as if they were ready to speak. She found herself waiting to hear the words when they came.

She was almost glad when Katy clattered in with a tray of lunch. "Sixes and sevens downstairs," Katy said soberly. There were new lines on the old face and she was bent with a weight that had nothing to do with the tray. "Not fit for a young, healthy person to see and hear, not fit for anybody. Mrs. Mundy's got her hands full this time and she looks as if her heart was breaking if you can make yourself believe she's got a heart. No gentlemen home for lunch, not counting Mr. Max, so it's trays for you and the madam. Where'll I put it?"

Regan closed the trunk. "Here, on the lid."

Katy deposited the tray. "You can thank your lucky stars you're leaving and I never thought I'd live to say a thing like that. Wish I was going too." She turned and saw Miss Etta's present. "Blessed Joseph, what's that you've got!"

"Forget you saw that, Katy," Regan said quickly. "It belonged to Mr. Hurst and it came here by mistake. I'm taking it back where it belongs."

Katy edged between the table and the trunk and stood with her back to the window, staring at the figure. "Looks human, don't it?" she observed fearfully. "What's it smiling at?"

"Nothing, Katy, that's your imagination. It's just a piece of statuary." She went on carefully. "Katy, why do you wish you were going away?"

"I don't feel so good, that's why. I'm unsettled in my mind and I can't put my finger on nothing . . . I think you ought to get rid of that statue, Miss Regan, right away. It's the wrong kind. It's no saint. I know the saints like the palm of me own hand and it's no saint. I saw a moving picture once about an unreligious scientist that shrunk real people into little people, like that one. Like you'd shrink a flannel shirt, same shape and all but you can't so much as put it on a cat. I hollered fit to wake the dead and Jenny had to take me home. Don't know why I'm thinking about that now, must be the statue sets me off, that and downstairs."

"What's wrong downstairs? What happened after I left?"

"Happened!" Katy's lip trembled. "Only the madam herself comes down, first time since I've been here, and she sees Miss Rosalie and takes the place. She don't raise her voice, I'll give her that, but she has a way with her just the same. Gives orders for this and orders for that and says she's not to be disturbed unless she rings. Miss Regan, look." She led the way to the window. "They were getting ready to go when they ran me out with the tray." She pointed downward. "Look. Miss Etta says she's seen it all before, she says it'll be hours before they come back. Look." Katy crossed herself.

Rosalie and Mrs. Mundy were tramping down the lawn to the water. They forged ahead like people on shipboard with miles of deck to cover.

"I don't want money," Katy said quietly. "I used to want money. I used to worry all the time, and Jenny did too, but we never let on to each other. We were speaking of it just now. We used to hope and pray we'd never lie in a charity bed, and when the Little Sisters of the Poor came down our street collecting for their work we'd always try to have a nickel ready. For them that didn't have a nickel even, for hope the saints would notice what we done and mark us good. Insurance, like, against receiving alms. But I don't know, I don't know now." Katy blinked and stared ahead. "Today I keep on saying to myself there's worse than charity. It won't be bad. There's people like yourselves for company and we'd like that. I keep on saying to myself there's something nice about the Little Sisters of the Poor."

They watched the figures on the lawn. Down to the water, turn, back to the house. Down to the water, turn, back to the house. Heads down, tramping, plodding, not talking. Down, turn, back.

"You sure you don't need somebody to work for you, Miss Regan?"

Regan put her hand on the thin, bent shoulder. "We'll see." She didn't look at Katy because she knew Katy was close to tears herself.

After Katy went she sat at the trunk and tried to eat the food she didn't want. She tried not to look out of the window but trying wasn't enough. The window became the only thing in the room. She saw the spire against the gray sky, like a beckoning finger again. It was like the first night, like last night, like all the other times when familiar things took other shapes and moved in aberrant patterns.

The room slowly filled with more than gray light. The window was closed but she thought she could hear the water washing up on the beach and foaming around the dock. She thought she could see it, foaming around the dock, rolling up the slope like a tidal wave, rising like a wall, covering the pavilion and the cypress trees, rolling on to the house, higher than the house, higher than her windows. She closed her eyes and waited for it to cover her. She waited for the feeling that she knew would come. Her body would turn over and over in the deep water, there would be nothing to grasp, nothing to cling to, nothing but the deep rolling water. Like Claudine. She would see a face under the water and it would be Claudine's, but when she tried to save Claudine the face would become her own. She would be trying to save herself.

When she opened her eyes again she was gripping the edge of the trunk and crying. She got to her feet and steadied herself against the table. The little figure rocked and she caught it before it fell. That was another terror. If the little figure broke . . . She returned it to the table with

trembling hands and saw that her hands were wet. She
touched her face and it was wet, too. Go out, she told herself, go out and walk like Rosalie. Go out of the house. It
doesn't matter what people think or say when they see you
walking up and down like Rosalie. Keep away from the
garden, go out and walk in the street, among strangers. Go
out and walk among strangers, like Hurst, and watch the
faces of the passersby. Go out and see what you can read in
other faces and perhaps you can see what they read in your
own.

"I've got to pack," she said aloud. "I've got to get ready,
there's so little time." But she took her coat from the closet
and left the room without looking back. Halfway down the
hall she knew she had forgotten something and she tried to
remember what it was. She went back and looked at the
empty room but it told her nothing. When her hand closed
over the key in her pocket she took it out and mechanically
locked the door.

Down the front stairs to the second floor and all of the
doors but one were closed. At the other end of the hall
Hurst's sitting room was like a picture fragment. The fire
was a low heap of red ash and the chairs that stood beside
it were empty.

Down to the first floor. The fringe on the red portières
hung straight and motionless. There were no flowers to
smell, there was no rustle of good black clothing, no subdued clearing of throats. Comparisons are odious, she said
to herself, comparisons are odious, she chanted. When she
found she was walking in step to that rhythm she quickened
her pace.

She closed the heavy door behind her and made a slow and
careful study of the carving. She told herself it was a work
of art, that she had never examined it properly, that it was
worth her time and attention. She traced the smooth, worn
feathers of the birds, investigated the hearts of the roses, admired the tendrils of the vine. Not until she found the small
round hole that held the nail did she admit she had been looking for that and nothing else. She covered it with her finger

and rubbed the wood as if she could erase it. But it was deep, and it was there to stay. It's been used at least four times, she told herself; four or five. It's almost as permanent as the carving and it's a necessity.

The sky was low and heavy and the few leaves on the sidewalk had lost their color. She walked slowly to the corner, hearing the noise of the traffic grow as she drew near.

She watched three women backing out of an interurban trolley. They were laughing at each other, they were all fat and they all carried bundles. One of them had a piping, childish voice. "He gave me five dollars for my birthday," she shrilled happily, "and he said you spend it on yourself, hon, don't spend it on the table." The others nodded. You have to spend it on the table, their looks said; they always tell you to spend it on yourself but you have to spend it on the table.

She walked by the church on the corner and crossed to the tearoom. The tearoom window held a pair of brass candlesticks with orange candles and a plate of cakes with orange icing. A woman in a print dress stood behind the window and smiled at her. She smiled back and the woman withdrew with a look of surprise. She moved on.

Next door a line of children stretched across the sidewalk in front of the movie theater. They dropped their money and scuffled for it, they kicked each other while gazing skyward and held loud conversations with friends at the far end of the line. A sign said "Children Under Sixteen Not Admitted Without Adult." The line dwindled noisily. They all got in.

Beyond the theater there was a small side street lined with two-story houses, each with three white painted steps. She walked down the street, reading the cards in the neat windows. In almost every house someone had something to sell. Hemstitching. Lace Curtains Stretched. Midwife. Canaries For Sale. Expert Radio Repairing. Puppies For Sale. Blankets Done Up. Midwife. God Is In This House Every Friday Night, Come One Come All. Mrs. Purvis, Hairdresser. Midwife.

Two girls came out of the hairdresser's. One of them looked anxiously up and down the street before she started down the steps with an arm around the waist of the other girl. The other girl walked with her eyes closed and her lips were turned under her teeth. When she reached the bottom step she sat down and leaned against her friend. A hand appeared in the window behind them and rapped smartly on the glass. It was only a hand with red knuckles. It waved them away and they got up and moved on.

Regan walked to the end of the block, turned and came back to the four corners. Already some of the shops had turned on their lights. Across the street from where she stood she saw Mr. Mayer standing in his doorway, looking at the sky. She looked, too, but there was nothing to see but heavy clouds. More rain, she thought, more rain and wind and cold. The night was coming and the sky was ready for it and the rain would fall the whole night long. Pattering on the laurels and magnolias down by the pavilion, dripping from the roof above her window, smoothing the rough clay mound in Memorial Park. The sign in the Park would swing on its rusty standard all night long and the rain would run in the feathered grooves of the angel's crumbling wings.

She didn't want to talk to Mr. Mayer. He was rocking back and forth with his hands in his pockets, calling greetings to the passersby and discouraging the advances of an over-friendly dog. When the dog attached itself to a shambling colored man, Mr. Mayer retired hastily and closed his door.

She sat on the church steps because other people were sitting there. The others were waiting for the trolley. They talked about their dinners, about closing up their shore cottages, about putting up the boat. Putting up the boat was a complicated matter.

She listened gravely, as if their problems were hers. It took two men to put up a boat. She was glad to know that. A trolley clanged around the corner and the people on the steps ran out into the street, still talking to each other. One of the men carried a rolled umbrella and it struck her shoulder as he passed. It was a hard blow and it threw her to one side, but the man went on without stopping. He doesn't know he struck me, she told herself. He acts as if he didn't even see me. He's going on as if I weren't here. She sat on, watching the traffic increase as the day faded.

The first drops of rain began to fall and she left the steps and started home. Young Sheffy's place of business was next door to the church. She looked resolutely across the street because she didn't want to see it. A few doors beyond Young Sheffy's she came to a white house with a black and gilt sign on the gate. She had seen the house before but had never noticed the sign. Now she read it carefully, as a stranger reads directions on a lamppost in a strange town. Dr. Poole.

Dr. Poole. Once she had told herself to call on Dr. Poole. When had she done that? After one of those talks with Fray? With Cousin May? After the pavilion? After one of those times. She had told herself to call on Dr. Poole and ask him about the headaches and the things she heard and saw and thought. Perhaps this was the time for that. Perhaps her subconscious mind had urged her from the house and guided her steps. She would tell him about the voices, about the people who walked by her bed at night, about the water.

She saw Dr. Poole as he had looked on the day of Hurst's funeral. He'd stared across the lunch table with owl's eyes behind gold rimmed glasses, he'd worn too many gold rings and a gold watch bracelet and he'd written Max's prescription with a gold incrusted pen. She wished the sign said Slocum instead of Poole. But Dr. Slocum was miles away in the country and even if she could find a cab she wouldn't know what directions to give. Even if she knew the directions she had no money for fare. And Fray was at Dr. Slocum's. She didn't want to see Fray.

She put her hand on the latch. She'd ask him for some sleeping pills, that was all. She wouldn't tell him anything. If she had some sleeping pills she could get through the night and that was all she wanted now. To get through the night.

The latch clicked and she swung the gate inward. At the same time the door of the house opened and three men came out on the porch. They were talking and they didn't see her. Dr. Poole, Dr. Slocum, Fray. She heard Fray's voice above the others. "You're not giving me much time," he said.

She backed away and threw a frantic look over her shoulder. The street behind her was filled with traffic. The interurban trolleys clanged around the corner, the country busses lumbered to and from the curb. In the middle of the street an endless line of large and small cars trailed each other. She dodged through it all, followed by the outraged cries of horns and bells and people. When she reached the other side of the street she slackened her pace and walked as if time didn't matter. She crossed the street again in front of the iron gates and went up the path.

Henry let her into the house. He was full of solicitude. "I thought we'd lost you," he said tenderly. "I went up to your room but your door was locked." He tried to take her coat with lingering hands. "Where've you been?"

"Walking. I've got to pack, Henry, I can't stop."

He dropped his hands. As she went up the stairs she looked back and saw the red portières close behind him. That's the first time I've seen anyone go in there, she said to herself. That's the first time since—

She unlocked her door and went immediately to work. The contents of the closet and chest were meager enough when she collected them. The lunch tray was still on the trunk and she moved it to the bed. The little figure on the table looked as if it were watching.

First a pair of old shoes. She dropped them into the empty trunk and they struck the bottom with a hollow thud. She examined the trunk fearfully, remembering Cousin May's conviction that it wasn't strong enough. It wasn't, she decided, but she'd have to risk it. One by one she packed the skirts and sweaters, the cotton underwear, the old bathrobe. When she came to the rabbit slippers she hesitated. She held them in her hand when she went to the window but the garden was empty. The rain fell quietly in straight, gray lines and the sky over the water was dark. It will soon be dark all over, she thought. I've got to hurry, I don't want to go down there in the dark. She turned on the lamp and wrote on a page of her tablet, "For Rosalie." She put this on the chest with the slippers. Fray might forget his promise but Rosalie would not be disappointed.

When the trunk was full she closed and locked it and turned to the suitcase on the table. What happened then was so deliberate and so direct that she felt as if she were watching the action of a scene that had been rehearsed to perfection. She drew the suitcase forward and the peeled stick swung like a hand and struck the porcelain figure. One little arm broke at the elbow and dropped to the table with a gentle ring.

In her ears it was a gentle ring but it echoed in her mind like a gong. She picked up the little arm and laid it on her palm. The gong thundered in her head. She saw the arm lying in Hurst's hand, she saw him looking down at it as she was looking. It was rosy in the lamplight then, as it was now. He was standing by a table, as she was standing. In the pavilion, at night, beside the table and the lamp. There was a red welt across his face and a whip on the floor at his feet.

"I've got it," she said. "I know what he wanted now!" The gong rang triumphantly and the past returned without shadows.

She saw herself outside the pavilion door, looking in. Hurst was in the center of the room talking to someone over by the mantel. She couldn't see the mantel but she heard the other voice, vindictive, spiteful, goading. She didn't recognize the voice because its normal tones were choked with rage, but she remembered the words. Someone hated Hurst and wished him dead. Someone lashed at his face with a whip, she could see the whip. It belonged to the old carriage in the stable. She covered her eyes. The voice went on, hate, hate, hate. It said he had spent too much money for a piece of china when other things were more important and needed. It said he had spent his money for a piece of china because the china looked like Claudine. She opened her eyes when she heard Hurst cry out. She saw him dash across the room, out of sight, and then she heard a gentle ring and a burst of laughter. She heard Hurst say, 'I will find it hard to forget this.' She saw herself running away, back to the dock.

He came for her there and she told him what she had seen. He took her back to the pavilion and closed the door. They were alone. He took her on his lap and told her she had imagined everything, that what she had seen and heard was all a bad dream. The porcelain figure was lying on the table and he said he had broken it himself. She told him someone else had done that. He said no. He held the little arm in the palm of his hand and pointed out the perfection of the blue flowers that still trailed miraculously from the curving fingers. She stopped crying when he showed her the flowers. Then he locked the figure away in a cabinet and told her again that it was all a bad dream. He said, 'Wash it out.' He said she had never left the boat. If she loved him she would believe that. Wash it out.

Everything he had said to her that night she heard again. Everything she had seen, she saw now. And under it all the vengeful, goading voice was an obbligato of hate. She ran into the hall crying, "Miss Etta!"

But Miss Etta's room was empty. She stumbled down the back stairs and along the second floor hall. The doors were all closed. She forgot the need for secrecy, she was almost completely demoralized. She ran down the hall toward the front of the house, crying "Miss Etta! Miss Etta!"

One of the doors opened and Henry came out. He was in his shirtsleeves and his eyes were half-closed. "What in the name of—" He stopped short when he saw her.

"You're acting crazy again," he said slowly. "You even look crazy." He gripped her shoulder and stared down into her face. "What's the matter with you? What's up? What have you got in your hand?"

She pulled away. "I haven't got anything. I want Miss Etta."

"Don't lie to me." He pried her fist open and saw what she held. "Oh," he said.

"I'm taking it back, I'm returning it! It hasn't anything to do with you! Where's Miss Etta?"

He looked as if he were trying to think. "I don't know," he said thickly. He went back into his room and closed the door, but when she vanished around the bend in the front stairs he reappeared and rocked unsteadily on the threshold. He looked up and down the hall, frowning, as if he were still trying to think.

On the first floor she found Miss Etta in the music room. Miss Etta listened to her story. When it was over she closed her eyes.

"What shall I do?" Regan begged.

"Go back to your room," Miss Etta said. "Go back and stay there." She mumbled under her breath and twisted her hands. "I didn't know what it was. I didn't know. Go back to your room and stay there and don't let anybody see what you've got. Don't let anybody see it." She pushed Regan to the door, pushed and clawed and prodded.

They both heard the footsteps on the veranda and the click of a key in the lock.

"The back stairs," Miss Etta whispered. "Hurry!" But she went nowhere herself. She stayed where she was, listening with bent head.

Up in her room Regan went to the window. The garden was dark, the pavilion was invisible, but the light in the kitchen made a dim circle on the flagstones. They haven't drawn the curtains all the way, she thought. If I go out there now I'll be seen. She stood without counting time, her forehead against the cold glass. Something is happening, she thought, to the house, to me. Something is being planned, put into motion, executed. Someone is in trouble. Something is being executed.

The cypress ring was The Island of the Dead. It was the last haven for lost souls. She knew that now, irrevocably. She wasn't surprised when she saw someone walking toward it.

A single figure came around the corner of the house by the conservatory. It was black and shapeless, veiled by the rain. It walked on the grass, avoiding the circle of light and the flagstones, and disappeared in the direction of the pavilion. Miss Etta? No, it was too big for Miss Etta. Miss Etta was a tiny thing.

She caught her breath when she discovered that she was not the only watcher. Three more figures came from the driveway in single file and followed the first one, keeping to the dark places, crouching and moving forward like trappers. Someone is in trouble, she said again.

She left the window and walked to the door as if she were both driven and led. She knew she was going to the pavilion. She was completing a cycle, closing a gap, finishing a story.

She went to the front stairs as quietly as Claudine must have gone. If there were people in the rooms below they wouldn't hear her. She opened and closed the front door as Claudine must have done, without a sound. She went around the house by the conservatory path and changed over to the grass because it was quieter. She was following in the steps of someone she didn't know.

Thin lines of light showed through the cracks in the pavilion shutters. All of the lights are on in there, she told herself. They want to see what they're doing. They don't know the light is showing. Perhaps they don't care. They. Who? Four people.

She remembered the sandy steps and crept through the shrubbery and trees until she was under one of the windows. It was open but the shutters were fastened. She could hear but she couldn't see. The rain was all around her, falling on the hard green leaves of laurel and magnolia, on the sloping roof of the pavilion. It fell on her upturned face.

She heard a voice, low at first then rising slowly. She put her cheek against the wet shutter and listened.

Fray. At first she thought he was reading aloud, his voice was even and monotonous, but soon she knew he was talking to someone.

"I've been watching you for two days," he said. "I've known where you were every minute and what you were doing and thinking. I planned to have a talk with you after dinner tonight but Etta changed all that. A few minutes ago she told me about the porcelain figure and I knew I had to find you at once. I knew where to come, didn't I? And I even know why you're here. You came to kill Regan Carr. Did you think you could get away with that one too?"

She heard him without surprise. He was only verifying what she had felt. It was the other voice that wrapped a cold hand around her heart. It was low and harsh and strange and the words were almost indistinguishable. No one in the house talked like that.

"Did you say why?" Fray asked. "You mean why kill Regan? That's easy. She's a Herald, for one thing, and she was beginning to put things together. Beginning to get smart, so it was time for us to have another accident. And if anybody was fool enough to yell murder you were all set to accuse me, weren't you? Well, it wouldn't have worked. I've got a fine accusation all ready to throw back in your teeth. See? Hurst's writing. And when I've finished with you, you're going to sign your name under his."

There was a scuffle, and he laughed. "No unseemly grabbing, please. You're not dealing with children, young women and old men this time."

"You devil!" Hate boiled over the words.

"Who, me? Praise from Sir Hubert! Now that's over and we understand each other. Time to get down to business. I want you to listen to a bedtime story because it's getting very close to bedtime for you. And you can thank old Etta Luders for the long, long night that's ahead of you. Old Etta is one of the gifted fools of this world. She was born a scavenger. She instinctively digs, although she doesn't know what for or why. She roots in the dark places out of pure spite because she knows the things people discard tell more about them than the things they keep. That's how she found the porcelain figure in Hurst's study, behind a row of books nobody ever read. I didn't know about the figure,

Etta didn't know. But she found it, liked it, and it said something to her. So she mended the old break and gave it to Regan. Then Regan broke it again and it said something to her too. Regan, in a panic, began to remember what Hurst wanted her to remember. She knew where she'd seen it before, she knew Hurst had bought it because it looked like Claudine. I haven't seen it myself, not yet, but I know that's the truth because your face says so."

She heard something strike against wood. The table? A fist?

Fray went on. "That poor little figure cost a lot of money, too, enough for a trip to Europe, enough to square the unpaid bills and accounts that Hurst didn't know about. But most of all it looked like Claudine. So one night when your finances were too much for you, you came down here to the pavilion and asked him to sell the figure and give the money to you. He refused, and you slashed him across the face with a whip. You cut his face open because he was better than you could ever be. You were always conscious of that and you hated him for it. You knew he'd never tell anyone about the whip, you knew you could trust this common man. You probably saw shame for yourself in his eyes. That was hard to take, wasn't it?"

"Lies, lies, lies," the voice chanted. "Lies, lies, lies!"

"Oh no! Truth! There was somebody else down here that night. You didn't know it then but I think you guessed it a few days ago. You had an audience, a six-year-old who was afraid of the dark but came through it alone to help somebody she loved. She was outside the door and she heard. She heard you accuse Hurst of an old affair with Claudine. And you said things about Gretel and my father that sickened him. He thought you were ill, out of your mind, and planned to send you away somewhere. Later that night, when you left him, he went back to the dock and found that weeping baby. He used all of the arts he knew to wipe the ugly business from her mind, and he succeeded because she trusted him. And when he wanted to bring it back he succeeded again, and for the same reason, even though he was dead."

The voice refuted with a guttural roll of sound but he understood.

"Wait," he said. "I don't know what made him begin to suspect you but I think he caught a look in your eyes, the same look I caught the day of the funeral when we all lunched together. It told me what you were capable of and I think it told him the same thing. He thought he was mad to think as he did, he told himself he couldn't be right. He became an obsession to himself. He looked for a taint in our blood. You may not believe me, but when I think of that I want to kill you myself."

She clung to the shutter. Don't let it be what I'm thinking, she prayed silently.

"But you're lucky," Fray continued. "We're both lucky. You, because you'll never hang for this. You're insane. Your body will be locked up and fed and cared for the rest of its life. And I'm lucky because I don't have to do anything about it. I don't have to touch you, even put a hand on you. I can keep this table between us and whip you with words. Hurst's dead hand will do the actual avenging, the hand that covered this paper with fine writing and hid it under the clock. That's where I found it late last night, under the clock in his sitting room. The same clock that Regan signed with her initials. That's a nice touch, isn't it? I could scare myself by wondering what led her to do that . . . By the way, was it you who searched Regan's suitcase for the letter Hurst wrote?"

She waited for the answer and when it came it was a throaty chuckle. She heard the rustle of stiff paper, the scrape of a chair. Who was sitting down? Was Fray standing, with the table between him and the other one? There were two more, there were four of them altogether. But she had heard only Fray and the one who wanted to kill her.

"Here's the little paper that tells the story," Fray said

smoothly. "I'm going to read it to you, and when that's
done I want your signature at the bottom, under Hurst's.
After that I'll tell you what I think you ought to do. I'm no
judge, I'm just a common guy, like Hurst. You played the
game, you can call the decision. Now. You know what day
October fifteen was? The day Hurst died. Listen.

" 'October 15, 1945: I leave this under the clock in my
sitting room. If I should be unable to regain it for any
reason, if I should be ill or if I should die, I ask the one
who finds it to take it at once to my brother Fray
Herald.

For some weeks I have suspected that my father, my
sister Carlotta Maria, known to us as Gretel, and my
sister-in-law Claudine Herald did not die by the hand of
God but as the result of inhuman endeavor. I am con-
fident that the name of their murderer is known to me
but until I can prove it without a doubt and have less
troubled minds to help me, I cannot write this name.
When I have this help, I will obtain a signature. After
that I do not plan. I will put down what I believe to be
the truth, or as much of the truth as we will ever know.

My sister Gretel and her playmate Rosalie Beauregard were the victims of a scheme which could be explained away as a joke if it failed. It did not fail. One
of those children is living today, if it can be called
living. The situation is covered in my diary. The children were in the pavilion, handling my guns. There
was no one at any window of the house, no one to see
who came and went. Guns were forbidden to Rosalie
and she was all too conscious of disobedience. It is easy
to believe that her mind was dwelling on old Beauregard's disciplinary switch, the one that cut the mind
and not the flesh. It is easy to believe that she told
Gretel. Old Beauregard had been dead for years but
he was always alive for Rosalie. She heard him in the
treetops when the wind blew. So someone who was
familiar with that ugly story crept up to the pavilion
with a leafy branch and struck it against the steps.
Panic in the hearts and hands of two children. One

dead, one better off dead. Why? Why? I do not know. But it was premeditated murder.' "

Someone laughed, not a loud laugh but a low, introspective chortle. Someone was recalling the past with pleasure.

"You don't have to tell me why you hated Gretel," Fray said. "I can guess. She probably didn't pay you enough attention. She had poise, good looks, assurance, and she wore her mother's pearls with a little cotton frock. Herald pearls, fine pearls. She was entitled to them. She was the only girl we had then. And she had a good, clean, sound mind. Sound! I've got that one right, haven't I? . . . Now the next. Claudine. I won't read this because I can't. Hurst let himself go with this one. You got two that time, Claudine and her baby. Same reason, too. Claudine didn't pay enough attention to you. She had everything she wanted and you didn't. Or you thought you didn't. You could have the whole world, but unless it crawled to you on its knees and lay flat on its face at your feet you'd feel cheated. Claudine had everything, and she was modest and retiring. Not your style. And she was going to have a child, another Herald. You got the idea for Claudine's death the afternoon Hurst went into the water, didn't you? You removed the dock board and when Claudine was in bed that night you went to her room and said that Max suspected her fidelity. You said that Max was down at the dock and you feared suicide. That was pretty crude and anyone but Claudine would have thrown you out. But Claudine was unworldly. And Max's talk about a new will clinched it. Premeditated murder again, without a weapon. That makes three. That's the way Hurst and I figure it, three. My father was the fourth . . . Are we right about Claudine?"

"Right, right, right!" The words were like drumbeats. There was another beat running underneath, outlasting the voice. The other beat went on until Fray shouted, "Stop!"

She knew what it was. A fist striking the table. Two fists. Fists, fingers, drumming. Above the drumming she heard her own voice. Stop. Stop. Stop.

Fray went on and she knew he was reaching the end of his endurance. "I won't read what Hurst says about my father either. I'm not enjoying this as I should. I thought I'd get a kick out of watching your face but I don't. You're hideous. I wonder why I didn't get on to you before. I've known you all my life and tonight is the first time I've ever really seen you . . . Now, my father. An old man who knew the world, a self-made man who had learned to classify people. Hurst and I were soft but my father wasn't. Neither Hurst nor I know how you gave yourself away to Father but I think it began when he saw the greed in your eyes. It was always there. He saw it, too often, and added it up. The last time he was here you knew he suspected you, and you knew he was ready to talk. We think he purposely let you see that, to find out what you'd do. He was probably looking for indisputable proof, as Hurst was. He asked for a family conference, he said he wanted to talk about the past and the future. He was drawing you out then, drawing you out into the open. But you don't work in the open. You went to his room when he was asleep and you set the stage for an illness that was almost certain to be fatal to a frail old man. And you planted an empty bottle, to make him appear irresponsible, and it worked."

Another voice intervened. A new voice. It was familiar but it didn't belong in the pavilion. An old voice with a trace of compassion, full of weary authority. "Cut it short. That's enough. Finish it. Coup de grâce, boy, for God's sake!"

There was silence. Then, "I suppose you're right," Fray said. It was almost a whisper but she heard it; she even heard the long, painful breath he drew. She thought she knew how he looked, standing in the lamplight with the table between him and the other one. He would be looking down, and his mouth would be thin and hard. Cruel.

"One more thing," he said. "You killed Hurst too. You killed him with the things you said to him and you watched him die. You could have saved him, he had medicine, but you wanted him where he was, dying at your feet. The upstart, the immigrant boy. A natural death. Heart failure. A straightforward certificate. You thought you were safe, safe for all time. But you were never safe. Every hour of your life, from the night you cut his face with a whip and broke the little figure he loved, a child was growing up to accuse you. A child who could verify everything you said and did before a jury of medical men. How are you going to feel when that happens? What are you going to say for yourself then?"

Silence, then a rustle of paper.

"Sign this," Fray said.

"No!"

Silence again.

Then, "All right," Fray said. "The paper without your signature isn't enough to hang you but the testimony of these witnesses can put you in a madhouse for the rest of your life. Think that over. A madhouse. You . . . We'll leave you here alone for a little while. We'll give you time to think. Then we'll come back and get the signature, if you're ready to give it. Stay and look around you. Nothing has been changed in this place, nothing has been altered. Open the cabinets, open the table drawers. The same things that were here when Gretel was a child are here now."

She crouched on the wet earth and covered her face with her hands. Footsteps crossed the pavilion floor; the door opened and closed. Shoes scraped on the sandy steps. She heard their steady march across the grass to the flagstone walk. Three of them now, only three. And there was no more need to be quiet.

It was quiet in the pavilion. She crouched under the sheltering leaves, waiting for a sound. When it came it was not what she expected.

It came slowly at first, struggling up from a great depth, subsiding, rising again. When it reached the surface it broke and spread. It was never loud but it overflowed all bounds. It was some time before she knew it was the sound of crying.

Who would cry like that? The last person in the world when he knew he was the last. The Devil, after he had fought for possession of a soul. That was the way the Devil would weep if he won.

She ran, openly, until she reached the kitchen windows. The half-drawn curtains showed Katy standing at the stove stirring the contents of a kettle. There was no one else there. She opened the door and went in.

"Well who looks like a drowned rat?" Katy scolded. "Get right upstairs and change those clothes!" She made too many gestures and her voice was too high. "Dry clothes from the skin out and I mean what I say!"

Regan went wordlessly to the long table and sat down facing the stove and The Box.

"You heard me!" Katy went on. She tasted the soup she was stirring and smacked her lips. "There's nothing like a good thick soup to put the heart in you!"

There was too much enthusiasm in Katy's voice, too much abandon in the tossing old head. She couldn't keep it up although she tried. When she spoke again it was almost in a whisper. "Don't you want to go upstairs?"

"No," Regan said. "I'll stay here with you."

"I'll be glad to have you," Katy replied. She crossed to the table and sat beside Regan. "We've had a lot of bad weather," she said tonelessly. Her eyes followed Regan's to The Box and they both watched the dial without speaking.

Then Katy said, "Something happened. Mr. Max . . ."

"No," Regan said. "No."

"He rang from his room a while ago and Mrs. Mundy went up. Then she rang for Mundy and he went. They said he was getting up, dressing, and needed help. That's what they said."

"Where are the others?"

"I haven't seen a living soul. Mrs. Mundy told Jenny to set the table, she said dinner would be early tonight. She said six-thirty."

Together they looked at the clock. Six-fifteen. They returned to The Box.

"Jenny's doing the table now," Katy said. "But it's funny

I don't hear her. She clumps. Usually I hear her but I don't now."

"Maybe someone sent for her."

"I guess that's it . . . Or maybe she's standing still."

They both thought about that. Jenny, upstairs, was standing still.

Katy said, "Are you watching The Box because you're waiting for it to ring?"

"I'm waiting for it not to ring because I want to know who isn't in the house."

"Somebody who isn't—" Katy drew away, slowly. "I better be getting dinner on. It's done. I better be getting it on . . . Miss Regan, where have you been?"

The Box whirred. Regan sat without moving. Katy braced her hands on the table and leaned forward. The little hand went round the dial three times before it stopped.

Regan said, "Dining room."

Katy said, "Jenny. Dining room. Jenny." She went to the dumbwaiter. "Jenny?" she called.

Jenny answered. "I'm ready if you are. It's almost time."

Katy went to the stove. She filled a tureen with soup, took toasted crackers from the oven and transferred them to a plate. Butter from the refrigerator, a silver pitcher of water. She put these on the dumbwaiter and called up to Jenny. "Ready."

The shelves glided out of sight. She went back to the stove and drew the kettles forward. There were covered dishes and platters on the work table. She moved these back and forth. "You better go on," she said.

They heard Jenny in the room above, clumping from dumbwaiter to table and back again.

"She was standing still before," Katy said. "I wonder why."

Then another set of steps, quick, light, like a child's, crossed the floor overhead. "Somebody couldn't wait, somebody's in a hurry," Katy said.

The empty waiter returned and she fastened it. The gong

rang, clear and deliberate. "You better go," Katy repeated.
"If the Mundys don't get down in time to serve, I'm helping.
I'll be there."

Regan went up the stairs.

Jenny stood by the serving table. She didn't look at Regan,
she was staring at the other occupant of the room. Miss Etta
had already taken her place and was sitting in a shapeless
huddle, as if she had no bones. Her head was sunk into the
feather boa.

Regan went to her own seat at the end of the table, next
to Max's chair. No one spoke. Finally she heard Miss Etta's
low whisper. Miss Etta didn't turn or raise her head. She
spoke softly and distinctly into the boa. "Slocum and Poole
are in the conservatory. With two other men. Can you
hear me? Slocum and Poole are in the conservatory with
two men. They're watching the hall, watching who comes
in here."

Slocum and Poole. They were the two in the pavilion.
Slocum was the one who said, 'Coup de grâce.' The others
were police.

"I know," she said to Miss Etta.

"Do you know anything else?"

"Nothing."

"We'll wait. We'll know soon. We'll wait."

Jenny filled two soup plates and served them. She held the
plates with both hands but even so they shook.

Regan took up her spoon but Miss Etta made no move.
Jenny went back to the dumbwaiter and called in a faltering
whisper. "Katy?"

Almost at once they heard Katy coming up the stairs.
When she entered the room she took her place beside Jenny
at the serving table. They stood close together, holding each
other's hands out of sight in the folds of their black uni-
forms.

"Ring again," Miss Etta said. "Ring again. Maybe somebody didn't hear before."

Jenny struck the gong with more force than she intended.

She gripped the inverted bronze cups with terrified hands and tried to muffle the sound.

Only Regan's spoon, striking against the edge of her plate, broke the silence after that. She kept her eyes on the plate. She was afraid to watch the door.

Someone came down the hall and entered the room. She knew that step even though it was slower than usual. Some-one drew out the chair on her left.

"Glad to see you," Fray said. She knew he was talking to her. She saw his hands unfold his napkin but she didn't look up. "We won't wait for the others, Jenny," he said. "Get right along with it."

She spooned her soup steadily but afterwards she couldn't remember what kind it was. She drank some water and crumbled a cracker and when the next step came to the door she closed her eyes.

This one she knew too, because the heavy table shook. It was someone who usually had assistance and was now without it.

"Good dinner tonight, Rosie," Fray said.

"I can't find anybody," Rosalie mourned. "Everybody's gone away again."

"I'm here," Fray said. "You don't need anybody else when you have me, Rosie . . . Good dinner!"

There was doubt in Rosalie's voice. "Good," she repeated vaguely.

More steps in the hall. Slow, careful steps. Three people this time. Three. Not Miss Etta, Fray, Rosalie or the Crains. Not those in the conservatory. Three others. Three.

Miss Etta sighed. She knew it was Miss Etta because it came from her side of the table. And Fray was talking.

"Congratulations," Fray was saying.

Max's voice said, "Thank you, little brother."

She heard Max behind her chair; he stopped and put a hand on her shoulder. "I told you I'd see you again," he said. There was something new in his voice. No, not new. It had been there all along, stifled, and now it was free and clear. It was life, come back.

Still she couldn't look up. Max went on talking, to Fray, to Miss Etta, to Rosalie, perhaps to herself. She didn't know.

"Mr. and Mrs. Mundy had to dress me like a baby," Max said. "A very degrading performance, for me. Mrs. Mundy, I want one of you at my side, within reach of the knives and forks I shall certainly drop to the floor. I've been spoon fed too long."

The Mundys. The other two were the Mundys. She saw the prim lace cuff of Mrs. Mundy's sleeve as she unfolded Max's napkin and placed it in his lap.

"Thank you, Mrs. Mundy," Max said. "You might see if Miss Rosalie needs anything." Mrs. Mundy's steps went around the table.

"Henry?" Rosalie quavered. "Where is Henry?"

"Hush," Mrs. Mundy said. "I'm here."

What happened next was the end. It came in three parts, one after the other, each one crowding the other. That was the way it seemed when she thought about it later. There must have been minutes between the parts, seconds, but she couldn't remember them. All she could remember was sounds.

The first sound came from outside the house. From a distance, not too far, not too near. From the direction of the water. A clean, single shot.

The second came from the conservatory. A chair overturned and running feet went by the dining room door. They clattered down the kitchen steps. The kitchen door slammed faintly.

Then came the voice in the hall. It was high and happy. It was singing something unintelligible but the happiness was plain. She waited until the voice subsided and unsteady steps found their way to the chair on the other side of Max. Henry.

She raised her eyes then and looked beyond Henry and Rosalie to the chair at the head of the table. It was empty, of course.

She went back to Rosalie and Henry. Henry was talking to himself and she knew it would be hours before they could make him understand, but in Rosalie's face the past and present were in open conflict.

Rosalie turned to Fray and the look she gave him was full of numb distress.

"Somebody played with the guns," Rosalie said anxiously. It was both question and statement. "Somebody played with the guns but it was an accident."

"That's right," Fray said. "It was an accident . . . Now eat your good dinner, Miss Beauregard."

They both watched Rosalie receive and embrace her new title. She said the beloved words over and over, silently. Miss Beauregard, Miss Beauregard.

"Good," she said. And her face broke into smiles.

Fray's hand took Regan's and held it. She clung to his hand as she had once clung to Hurst's, and the white wreath on the old, carved door faded in her mind as it had faded in life and the voice in the pavilion was hushed for all time. When she looked at him she knew that they had both come home.